GROW UP ALREADY

DANIEL URBAN

PAGE PUBLISHING, INC.
New York, NY

First originally published by Page Publishing, Inc. 2018

ISBN 978-1-64214-283-9 (Paperback)
ISBN 978-1-64214-285-3 (Digital)

Printed in the United States of America

FOREWORD

Teachers sent notes home to my parents each school year, and I could almost pinpoint the day when my brother and sister would be excused from the supper table while I remained seated for my annual talking-to. It was always during the first week of November. There was still Halloween candy from trick-or-treat night in the big orange bowl on the kitchen counter, but the melted plastic popcorn decorations displayed in the front windows depicted pilgrims, Indians, and a turkey. Thanksgiving was just a few weeks away; the first marking period of the school year was over, but the first report card was not yet issued.

"We got a letter from your teacher. We have to have a talk about it," my father would start as he placed the letter next to his coffee cup.

I wasn't acting out violently. I wasn't bullying or being bullied. I wasn't being disruptive or disrespectful. There was no property damage, and I injured no one. In all actuality, I did nothing wrong. The letter was sent home because I was being me. Me being me apparently didn't meet the standards of normal behavior set forth by the Panther Valley School District, but I do believe the teachers who penned the letters were genuinely concerned for my academic well-being.

Each year the teachers were different, but the letters alluded to the same problem. One teacher said I had difficulty concentrating. Another said I lacked focus. One said I often appeared lost and confused. Each school year's talk about my inability to pay full attention in class was accompanied by the same series of questions from my parents.

"Are you having trouble seeing the blackboard?"

"No."

"Do we need to tell the teacher to seat you in the front of the classroom?"

"No."

"Is a classmate distracting you?"

"No."

"Are the lessons too difficult to understand?"

"No."

Once I said no to all the logical questions, it was put to me to elaborate on my problem.

"If none of those are the problem, then what is the problem?"

"I don't know."

I was in elementary school. Of course, I had no idea what my problem was. I didn't have the vocabulary or enough worldly wisdom to articulate what was going on with me. Most of the time, I wasn't aware there was a problem until I was held over at the dinner table for my yearly inquisition and pep talk.

There was one letter that accurately stated my problem. It said that I was a daydreamer. I found grade school repetitive. Two plus two was always going to be four. The times table didn't change. Verbs were always words of action, being, or doing. Nouns were always a person, place, thing, or idea. I couldn't relearn things I already knew or didn't forget. When nothing new was holding my interest, I would tune out of the classroom and tune into my imagination.

By today's standards, I would probably have been diagnosed with attention deficit disorder (ADD) or attention deficit hyperactivity disorder (ADHD) and be prescribed medication that would retool my brain so I could function according to the standards of normal society. Unfortunately, or fortunately—I'm not sure which—I grew up in the seventies and eighties. Forced conformity was how abnormal kids were handled. Uniqueness was viewed as weakness or a challenge to authority. The proverbial square pegs were pounded into round holes in the interest of uniformity.

The week after my annual talk at the supper table was when the first report card of the school year was sent home. In elementary school, students didn't receive traditional letter grades of A, B, C, D, or F. For *satisfactory* work, a student received an S. For *unsatisfactory* work, a student received a U. When I brought home a report card with straight Ss, my parents spoke no more of the letter from my teacher, my struggles with concentration, my lack of focus, or my appearance of being lost. I'm guessing they thought their talk at the supper table did the trick and sent me on the right path.

In my entire grade school history, I only received one U, and that was for *conduct* in the second marking period of the second grade. I drew a picture of a fireman peeing on a fire. When I was questioned about my drawing, "When you gotta go, you gotta go" was my response. My answer was honest and not meant as comedy, but it inspired raucous laughter from my classmates. Perceived class clowns were dealt with using isolationism. Clowns don't perform without an audience. I was ordered to take my desk and sit in the hallway, away from the other students. My time in the hallway didn't last too long. Teachers on a coffee break and other adults wandering the hall of the elementary school would ask why I was ejected from the classroom and forced to sit in the hall. When I told them it was because I drew a picture of a fireman peeing on a fire, they laughed. The Coca-Cola guy who filled the soda machine in the teacher's lounge thought my infraction was so funny that he plunked two quarters on my desk, gave me a cold can of soda, and patted me on the back before walking away and laughing hysterically. When my punishment became profitable for me and entertaining to adult audiences, my teacher, Mrs. Whitehead, had me promptly return to the classroom. Giving me the U in conduct ruined my reputation as a straight-S student. It was the only option that would lend Mrs. Whitehead peace of mind. She couldn't afford to let the laughter of my seven-year-old classmates and her adult peers diminish her authority.

Each grade the letters continued, but I didn't stop daydreaming. After each talk, I tried harder to pay attention. My efforts didn't last long, though; I just got better at masking my daydreaming. In hindsight, I wonder if my family noticed how often I would get lost in my head. I'm pretty certain they did. I'm pretty sure they chalked my daydreaming up to being a personality trait. When I would overhear my mother and grandmother answering questions about us kids, my older brother and younger sister conformed, so they could easily rattle off a list of their accomplishments and activities. When it came to me, the answers were different. "Danny is come-day-go-day," "Danny marches to the beat of a different drummer," and "Danny is Danny" were the top three answers offered on my behalf. So I'm pretty sure these answers were derived from my propensity for living in my head.

My daydreaming wasn't always forgiven and overlooked. It caused me a lot of trouble. I was often scolded for not paying attention. When caught tuning out of conversations that didn't capture my interest, I was called out and quizzed on what was said. When I failed to accurately regurgitate the stated information, I was reprimanded. If I would exude a blank expression, fingers were snapped in front of my face to get my attention and I would sternly be ordered to focus. It was often a source of entertainment. If I was thought to be tuned out, people talking to me would make outlandish statements often involving flying pigs exiting a butt or talking unicorns to see if I noticed. When I didn't, it was a reason to make sport of me. Sometimes, I was taken advantage of. If I was hovering halfway between an inward trance and conscious presence, they would ask me for favors. Later, I would be berated for not keeping promises that I couldn't remember making.

With the benefit of hindsight, there's one main sticking point I find puzzling. Not one person asked me what I daydreamed about. The teachers who wrote the letters to my parents, not one of them ever asked me what was on my mind. The guidance counselors who met with me to make sure I wasn't a danger to myself or others or a serial killer in the making, they quizzed me on basic classroom stuff but never asked where my mind went when I tuned out. My parents never asked. My siblings never asked. None of my friends, girlfriends, or coworkers were curious enough to know where my thoughts went in my moments of quiet contentment. Not one person asked, until Tracy. It was probably why I fell in love with and married her.

Grow Up Already is my first book. It would have never been written if Tracy didn't ask me what I was thinking about when I zoned out while having dinner with common friends of ours one night. I was thrilled and scared to be asked. Thrilled, because it was the first time I was asked. Scared, because it felt like my defenses for masking my inattentiveness were compromised and my internal monologue would be made public and ridiculed. I don't remember what answer I offered. It could have been a poop or fart joke, but whatever it was, she laughed and continued to engage me in a conversation that held my interest.

That dinner with common friends of ours was at least half a decade before we even started dating. Our conversation, though I don't remember the content, I remember how freeing it felt and how comfortable I felt sharing my mind with her. At that time, I didn't know she would be the one who would give me everything I needed to follow my dream of becoming a writer. I had no idea that she would be my biggest cheerleader and source of inspiration. When my dream became difficult and frustrating, I had no idea how calmly she could show me my progress and how far I'd come. She has a knack for pointing out how silly it would be to give up on my dream after I put so much work into it. Her chapter in my life is still being written, but her appearance in it is the turning point that will guide me to happy endings. If I had the ability, there are not many people I would want to take by the hand and walk with through my imagination and give them a tour, but Tracy is the first one that comes to mind. It's only right that I dedicate my first book to the first person to ask where my mind was taking me.

Tracy, I love you with all my heart and soul. This book is the first of many, and it is the product of the mind you encouraged me to share with the world. This one is for you and because of you. I couldn't ask for a better person to share a life with. Your love brings out what I kept trapped inside for too long.

CHAPTER I

The curtains on the alcove windows above the large oak desk are drawn. Inside the main area of the study, among the tall bookshelves, Theodore "Furshizzle" Graham, in his khaki cargo shorts and comfortable button-down shirt, sits in a black leather recliner. *Jeopardy* is on the television. Wayne Arnold, a white kid with dreadlocks, kneels on the floor in front of the other recliner. He's rolling a joint on the coffee table.

"Who is Edward R. Murrow?" Theodore says as Wayne looks at the television to see if Theodore is correct.

"What is *string theory*?" Theodore says. Wayne again looks at the television.

"Who is Louis Pasteur?"

Shaking his head, Wayne says, "Damn, Mr. Graham, you haven't gotten one wrong yet. You should go on that show. You would kick some ass."

"I'm more of a *Press Your Luck* kind of guy, no Whammies, big bucks."

"Yeah, man, I remember that show. Those cartoon guys would be a bunch of dicks. They would act all stupid and shit and take all your money. The contestants could be dicks too. They could pass spins they didn't want and ruin other people's shit with Whammies."

"Yeah, that's the show. I never heard it described quite so accurately. You should have written the *TV Guide* blurb for them."

"No way! Is *TV Guide* still a thing? I never understood that. Who wanted to read about watching TV? I don't think my grandmother ever read her *TV Guide*, but she sure as hell threw it at me and my brothers when we acted up during her stories," Wayne says before he licks the sticky side of the rolling paper and twists the joint together.

"Who is Phil Hartman?" Theodore says as he answers another *Jeopardy* question.

Wayne pats his pockets then reaches into his pants pocket to pull out a BIC lighter. He offers the joint and lighter to Theodore. He takes them and runs the joint under his nose and nods with approval.

"Seriously, Mr. Graham, what are you doing in this old-money town working for the Douglas family and living in their great-grand-father Lord Money Bags's study house?"

"What do you mean? You know what I do. You're one of my students at the community college. You know I teach at the youth college. This is my job. The Douglas family includes housing with my employment."

"My old man says you were some fancy Harvard lawyer and super rich people would pay you butt loads of cash to keep them out of trouble. He says you're probably working off some debt to the Douglas family."

Theodore puts the joint in his mouth, flicks the lighter, and takes a long drag. At the beginning of his exhale, he says, "Yeah, I was a lawyer for a bunch of years. I hated the job. I hated Washington, DC. So I finished my English doctorate and wrote a few books. Gene Douglas was one of my Harvard buddies. He offered me the jobs. I can publish my books through his publishing house. It's mutually beneficial. I make a few bucks, and the publishing house gets 10 percent. He pays me to teach at both schools. His schools use my work's notoriety to attract students, and I enjoy coaching the debate team. It works out for everybody."

"Couldn't you be doing way better somewhere else? The lawyer thing seems like your ticket to the big time. If you were still doing that, you could probably buy the Douglas family estate. The teaching seems like a waste."

"You're one of my students. I'm teaching you. I'm helping you prepare your mind for the future. Are you saying I'm wasting my time?"

Wayne exhales a hit of smoke and passes the joint to Theodore. "Don't get me wrong, Mr. Graham. I love your class. Yours is the only one I actually do the work for, but I'm already off to a good start in my career."

"You gather shopping carts at the Stop & Shop. I hardly call that a career."

"For the guy with all the brains, you don't seem too smart. Selling weed is my job. You buy weed from me. You're my best customer. I'm working right now. You're a customer."

"Being the neighborhood weed dealer, that's going to be your career? You don't aspire to be more?"

"Look, Mr. G, I'm only in community college for my old man. My dad is an electrician. My mom is a lunch lady at the Carter public school. They worked hard to send me and my two brothers to college. My older brothers went to state schools. They're both in finance and do well. I play the part of the dumb, spoiled baby of the family and go to community college. My old man doesn't think I'm such a waste if a bring home a few good grades here and there. He just thinks I'm a late bloomer."

Exhaling a hit of marijuana smoke, Theodore says, "You're not a waste. You're a smart kid. I've graded your writing, it's decent. We've had some intelligent conversations while we got baked. You play a decent guitar and are dependable when selling me weed."

"I know I'm not a waste. I just go through the motions to appease the old man. I work hard developing my career selling weed. I hustle. Last year, between my regular buyers and the music festival circuit, I cleared ninety-eight grand after I paid my supplier and expenses. I made twenty grand more than my father. This year, I'm growing my own product. I don't need a supplier now. My brothers project that I will triple what I did last year."

"So this is a family business? Your brothers are in on it too?"

"I can't be twenty years old and have my parents know I make three times what they do. It would shatter my old man's soul to know I am making more than him by selling something he tried to teach me to stay away from. My brothers are in finance. They're going to manage the money until I get done with school. I'm getting an associate's degree in accounting so when I move away, the old man will think I'm a certified accountant and doing well for myself. My brothers are just covering for me to protect the old man. He worked hard for us. We can at least help him feel proud of his sons. My old man is one of the good guys."

Theodore nods in agreement. "Oh, how the times have changed. I can relate. My old man was a union welder and worked his ass off so I can have an Ivy League education. My education may have been the death of him. He was from a generation that when you worked hard for a company, it was possible to get ahead and be secure. It's not that way anymore. When I was a lawyer, my job was to make sure middle-class labor didn't get ahead but just kept satisfied enough not to quit. It's the way the wealthy corporate types rig the system."

"I know, Mr. G. I watched my dad's company screw with him his whole life. They would dangle the carrot of a raise or a supervisor spot in front of him. He would brag about the opportunity to get ahead and be so proud to work to advance. A couple of months down the road, he would say that they eliminated the position for financial reasons but, if he worked a little extra and pushed a little harder, the opportunity might be there when the company was in a better financial position. Meanwhile, the family that owns my old man's company has new expensive cars, summer homes, ski homes, and their hideous daughters got much-needed nose jobs and plastic surgeries. It was a trap my old man got caught in. It kept him from ever quitting. It kept him working harder, and it gave him false hope. He still believes he will get the regional foreman job before he retires. Truth is, the boss's eldest son is getting the job when he's done school. It doesn't matter if he doesn't know anything about electrical work—my old man will get stuck doing the work for him. I watched my old man being made a fool of throughout his career, yet he remains loyal to people who treat him unfairly. I'm not falling for that trick, but I can't shatter his dreams by letting him know that I'm doing better than him selling weed," Wayne says and offers the stub of the joint to Theodore.

"Na, I'm good with that for now. I'm also good with television. I hate *Wheel of Fortune*. It's just white-trash noise to me. This weed is weed you grow? I'm definitely going to be a frequent, regular customer. Hey, what's the advancement situation look like for you at the grocery store?" Theodore asks as he shuts off the television.

Wayne snubs the joint in the ashtray and throws the roach into a baggie full of joint stubs. "Well, if I get six more customer comments that are positive, I will have the chance to get twenty cents more an hour to stock the grocery shelves. There is a ninety-day trial period I will have to work at my present rate while they decide if I qualify for the raise. By their policies, I could work myself out of poverty in 109 years. So I got that going for me."

"Yeah, you're fortunate." Theodore laughs. "At least you can work inside the store if you move up. You won't have to push carts in the elements."

"I don't want to work in the store. Inside is a drama fest between slutty cashiers, pervert managers, power-hungry department clerks, and slick salesmen. I like it outside. I can sell weed without raising suspicion. I hook up with rich cougars and MILFs when I carry their bags and load their groceries. I only work twenty hours a week. It's not bad at all. My old man thinks I'm being responsible. He is happy that I don't ask him for spending money. I always tell him I am saving up for something a few weeks before I buy it. I have a pretty good gig," Wayne says as he sticks the bag of roaches into his backpack.

"You do have a good gig. You have a well-thought-out plan. Are you hiring?"

"I would say you have it made. Every girl in English class would love to hook up with you. You can be rich if you want. You are an amazing guitarist. You're good at *Jeopardy*, and you can afford to buy weed by the ounce. I have to save the roaches from social smoking deliveries for the broke moochers. When I get a baggie full of roaches, I get all the weed out of them and sell cheap bags of shake to people who never have money but always want to get high. People with no money are pests and persistent hagglers."

Theodore, laughing, says, "You have created your own generic label of weed. I have to give you credit. You are quite business savvy and make more money than I do teaching. I can't be hooking up with girls from your English class. That's the forbidden fruit and the line I won't cross. Don't get me wrong, the temptation is there, but I have enough trouble with women my own age."

"Oh, yeah, you hooked up with Claire Peterson. She is quite the fox. Mr. Peterson hates your guts. If he could get you out of this town, he would in a heartbeat."

"How do you know about Claire Peterson?"

"Mr. G, this old-money town talks. Plus, I sell weed to his eldest son, Jeff. Jeff has to tell his old man that he is tutoring me in math when we make weed deals. That entitlement kid is dumb as fuck. He is lucky he knows how to wear pants."

"Yeah, I know his kids. His youngest son, Kurtis, is in my English class. He is as dumb as a boot too. We had to create a third-string alternate position on the debate team so he could have an extracurricular that makes him appear smart on his transcripts. No matter what, though, I don't want to be the talk of the town."

Wayne packs up his backpack, throws it over his shoulder, and stands up, ready to leave.

"Like it or not, Mr. G, you're the only interesting thing in this town. People are going to talk. Plus, women are jealous, so all the rich wives fantasize about an affair with the great Theodore 'Furshizzle' Graham. You should get the fuck out of here. You could do so much more and so much better somewhere else. Tell the Douglas family to suck it, and move on to better things. Look, I gotta be moving on. I'll be back in two weeks with another ounce, but do you want to get together on Thursday and play some guitar?"

"The last thing I should be doing is taking advice from my twenty-year-old weed guy. Thursday should be good—wait, shit, I can't. The debate team has the qualifier for nationals on Thursday. I will call you. Maybe we can jam on Sunday afternoon."

"Ooh, the National Youth College Debates, that's a big deal. Gene Douglas will probably blow you if you win. All right, dude, call me when you can jam. We'll figure something out," Wayne says and leaves Theodore's place.

Theodore goes back into the study and pulls a thick book off the shelf and opens it. The book is a fake, and it is hollow. It's filled with rolling papers, a grinder, glass pipes, pipe cleaners, and other smoking devices. He sits down on the edge of his recliner and clicks on the stereo. "Stephen's Cat" by Widespread Panic is playing. He sways to the music and leans into the coffee table as he begins rolling joints from his new bag of weed.

CHAPTER 2

Theodore is sitting in the front office's waiting room as if a child waiting to be reprimanded by the principal. He knows of doing no wrong deed and has no cause for alarm. Scanning and studying the surroundings of the reception area and tapping out a rhythm on his knees, he sits content, smiling widely and saying hello to anybody passing him in the busy of the morning office. Ms. Daniels exits her office with a very cross look and motions Theodore to come to her.

Theodore makes his way to Ms. Daniels's office with a casual come-day-go-day, carefree strut. "What's up, Delores? How's it going?"

"Mr. Graham, I will be addressed as Ms. Daniels. There is a chain of superiority at this school, and I have achieved a level that commands respect."

"I'm sorry, Mrs. D, I thought you were super stoked that we won the debate last night. Our school qualified for the qualifier that qualifies the qualified team for nationals. That's huge. I figured I was here to be thanked or given a prize or something."

"It's Ms. Daniels, not Mrs. D. The debate performance aside, we have other problems to address," she says. "Have a seat, Mr. Graham."

Theodore grabs a chair, spins it around, and seats himself. "Call me Furshizzle, Ms. Daniels."

"I will not call you . . . Furshizzle!"

"How about Grandmaster T? You can call me that, Ms. Daniels."

Ms. Daniels looks at Theodore with anger. He notices her raised ire and backs off.

"Okay, Mr. Graham is fine. Call me that," he says. "So what's going on?"

Gritting her teeth, she picks up a legal pad from her desk. "You honestly don't know why you're here? Of course you don't!" she says. "I'm the one tasked with handling calls from parents about your behavior. I'm responsible for reprimanding you and doing damage control for the school."

"What did I do?" Theodore asks. "We won the debate and qualified for nationals. I didn't get caught skinny-dipping with the librarian for a few months. You stopped letting the police have the drug dogs sniff around my office and confiscating my glaucoma medication. The kids in debate club made high honors and are auditing my contemporary English class at the community college. I've been doing good, not harm."

"I am not about to praise you for graduating from monkey status to near-human status," she says. "Tell me something, Mr. Graham. How does a man with two doctorates, six published textbooks, and four top-selling novels become such a sophomoric . . . wasteoid?"

"I blame Obamacare mostly."

With a deep breath to calm herself, Ms. Daniels raises her eyes to look at Theodore. "The debate performance aside, I got a call from Mrs. Douglas."

"Oh, Ernie's mom. That kid came a long way. He was a shy, scared kid, but since he's been writing and taking guitar lessons with me, he's like a rock star. He scored six points in the science part of last night's debate. He's a smart kid. He got some confidence and swagger now."

"Yes, Ernest is doing quite well, but his mother is not happy. It is something she heard Ernest repeat. When asked where he heard it, he said on the bus ride to one of the debates."

"Oh, yeah? What did Ernie say, Mrs. D—errr, ah . . . I mean, Ms. Daniels?"

Rolling her eyes at Theodore then looking down at a legal pad, Ms. Daniels says, "Mrs. Douglas said she overheard Ernest telling their neighbor's daughter that he wanted to . . . let's see here, yes, here it is. He said he wanted to 'pop that pussy, pop, pop, pop, that pussy.'

He heard it on the debate team bus when you, the expected-to-be-responsible adult, played it."

"Cool! Ernie is into 2 Live Crew. Well, I guess I should talk to him. The song is fun to sing, but it's disrespectful to sing to girls."

"I don't think you understand, Mr. Graham. Mrs. Douglas is threatening to go to the board and ask that you be terminated. I would be more than happy to recommend the board fire you, but your students give the school the ranking we need to attract students from wealthier families. I'm not sure how to handle you."

"Okay, Ms. Daniels, no more rap music on the debate team bus. I will talk to Ernie, and I will talk to Mr. Douglas."

"It was Mrs. Douglas that made the complaint, not Mr. Douglas. Why would you have to talk to him?"

"I will talk to Mr. Douglas because, ever since I had some steamy relations with Mrs. Peterson in the cloakroom at the alumni donor dinner, Sandy Douglas has been nothing but a pain in our ass—well, your ass mostly, you get the phone calls. I think she is just jealous of Mrs. Peterson for being a rich divorced woman. Hmmm?" Theodore pauses to ponder. "Was she divorced when we were in the cloakroom? That's interesting. I should find that out. Anyway, I will talk to Mr. Douglas and tell him to take better care of Mrs. Douglas in the bedroom. Maybe if she is getting some action, she won't be a grouchy busybody."

"The placement of your penis, Mr. Graham, is a real liability for this school. When Mrs. Douglas talks to the board, I am going to recommend you are terminated so I will no longer have to take responsibility for your boorish behavior."

"Come on, Ms. Daniels! That's not fair," Theodore defends. "I love teaching these kids. I feed off their imaginations and want to do more to explain and explore this world with them. These kids are in my English classes. The words Ernie repeated from a song are English words expressed by a genre of artists that represent a portion of our population. Aren't we supposed to expose kids to culture? All cultures? Not just our own stuffy, waspy culture? These kids thirst for knowledge. You pay me to quench that thirst. I'm doing my job well.

I've raised the GPA ratings of this school a full percentage point. The board would be foolish to fire me."

"Mrs. Douglas, her husband's family founded this school. Her husband chairs the board. She sits on the board as president of the parents' association. I'm sure Mr. Douglas, Mrs. Douglas, and the rest of the board will look at your destructiveness versus the bottom line and see things my way."

"I will make you a deal, Ms. Daniels. You go to the board and cite my academic records and tell them about the national debate final, and I promise I won't poorly influence the kids. After you do that, if we don't win the national debate for the school, I will resign and will be out of your sight for good. If I win, I get to stay, maybe be promoted to the head of the English department, and replace that old fossil Lord Dingleberry."

"I will not wager with you for your job, Mr. Graham. Professor Dannonberry's penis doesn't cause me to get phone calls."

"If the school wins the national debate, you could plaster the school's win all over the media and school's literature. You can charge all these 1 percent families a shitload more in tuition fees. The school loves donations. It would be a huge feather in your cap. They might finally let you have a tenured spot on the board. You've been working for that opportunity for a long time. I would credit you for your guidance in media interviews when we win. That seat on the board would be nice, huh?"

"A shitload? How are you a professor of English? You talk as if you were from a backward, inbred section of Appalachia."

Taking a moment to think about what Theodore proposed, she weighed the benefits in her mind. Ms. Daniels exhales a conceding breath.

"Okay, Mr. Graham, you've appealed to my good business sense. I'm not sure if I should root for you to win or lose."

Theodore stands up, spins his chair around, and places it back where it came from. He begins to leave Ms. Daniels's office but turns back toward her.

"You know, Ms. Daniels, we work well together. You are a lot nicer when I can benefit you."

"Get out of my office, Mr. Graham. I've had enough of you for today."

"You know, if you were a little nicer to me, Delores, I would like to pop, pop, pop that pussy."

"Fuck you, Furshizzle. Get out of here."

"Not now, Ms. Daniels, I think I got to give it up for Mrs. Douglas first. Peace out, Mrs. D," Theodore says as he leaves and closes the office door behind him.

CHAPTER 3

Theodore pulls his beat-up olive green '72 Buick Skylark past an obese security guard, through a tall gate, and up a wide horseshoe driveway set in front of an enormous brick house resembling a castle. Blaring from Theodore's classic car windows is 2 Live Crew's hip-hop hit "Pop the Pussy." There is a limousine, a Porsche, and a cherry-red convertible parked along the side of the driveway. Theodore parks his Buick so the red convertible can't pull out. He revs the Buick's engine a few times and smiles as the big seventies engine warbles. Theodore shuts the engine off and pulls down the dashboard-mounted ashtray. He takes a joint out of the half-dozen in the ashtray and drops it in the front pocket of his shirt. He gets out of the car and strolls to the front door. As he is about to ring the doorbell, the door swings open and Sandy Douglas is standing there with a cocky yet come-hither expression.

"Mr. Graham, I have a complaint against you filed at the honor school. Your behavior in front of your students is unacceptable. I'm having you fired, and you won't be able to ruin our young minds any longer. I don't think it is wise to be here. I may have to tell the board you are harassing me at home."

Theodore grimaces at her pit bull–style attack at the front door and steps back. He puts his hands up.

"Sandy, I come in peace. I am only here to see Gene regarding another matter."

She leans into Theodore and looks at him with inquisitive yet flirty, playful eyes. "What could you possibly want to talk to my husband about? Hmmmmmmm? Maybe his vote on the board? Hmmmm?"

"No, Sandy, I just came to ask him what it's like to get to play with those nice plastic boobies every night. Plastic surgery has been good to you, Sand-Double D-Bags, hasn't it?" Theodore says and points to Sandy's breasts accentuated by her tight top and underwire bra.

"I want you off my property, you slimy snake. I have to get to the country club. I don't have time for your games. Issac, call security. We have an unwanted guest I want removed."

"Don't call security, Issac. I'm leaving peacefully," Theodore says as Issac rolls his eyes and closes the door behind Sandy. Theodore follows Sandy to her little red convertible.

"Cut the shit, Sandy. You're just looking for some way to get back at me for having sex with Claire Peterson in the cloakroom at the alumni dinner. You hens are always in a competition of merchandise, money, and the attention of men. I'm not a trophy for ladies to fight over. You only think it's wrong that I was with Claire because I wasn't with you. I remember your playful ways. Remember the dedication ceremony of the Douglas Musical Studies Lounge? Gene was conveniently away on business. The guy is filthy rich, so he works, like, three times in a year? Hard to find a more convenient time for the dedication with his busy schedule, huh? Please! You got horny and drunk at the dedication ceremony. You flirted with me all night and threw yourself at me. Then you showed up at my place, trying to seduce me, and ended up passing out on my living room floor. You were more than willing to cheat on your husband then, your husband, my college schoolmate. That dedication wasn't that long ago. What was that, like, two sets of tits ago?"

"Thankfully, nothing happened that night, but it's not about that night. It's about you being a bad influence on my son. Playing 2 Live Crew on a bus full of seventeen-year-old students? My son was serenading my neighbor's college-age daughter with 'Pop the Pussy.' That's not right."

"Is the college-girl neighbor hot? Maybe a little slutty?"

"You are an absolute pig, Teddy. I can't wait to get your ass out of that school. You're blocking me in. You're going to have to move your car."

"Come on, Sandy, we're around the same age. You contain more silicone than I do and will preserve better after death, but we're around the same age. I remember when you would visit Gene at Harvard. We were young and had fun, drunken and drug-induced fun. That was when you had your own breasts," Theodore says and hops in the passenger seat of Sandy's red convertible.

"You and Gene got inheritance-rich and boring while I kept learning, writing, publishing, and teaching. I kept enjoying life. I didn't get wrapped up in the money and the quest for material goods so I could hide in a big rail-baron's castle. You have all this money and all this stuff, yet you are so joyless that you have to give me, the working man, a hard time. Is it just so you can get some pleasure out of life? It was you guys who convinced me to come here and teach at the school. You asked me to help build the reputation of the Douglas Community College so you can play the Ivy League martyrs while raking in the earned pay of middle-class families. Now you want to have me fired? I don't get it. It has to be about my romp in the cloakroom with Claire Peterson. It can't be about your kid singing rap music with explicit sexual content."

"My kid also caught you smoking a joint in your office when he came for a guitar lesson the other day," Sandy says as she glares at Theodore reclined in the passenger seat with his legs draped over the door.

Theodore rolls his eyes. "Your kid got to learn to knock. He was half an hour early for the lesson. I like to get baked before we jam. I offered him some, and he turned it down. You're a good mom, in that way, anyway. He just said no. Hooray, you! Way to go, Sandy," Theodore says. "Besides, I remember you used to be pretty fond of having that straw up your nose and doing cocaine to stay skinny for your pretty-girl pageants on the county fair circuit. I kind of recall your real boobies being featured on the *Girls Gone Wild #9* DVD as a result of an all-night sniffy sniff coke bender at Daytona Beach. Remember that? You're a MILF, you probably have prescription medication to keep your body nice and toned now. Are you a MILF yet, or did you move up to cougarhood? When does one become a cougar? I guess when Ernie leaves the nest next year, you will be a cougar,

23

then you can go to the country club, seduce a horny caddie, a busboy or two, or the studly, cock-of-suburbia tennis pro."

"I'm going to be late. Get out and move your piece-of-shit Buick out of my way."

Theodore spins his legs into the car and sits up in the passenger seat next to Sandy. "I'm only here to see Gene. I want to talk to him for a little bit about the community college and maybe expanding some of the departments. I will make a deal with you. If I can prove your complaint to the board is because I slept with Claire Peterson and not because your son was singing dirty rap lyrics, you will tell me where Gene is so I can talk to him. We got a deal?"

"How can you prove that?"

Theodore turns on the satellite radio of Sandy's car and begins to press buttons.

"Preset button A-1, Jam On, very nice. You're expanding your Dead Head mind to other jam bands. Not bad. Preset A-2, the Grateful Dead Channel. Why aren't they number one? I don't totally disagree with your programming choices thus far. Preset A-3, Classic Vinyl. It's always a good staple for reliably good classic rock. Preset A-4, the Coffee House. This is just a channel of girls with daddy issues singing acoustic versions of classic rock. Still got daddy issues, Sandy? Maybe a lesbo fantasy or two? Nice! Preset A-5, Sirius Satellite Radio, channel number 40 and a fucking 3, BackSpin. The hip-hop channel we were listening to so we could get pumped up on the bus for the debate the other night. Ha! How can you get mad at what the coach plays on the radio in front of your child when you have the same station as a preset in your car radio? It's because of the cloakroom with Claire, isn't it?" Theodore says with a playful, satisfied smile.

"Gene is out back, sitting by the pool. Let yourself in."

"See, Sandy, that wasn't so hard. I like when we're getting along."

"Don't think for one second that I am going to drop my complaint to the board about you. I will still have you fired, and you can be easily replaced at the community college."

"You know what, Sandy?"

"What?"

"When you were passed out in your sexy black cocktail dress on my living room floor, I debated giving you the Bill Cosby treatment and taking advantage of your drunk condition for my own sexual pleasure. I didn't because I'm a gentleman and I didn't want you to do the walk of shame in the morning. You are already carrying enough shame as the oiled-and-ready, topless, horny slut from *Girls Gone Wild #9*. Besides, Claire was mostly sober, conscious, and moved around real nice."

"Gentleman my ass! Fuck you, Furshizzle! Get out of my driveway already."

"If Gene doesn't start putting out, I'm going to have no choice but to fuck the rich-bitch bitchiness out of you. Until then, give this a try," Theodore says as he offers her the joint from his pocket. "Take it. You might feel what happiness is again."

"I hate you, Teddy," she says and looks away from him. She looks back, leans over, and swipes the joint out of his fingers.

Theodore walks away from Sandy's convertible and gets into his old Buick. He starts it up and revs the engine a few times just to enjoy the warble. He spins his car around and gives a beauty pageant wave to Sandy as he passes. She flips him the middle finger and quickly speeds out of the driveway. Theodore reparks his car in the driveway.

CHAPTER 4

Theodore checks his hair in the mirror of his '72 Buick Skylark. He brushes his hand over his shirt pocket and gently pats it. Realizing his pocket is empty and remembering why, he reaches down to the dashboard-mounted ashtray and removes two tightly rolled joints from the bunch and drops them in his shirt pocket. He revs the engine a few more times to hear the warble and twists the keys in the ignition to turn the car off. He closes the joint-filled ashtray and goes to the front door and lets himself into the Douglas castle. When Theodore closes the big wooden door behind him, he sees Issac, the Douglases' butler, clearing coffee cups from the parlor table.

"Good morning, Mr. Graham. Wasn't it but ten minutes ago the lady of the house was instructing me to summon Jeremy, the four-hundred-pound security guard, to remove you from the premises? Need I call that mouth-breather now?" Issac says.

Theodore steps into the parlor and smiles at Issac. "We made nice, and the madam told me to let myself in. How have you been, Issac? What's cool in your world?"

"Life's good for me. I get to roll my eyes and hold my tongue while witnessing how far out of touch these rich-ass white folks are with the way the real world works. How can I, with a straight face, ask for more out of life? How did the famous Furshizzle make nice with Mrs. Douglas? Not with your penis, I hope? That, indeed, would be an entertaining drama to watch unfold in this household."

"Sometimes, Issac, you have to weigh the consequences of your penis. Weigh the estimated sexual satisfaction one could obtain from intercourse with a woman against the drama and nonsense one would obtain as a result of said sexual intercourse with that woman.

There is a formula, and that's what I used. It's that formula that tells me that sex with the hot Mrs. Sandy Douglas would not be worth the aftermath of the encounter. Besides, I can't be testing the thin ice I'm on by jumping on it a little more."

"Yes, Mr. Graham, she's a beautiful tree, but the cherries are sour. I take it your business is with Mr. Douglas?"

"Yes, I'm here to see Gene. Where can I find the man of the house?"

"Mr. Douglas is on the patio by the pool, watching the news and studying the public opinion polls. I take it you know how to get there, Mr. Graham. Do you need me to announce you?"

"No, Issac, you have been most helpful, and I enjoyed our exchange. Here's something for your troubles," Theodore says and removes one of the nicely rolled joints and hands it to him.

"The missus and I will enjoy this gift after dinner tonight. Thank you, kind sir."

"It's my pleasure, Issac. Tell your beautiful wife I said hello. Just think, Issac, if Mr. Douglas ends up being governor in two years, you will get to do this job in the governor's mansion."

"Fuck you, Furshizzle! I hope my black ass is retired by then."

Theodore walks through the hallway to the glass doors of the tea room. He sees Gene sitting at a patio table covered with stacks of newspapers and political polling data. Gene's face is covered by a newspaper, and his back is toward the pool. Theodore makes his way through the sliding glass door and walks toward him.

"Yo, yo, Gino, come out and play!"

Gene drops the newspaper down and sees Theodore. With a look of disappointment on his face, he says, "Teddy 'Furshizzle' Graham, haven't you caused enough headaches and heartaches in my life? Why must you antagonize my wife? You know what an absolute torment she can be."

"You were the one who said 'I do' to her. Her vagina was her gateway to your wallet. That's what happens when you marry the cheerleader type. I'm digging the new set of fun bags, though. How much did they set you back?"

"What are you doing here, Teddy? You know my wife has a complaint with the board against you. You know how she expects me to side with her and help get rid of you at the disciplinary hearing, don't you?"

"You know better than that, Gene. I'm doing good by you. I have the GPA of your great-grandpappy's legacy ranked near the top in the nation. Your son, Ernie, may be in the National Youth Debate, and he's an amazing musician. I publish my adventure novels and blog through your granddaddy's publishing house. At your daddy's community college, I teach. And because I am a noted author, I attract tuition fees. Those tuition fees are all tax-exempt and all profit for you. It probably pays for your wife's seasonal silicon-titty tune-ups."

"Look, Teddy, I look at you and I wonder, How in the hell does a middle-aged real-life Jeff Spicoli accomplish the things that you do? You are one of the most brilliant lawyers I know, but instead of continuing to practice law and build a litigation empire, you quit and decide to write trashy romance and adventure novels and teach classes to kids and community college students. You have all this brilliance, but you have my kid singing dirty hip-hop songs to my neighbor's hot daughter, and—"

Theodore interrupts, "So your neighbor's college-age daughter is hot? Ernie's got some taste. He may be a Jersey player, after all."

"This is the problem with you, Teddy. You're a hindrance to my future. For all the good things you do for me, there is all the bad things you do. You got caught skinny-dipping with the librarian in the swim team pool. I had to pay Jim Peterson seventy grand to get him to turn the surveillance tapes over to me. I had to pay that much because he is still pissed, a week after I get you hired at the school, you fuck his wife in the cloakroom at the alumni dinner. You got caught by their teenage daughter, Amanda. I had to be blackmailed for those tapes so they wouldn't haunt me in the future. He is a definite 'no' vote when the board takes up my wife's complaint about you."

"Do you still have those tapes? Pam the librarian has a smoking-hot body. Can you burn those tapes to DVD for me? Sometimes it's nice to have video to accompany the spank bank."

"I'm serious, Teddy. You're a bad influence on my kid. If he picks up your behavior, it's going to hurt me and keep him from fulfilling his part in the family legacy. You aggravate my wife by just existing. Ever since you had to stick your pecker in her archrival, Claire Peterson, I haven't heard the end of it. Your penis has become a *Where's Waldo* mystery for her on Facebook searches. She's more interested in your penis than mine. I'm the one that has to deal with her drama when you piss her off. Comforting my wife costs me a fortune in cute convertibles, plastic surgery, and expensive retail therapy sessions. Oh, and I donate a bunch of money for local police to have a drug task force, and when they are doing a training exercise in front of the media at my family's school, they find not one student with drugs but find your desk drawer full of doobies. Getting the police and media to not report that cost me an additional hundred grand in donations. I'm running for governor next year. I can't risk one of your little sex-capers, pot parties, or protests being hung on me because of my association with you. I am seriously considering swaying the board to let you go and terminating your employment at the community college. You're a hazard to me. I'm kind of leaning toward cutting you out."

Theodore reaches in his shirt pocket and pulls out a joint. He reaches in his pants pocket for his lighter, flicks it lit, and lights the joint. He takes a nice, deep hit, and as he is holding the smoke in, he offers the joint to Gene.

"What the hell is wrong with you? I just told you that I am going to have you fired because of your behavior and you light a joint in front me? Is there something wrong with you? Seriously?"

"We're still friends. Right? We can still get high together. We haven't been baked together for a long time."

"I can't be getting baked in the middle of the day. I have polls and survey results to review. New numbers are coming in this afternoon. I got some potential donors to call. I can't be getting high."

"Suit yourself. I thought it would be fun to hang out. You have to fire me to protect your political career. I understand, fine, no hard feelings, but I came here because of our friendship, not because of the teaching jobs and the convenience of publishing at your publishing house."

Gene gives in and takes the joint from Theodore. He takes a hit and goes into a coughing fit.

"I probably should have told you to hit that easy. You should probably have some beer to soothe that cough," Theodore says as he makes his way over to the refrigerator behind the patio bar.

Gene, still coughing from the hit, follows Theodore over to the bar and sits on one of the stools. Theodore stands behind the bar and places a beer in front of Gene and one in front of himself. Gene takes another drag off the joint.

As he exhales, Gene looks at Theodore. "Why can't you grow up already? You're the smartest guy I know. I was hoping you were just taking a break from practicing law and blowing off some steam. I knew you would help the family schools and was hoping that when I announced my candidacy, you would run my campaign. Instead, you're the circus act that I have to put an end to before you destroy my family name and what I have been working my whole life for."

"Working for? You don't know what work is. Your great-grand-pappy was a crooked, corrupt rail baron. He made a lot of money off the blood, sweat, and tears of the people that worked for him. When the antitrust lawsuits started to come, he cashed out with billions of dollars, turned his back on the people that made him rich, and left them for dead when the Gilded Age began to crumble and fade. He got old, feeble, and afraid to meet his Maker because the guilt of his corruption was eating his dying mind. He wanted people to praise his name, not curse it. That was why he started these schools, invested in the community, started foundations, and gave to charities. In his will, he had it written so he could still control the family and be the boss. He gave each generation of males a duty, your grandfather, your father, you, and even Ernie. Ernie's unborn son already has an obligation to fulfill. He had a plan for all of you, and the only things those plans do is get his name mentioned all throughout history.

With his money, you never had to worry. You always had the best money could buy, the enormous house, the expensive cars, the Ivy League education. Do you call sitting on boards, going to quarterly business luncheons, and chairing pointless committees, doing actual work? You get your ass kissed and sell your board votes to the highest bidder."

Gene takes a sip from the beer bottle in front of him and passes the joint to Theodore.

"That's not fair. I'm not going to feel guilty for being fortunate."

"I'm not trying to make you feel guilty because you're fortunate. It's what you are doing with that fortune. You have so much power and influence. You can make such a difference in the world. Your schools could do so much more. The Douglas Youth Honors College, it's a few financially recruited brilliant young minds surrounded by clueless, superrich entitlement kids. They pay you a shitload of money for a certificate to say that their stupid kids are super smart. The community college could serve to better so many more, but you don't invest in the community around it. These are just educated locals with no place to work that are going to move away for opportunity or stick around for heroin and welfare. Your legacy should be because of something good you do, not for how many centuries the Douglas fortune can live on with notoriety."

Theodore takes another sip of his beer.

"You know why I quit practicing law?"

"No, Teddy, why did you quit law?"

"I got tired of litigating laws, contracts, and collective bargaining agreements for superrich assholes. It's not the class that I came from. I felt sick for getting paid well to keep people like my father down. I lost my mother to a car accident when I was three. My father worked as a union welder in a hot, dangerous factory. He never recovered from the loss of my mother, but he made sure I was being the best I could be. He didn't want me to be stuck working in a place like him. He taught me a work ethic and the value of knowledge. I came from a blue-collar town, had a twenty-five-hour workweek at the local grocery store, and had full-time schooling at the age of thirteen. On weekends, I did side jobs with my dad, putting decks on, laying concrete patios, and doing tree removal. He worked all the time, overtime, and anytime, just so he could try to get me the best the world could offer. The guy never enjoyed himself. He died at work, for Christ's sake. When I was in grad school and got the call that he had a massive heart attack and died, I went home and had to handle all his affairs. I got to see how he lived. It was sad. He lived with nothing but what he needed to survive and without love and companionship. He lived like that for me so I could have opportunity. He did it so I wouldn't fall into the bitter, blue-collar mind trap that makes one mad at the world. My old man died providing me with the real American dream. As a lawyer, I didn't want to help rich people save money by hurting hardworking people like my dad. When I got to Harvard, I don't think there was a prouder man on the planet. My dad saw the toil of his shitty life finally paying off. I owed it to him to work just as hard in school and not let his hard work be in vain. If you failed out of Harvard, you came back to your castle, cars, cash, and unlimited second chances. If I failed out of Harvard, I failed that man. I couldn't disrespect him like that. I couldn't be that lawyer that manipulated collective bargaining agreements for profiteers that wanted to cut benefits and salaries for regular working folks. I made more than enough in law to go back to school for my English doctorate, and you hooked me up with my gigs here. Teaching is my outlet to help others have a chance at a better life. I don't have children of my own to shape, so I try to shape my students. I'm not interested in running your campaign, because I do not want to take cues from your crusty old fossil-fuel friends that are protecting their old dirty money from regular folks. I don't want to give legal advice to lobbyists that litigate to keep the wealthy class wealthy and in power. When we were in college, you still had the ability to empathize. Now you just read papers and opinion polls that tell you how to behave so you can get elected. You had a social conscience, Gene. You used to believe that people could make a better tomorrow. Now you shape-shift to appeal to people so they will vote for you and so you can fulfill your duty to your great-grandpappy. What the hell happened?"

"Don't give me your rags-to-riches bullshit. You chose not to chase the wealth. If you go back to litigating, you would have as much as I do. Maybe even more."

Teddy turns around and takes two more bottles of Heineken out of the refrigerator. He places one in front of Gene and sips his before setting it on the bar in front of him. Gene offers the joint to him. Teddy takes it and takes a long hit and looks toward the tea room inside the house.

"I always thought about gold-digging the nursing home, assisted living, and elder community circuit. I could parade around with these rich, golden-year, old-money women, treat them like trophies, and they would put me in their wills, marry me, leave me their fortunes, or hook me up with their sexy, rich daughters. Old ladies like me. That might be my calling, and there is no way for me to lose," Theodore says with a thoughtful grimace.

"You will have plenty of time to chase that dream after I fire you."

"You're pretty baked, aren't you?" Theodore asks. "You got a nice high going, don't you?"

"Yeah, I don't know how you get me to behave like this. I got shit to do. New polls are coming in. Sandy is gone for the afternoon. I wanted to get a lot done today. I have a long gubernatorial race to run starting this spring. Now here I am, two beers before noon, and I am completely stoned."

"You're welcome."

"No, Teddy. This is exactly what I mean. You are a hindrance. You are a distraction that prevents me from fulfilling the demands of my family legacy."

Theodore reaches across the bar and puts his hand on Gene's shoulder. "I miss hanging out with you. We used to have fun. I'm having fun now. Besides, the Democrats are going to run Sherman Jones. He's the fall guy that will be well paid to lose to you. When your two terms are up, you guys will run a fall guy so some rich Democrat can have his turn. You don't need to do all this stuff. You're a lock to win."

"It's not that easy. I have to make appearances. I have to make speeches. I have to fund-raise. I have to get media support. I have to appeal to voters at town hall meetings, and I have to get those new voters so the Democrats aren't in a position to get a turn after my terms."

"I would be so good at coordinating all that stuff for you. It's kind of my thing."

Gene gets up from his barstool and looks at Theodore with cold, piercing eyes. "I wanted you in that position, then you gave up law. I hired you here at my schools, hoping the teaching bug would leave your system and you could be my chief executive and run my campaign and office. But no! The great Teddy Furshizzle has to be the pothead man-child that can't stay out of trouble and has become a liability to me and my family name. You should probably go, Teddy."

"Hey, look, there's Issac in the tea room!" Theodore cheerfully exclaims and waves to him and flails his arm wildly.

Issac sees Theodore and turns his head back to his work dusting off the tea tables. He shakes his head disapprovingly at Teddy's antics.

"Did you ever sit in that tea room?"

Puzzled, Gene looks at Issac in the tea room and then back at Theodore. "I guess. Sandy hosts her pageant committee meetings there and country club fund-raising luncheons in there. I don't go in there often."

Theodore gets out from behind the patio bar and makes his way to the big glass windows and looks inside. Issac finished his dusting and left the tea room for the hallway. Theodore stoops down and looks closely inside the window.

"The furniture in there is hideous. I bet the wife picked it out. I bet you paid a nice penny for that ugly stuff."

"Teddy, this has been . . . fun, but it's been a horrible waste of time for me. You should get going."

Theodore comes back over to the patio bar and sits on the stool next to Gene. "Look, Gene, I'm sorry I've been such a liability. I wasn't born into this culture. I don't understand it. I still like to enjoy life and don't want to feel like I have to be putting puzzle pieces in the right spots so my legacy is perfectly put together. I don't have a legacy to pass on or fulfill. But you're my friend. I don't want to ruin things for you. I would actually love to help you with the campaign. It's the least I could do. If you don't want me on the campaign, I understand—at least keep me at the schools. I like teaching. I like the debate team. The publishing house is a huge help. I hope to have a book ready to publish at the end of the school year. I can stop the nonsense. The last thing I want to do is hurt the happiness of a friend."

"I don't know, Teddy. If I get rid of you, Jim Peterson will be off my back, Sandy will stop being such a pain in my ass, and I don't have to worry about getting caught up in or having to spend money to cover up your bad behavior. It just seems smarter to get rid of you."

Theodore stands up and walks behind the patio bar and gets another beer out of the refrigerator. "Do you want another one, buddy?" Theodore asks as he offers one of Gene's beers to him.

"No, Teddy, I got to get back to work."

"Do you mind if I take one for the road?"

"Yeah, Teddy, help yourself."

Theodore grabs one of the folded six-pack holders next to the wastebasket, unfolds it, and begins filling it with bottles of Heineken. Gene is disgusted but says nothing. Theodore puts the six-pack on top of the bar. He turns back to the refrigerator, opens it again, and takes another bottle of beer out and uncaps it.

"You're almost out of beer, you're going to have to restock this fridge."

"Just go, Teddy. I have work to do."

"Hey, was the Douglas Youth Honors College ever in the national youth debate before?"

Gene thinks for a moment. "No, they never even made it to the qualifier."

"The school is in the qualifier Thursday, but after my hearing with the board, I will be gone. I guess Earl Dingleberry will have to rally the team and get them in the nationals," Theodore says as he picks up the six-pack and begins to make his way toward the house to leave.

"Professor Dannonberry will do just fine, I'm sure. I'm sorry, Teddy, this is what's best for me and my family."

"That's cool. I hope he does."

"Yeah, he'll be fine, I'm sure."

"You know, if the school won the national debate, even if they only qualified for it, it would look so good for your family name, and it would be a strong positive to campaign on. If my new book sells as good as the last one, I will have to do media interviews and appearances. I could talk about the youth school, your contributions to the community with the community college, and how you made the decision to bring me here. I would even announce that I am taking a year's leave from teaching so I could work on your campaign because I want to help you do even more for education. Anyway, you saved me a lot of trouble and talking. Thanks for the beers," Theodore says as he opens the door to the house.

"Wait, Teddy. You would seriously work for my campaign? Speech writing? Navigate the legalities? Help me appeal to new voters? You would do all that and stay out of trouble?"

"This is what you've been working your whole life for. I'm your friend for a long time. Of course I would help you."

"I don't know, Teddy. This offer seems too little too late, and you've already caused me enough headache, expense, and stress. I just don't know."

"I told you I understand the danger I pose. I will see you at my disciplinary hearing. Hopefully, I can convince the board to at least let me finish out the year. Odds aren't in my favor. Delores Daniels is a no vote from the administration, Jim Peterson is a definite no, your wife as head of the parents' association is a no, and if it's a tie, you will vote no. I don't know who else will be on the committee, but it is what it is."

"Try not to give Jim Peterson a hard time at the hearing."

Teddy is in the doorway of the house, and as he is about to leave, he says, "Sandy treats you like crap. Let's get back at her. We can make a video of us leaving beer farts on this hideous tea room furniture, and I will post it on my Facebook page."

"That would make home life worse for me."

"Yeah, I guess you're right. Hey, can you text me a picture of her latest breasts? I'm curious."

"Fuck you, Furshizzle. It's going to be a sweet sorrow that brings peace to my life when I let you go."

Teddy makes his way into the house. Gene watches through the big glass window. Teddy goes into the tea room, drops his shorts to expose his butt, and sits on one of the tea tables. He pulls out his cell phone and snaps a selfie. After Teddy pulls his pants up and puts his phone back in his pocket, he gives Gene a thumbs-up and waves to him while he watches from the patio. Teddy picks up his half-finished bottle and the six-pack of Heineken and disappears and into the hallway.

Chapter 5

The Douglas Youth Honors College boardroom resembles council and committee rooms of the finest Ivy League colleges and law schools. Cherrywood decor depicts symbols of education, justice, integrity, tradition, and honor. The spectacle of the room hints of a self-praising hierarchy of a wealthy class. There are large centuries-old dark wood tables set on a wood-railed platform that sits three feet above the main floor. There are three high-back leather chairs on either side of a further-raised board chairman's booth. Each chair has gold name and title plates placed on the table in front of them. On the main floor facing the committee tables and the chairman's booth six feet above is a two-seated, gated wooden booth with a podium. On the gate to the booth is a gold-plated sign that reads, "For those having business with the Douglas Youth Honors College Board." Behind the board table, in one corner, is an American flag, and in the other corner, a flag with the school crest, which is also the Douglas family crest.

Gene Douglas takes his seat in the board chairman's booth, and all but one member of the board is seated in the high-back leather chairs. The center booth on the floor is unoccupied as an attractive stenographer sits adjacent and ready to record the board hearing. The four rows of public seating in the back of the room are empty.

"This hearing is to start in five minutes, and that man-child isn't here yet. Has he no respect for this school at all?" Jim Peterson asks Gene Douglas, the board chairman.

"Calm down, Jim. Rose Fayweather isn't here yet. We can't start without her. If Mr. Graham doesn't make it, our decision today will be very simple to make," Gene responds.

"The sooner that man is out of here, the better. If we don't do this now, Gene, he will take your school and your candidacy for the governor with it."

The wooden door at the back of the boardroom opens. Rose Fayweather and Theodore are laughing as they enter the room. Following the two are six uniformed students with the Douglas family crest on the breast of their blazers. Rose and Theodore get to the center booth on the main floor. Rose whispers to Theodore, and she spins around. Theodore zips the zipper on the back of her judicial robe. Rose turns around, gives Theodore a hug and a peck on the cheek, and makes her way to the empty board member chair. Theodore goes through the gate of the protestants' booth, places his briefcase on the chair, and places a legal pad and pen on the podium.

Jim Peterson and Sandy Douglas shoot angry looks at Theodore as he instructs the students to sit down.

"Who are these students, Mr. Graham? Why are they present at this hearing?" Jim Peterson asks.

"These students are political science underclassmen that will be eligible to run for student union offices next year. One of them may replace Mr. Winters, who will be going to Princeton in the fall. Professor Peterson—wait, is it Professor Peterson, or did Claire remarry, or did she go back to her maiden name after the divorce?" Theodore asks.

The look on Jim Peterson's face turned from angry to furious, and Theodore gives him a playful wink.

"Anyway, Professor Claire, the stunning and brilliant dean of social sciences, thought this hearing would be a great opportunity for these students to learn the proceedings of this board and to see the role Mr. Winters plays as president of the student union," Theodore says.

"I am not so sure that this hearing is appropriate for these students, Mr. Graham," Jim Peterson snaps.

"Are you going to do a lot of cursing and swearing, Jim?" Theodore asks. "Will there be brief nudity? I was to the understanding that this would be a fair hearing where the board is to take a vote after a period of inquiry. Is this not an educational institution tasked with educating these young minds?"

"I think you ought to address this board with a little more respect, Mr. Graham. This is, after all, a hearing called to address your conduct at this school."

"It is a hearing about my conduct, yet I care more about these students learning from it than I do about my own reputation. I think I should get credit for being a teacher first and being a defendant in front of this board second."

Jim Peterson stands up and points down at Theodore. "You are not going to make a circus out of this proceeding, Mr. Graham, and these students are not going to gain you any credit."

"Sit down, Mr. Peterson!" Rose Fayweather shouts. "As dean of education at this school, I think this is an excellent opportunity for these students to learn about these proceedings, and I personally would like to discuss what they learned in a panel discussion afterward. Does anyone else besides Mr. Peterson object to these students being here?"

No other members of the board raise their hands or indicate that they don't want the students in the proceedings. With an angry scowl, Jim Peterson sits down. Theodore turns around and gives the quietly seated students a thumbs-up.

"Thank you, Mrs. Fayweather. A panel discussion after this proceeding is an absolutely wonderful idea. It didn't even occur to me. I guess that's why you are the dean of education," Theodore says.

Gene picks up the gavel and slams it three times. "Let's get this proceeding moving. The students can stay as long as they aren't disruptive."

Gene taps the gavel three more times. "I, Eugene H. Douglas, chairman of the board, call this meeting of the Douglas Youth Honors College to order on the date, Wednesday, March the sixteenth in the year of our Lord 2015. Will members serving on this board make their presence known for the record."

The young student at the board table rises. "Carl Winters, president of the student union, is present, Mr. Chairman."

"Burt Lewis, controller of the Douglas Youth Honors College, is present, Your Honor."

"Sandy Douglas, president of the parents committee, is present, Your Honor."

"Rose Fayweather, dean of education is present, Your Honor."

Theodore gives her a playful wink and little wave as she returns to her seat. She shyly waves back.

"Jim Peterson, campus trustee, is present, Your Honor."

Theodore makes a masturbation motion. A series of brief snickers and giggles from the students erupts.

"Dolores Daniels, school administrator, is present, Mr. Chairman."

"The board meets quorum for this hearing. May we hear introduction from those having business with this board?" Gene says, looking down at Theodore sitting in his chair.

Theodore remains quietly seated, facing the board members at the table in front of him. He then turns his head, scanning the room to see if anyone else has risen.

"Mr. Graham, you are the one that has business before the board. Please make your presence known for the record," Gene says.

Theodore remains seated. "Gene, I have no business with the board. The board requested my presence at this hearing. You already mentioned my name, so I see no need for the redundancy."

"Introduce yourself to this board for the record, Mr. Graham."

Theodore stands. "Theodore 'Furshizzle' Graham, teacher and debate team coach, is present."

"Mr. Graham, you are called in front of this board because there have been complaints registered by parents about your behavior and actions. These complaints will be discussed before the board. You will be given a chance to defend and clarify your position, and the board will determine and vote on necessary actions to be taken," Gene says.

Theodore stands. "Gene, I believe I have the right to know my accusers."

"You will address me as Your Honor or Mr. Chairman."

"I'm sorry, Gene, Mr. Your Honor Chairman, but I believe I have a right to know my accusers."

"The parents registering the complaints have chosen to remain anonymous, Mr. Graham. It's your behavior that is in question, not the identity of the parents registering complaints against you."

Theodore nods. "Well, I have heard from Delores Daniels, the administrator, that Sandy Douglas was registering a complaint against me, and I suspect that Jim Peterson was following her lead. They have both voiced their distaste for my existence. If those are the parents registering the complaints against me, I believe they should both abstain from this hearing since they are both complainants and board members. It is in the best interest of fairness."

"The parents registering these complaints shall remain anonymous, and you will be given fair opportunity to defend yourself, Mr. Graham."

"I want the record to show that I question the fairness of this proceeding in the event that the events of this hearing will be brought up at a future Department of Labor hearing. Oh, wow, your glasses are really pretty and you look good in them. Don't type that part into your little machine," Theodore says to the stenographer.

She nervously giggles.

"Mr. Peterson, will you present the issues regarding Mr. Graham's behavior for the board?" Gene says.

Jim Peterson stands and stares directly at Theodore. "With pleasure, Mr. Chairman. First, Mr. Graham has been accused of exposing students to lewd and offensive material. Second, Mr. Graham has been accused of using marijuana on school property. Third, Mr. Graham is disrespectful to the traditions, values, and conduct of the Douglas Youth Honors College. These are the charges brought to be resolved here today, Your Honor."

"Thank you, Mr. Peterson. You may be seated."

"Mr. Your Honor, can I address these charges one at a time?" Theodore asks.

Gritting his teeth, Gene answers, "It is Mr. Chairman or Your Honor."

"Yes, Your Chair, apologies, Mr. Honor."

Jim Peterson quickly stands up. "This man is making a mockery of this hearing. He cares nothing about his consequences. He is out of order."

"I'm out of order! You're out of order, the whole freaking system is out of—"

Teddy says until he is interrupted.

"Enough, Teddy!" Gene shouts.

"It's Mr. Graham, Your Honor, as the record will show. Do I need the stenographer to read back my introduction to the board? I thought Mr. Peterson was quoting the film *A Few Good Men*. I was just playing along. It's a great freaking movie, Mr. P."

"Mr. Graham, the first charge is that you exposed students to lewd and offensive material," Gene says.

Theodore stands. "Your Honor, I do not know of which material the board is referring. I need more information on said material so I can form an informed argument in my defense. I do know for a fact that I didn't show the students *Girls Gone Wild #9*, but perhaps I can borrow your copy."

Gene's expression turns irate as Sandy Douglas lowers her head and stares at the table, not wanting to make eye contact with others in the room.

"Mrs. Douglas, you've taken the complaints registered by the parents and brought them to this board. Please elaborate for this proceeding," Gene instructs his wife.

"Yes, Your Honor. Mr. Graham played offensive hip-hop rap music on the bus to the debate team competition last week," Sandy Douglas says.

Theodore returns to his feet. "Can you be a little more specific, Mrs. Douglas? I doubt that all hip-hop or rap music is offensive. Because the majority of artists excelling in those styles of music are nonwhite, not being specific would, in a transcript of this hearing, appear racially biased."

"Yes, Mr. Graham, the song 'Pop the Pussy' by 2 Live Crew was played on the bus ride to the debate," Sandy explains.

"I remember hearing that song. I thought it was about a cat," Theodore says.

The students seated behind him snicker and giggle.

"Mr. Graham, do you think it's funny exposing impressionable youth to music with foul language and sexual undertones?" Gene asks.

"The bus is property of the Douglas Youth Honors College. It is equipped with satellite radio that the school pays a subscription for. There are parental controls on the receiver of the radio that can be used to block out content and channels that may be considered inappropriate for impressionable youth. It is not in my job description to determine what is acceptable or unacceptable. The students control the radio. I think the campus trustee should be held accountable for not using the parental controls that would have prevented the students being exposed to the material in question," Theodore says.

Gene shuffles through some papers in front of him. His expression grows more irritated. He flips through a couple of loose leaf pages and pulls one out and places it on top of the pile.

"The second charge, Mr. Graham, is that you are using marijuana on school property. Marijuana is illegal in this country and in this state. It is forbidden on this campus. It was reported that the smell of marijuana was coming from your office," Gene says.

"Mr. Chairman, I will not lie to you. I did try marijuana back in college. Oh, that's right, you and I went to college together. Didn't you try it with me? Wasn't your wife, Sandy, there too?" Theodore points to Sandy Douglas seated at the table.

Gene and Sandy lower their heads as Theodore opens his briefcase and pulls out a small square of paper that appears to be an invoice.

"Anyway, enough about our crazy college days. I think this slip of paper will help. It's a request to the maintenance department asking them to address the skunk problem near the faculty building. I had the windows open because I burned a Hot Pocket in the microwave and it was smoky in my office. That was when I noticed a strong skunk smell coming in. Sometimes the odor of skunk urine can resemble the smoke of a burning marijuana plant. I just didn't have time to drop the request slip off at the maintenance office. I will drop it off after this hearing," Theodore explains.

"He knew he was being charged with this and just filled that slip out to try to fool us with this skunk story. This board isn't buying that fabrication, Mr. Graham. You are using illegal narcotics on this campus, and it won't be tolerated," Jim Peterson scolds from his chair.

"May I address the board, Mr. Chairman?" Carl Winters, the student union president, asks.

"Yes, Mr. Winters."

"When we were out for a run with the cross-country team last week, Charlie from maintenance told us not to run by the faculty building after dark because of the skunks. He said somebody from animal control will be in to trap them soon."

"Thank you for helping me clear up this misunderstanding, Carl," Theodore says.

"There is the third charge. Mr. Graham is disrespectful to the traditions, values, and conduct of the Douglas Youth Honors College. Can you elaborate on this for us a little more, Mr. Lewis?" Gene asks.

"Yes, Mr. Chairman. It's obvious by the behavior of Mr. Graham at this hearing that he does not respect this school or anything that it stands for. He doesn't appear to respect himself. I've have yet to see him in a school blazer with the school crest as the students seated behind him are wearing. I haven't seen him in one as a teacher, at a debate competition, or at any formal social engagement of this school. His refusal to wear the blazer with the school crest is clearly an indication of his distaste for our rules, values, and conduct," Burt Lewis explains.

"Mr. Lewis, with all due respect, I do not own a Douglas Youth Honors College blazer with the school crest. I am not a student at the school, an alumni of the school, or a tenured educator at this school. According to school bylaws, I have to be one of those to wear the blazer. I was up for tenure at the end of last school year, but I didn't push Mr. Peterson for my tenure review hearing because he was going through a rough divorce and I didn't want to add to his stress. I was also busy helping to console Claire Peterson through a tough time," Theodore says.

"You are a snake, but that is correct, Mr. Graham, you are not tenured. I didn't think of it until now. You made the job of this board real easy. You are not a tenured teacher at this school and therefore are not entitled and have no right to defend yourself at a hearing. It is up to the board, and you have no say. I make the motion that the board take an immediate vote on the employment status of Mr. Graham," Jim Peterson says with a look of satisfaction.

"I second the motion," Sandy Douglas declares.

"According to the rules, Mr. Graham, you are not tenured and have no right to be present at this vote. You are dismissed from this boardroom. I ask that you please wait in your office. I will notify you of the outcome and the next steps that need to be taken," Gene says.

"You guys invited me, but no problem, dudes. I will see you in my office a little later, Gene. Mrs. Fayweather, no matter the outcome, I would still love to come over Saturday for lasagna and check out some of your Buddy Rich albums. That is, if you'll still have me, of course," Theodore says, closes his briefcase, and leaves the boardroom.

The door closes behind Theodore, and the room settles. The students face forward, and the board members sit straight in their seats. The shuffle of people turns to respectful silence.

"All right, let's get this over with. We will conduct a procedural vote. With each vote, each board member should make a brief statement on their reasoning for the record. A *yay* vote means Theodore Graham remains in his current position as a teacher and the debate coach. A *nay* vote means he will be terminated immediately and be given forty-eight hours to vacate his faculty housing. Does any board member have questions?" Gene says.

Gene scans and looks around at the board members and sees there are no raised hands.

"All right, let's start the voting. Burt Lewis, how does the controller vote?"

"Theodore Graham, he behaves too middle-class for my liking. There is no place for his antics at this school. He is a liability. I vote nay."

"Campus Trustee, how vote ye?"

"That man is the most vile human I ever met. He is poison for this school, and he is poison for the minds that attend it. I vote nay," Jim Peterson says.

"Sandy Douglas, how does the president of the parents committee vote?"

"That man is a bad influence on our children and sets a bad example. I vote nay."

"How about the student union president, how do you vote, Mr. Winters?"

"I've had Mr. Graham for only one class at this school. I've always been the athletic type and not the scholastic type, but in his class, Mr. Graham taught me reading tips and critical thinking skills that I credit for helping me get into Princeton next fall. He is a good teacher. I vote yay."

"Mrs. Fayweather, how does the dean of education vote?"

"Gene, dear, Theodore is the only interesting friend you have. He has a brilliant mind and a caring heart. He is not from our class, so he is rough around the edges. He has a zest for life and the pleasures in it, and that's how he inspires students like Mr. Winters sitting next to me. Don't you think he only fights authority because authority needled his class his whole life? He is very loyal to the ones that are not holding their wealth over his middle-class roots. He is the life force this school needs to move forward. I vote yay."

"How does the administration vote, Ms. Daniels?"

"Mr. Graham is nothing but a headache for me. Each complaint about him lands on my desk first. I despise being his babysitter. I abhor the man. I did, however, crunch some numbers. If Mr. Graham at least qualifies the team for the national debate, there will be a greater interest in the school and we can raise tuition fees by 8 percent and have full enrollment. If Mr. Graham wins the debate, the school can raise tuition fees by 30 percent and we will have to turn students away. Mr. Graham has, I believe, a probable chance of winning. I don't think Professor Dannonberry has the skills needed to take the team to victory, and the qualifier is tomorrow night. The tuition fees alone would improve the school's profit, but donations from families trying to secure spots for their family members in the

Douglas School would be in the millions. It only makes good business sense to keep Mr. Graham. I vote yay."

"The board is tied. The deciding vote is yours, Gene," Burt Lewis says.

"Hearing of Ms. Daniels's research and the benefit to the school, I have to vote yay and grant Mr. Graham tenure so the school's crest will be displayed on his blazer at the national debates," Gene says.

Sandy Douglas looks at her husband with a scowl. Burt Lewis stands up and leaves the room without saying a word. The students sitting in on the board meeting applaud. Jim Peterson looks as if he wants to kill. He approaches Gene like he wants to scream and holler but is so defeated with fury that all he can do is mutter and mumble incoherently.

"As chairman of this board, I declare this meeting adjourned. Jim, please make sure that Mr. Graham gets a blazer with the school crest so he will be wearing one for the qualifier debates," Gene says and pounds the gavel.

*   *   *

Down the narrow old corridors of an institution that old money built and modernized with the hum of thirty-year-old fluorescent lighting, Gene makes his way to let Theodore Graham know the fate of his employment. He still isn't 100 percent sure of why he has voted in favor of keeping Theodore. The reasons range from profit, a tool to prestige, a reward for loyalty, to friendship. Gene chooses to believe it's friendship, though the other reasons are to his benefit. It is always a pleasure to deliver good news, and Gene makes his way to the dark chestnut-wood door of Theodore's corner office overlooking the campus quad.

Knock knock knock.

"It's Gene Douglas. Teddy, are you in there?"

"I'll buzz you in. Come on in, Gino."

Bzzzzzzzzzzz click.

Gene enters Theodore's office. There is marijuana smoke hanging in the air, a bong and beer bottles on the coffee table, and

Theodore is on the leather sofa, kissing the stenographer from the hearing. Her hair is down, her glasses are off, her blouse has a few buttons undone, and her black lacy bra is exposed.

"You remember Jennifer from the hearing? Jennifer here was just telling me about her job as a stenographer. It's a really interesting profession."

"I'll bet it is, Mr. Graham. Ms. Boyle, can you excuse us? I need to talk with Mr. Graham for a while."

"Sure thing, Mr. Douglas. Teddy, if you want to learn more about dictation, call me later," Jennifer says as she buttons her blouse.

She gives Theodore a playful wink as she puts her dark-rimmed glasses on. She puts her suit jacket on and gathers her purse and makes her way to the door and turns around and to give Theodore a little wave of her hand and then exits.

"I take it you heard about the board's vote already. I think I might already be regretting my vote," Gene says as he waves the marijuana smoke that hangs in the air.

Theodore points to the bong sitting on the table in front of him. "You want a whack of that? I just packed a fresh one. I thought we would celebrate."

"No, I don't want a whack of your bong, Teddy. I came here to let you know the good news, but I see Ms. Boyle beat me to it. How do you do it, Teddy? The hearing about your conduct ended less than an hour ago, and I find you smoking pot and making out with the stenographer."

"I'm a people person, I guess," Theodore says. "Sit down. Let me at least grab you a beer."

Theodore takes a bottle of Heineken out of an ice- and beer-filled Coleman lunch cooler on the floor next to him and offers it to Gene. Gene takes the beer out of Theodore's hand and takes a seat on the leather sofa next to him.

"You don't know how close you came to being tossed out of here, Teddy. Jim Peterson is furious. All he could do after I voted was murmur, stutter, and mumble. It will be a while before Sandy talks to me again, and when she does, it's going to cost me a fortune."

Theodore motions to the bong, shrugs, and motions to the bong again.

"Yeah, you're right, Teddy, I might as well make the best of it." Gene picks up the bong, lights it, and takes a long hit.

"Attaboy! If only Jim Peterson could see us now."

Gene exhales and chuckles. "That guy hates you. My wife hates you. I probably should too, but you are a good friend, a loyal person, and I can use you in my corner. Were you serious the other day on my patio when you said you would run or at least work on my campaign?"

"Yes, I was serious. I know you have a great shot at being governor, and I know you have the power and the influence to do great things. You can help so many people, and you can pay it forward. If you want me on board to help you do those things, I'm on board. You can fulfill your family legacy and leave one of your own, one that you made. I'm in, let's do it."

"Needing you on my campaign, I think that's what made me vote in your favor at the hearing today. I hope that doesn't make me a bad person."

"What are friends for? You've done a lot for me, and for that, I'm grateful. I promise you this, I will tone down the circus of me. I can't let the next governor of our state be dragged down by scandal. Let's get Eugene H. Douglas elected governor."

"It's a deal," Gene agrees and shakes Theodore's hand.

"What is the missus going to say when she finds out that not only am I not getting fired, I am becoming your campaign manager also?"

"Oh, fuck. I don't even want to think about breaking that news to her."

"If you want to be the next governor, tell the voters your wife will show her tits. That's it! That's our strategy. Ballots for boobies. It's fucking genius," Theodore says. "The voters will eat that shit up, especially college-age male voters and bi-curious female scholars."

"Umm, that's one idea, but let's look at some others, maybe after I get an election team together."

"Okay, at least that idea is on the top of the pile for now. Do you think I can at least see them?"

"Fuck you, Furshizzle! Please don't torment her too horribly through the whole campaign ordeal. I beg you."

"I will promise to do my best to make nice."

Gene stands up from the sofa and takes the last swig of his beer. He picks up the bong and takes a hit off it.

"I got to go. I probably shouldn't be smoking pot on school property," Gene jokes.

"It's those goddamn skunks. Maintenance better get on that."

Gene is shaking his head and laughing as he makes his way to the door. At the door, Gene turns around. "Win me that qualifier, Teddy. Those kids can't do it without your guidance."

Theodore, with the bong at his mouth, offers a thumbs-up. Gene leaves, and the door closes behind him.

CHAPTER 6

Theodore and Ernie are jamming on their guitars while in a studio recording session. They take turns leading; they mimic riffs, expand on them, draw them out, and play the notes and chords simultaneously. A bald middle-aged man in the studio booth can be seen moving his head to the music as he monitors levels and adjusts knobs on a mixing board. To the observer, one would conclude the guitarists are either competing against or complimenting each other. The two come together for one last series of bars and bring the song to an end.

Through an intercom speaker, Sid says, "You two guys should start a band. Having you guys record in here is refreshing. It's a nice change from recording audition tapes for untalented entitlement kids with their helicopter parents hovering over me. Is that it, Teddy, or do you guys want to lay down some more tracks?"

"That should be it, Sid. Can you make copies of all the tracks of us playing together and isolate Ernie's guitar and make copies of that?" Theodore asks.

"You got it, Teddy. You want copies of your playing isolated too?"

"No, just Ernie's."

"I will have them ready in half an hour, forty minutes, if you guys want to hang tight."

"Hey, Sid, how does a stubby middle-aged recording studio attendant get a hot girl like the one I saw you with at the store the other day? You didn't promise to help make her famous, did you?"

"Fuck you, Furshizzle! She happens to think I am a good guy. It's just a coincidence that I can help her with audition tapes. Don't knock it, man. The regular sex and blow jobs are a refreshing change from internet porn and whacking off. I got to take it where I can get it."

"I can't blame you. She is a good-looking woman. I hope she can sing."

"Her voice is hideous, so I can almost count on getting laid regularly for a while, at least until some producer is honest with her. Sit tight, I will get these copies to you in a bit."

Theodore and Ernie disconnect their guitar straps and wrap their amp cords. They place their guitars in their cases and grab bottles of water before sitting on the stools inside the studio.

"How come they call you Furshizzle?" Ernie asks. "Is it because you made some white guy hip-hop music or rap or something?"

Theodore laughs. "I wish it were because of that, but it's a pretty embarrassing story. It's been with me since I was a freshman at Harvard. I wished it would go away, but some people, like your mother and father, retell it, so I never escape it. I am surprised your old man never told you."

"The old man doesn't tell me much. He just tells me to stick to my legacy plan and don't get wrapped up in nonsense. So why do they call you Furshizzle?"

"Well, kid, you're going to laugh. It's not for flattering reasons. I grew up in an area that was mostly white. There was not one non-white kid in my high school. We had one kid from Thailand that was adopted by a white family. That was the extent of diversity where I grew up. I remember a youth bus trip to the city. The kids were more amazed by seeing for real black people than they were seeing the museum exhibits and skyscrapers."

"That is definitely a white area. Sounds like the country club."

"The country club is full of rich people that can afford to keep brown people out. My area was mostly middle-class, working families. Ethnic mobs and hooded organizations didn't let people of color settle there peacefully for any extended amount of time. It wasn't right, but it was the way it was. It was hard enough for Eastern Europeans, Irish, Italians, and Germans to get along with one another under the power of the waspy English folks that thought it was their God-given duty to rule over all. Diversity with nonwhite cultures in that kind of area was viewed negatively. It was feared because it would upset the balance of power. One politician from my neighborhood used to get drunk at a local bar and loudly proclaim when he made toasts, 'If the area is all white, I'm doing something right!' That kind of shit doesn't fly in the evolving world today."

"So what does this have to do with your nickname being Furshizzle?"

"I was raised culturally ignorant because of my surroundings growing up. College was an awakening for me. When I was at Harvard, I used to study at this little family-owned sandwich shop off campus. The sandwich shop was owned by the Gatley family, a black family. One of the waitresses was their daughter, whom I hit it off with. We used to talk about books, music, and movies. We had a lot in common, so we started dating. Her name was Sally Gatley, and I used to take her to the student union to hang out with me and your dad and other friends. There was a junior named Raymond Whitney in the fraternity that your dad was pledging, Delta Gamma Dollar Sign or whatever it is. My family credit rating and public school education excluded me from membership, which was fine with me. Fraternities to me were places where asshole kids experimented with homosexual acts, fucked one another's girlfriends, and pretended it was a sacred brotherhood. I had no interest in fraternity life. I shouldn't tell you that. Your father will probably insist you join the same fraternity."

"Yes, Father Gene already gave me the rundown on being a pledge because I am a legacy."

"Anyway, Ray Whitney saw me hanging out with Sally in the student union and around the commons a few times. One time, when I was hanging out with your old man, Ray came over and asked me why I was dating a black girl. He told me he dated a few black girls and that I should know a few things and some terminology. Being a naive freshman and culturally ignorant, I listened to what he had to say. He told me that black women don't call the penis dick, cock, or wiener, they call it a furshizzle, slang for a chisel used on a furry woman's part, the vagina. One night, Sally and I were alone, making out, and things were getting hot and heavy. I told her that her kisses were making my furshizzle hard. I was proud. I thought I had the slang mastered when I said it. She thought I was being a racist jerk. Sally started screaming and yelling at me. I froze. I didn't know what I did wrong. One of her brothers, Marcus, busted in on us and grabbed me. I tried to explain, but Sally or Marcus wanted to hear none of it. Her brother beat me senseless, duct-taped my ankles together and my arms to my side. He also staple-gunned a sign to my back: WE DON'T CALL DICKS FURSHIZZLES. Marcus and a few of his buddies dumped me on the front lawn of the student union, bloodied and duct-taped together. I became a campus punch line for a while, and they pinned the nickname Furshizzle on me. That was where the name came from."

"Oh my god, that's awful! Did you ever get even with Ray Whitney?"

"One weekend, I had a bunch of buddies from home come up for a visit, and we were going to get even with Ray. Your dad and grandparents talked me out of it. Apparently, the Whitney family was pretty well connected and somehow owned the company my old man worked for. I was the talk of campus until somebody shit their pants in a speech comm class and took the attention off me. I hated the nickname at first, but over time, I embraced it. If I was doing better with women at parties and gatherings than your father, he would tell that story to turn the table and make him seem impressive to the ladies. It never worked. I still did better than him."

"Wow, some kind of friend my dad is."

"When women enter the picture, young men get competitive and friendship goes out the window. Women have that effect on guys that want to get laid. Your dad has been a good friend, and his parents, your grandparents, were always pretty good to me. I was a fish out of water at Harvard, but my dad worked hard to get me there, and he made me work hard to belong there. I had to overcome the poor-kid-in-a-rich-kid's-world scenario and focus on getting my law degree. Your grandparents took a shine to me and helped me overcome it. They made me feel at home."

"So that's where Furshizzle came from. All this time I thought it was for something cool," Ernie jokes.

"You got to promise me that you won't tell your classmates and the guys on the debate team this story. It will be a distraction, and it will probably piss your mom off even more."

"The Furshizzle story is going to be a tough one to keep to myself, but I owe you, Teddy. You really helped me with everything. Because of you, I have an interest in learning and using my brain. I found confidence because of you. You encouraged me with guitar, worked with me, taught me, jammed with me, and made it fun. I promise I won't tell the story of Furshizzle. My mom is always pissed off at you, anyway. You always call her out on her bullshit."

Sid exits the mixing booth and comes into studio with Theodore and Ernie. He holds up a couple of CDs and flash drive.

"I'm not sure what format you needed these in, so I just gave you copies on CDs and a flash drive. You would be amazed at how many auditions still have to be sent in on CDs. People can't get with the times. Anyway, you have both. You are talented, kid, keep working hard," Sid says.

"Thanks, Sid, I owe it all to Teddy."

"Fuck him. Teddy is a piece of shit. Don't let him drag you down."

Theodore laughs. "Listen to Sid. If you want to be a bald, chubby middle-age recording studio guy, this is the guy you want to look up to."

"Fuck you, Furshizzle," Sid shoots back.

"Seriously, though, thanks for doing me this favor. You are one of the good ones, Sid," Theodore says.

"You got it, brother. If you guys want to record again, just give me a call. It was nice to work with talented people for a change," Sid says and leaves the studio and goes back in the booth.

Ernie, with a puzzled expression, asks Theodore, "How come you isolated my tracks and not yours? How is he doing you a favor? Am I missing something?"

"You told me a counselor at a summer camp put a guitar in your hands when you were eight. You owe that counselor many, many thanks. You have a way with the instrument and a talent that most musicians would envy. I wish I had your aptitude for it. I think it would be a waste if you didn't explore your talent and make the most out of it. You are better than playing in garage bands with your buddies and not pretentious enough to be the douche-nozzle that shows up to parties with a guitar to hook up with women. You have to develop, work, and play with other musicians that play on your level. I brought you here with me today to have an audition tape made. There is this musician's colony that I think you should apply to. I can almost guarantee you will get in if you fill out the application and send them the audition tape."

"Teddy, you know my family legacy has other plans for me. You will just make my parents hate you. I'm taking a year off to campaign with my dad, and then I am going to Harvard the fall semester afterward. Once I get out of Harvard, I'm supposed to do whatever. I will probably sit on boards and committees like my old man, and then when it's time, I will run for the Senate. My family will kill me if I deviate from the legacy. My dad will kill you for putting the idea in my head."

Theodore runs his hand through his hair. He opens his guitar case and removes a thick manila envelope from the pocket and hands it to Ernie.

"I know your legacy. I am not telling you to rebel against your parents or family. I am asking you to think about it and talk to your parents. You are on the debate team—make it a real-life debate with your parents. This envelope has some literature on the musician's colony and the application. There is no deadline to apply. If you apply and get accepted to the colony, they will tell you to report when they have an opening or a need for your ability. You stay at the colony for two years. You can stay longer and work at the colony if you choose and if they want you to. It's not like college where you sit in classes and learn shit that you will never need to know. This is where you can develop as an artist and find other artists to work with. Some solid bands have formed in that colony, and it's only been in operation for a few years. I think you would stand to benefit greatly from it. All I ask is that you look at it, think about it, and talk to your parents. If you decide on it, you have your audition tapes ready to go. Please think about it."

"I will look at it and think about it, but you know how my family is about preserving the plan that my great-great-grandfather Douglas willed. I am his namesake. It's going to be a tough sell."

"All I ask is that you seriously consider it. Think about it after the national debate, though. I need your head in the game. Have you guys been working on the proofs and arguments for the debate?"

"We had a couple of meetings and research sessions. We have a work session and a mock debate tonight in the study lounge. Stop by if you want."

Theodore picks up his guitar case. "We have official practices starting in a few days. I will see plenty of you guys for the next three weeks. Tonight, I need to sow some wild oats, get drunk, and hopefully get naked with an attractive woman, preferably one that isn't pretending to be single. I always get beatings because of the ones that lie about their marital status. Go figure, they lie and I'm the bad guy. Anyway, I gotta get some nonsense out of my system. I promised your old man I would buckle down so we win the national debate, finish the semester with high rankings, and begin working on his campaign."

"We will be ready for nationals. If we win, it might be easier to convince my parents to let me go to this commune you are trying to send me to. My mom is still pissed that you are going to run Dad's campaign, but she knows he needs you," Ernie says as he picks up his guitar case.

Theodore goes over to the booth window and taps on the glass. He waves goodbye to Sid, who is sitting at the mixing board with headphones on. Sid waves back.

"Your mom, the plastic-breasted humanoid Sandy Douglas, was never a fan of mine. We've had our issues. Just take a look at the stuff in the envelope, Ernie. You may not even like the requirements of the commune. Read the literature, decide for yourself. If I had that opportunity when I was your age, I probably would have chosen another direction. If I didn't at least show you this opportunity, I couldn't consider myself a caring teacher," Theodore says to Ernie as they exit the studio.

CHAPTER 7

The auditorium is silent. The last student has made his counterpoint rebuttal. Suspense hangs in the air while the judges seated at their table begin jotting and passing notes. The moderator for the finals of the National Youth Scholars Debate offers the cliffhanger phrasing to television cameras.

"The judges will have their final decision, and the winner of this year's National Youth Scholars Debate will be announced after this short break. Stay tuned!"

The red ON-AIR light goes off. The debate team coach Theodore Graham walks onto the debate stage behind the Douglas Youth Honors College team. He pats students on the back and compliments them on a job well done and has them all turn around in their seats and huddle around him.

"When we come back from this commercial break, we will learn if we finished ahead of twenty-eight of the top youth honors schools in the country or twenty-nine. No matter what the outcome, you have nothing to be ashamed of and everything to be proud of. You guys worked hard to get here. All of you have bright, prosperous futures ahead of you, and I am proud to have had the opportunity to be part of this chapter in your lives. I took some time to know all of you and be in the presence of your brilliant minds. Thirty years from now, you will look back to today and think about the people sitting here right now, and you will all still be amazed by how perfect this team functioned. This type of perfection is rare in this life, and you are all fortunate to be a part of it. When the cameras come back, heads up, smiles on, and good luck. You debated like winners, you should win," Theodore encourages his team.

"Thirty seconds. Quiet, please!" a stage director shouts.

The auditorium goes from a roar to a hush, to silent. Theodore exits the stage, and the young debaters face forward and sit up straight. The crests of their schools are sharply displayed on their blazers.

The ON-AIR and APPLAUSE lights are illuminated, and the audience applauds as the moderator appears onstage, clapping as he makes his way to a podium at center stage. The judges at the table still appear to be comparing notes and discussing the competition.

"Welcome back to the National Youth Honors Debate. I'm Pat Gladstone, host and moderator of this tough-fought battle of young scholars. The judges will be handing me the envelope with the winner momentarily, but let me just say a few things first. I have seen some of the brightest minds on this stage in the last few days. Though only one team can leave here tonight as the champions, I have to say you are all winners to me. Thank you to the parents that encourage these brilliant leaders of the future. Thank you to all the teachers, professors, trainers, and coaches for the guidance given, and a big thank-you to our sponsor, Feelgood Gas and Fracking Industries, for making this all possible and for their commitment to educating our young minds and providing safe and affordable energy."

A stately-looking woman in a red dress appears onstage carrying an envelope. She makes her way to the center of the stage and hands the envelope to Pat Gladstone. He takes the envelope, shakes the woman's hand, and watches as she exits the stage.

"Thank you, Mrs. Pentworth. Okay, folks, here we have it," Pat Gladstone says as he opens the envelope. "With a score of 7 to 3, the Douglas Youth Honors College beats Burlington Youth Preparatory Tech. Douglas Youth Honors College is this year's winner!"

The audience cheers and applauds loudly. Pat Gladstone makes his way over to the Douglas debate team to congratulate them as they are celebrating. Theodore is now onstage, celebrating with his team. Burlington's coach comes onstage and lines his team up for the congratulatory handshakes. Both teams shake hands, and Theodore greets the coach of Burlington's team.

"We'll be right back. Grace Downwood will be doing postdebate interviews with team captains and their coaches when we return. Stay tuned!" Pat Gladstone says to the cameras.

The ON-AIR light goes off, and the audience begins to file out of the auditorium.

Theodore stands onstage as a young Native American reporter prepares the team captains for their television interviews. Gene Douglas makes his way backstage and stands next to Theodore, watching the reporter talk to his team captain.

"You did it, Teddy. I can't believe it, you won my family's school a national debate championship. And to think I could have fired you two months ago!"

"Yeah, glad you didn't. Hey, do you know that reporter Grace Downwood?"

"Just from Channel 6 News, not personally. She's pretty new there. Why?"

"Look at her. She is beautiful, sexy, but sharp as a whip. Her Native American heritage makes her tough as nails. I fear and respect her. Look at her organizing her cameraman and the debate captains. She is downright intimidating."

"Keep it together, Teddy. She's interviewing you next. You're not afraid of her, are you?"

Teddy looks Grace Downwood over again. "I'm turned on by her. Maybe a little scared too, definitely turned on, though. She's professional. It makes her even more attractive."

"Teddy, don't hit on her during your interview. Don't embarrass the school and me. Please," Gene pleads.

Theodore looks away from the reporter. "Gene, I've been doing what I promised. I am not going to stop now. I'm just saying that woman is captivating and raises my curiosity. I got it under control."

"There is something about her, definitely something about her. I will trust you with this, but I do want to talk to you at some point soon."

"You still want me to run your campaign. Right?"

"Yes, definitely. I need you on the campaign. We'll talk about it later. Can you swing by for brunch tomorrow?"

"I'll be there. You're going to run for governor, aren't you?"

"Yes, I am going to run. We'll talk tomorrow."

Grace Downwood walks with her cameraman toward Theodore and Gene at the wing of the stage. She points to an area for her cameraman to set up. She turns and motions for Theodore to come over for his interview.

"I got to go, Gene. You hang right here. I'm getting interviewed by the sexy journalist. As your campaign manager, I have decided to give your candidacy a cold open right now."

"What? Teddy, *no!*" Gene says on deaf ears as Theodore goes to the reporter.

Theodore and Grace Downwood make small talk while the seconds-till-on-air clock counts down. The clock reaches ten seconds till air. Teddy straightens his posture and pulls his Douglas Youth Honors College blazer tight. Grace Downwood takes her mark at the 5 count.

"This is Channel 6, Grace Downwood back live with coverage of the National Youth Honors Debate finals, where the Douglas Youth Honors College handily defeated Burlington Youth Preparatory Tech and robbed them of a three-peat. Here with me now is coach of the Douglas Youth Honors College team, Theodore Graham. Coach Graham, how do you explain the victory here tonight? How did you take a school that hasn't finished in the top ten schools during its one-hundred year history, to number one?"

"First, just let me say thank you to you, Grace Downwood and Channel 6. You were fantastic to the kids all week long. I know it was a great honor for my team to meet you. It's a great honor for me to meet you as well. I think it would be nice to have you talk to our students about your career and your hard work. How about you come to Douglas and speak to our students? You are a brilliant talent, it would be quite an honor to learn about you."

"That is a wonderful compliment, Mr. Graham. Thank you! I will consider it, but what about the victory here tonight?"

"The victory is a result of the hard work of these amazing kids. It was an honor to help them learn and watch their brilliant minds question and explore. They wanted to win, and they worked hard to get what they wanted. It's a true victory. I'm so happy for them."

"Obviously, you had something to do with this victory. All these kids sing your praise, and the school's GPA rating has climbed every year since you arrived at the school three years ago."

"I would like to think it was me, but it's not. It's the chairman of the school, a member of the family that founded this wonderful institution, Mr. Gene Douglas. He wasn't happy with the direction the school was heading. He had better ideas about education. He told me his ideas, and I said, 'Hell yeah, I'll help you with that.' He put together a smart and caring staff, Ms. Delores Daniels, our administrator; Mrs. Fayweather, our dean of education; Mrs. Claire Peterson, our social sciences dean; plus all the people that work hard to keep the school running. It is a team effort. Gene Douglas reorganized this school, and his ideas led this team to victory tonight. We tried as a team to fine-tune and perfect Mr. Douglas's ideas until they showed results, and that's what we all witnessed here tonight, the results of Gene Douglas's ideas. I hear he may run for governor. If he can do what he did for Douglas, the National Debate Champions, there is no reason he can't do it for education for all kids across this great state. In fact, there he is standing right over there," Theodore says and motions for Gene to come over.

Gene walks over to Theodore and Grace Downwood from the wing of the stage. The cameraman carefully pans his camera so he doesn't blow the live broadcast shot.

"Coach Graham tells us you are thinking about running for governor to apply your education plan to all students across this state. Is your coach telling us the truth?"

"I'm proud of our students tonight and my son, Ernie. Great job, son. Mr. Graham may have told you right, I am thinking about it, but only thinking right now," Gene nervously answers.

"There you have it, Channel 6 viewers. Gene Douglas, chairman of the school that won tonight's National Youth Honors Debate, is thinking of running for governor to improve education in our state. We will be back with Burlington's coach after this."

"Thank you, guys. Coach Graham, give me a call about speaking at the school or if you have any more juicy political scoops. We can set up a meeting or a lunch or a dinner," Grace says. "Mr. Douglas, I would like to learn more about your education plans. Maybe we can do a story on you and your school."

Grace Downwood quickly walks away to prep Burlington Preparatory Tech's coach for his interview. Gene shoots Theodore an angry look.

"How could you, Teddy? That's not how and when I wanted to launch my campaign," Gene scolds.

Theodore puts his arm on Gene's shoulder and pats him on the chest. "I will see you for brunch in the morning. You can thank me then. I got to run. I'm going to celebrate on the bus with the team. I'll see you about ten-ish," Theodore says and walks offstage to high-five a few members of his team.

*　　*　　*

Theodore pulls his '72 Buick Skylark past the overweight security guard at the gate of the Douglas mansion. He parks in the driveway and enjoys the warble of the engine as he revs it a few more times before shutting it off. He checks his hair in the mirror and pulls the dashboard-mounted ashtray down, removes a few nicely rolled joints, and places them in his shirt pocket. He exits his car and makes his way to the front door of the Douglas home and rings the bell. Issac, the Douglases' butler, answers.

"Mr. Graham, welcome. You will find yourself on the excrement list of the lord and lady of the manor. Did Jeremy, the Shamoo of security guards, tell you about his new diet? He set a goal to lose one hundred pounds. If he is successful, he will be able to see the tips of his feet," Issac says in greeting to Theodore.

"When he can see his pecker, I'm sure he will ask for some vacation time to whack off."

"That's a brain image that I am sorry you painted for me, Mr. Graham. Mr. and Mrs. Douglas are on the patio, waiting for you. Brunch will be served shortly. The lady of the manor is especially hostile to your presence today. I made sure nothing sharper than a butter knife is on the table."

"Mrs. Douglas is always angry with me. Maybe I will give her one of these. It might help. Of course, I brought one for you," Theodore says and offers him one of the joints from his shirt pocket.

"One of these may make Mrs. Douglas a little more friendly. I know when I go home with one of your joints, the wife and I have some ribald adventures. It feels good to get some sexual affection. She will be pleased to see this tonight."

"I've met your wife, Issac, you better be doing her right. She's a beautiful woman."

"Indeed, she is, Mr. Graham. I trust you can find the patio so I can excuse myself and get this brunch served?"

"I will find them, Issac. Thank you."

On the patio, Theodore sees a table set for brunch. Past the set table, Sandy and Gene are sitting in a lounging area next to the pool, drinking coffee and watching *Say Yes to the Dress* on the television. Sandy hears the patio door close and turns around.

"What the fuck did you do, Teddy? What the fuck were you thinking? That was not how we were going to announce the campaign. You ruin everything, you ignorant fuck!" Sandy says as she approaches Theodore and yells in his face.

"Sandy! Calm down," Gene urges.

"I thought you were going to congratulate me for the team winning the national debate last night. Apparently, I am wrong. I didn't launch the campaign, Ms. Plastic Tits. I said Gene was thinking about running. He confirmed he was thinking about it on TV. I did you both a huge favor last night. Don't you guys watch *State of the State This Week* on Channel 6 on Sunday morning?" Theodore asks.

Theodore points to the television. "Of course you don't. You are watching *Say Yes to the Dress* on the ironically named The Learning Channel. Obviously, you don't have control of the remote, Gene. Put *State of the State This Week* on Channel 6 at ten thirty. You will thank me."

Sandy goes back and sits down next to Gene, who turns the television to Channel 6. Theodore follows Sandy. He sits on one of the lounge stools at the bar and pours himself a cup of coffee. He reaches in his pocket and removes one of his joints and lights it. He takes a long drag of the joint and offers it to Gene, who is sitting on a chair facing the television.

"Really, Teddy, a joint already? Come on! We have to talk seriously today."

Sandy reaches over Gene and takes the joint out of Theodore's hand. "This better be good news, or we will put an end to you before you ruin Gene's legacy."

"You will be nice to me when you see what my interview with Grace Downwood did for Gene. Then I have another joint, so we can turn this brunch into a party with drinks and everything. Here it is, Gene, turn up the volume."

"Welcome this Sunday morning to State of the State This Week. I am your host, Walter Carl. Joining me today are political analysts and editorial writers for The Morning Sun Gazette, Brad Utes and Joan Mowrey. Welcome. Last night, after the Douglas Youth Honors College won the National Youth Debate, one of our Channel 6 reporters, Grace Downwood, interviewed the debate team coach, who revealed that Eugene Douglas, proprietor of the Douglas family estate, which includes the youth school, a community college, and a publishing house, is thinking about a gubernatorial run. At the end of the interview, Eugene Douglas came on and said he was thinking about it. It didn't seem like Eugene wanted that information out, but it's out now. What do you think of this news, Brad?"

"It's a little too early to tell, but after I learned this last night, I made a few calls to get some polling information and start some data polls in the field. A few other competing newspapers and local TV outlets did the same. His name polls really well with conservatives. He is tied in with business leaders and developers. He turned a youth preparatory school that was a year away from bankruptcy into the top debating school in the nation. The GPA performance for that school has increased steadily for the past three years. Three years ago, the Douglas school had to lower its tuition rate to attract students. Today, I learned that the school is booked to capacity for next year and there are five hundred students on a waiting

list to get in. Obviously, Eugene Douglas is doing something right. His leadership ability should be looked at and considered."

"Give me that joint, Teddy. This is unbelievable! How did you do this?" Gene asks.

Theodore reaches to hand the joint to Gene. Sandy quickly takes it out of his hand and takes two quick hits off it and passes it to Gene.

"What about the backing for Eugene Douglas? Is he a feasible candidate? What do you think, Joan?"

"He is definitely a feasible candidate. He now has a proven record of getting things done with education, and the liberal voters in the state will support him for that. He has a lot of friends in the business community. I got a text last night about Mr. Douglas thinking about running. I checked my e-mail, and three hours after he appeared on television, there is already polling information in the field about him. One of the sets of polling data that stood out was financial. There are a lot of constituents, organizations, and industries looking to endorse this campaign. It hasn't been a day since he said was thinking about running—he didn't say he was running—and already there is at least fourteen million dollars of endorsements on the table that are his for the taking."

Gene jumps to his feet and shuts the television off. He takes a long drag off the joint, exhales, and shouts, "We are having mimosas with brunch today, Issac! How did you do it, Teddy? How do you do this stuff like you do? I don't know why I ever doubt you."

"What does all this mean?" Sandy asks.

"It means that little announcement I made last night, the one that you screamed at me for twenty minutes ago, has done you much good. Competing news networks are doing the polling information on Gene at their expense. Gene doesn't have to pay to use it because it's information about him. It also shows that there are wealthy donors already itchy to launch this campaign. Gene will have little out-of-pocket expense, and he has Channel 6 in his corner if he breaks stories with them exclusively. The two biggest costs to any campaign are taken care of. When the campaign is over, the donor money that is left over is yours. It could be millions. You can get another new set of tits," Theodore explains.

"What do we do next?" Gene asks.

"You have a little over four months to get your people together. You will have to form your election team, and you will have to get your super PAC in order and secure your big financial donors. You can also start grassroots funding with contributions from constituents. Many of the people will donate a lot of cash to try to buy their kids' way into Douglas Youth Honors College. The grassroots fund will pay for your administrative costs and transportation. Once you announce your candidacy and go on the ballot in the first county, you can no longer communicate with your super PAC until after the election. The money left in the super PAC after the election is yours, and it could be millions. I will have the agreements drawn so I can be the liaison between the campaign and the super PAC and make sure it represents you right in campaign ads. Those are the next steps. That little television segment on Channel 6 last night made you millions and gave you a four-month head start in the election."

Sandy stands up, lifts her shirt, and exposes her fake breasts to Theodore. "You wanted to see them since I got them. This is the best way I can thank you, Teddy. Get a good look, because you have a history of making me hate you again quickly."

"Put your shirt down, Sandy! For God's sake!" Gene scolds.

Theodore looks to the brunch table and sees Issac getting ready to serve. He wants to see if Issac has gotten a look at Sandy's exposed breasts. Issac shows a thumbs-up to Theodore.

"They are very nice, Sandy, but this is great news I made happen for you. Would a blow job be too much to ask?" Theodore asks jokingly.

She doesn't answer but gives him a cunning wink.

"I might be inclined to give you that blow job after that other joint and mimosas, Teddy," Gene jokes. "I can't believe it. You're a genius at politics! I should never doubt you, Teddy. Let's go eat. It looks like Issac is ready for us."

Gene leads the way over to the brunch table, Theodore follows, and Sandy puts her hand around Teddy's waist and playfully thanks him for the morning's good news.

*　　*　　*

Issac clears the brunch table. Theodore, Sandy, and Gene sit at the brunch table with cocktails, celebrating the good news about Gene's gubernatorial campaign. They are passing a second joint around.

"It's a really nice day. It's getting pretty warm. I think I am going to put my bikini on and have a swim," Sandy says as she puffs the joint one more time before leaving for the pool house to change.

"So what did you want to talk to me about, Gene?" Theodore asks. "It sounded like something was eating at you last night."

Gene sits up in his chair and adjusts his glasses. "Tell me about the Black Rock Valley Musical Artists Colony. I found a thick manila envelope with literature about it, audition CDs, and a completed application with Ernie's name on it. It was complete with essays of why he wants to attend there for two years. I know you have everything to do with this."

"Ernie is a talented musician. I don't know how you don't recognize this. This artist colony is the perfect environment for him to grow, develop, and branch out. There, he can work with other musicians playing at his level. He can explore music, play music, and maybe launch a musical career. A lot of good bands are forming in that colony. It has a whole touring festival circuit in the summer. It's a new concept school for musicians to make and produce music. I think it would be great for Ernie. I suggested it to him."

"Don't hand me that crap, Teddy. I did a little research into this colony and made some phone calls. It wasn't hard to figure out that T. F. Shizzle Holding Company is you. You own the colony. You formed the colony. It is in the town where you grew up. You left that colony and came here to work for me at my schools. Why did you come here? Why didn't you tell me about it?"

"You called me and asked me to come here because your schools were losing money and your publishing house was in danger of closing because nobody of any notoriety wanted to publish with you. You never once asked what I had going on. I came here because my friend from college asked if I could help. You and your family helped me get through Harvard, twice. Coming here was the least I could do for a friend who helped me navigate a wealthy environment."

Gene readjusts himself in his seat and takes a moment to put his thoughts together. "When I heard you went back to where you grew up, I just thought you went back there to drink or party or drug yourself to death. I just assumed your time as a corporate and legislative lawyer burned you out. I wanted to give you a hand up. You built a successful artist colony and took three years away from it to save my schools."

"I don't regret coming here, Gene. I did good work and enjoyed myself. I will be away from it for nearly five years when I return. We have to get you elected governor before I leave."

Sandy returns from the pool house in a fluffy white bathrobe. She places a towel on the back of one of the chairs at the brunch table.

"Is there any more of that joint left?" Sandy asks.

Theodore hands her the half-smoked joint and lighter sitting on the table. She takes it from him, lights the joint, and takes a long drag. She hands the lighter and the lit joint back to Theodore and touches his arm playfully and longer than necessary.

"You two boys have your serious faces on. I'm getting in the pool," Sandy says as she takes off the fluffy white bathrobe and exposes her bikini-clad body. She walks away from the two with a runway model strut.

"This is why you didn't care if I fired you at your board hearing. You have a place to go. You were planning on leaving here after the semester was over, anyway. You weren't going to renew your contract," Gene says.

"That was my plan. Obviously, things have changed. You didn't fire me and you are about to prepare to run for governor. I agreed to help. I am going to stay and help you win."

Gene stands up and looks down at Theodore. "You were going to take my son with you. You know what his legacy is. You know he has family duties to carry out. You weren't going to tell me. I feel betrayed."

"I want Ernie to go to that colony because he belongs there. I cut an audition tape with him and gave him the literature. I told him to talk to you and Sandy about it after he decided if the colony was right for him. Did you talk to him about what you found? About the colony? About the guitar? Do you even listen to him play?"

"I wanted answers from you! Why would you distract him with this? He is to be with me on the campaign trail and then go to Harvard. He's going to be good for the photo ops and family values credit with voters. When the time is right, when he is ready, he is supposed to run for Senate. That's his legacy. Governor is my legacy, senator is his. If he is any good at it, a presidential run is not out of the realm of possibility."

"You should really listen to him play, Gene. He is on a level that I wish I were on. The colony would be a real-world introduction into the industry. He can play with other artists, find a style he likes, form bands, and test his art out at festivals and small venues. The colony connects artists. I believe this is where Ernie can excel, and there is nothing that says he can't be a senator down the road."

"He's really that good?"

"He is amazing, and when I watch him and listen to him play, I can see he is enjoying himself. He plays the legacy role for you out of respect, but he's not enjoying himself. Ernie has rock-and-roll dreams. Times have changed. Let him leave a legacy of music."

"We are a political family. We serve to preserve the Douglas name throughout history. Those that govern are history. That's why Ernie is to become a senator."

"Who is John Lennon?" Theodore asks.

"What? He was the leader of the Beatles."

"Paul McCartney may disagree with that, but he was a member of the Beatles. Who is Angus King?"

"He is the guitarist for AC/DC."

Shaking his head, Theodore says, "Nope, that's Angus Young. Angus King is a senator from Maine."

Theodore gets up from the table and gets a beer from the patio bar's refrigerator. Sandy is in the pool, floating on a raft. When she sees she is in Theodore's line of sight, she gives him a playful wave and starts flirtatiously adjusting herself in her bikini.

"Hey, Sandy, who is Bobby Weir?"

"Grateful Dead! Woooo!" Sandy shouts back.

"Hey, Gene, who is Mark Kirk?"

"Um, oh . . . Jefferson Starship."

"Kirk. Starship. I see how you made the Star Trek connection, but no. Mark Kirk is a Republican senator from Illinois," Theodore says. "Hey, Sandy, who is Pete Townsend?"

"He's the best guitarist ever! From The Who. The Whooooooooooooo!" Sandy yells as she thrusts her arms skyward. She loses her balance and falls off the raft into the pool.

"Your baked and well-on-her-way-to-drunk wife knows her music," Theodore says. "Who is David Vitter?"

"Isn't he that guy from Stone Temple Pearl Jam?"

"Oh, Gino, turn on a fucking radio, you are way out of touch. Pearl Jam and Stone Temple Pilots are two different bands. Eddie Vedder plays in Pearl Jam and is amazingly talented. David Vitter is a Republican senator from Louisiana."

"What's your point?"

"My point is, Ernie has the potential to be a famous musician or a footnote politician. I don't know that for sure, he's a bright kid, he could probably excel at both. A guitar-playing senator. Ooh, that has *sitcom* written all over it. I got to make a note of that. I just think he would master his craft in music and only fulfill an obligation in politics. A rich man's family obligation doesn't have to be his cross to bear."

"Am I going to be a footnote governor?"

"Not since you brought me on board to run your campaign. I'm going to try to make you interesting."

"Hey, I'm interesting."

Sandy overhears what Gene says to Theodore and can be heard laughing hysterically from the pool. Theodore can't help but laugh himself.

"You have your charms, buddy, we'll fine-tune them. Are Ernie's audition tapes here?"

"I think they are in his room."

"Why don't you go get them and actually listen to your son play? We can put the CD on at the patio bar."

"I'll go see if I can find them. I should at least hear him play."

"I see a Father of the Year title is in your future," Theodore says sarcastically.

Gene leaves the patio and disappears into the house. Theodore goes back over to the patio bar and gets himself another beer. He pulls another joint out of his front pocket and lights it. Sandy gets out of the pool, takes her towel from the back of a chair, and does a modeling strut over to Theodore at the bar.

"With the campaign ahead, I'm going to be seeing a lot of you, Teddy. You're going to be seeing a lot more of me too," Sandy says flirtatiously.

"You showed me your tits already, and that was just because I told you the governor run is going to make you a lot of money."

"The alumni dinner is coming up soon. Maybe you can meet me in the cloakroom, and I will show you a whole lot more."

"I promised Claire Peterson I would meet her there again this year. It's sort of becoming a tradition. Maybe we can hook up in a janitor's closet some other time."

Sandy drops her towel on one of the patio barstools. She stands toe to toe with Theodore and touches his chest. "How could you hook up with that bitch Claire when she was married and you won't even flirt with me when I'm throwing myself at you?"

"I don't know why I hooked up with Claire, it just happened. It may not have been the right thing to do when I think about it in hindsight, but I enjoyed it. I like her. I know why I won't mess around with you, though. You are my best friend's wife, and I can't disrespect Gene like that, or your son, Ernie. I do have some scruples, not many, but some."

"If we hooked up, Teddy, Gene would just give us a lot of money to keep us quiet and discreet so we wouldn't bring shame on the Douglas name. If you had stayed with law instead of slumming here as a teacher, I would have left Gene for you. You were making a ton of money. We could have had a lot of fun."

"It's always the money with you. That was your legacy. Marry somebody with tons of money and lavish yourself in the finer things in life. You fulfilled your legacy. It's too bad that doing so has made you so cold and unhappy."

"And to think I was going to sunbathe topless and ask you to rub lotion on my breasts. You definitely would have enjoyed that," Sandy says and picks up the joint sitting on the patio bar.

"I never said I wouldn't do that."

"Too late, Furshizzle, you blew your chance," Sandy says and returns to the pool to sunbathe.

Gene comes out of the house carrying CDs and makes his way to the patio bar with Theodore, who is puffing on the joint.

"I found them. Which one should I put on?"

"Play the first one. It's me and Ernie playing together. The second one is Ernie's guitar isolated and playing solo."

Gene makes his way behind the patio bar and tries to figure out how to play the CD player. Theodore looks over at Sandy, who is now sunbathing topless. The music begins to play. Gene takes a hit of the lit joint in the ashtray on the bar and hands it to Theodore.

"This is my son and you playing?"

"Yes, he is playing lead. This is his guitar essay he put together."

Gene is moving his head to the music and tapping a beat on the bar. "He is really good. I can't believe this is my kid."

"I can't believe you never heard him play before."

"Who is this band?" Sandy shouts from by the pool.

"It is your son, Ernie, and Teddy playing!" Gene yells.

"Get the fuck out of here!" she yells and comes running over to the patio bar to listen a little more closely.

"Put your top on, for God's sake," Gene scolds.

"You don't have to do that on my account, Sandy, but what the hell kind of parents are you? I can't believe neither of you ever heard your son play."

"It was something he said he picked up at summer camp when he was eight, and he plays with his buddies and you at school. I figured it's better than having him at home playing Vice City and whacking off to internet porn like most teenagers. I'm not so sure his hanging out with you is a good idea, though," Sandy says.

"You truly are a foul woman," Theodore says.

Gene fist-bumps Theodore. "I guess I will have to at least talk to Ernie about this colony thing. We will have to figure out how to work it around his legacy. And to think I was going to yell at you all brunch long. You bring me awesome campaign news, and you turn me on to my son's music. I don't know how to repay you."

"Well, I got to see Sandy's tits a couple of times, that's a start. Can I rub a little oil on them, maybe?"

"Honey, let Teddy rub some oil on your tits. He brought us really good news today."

Sandy grabs a towel from the barstool behind her and quickly covers her breasts. "I will not! Teddy isn't touching me. Not after his hands were all over Claire Peterson."

"You know I can't unsee those surgically enhanced cans, right? I think I might think about them later tonight when I am trying to fall asleep."

"Fuck you, Furshizzle! You're a pervert!"

Theodore reaches in the pocket of his shorts and pulls out his cell phone to check the time. "Hey, guys, I got to run. I promised to play guitar with my friend Wayne. I have to meet him in half an hour. Thanks for the brunch and the breasts. Enjoy your son's talent. He is that good."

"Thanks again, Teddy, for everything. I will call you, and we can set up a strategy meeting and get this campaign rolling."

"Right on, Gino. See you later. Tits McGee, thanks for the peek."

"Get lost, Furshizzle!" Sandy shouts before returning to listening to her son's guitar music with her husband.

CHAPTER 8

A stage and folding chairs are set on the plush lawn of the Douglas Youth Honors College commons. To the right of a stage, a few local reporters are milling around with crews. The rows of chairs are mostly empty, dotted only sparsely with a few attendees. The first few rows are filled with students and faculty mandated to attend. Centered above the podium, above the stage, hangs a banner, "The Bambi Wilson Pageant Foundation." Well-dressed members of the pageant commission sit in a single row of chairs to the right of the podium. To the left, Ernie Douglas, Theodore Graham, Gene Douglas, Sandy Douglas, and Holly Herman wait for the event to begin. Sandy Douglas looks at the minimal audience and then to her watch. Sandy motions to her press coordinator, Wendy Uher, to begin in five minutes.

"Why am I here?" Theodore leans over and whispers to Gene.

"You are mandated to be here like the rest of the faculty."

"How come I am sitting up here and not down there with the rest of the faculty and staff?"

"It's important that you are up here with us. You are the debate coach that led the school to the national championship. I'm going to need you a little later to help me with the press."

Theodore straightens up in his seat. A look of fear comes over his face. "The press? You're not going to . . . oh, no, Gene, no. Why didn't you ask me about this? You can't officially announce your candidacy here. Not at this event."

"Sandy wanted it to be here. I knew you wouldn't go for it. She wants to draw attention to her beauty pageants. She asked for this favor while giving me head. I couldn't say no. Head is a rarity in my life."

"Would it be possible for you to get a different wife for your campaign?" Theodore asks. "Why on earth would you agree to this? I get the blow job thing, but couldn't you change your mind? Blow jobs are her currency. She will need more plastic surgery or shopping money soon, so get your blow jobs then. I don't have a good feeling about this."

"Just play along, Teddy."

Sandy Douglas looks at her watch and is disappointed by the mostly empty seats littering the lawn. She motions for Wendy to begin. Wendy instructs a sound technician stationed behind the audience to start the music. The chorus of "Isn't She Lovely" by Stevie Wonder can be heard over the sound system as Holly Herman makes her way to the podium at center stage.

The music fades. Holly Herman faces the tepidly responding crowd. "Welcome, all of you, to the Douglas Youth Honors College for the annual Bambi Wilson Pageant Foundation Luncheon. It's here where pageant season commences each year. Once again we have some exciting news for this new pageant season. Here today, daughter of Bambi Wilson and president of the Bambi Wilson Pageant Foundation, Sandy Douglas. She will tell us the exciting news. Come on up here, Sandy, and tell us what's new and exciting for this pageant season."

Those sitting on the stage respectfully clap as Sandy makes her way to the podium as "Isn't She Lovely" plays again. The echo of only a few clapping hands is heard from the crowd.

Leaning over to Gene, Theodore says, "Your wife is going to ruin Stevie Wonder for me."

Gene ignores Theodore's comment and faces the podium and claps for his wife.

"Thank you, Holly. Thank you, pageant sponsors. Thank you, students and faculty. Thanks to my husband, Gene, and my wonderful son, Ernie, sitting here onstage, and thanks to our longtime family friend, the coach that saw our team all the way to win the national debate finals, Mr. Theodore Graham," Sandy says. The crowd gives a slightly more enthusiastic round of applause.

"My biggest thanks of all has to go to my mother, Bambi Wilson, God rest her soul. She guided me through the beauty pageant circuit. From Junior Miss, to Young Miss, from Miss Teen, to Miss Kentucky, all the way to my seventeenth-runner-up victory in the Miss America pageant, she was my guide, my support, my comfort, and my rock. I started the Bambi Wilson Pageant Foundation to honor her commitment to helping young women display their beauty and reach their full potential," Sandy says, touting her mother. The crowd responds with a barely audible applause.

"Wasn't Bambi a stripper in Lexington?" Theodore asks Gene.

"Shut up, Teddy," Gene whispers.

Theodore leans over to Ernie. "Your grandmother was a headliner at a strip club in Lexington. She used to be able to shoot ping pong balls out of her cooter."

Ernie begins to giggle but tries to maintain his composure in front of the crowd and his classmates.

"Knock it off, you two."

"Does Sandy know how to do the ping pong ball trick?" Theodore asks.

"Come on, Teddy, stop."

"This year, the Bambi Wilson Pageant Foundation will host Junior Miss, Young Miss, Miss Teen, and our College Queen pageants, but this year, we are introducing a brand-new pageant." Sandy pauses to build suspense. "This year, we will have a Magnificent Moms Pageant."

The attendees applaud after the pageant foundation members onstage clap for the announcement.

"There are so many beautiful moms out there that go unrecognized and are underappreciated. This pageant is for them. When we talked about this new pageant, the committee said to me, 'Sandy, you should enter this pageant, you're a magnificent mom.' I didn't think much about it at first, but then I said to myself, 'Why not me?' I'm taking my pageant shoes out of retirement, and I will compete in this first annual Magnificent Moms Pageant here at Douglas."

"I can't believe you invited the press for this. Your wife may have sunk your campaign before it even started," Theodore whispers to Gene.

"Now, just to keep it honest and fair, I am resigning from the pageant foundation effective immediately. I am turning everything over to Holly Herman. She will do a fantastic job putting all these pageants together. She has been a loyal assistant for pageants of years past. This year, I am certain she will do an amazing job heading the commission. She better do well, because I can't help her. I have a beauty pageant to get ready for. Come on up here, Holly."

"I can't tell which is more fake, Sandy or her tits," Theodore says.

Ernie snickers. Gene tries to ignore Theodore's comments.

"I do have one more announcement to make, and I am glad you are all here to hear it. Some of you may have heard rumors, some of you may have heard my husband was thinking about it, but I am here to confirm it. Eugene Douglas, my husband, is running for governor of our great state," Sandy says with great enthusiasm but only receives mediocre applause.

"Come on up here, honey. Tell our friends what you plan to do for our great state."

Gene waves to the people and empty seats. The press to the right of the stage is now lively, lining up camera shots, jotting down notes, and shuffling for space at the front of the stage. Gene gives Sandy a hug and a kiss at the podium and motions for Ernie to join them. Ernie joins his parents in a group hug. Sandy and Ernie take their seats when Gene takes the podium.

"Good aftern . . .," Gene says, but feedback from the sound system screeches and whistles.

"Sorry about that, folks. Good afternoon, everybody, thanks for being here, and thanks to my beautiful wife, Sandy, for letting the cat out of the bag of secrets. I'm running for governor of our great state. I think that smaller education and investments in government are the keys, um, err . . . I got that backward. We need smaller government and smaller education to make this state great again. Low taxes and a guy that's going to get it right for fighting for you, that's me. It's an honor to make this announcement in front of you, folks, that are a nice, good audience. I will be proud to be your governor and honored to have your support. My campaign manager, Mr. Graham, is sitting right there. I'm confident he will get us there. The race is a long way off, and today is about my wife's pageant foundation. I guess it's Holly Herman's now, so let me turn it back over to them. You will all have plenty of time to get to know me better as the campaign goes into full swing. Thank you, everybody. I hope to have all your votes."

Theodore leans over to Gene when he takes his seat. "Public speaking much?"

"How did I do?"

"We have a lot of work to do, Gene. I was embarrassed for you. If you're going to pull stunts like this, run them by me so I can at least get you properly prepared. I hope to God a natural disaster hits so they don't show your speech on the six o'clock news."

The stage event concludes. Gene and Ernie stay onstage to shake hands and mingle with Sandy's pageant people and make small talk. Theodore tries to make a quick getaway after the disaster he just witnessed. He makes his way down the steps on the side of the stage and is confronted by Grace Downwood of Channel 6 News.

"Coach Graham, can we get a few words from you about the campaign?"

"This isn't live television, is it?"

"I hardly think Mrs. Douglas's beauty pageant commission luncheon is worthy of live coverage."

"I guess I can give you a few words. Where do you want me?"

Grace Downwood leads Theodore over to a tree at the edge of the lawn and instructs her cameraman where to shoot from. She places Theodore where she wants him to stand and takes her mark.

"This is Grace Downwood with Channel 6 News, and we are here with Theodore Graham, the campaign manager for Gene Douglas, who just officially announced his candidacy for governor. Mr. Graham, what do you think of Gene Douglas's chances in this gubernatorial race?"

"Well, Ms. Downwood, with the record-breaking crowd here today and the profound words of Gene Douglas, I ask you to judge for yourself," Theodore says in deadpan.

Grace Downwood breaks out of her reporter persona and starts laughing hysterically. "We can't use that footage. We'll try this again," she says. "Do you think you can give me an answer that's not delusional, Mr. Graham?"

"You mean that was no good?" Theodore answers with a smile.

"I think you and I both know this was a horrible event and a horrible campaign rollout. I will give you a chance to do some damage control."

"Thank you for your mercy, Ms. Downwood. Let me attempt to fix this disaster."

Grace positions Theodore again and retakes her mark. "This is Grace Downwood, Channel 6 News, here with Theodore Graham, the campaign manager for Gene Douglas, who just announced his candidacy for governor. Mr. Graham, what do you think of Gene Douglas's chances in this gubernatorial race?"

"I think Mrs. Douglas is really enthusiastic about her husband running for governor. She wanted to be the one to make the announcement, and she did. Unfortunately, Mr. Douglas had no idea she was going to make it here today. He was caught off guard and wasn't expecting to speak about it today. I think he and Mrs. Douglas will have to communicate a little better as the campaign moves forward."

"He did seem to be a little taken aback, judging by his speech. So as his campaign manager, what do you think his chances are?"

"We have a lot of work to do and a long road ahead of us. It's too early to speculate on his chances. We have to get out and talk to the voters, get to know them, and see what they need and expect from their next governor. Once we get to know the voters of this wonderful state, we will come up with a solid plan to serve the interests of the people. We can't make a plan without the voice of people guiding us. Gene is goal-oriented. His goals as governor will be to do right and work for the betterment of the great people of our state. Once the people tell us how we can serve them best, we will set those goals and deliver for them. I have no doubt in my mind, Gene Douglas will accomplish those goals."

"No other candidate has officially announced their bid yet, and this is not a race against an incumbent. Larry Richmond has some polling data in the field and is thinking about running in the Republican primary. Sherman Jones, he is doing the same and considering running in the Democratic primary. What do you think about these men as potential opponents?"

"Well, we are the first to officially announce. Sandy Douglas took care of that for us today. When others announce their candidacies, we will look forward to a competitive and challenging race. It is ultimately up to the voters, and we are still a year away from Election Day. We will handle the hurdles as we face them."

"Thank you for talking to us and our Channel 6 viewers. I am sure we will be talking to you a lot more as the governor's race moves forward. I am Grace Downwood, reporting from the Douglas Youth Honors College with Theodore Graham, campaign manager for the officially announced, Gene Douglas for Governor campaign."

"I appreciate the chance to do some damage control, Ms. Downwood. I owe you one."

"It's way too early to smear the Douglas name, but you do owe me one. Any more announcements from this campaign, I'm the first one you call. When the election gets closer, you can set up a one-on-one interview with me and Mr. Douglas," Grace Downwood bargains and puts one of her business cards in Theodore's shirt pocket.

"If Mr. Douglas mumbles and stutters like he did today, we won't be a campaign very long. Thanks again, Ms. Downwood."

A cameraman and a chubby balding reporter comes running toward Theodore and Grace Downwood.

"Mr. Graham! Mr. Graham! Barry Barnhardt with Channel 3 News. Could we get a few words from the campaign manager?"

"Watch Channel 6 News. You can report on my comments after their broadcast," Theodore says and winks at Grace Downwood. "Now, if you will all excuse me, I have a sunny Saturday afternoon to enjoy."

*　　*　　*

The sun is setting on the Douglas family mansion. Theodore drives by a very elderly security guard at the front gate and parks his '72 Buick Skylark in the driveway. He revs the engine a few times to savor the warble of the engine before he shuts it off. He pulls the metal dashboard-mounted ashtray down and removes a few nicely rolled joints. He places them in his shirt pocket, exits the vehicle, and rings the doorbell. Issac, the butler, opens the front door.

"Good evening, Mr. Graham. Mrs. Douglas is especially venomous because of you this evening. Your death would bring her great joy."

"What happened to big Jeremy, the security guard, at the gate? There's a really old guy down there now."

"That is Abe, the evening security guard. He is quite ancient. His flatulence is accompanied by dust. When I report for work in the morning, I must check to see if he is breathing."

Theodore reaches in his shirt pocket and hands Issac a joint. "I guess it is near the end of your shift. I'll give you this in case you leave before I do."

"With this governor's campaign, Mr. Graham, you are going to turn me and the wife into potheads. I am not complaining. I consider your joints ladies-undergarment-disintegration devices. Thank you, kind sir. The man and lady of the house are in the parlor. There was much screaming after they watched you on the news."

Then he continued. "Your visit this evening is unexpected, I better announ—"

Issac is interrupted by Sandy yelling from the parlor. "How could you, Teddy! You're an asshole! You made a fucking fool of me!"

"The lady of the house is aware of your presence, Mr. Graham. I am going home to get high with my wife before the gunplay starts," Issac says.

Theodore walks into the parlor. Gene is sitting on a lounge chair, watching television, while Sandy is furiously pacing the room. She is holding a gin and tonic.

"I have never been so embarrassed in my life, Teddy. You told that Grace Down syndrome Channel 6 News slut that my announcement that Gene was running for governor was a surprise to him. You told them that I leaked it. We planned to announce it there to get attention for my pageant foundation, but no, you made me out to be a scatterbrain woman that craves attention!"

"I kind of recall you announcing a Magnificent Moms Pageant and your coming out of retirement to compete in it. That's not calling attention to yourself? You should have called it the Pathetic Plastic Princesses Pageant."

Sandy throws her gin and tonic at Theodore. Gene gets out of his chair quickly and grabs ahold of his wife.

"Enough, Sandy! Teddy, what are you doing here?"

Theodore reaches in his shirt pocket and says, "I thought the three of us could smoke a joint and talk about the mess that happened today."

"We're not getting high tonight," Gene snaps.

Sandy snatches the joint out of Theodore's hand.

"Sandy seems like she wants to get high. It's Saturday night. Loosen up a little, Gene."

"Issac! Issac! I spilled my drink. I need you to help me clean it up!" Sandy yells.

"I think Issac left. He was on his way out when I came in."

"You're going to have to clean this up, Gene," Sandy says and points to the mess.

Gene gets paper towels and a dustpan from behind the minibar and starts to clean up ice cubes and uses the towels to soak up the thrown drink from the carpeting. Sandy lights the joint.

"I got to get a picture of this, Gene. We can use this picture to show you are like regular working people. Maybe we can get Sandy to give Issac a foot rub to let people know she cares."

"Very funny, Teddy. The announcement today wasn't that bad, was it?"

Theodore shakes his head and runs his hand through his hair. He puts his hand out, and Sandy passes him the joint. "Are you kidding me? Which television station did you watch? Did you write your own speech, or did you go to the *special* school and have a retarded kid write it for you?"

"I watched Channel 6 News and the interview you did with Grace Downwood. The clips from my speech were fine, but your interview made it seem like I did a terrible job and that Sandy went off the plan and caught me off guard."

"Do you have a computer handy, a laptop, or a tablet or something?"

"I have my laptop in here. What do you want it for?" Sandy asks.

Theodore takes the laptop from Sandy. "Let's see what's going on in social media. Let's check out what Channel 3 News posted."

Theodore logs onto the page and begins to scroll through pages. Gene and Sandy stand behind him to see what he finds on the screen.

"All the news is going to report the same thing about the speech. We had all the local networks there. It's going to be the same. It was your interview on Channel 6 News that ruined it," Sandy says.

Theodore types a few things and scrolls down the screen a little bit further. "Oh, here we are, Channel 3 News. They posted the video clip of your whole speech. But before we watch your entire speech, let's see what people, the voters you are trying to appeal to, think about your announcement. Shall we?"

Theodore begins to read the comments on the screen to Sandy and Gene.

"Darth Skywalker asks, 'How does a moron like this own an honors college, a community college, and a publishing house?'

"MartyMustang says, 'It's "let the cat out of the bag," not "let the cat out of the bag of secrets." *Where's Waldo* would be ashamed to publish with this guy.'

"Muffdiver69 says, 'I think that hot wife of his literally fucked his brains out. I've heard farts that made more sense than Gene Douglas.'

"ScribbleSid just took a freeze frame of your face during the speech and drew a penis going into your mouth. Ooh, wait. He also drew a penis coming out of your cleavage, Sandy."

"We should sue these people. They are ruining us!" Sandy says.

Theodore turns around to Sandy and gives her a disgusted look. "Really, Sandy? How do you suppose we serve DarthSkywalker and MuffDiver69 legal papers? These people are commenting anonymously. This is public opinion. This is what makes or breaks a candidate."

Then he continues, "Okay, let's see here. Channel 9 News. They posted your speech with the headline GOVERNOR HOPEFUL GENE DOUGLAS SHOULD LOOK INTO TELEPROMPTER TECHNOLOGY.

"BartBoogerFart says, 'The most interesting thing in this guy's speech was the feedback from the sound system.'

"ConstanceLyngus says, 'I wonder if that guy's wife had vaginal rejuvenation surgery and her asshole bleached. Her poop asshole, not the asshole making the speech LMAO.'

"GregGforce says, 'If this guy becomes our governor, Texas and Florida will no longer be our most embarrassing states.'

"MildredDavis86 says, 'Sherman Jones will coast to an easy victory if Gene Douglas is the best the conservatives have to offer.'

"VitoNsheila just posted a picture of Joe Pesci with the caption, 'You're a mumbling, stuttering little fuck.'

"SkinhoundDaddy says, 'I will definitely vote for that guy if he sends me a bunch of naked pictures of his wife.'

"CurleyShirley says simply, 'Stupid is as stupid does.'

"These are the people that watch television. A good chunk of them vote, and this is what they are saying publicly about your little announcement stunt today."

"What does the social media say about the Channel 6 News coverage and your little interview today?" Gene asks.

Theodore clicks a few more buttons and types a few words. The Channel 6 News social media page comes up on the screen.

"Well, let's see. Channel 6 News has a picture of the two of you at the podium with the headline SUPER EXCITED WIFE LEAKS GUBERNATORIAL CANDIDACY. I click on the article, and there is just a blurb about your candidacy being official and that Sandy couldn't keep a secret any longer and made you announce at her event today. Below the blurb is my interview with Grace Downwood."

"What are the people saying about this one? What are they saying about you and your interview, Teddy?" Sandy asks.

"Well, let's see," Theodore says. "PoliticalHound says, 'I can understand that Mr. Douglas's wife is excited about her husband running for governor, but where was her brain? He was totally unprepared and looked foolish today.'

"MindyMinx says, 'I don't know much about politics, but I might even make breakfast for Theodore, the campaign manager, after a long night of having my way with him.'

"I have to see if I can find out who this MindyMinx is. Free breakfast is free breakfast.

"HerculesHarry says, 'That campaign manager was doing some major damage control in this interview. If Sherman Jones had him, he could guarantee himself the gubernatorial victory.'

"CuriousChester says, 'I wonder if Sandy Douglas's vagina smells like Legos, because that woman is clearly made of plastic.'

"MaxMuslimHater says, 'I hope the campaign for this guy gets better. If this is how they roll out a campaign, they might as well hand the state over to stupid liberals and sharia law.'

"I-Heart-Beer says, 'I pulled something out of my belly button today, and it was more interesting than Gene Douglas. I wouldn't mind seeing his wife and that Grace Downwood doing some hardcore lesbo, though.'

"SingleMomStrong says, 'I hope this Douglas guy is better than he appears. I think his wife is probably sweet and means well, but she might have sunk this campaign before it started. I was hoping for somebody who cares and would invest in education. If that campaign manager wants to come by and talk about issues, he can park his boots by my bed and we can talk politics all night and naked.'

"So there you go, Sandy, that's what they are saying on the Channel 6 News page. Gene looks like an idiot, you look silly, and I did okay. I could get a free breakfast and a night of naked political talk. Curious Chester did bring up a good question, does your vagina smell like Legos?"

"Fuck you, Furshizzle! You're an asshole."

"So what do we do about this? How do we change the tone of what these people are saying?" Gene asks.

Theodore gets up from behind the computer. "First, the next time Sandy is asking for a favor in exchange for oral sex, when she finishes the oral sex, give me a call and run it by me."

"What? I can't believe you told him that."

"Sandy, if you are giving out blow jobs, I would be more than happy to listen to your ideas about the campaign. My penis is calling the shots," Theodore says.

"I wouldn't go near your penis, Teddy. It's been in some awful places."

"Well, that's fine. Keep your nose out of the campaign."

Gene appears frustrated and nervous. "You two, cut it out. This isn't helping. Really, Teddy, what do we do now? I can't let this blow my chances."

"First, listen to me and not her. I know what I am doing. Second, do not associate your campaign with your wife's pageant commission. It's shallow, and it will cost you women voters, especially working moms."

"What do you mean? My pageant commission just announced the Magnificent Moms Pageant. It's a pageant for working moms."

Theodore shakes his head. "This Magnificent Moms Pageant you created is for you. You want to compete again. You aren't a working mom. Your son goes to a rich kids' private school that your family owns. It's two miles away, yet you make him live in a dorm. You never listened to him play guitar until I played his audition tape for you. You are far from a magnificent mom. You look pampered and plastic. Real working moms, they look tired. They look tired because they work all day for less than they are worth and come home from an unrewarding job to take care of their kids, do laundry, clean their house, run kids to and from school activities, and cook to put food on their tables. That's a magnificent mom."

"Come on, Teddy, you don't have to be so hard on her. She does mean well."

"You're right, Gene. Sandy, I'm sorry. I just don't want this campaign to take steps forward and have poor performances like today take us all those steps back. I want to do this right. I came here tonight to let you know that I got a guest spot on *State of the State This Week* tomorrow. I'm going to see if I can do a little more damage control and get us some positive momentum to push us ahead."

"Do you want me to come on the show with you?"

"No, Gene, you've done enough damage already. We will work on you and your image soon enough. I will do this tomorrow, and we can watch the polls afterward."

Gene shrugs his shoulders. "I will trust you on this, Teddy. You've come through for me so far. I will run our ideas past you in the future, but can you and Sandy bury the hatchet already?"

"I'm sorry, Sandy. Watch the show tomorrow. I will try to help you out too. I don't like to constantly be at odds with you. I really don't."

"For Gene's sake, I am willing to bury the hatchet. I'm sorry too, Teddy. Let's hug it out," she says and opens her arms.

Theodore hugs Sandy and kisses her on top of the head. "You know I love you guys. You just have to learn to trust me. If you had run this beauty pageant idea by me, I could have made it so we would be celebrating tonight instead of arguing. Let's have one plan and stick to it, okay?"

"Sounds like a wise idea. Now you give me a hug, you sleazy old man-child," Gene says.

Theodore hugs his friend. "Now I got to get going. It's Saturday night. I have to blow off some steam with fun people."

"Do you want to stick around and have some drinks and maybe smoke another joint and relax?"

"I said with *fun* people. Besides, I've done enough damage to the Douglas name for today. Watch the show tomorrow, Channel 6, at ten thirty. I'll make you both happy. But now I have to leave your hospitality."

"Stop by after the show. We can have a nice lunch," Sandy offers.

Theodore, as he is making his way to the door, turns to them. "Sounds like a plan. I'll catch you then."

Theodore disappears into the hall. The front door of the Douglas mansion is heard closing behind him as he makes his way out of the house. The engine of his Buick fires up and warbles in the driveway. A quick squeal of the tires, and Theodore's car is heard vanishing down the driveway.

*   *   *

Theodore sits on the studio stage of *State of the State This Week* with host Walter Carl and two regular panelists, Brad Utes and Joan Mowery. He is polished, groomed, wearing a sharp-looking suit and sitting up straight. The show is about to begin as the theme music is cued and the ON-AIR light is illuminated.

"Good Sunday morning to you. I am Walter Carl, host of *State of the State This Week*. Joining me today is Joan Mowrey and Brad Utes of *The Morning Sun Gazette*. We also have a special guest with us this morning, Theodore Graham, campaign manager for the awkwardly announced gubernatorial campaign of Gene Douglas. Welcome to all of you. Let's start off with Mr. Graham. Tell us a little bit about the announcement of the Gene Douglas campaign. Many are saying it died as soon as it got out of the gate yesterday."

"First, Walter, thank you for having me on today. It's an honor to be on the show. I usually just watch it. Yesterday was a little awkward. Gene Douglas was caught by surprise. His wife's public announcement of his governorship intentions wasn't part of the plan. I was caught off guard as well. You have to know Sandy Douglas. She is a sharp woman with a big heart, and she is excited about her husband being the governor. It was hard for her to sit on that information. Her heart was in the right place. It was done out of love. It's not a setback at all, and now the people know Gene Douglas is officially in the race."

Joan Mowrey asks Theodore a follow-up question. "You don't think the rollout yesterday was a shameless attempt by Sandy Douglas to gain attention and donations for her beauty pageant commission by using her husband's political publicity?"

"That's a fair question, Joan. I am sure that Sandy Douglas would love to have more attention paid to her beauty pageant commission. Personally, I think her beauty pageants don't get the attention they deserve. I know that there are some out there that think the pageants are sexist and degrading. Out of my own ignorance, I used to believe that as well. But the more I got to know Sandy Douglas and see the work she does, my mind was changed. She does a lot for girls and young women of all ages, elementary school girls, teenage girls, and college women. Her pageants teach confidence, promote intelligence, independence, and the winners get scholarships that help them better themselves. Most of the participants in her pageants qualify for some higher education financing. In this economy, especially for working-class families, every bit of help counts. It may reward beauty to a degree, but since when do women have to be ashamed of being attractive, intelligent, hardworking humans?"

Brad Utes asks the next question. "Yesterday, Sandy Douglas resigned from her commission to participate in her commission's new Magnificent Moms Pageant. Don't you think she created this pageant just so she could have a category that she could compete in again?"

"Sandy Douglas was always a fierce competitor. Beauty pageants are what she is good at. She likes the competition, and she likes the challenge that comes with winning. I may have this wrong, and I hope Mrs. Douglas will forgive me if I am, but I believe she announced she will be competing to get other working moms to participate. Sandy Douglas is a beautiful woman, and I think she wants other women just like her to come out and give her a run for her money. I don't think she expects to win, but I know she is hoping to get women to come out and try to beat her. She wants real women to be appreciated, recognized, and seen for how amazing they are. I don't think her plans are sinister or selfish in the least. I am here to answer questions about the campaign, though. I'm sure if you want to learn about the beauty pageant circuit, Mrs. Douglas, Wendy Uher, or Holly Herman would be happy to talk to you about the work they do."

"So tell us, what's next for the Gene Douglas campaign?" Walter Carl asks.

"Our next step is to go out and get to know the voters of our state. We have to find out what the people of our great state want, older citizens, young citizens, parents, single parents, working families, middle-class families, women, men, and children. There are people struggling to make ends meet. Small towns are losing small businesses, and the tax coffers used to fund infrastructure are crumbling. People want better educational opportunities. People want lower taxes. People want smaller government. We are going to go to the people, talk to them, listen to them, and then come up with a plan. We haven't even fully put together our team. How can we put the right people on the team if we don't know the needs of the people we want to serve?"

Brad Utes asks, "Gene Douglas is very wealthy. He travels in wealthy circles. He has ties to institutions of wealth and industry. Is Gene Douglas going to step out of his circle and learn the actual makeup of this state?"

"Of course he is. He is wealthy, yes, but his wealth doesn't prevent him from feeling empathy for the struggles of fellow citizens. We are going to travel the state and meet people. We aren't going out to do credit checks on them. I know you, Walter and Joan, are residents of this state and the three of you are talented journalists. Maybe you guys would like to help us get in touch with the people. What do your readers want? Take some readers polls. What do your viewers want? Host a public call-in show. Come on out and talk to the people with us and see how we are learning from the people. You can participate as the media and keep us honest by questioning our intentions, but as fellow citizens, maybe you can help bring the needs of the people to us. If the media has a right to inform the people about politics, don't you think the media also has a duty to bring the voices of their subscribers to the ears of the ones that want their votes? We're not running a campaign to dodge the media, that's why I am here today. I am here to talk to you guys and ask for your help in getting the voices of the people to the 'Gene Douglas for governor' campaign so we can actually do the work to make a real difference."

"Thank you, Theodore Graham, for talking to us today. I am sure the three of us can work together in the future. We would love to have you back again. When we return from a short break, Joan, Brad, and I will talk about the state's possible budget crisis. Stay tuned!

There is more *State of the State This Week* when we return," Walter Carl says as he leads into the commercial break.

*   *   *

Gene and Sandy Douglas are sitting in their patio lounge, watching Theodore's appearance on *State of the State This Week*. The show goes to commercial break.

"Are you crying? What's going on with you?" Gene asks his wife.

Tears are rolling down Sandy's face. With a weak voice, she says, "Teddy said really beautiful things about us. Those were some of the nicest things that anybody has ever said about me, and they came from Teddy, of all people. I feel bad for being such a bitch to him all the time. I am going to hug him so tightly and thank him profusely when he gets here for lunch."

"He did a good job for us this morning. That's why I have him on my team. Don't get carried away and don't believe everything you see on television. This is, after all, politics."

CHAPTER 9

Gene is sitting at a dark-wood conference table with three other men dressed in expensive suits. The four men have their briefcases and are passing charts and graphs across the table and making notes. The door opens, and Theodore enters the room. He is carrying a student backpack, has headphones around his neck, is wearing khaki shorts and a Monsters of Rock tour T-shirt and a pair of sandals.

"Am I late? I thought we said we would meet at eleven. I was proud of myself for being ten minutes early."

Gene stands up from his seat and says, "You're fine, Teddy. We did say eleven, and you're early."

"Good, I was afraid that it's our first official campaign meeting and your campaign manager, me, is late."

"Teddy, I would like you to meet these three gentlemen here. This is Tim Collins, he is going to be our pollster and statistician. This gentleman, Robert Wermer, he is going to be in charge of our finance and expenses. And this gentleman over here, Russell Dewitt, from the Republican Council, he is going to be our strategy guide."

"Good morning, gentlemen. It's nice to meet all of you."

The three men greet Theodore with handshakes. Tim Collins and Robert Wermer welcome Theodore, while Russell Dewitt examines Theodore and gives him a disapproving look.

"Nice of you to get dressed up for the meeting, Mr. Graham."

Theodore appears puzzled at Russell's comment. "I didn't know we needed to dress up for a planning meeting, but I guess I will be the one that's comfortable. I think better that way."

Gene attempts to quell Russell's fear over Theodore's appearance. "Russell, Teddy here is one of the brightest legal minds that I have the pleasure of knowing. He is a gifted writer and educator, and he is the Douglas Youth Honors College Debate Team coach. He took our team to the national debate finals, and they won."

"With that résumé, Gene, I would think he owns a pair of slacks and a shirt with buttons."

"Okay, fellows, why don't we get started? Teddy, you're the campaign manager, why don't you tell us where to begin?" Gene instructs.

Theodore moves to the head of the table and puts his backpack on it. He unzips the backpack and begins rooting for a binder. Two bottles of Heineken roll out onto the table. Theodore quickly grabs them before they roll on the floor.

"Any of you guys want a beer?" Theodore asks. "They are cold. I just took them out of the refrigerator in my office."

Gene shakes his head while the other men decline the offer of a beer. Russell has an offended look on his face. Theodore pulls the binder he has been searching for out of the backpack.

"Ooh, a pen, I'm going to need a pen to make some notes," Theodore says. As he opens the small pocket on the backpack, a bag of joint falls out on the table.

"Is this some kind of joke, Gene? You can't expect me to work for a campaign that has the adult version of Bart Simpson as its manager!" Russell snaps.

"Is there a problem, Russ?" Theodore asks.

"I'm starting to regret coming to this campaign. I didn't know it was going to be run by a clown."

"Don't let me keep you here, Mr. Dewitt. Gene thought it would be good to hire an adviser from the Republican Council to help rally the party behind our campaign. I didn't think it was necessary, because I saw how well you did as a strategist for the last two gubernatorial campaigns. The people elected the Democrat governor we have now. Twice. I didn't see how hiring a losing strategist was going to help us win, but Gene wanted somebody from the party on board."

"Fellows, let's not start off our first meeting like this. We're all on the same team."

"Okay, if Russell is done with his little protest about me, we can get started. Robert, give us the rundown on how the finance for the campaign is going to work."

Robert opens a binder in front of him and searches for the correct page. "We have start-up capital of 350,000. Rent on the campaign headquarters office is set at 4,000 a month for twenty-two months, so that is eighty-eight grand in expenses right out of the gate."

"Where's our office going to be? I thought this was going to be the campaign headquarters?" Theodore asks.

"It is," Gene answers.

"You own this building already. You are going to pay rent to yourself on a building you already own?"

"Gene Douglas for governor is renting the building," Robert Wermer answers.

Theodore points to Gene. "Gene Douglas is right there. He is the guy we're trying to get elected governor. This is his building."

"Let's move on," Gene says.

Robert flips a page in his binder. "Top campaign staff, the four of us here today, plus the positions we fill in this meeting will get thirty-thousand-dollars-plus expenses, initially, anyway. The salaries will be increased or decreased every four months, depending on the performance of the campaign and the fund-raising."

"We haven't even been placed on a ballot yet, and we already spent 57 percent of our start-up budget," Theodore says.

"Politics is not a poor man's game, Mr. Graham, but a guy in shorts and a T-shirt wouldn't know that," Russell Dewitt says.

"Enough, Russ!" Gene snaps. "Continue, Robert."

"There will be additional sources of revenue to make up for initial expenses. We will circulate electronic mailing and snail-mail fund-raising brochures to regular individual contributors from the party. After those mailers are out, we will start mailing to small businesses and business owners throughout the state. There will be some meet-and-greet events to bring in some larger contributions, golf tournaments, luncheons, and chamber of commerce events in some of the larger counties. There will be more similar events as the campaign goes on, I'm sure."

"What about the super PAC?" Gene asks.

"Once we are on the ballot, the campaign itself can't communicate with the super PAC. That's according to the Citizens United laws of the state. The super PAC will take the larger contributions from big business, banks, fuel industries, and wealthy donors. Any contribution over ten thousand dollars will be made to the super PAC. There is already about eleven million pledged to fund the super PAC. We will have to appoint a chair to the super PAC and a liaison to legally coordinate with the campaign."

"I would like to be that liaison. I have experience with super PACs and aligning their message with a campaign," Russell Dewitt offers.

"I already have that job, Mr. Dimwit," Theodore says.

"My name is Russell Dewitt, Mr. Graham, and I have experience with these matters. This is why Mr. Douglas has me here."

"Is this true, Gene? You want Mr. Dewitt the dimwit to coordinate with the super PAC?" Theodore asks.

Gene seems a little uncomfortable being put on the spot. "Teddy, I need you guiding me, getting me ready, and helping me relate to the voters. I need you with me full-time, so I will let Mr. Dewitt do what he has the experience with."

"It's Mr. Dimwit," Theodore says.

"It's Dewitt," Russell shoots back.

"Do what?" Theodore asks.

"My name is Dewitt!" Russell shouts.

"Yeah, Russ, Gene introduced us at the beginning of the meeting. Don't you remember? What a dimwit," Theodore jokes.

"Enough. Let's move on to polling. Tim, what do you have for us?" Gene asks.

Tim turns on the overhead projector without a slide on it. The empty screen on the wall is now illuminated. Theodore makes a shadow puppet of a dog on the screen.

"Woof, woof, woof," Theodore says as he moves the shadow puppet around on the screen.

"Come on, Gene! I thought you were a serious candidate for governor, but with this clown on your staff, I see that it's not!" Russell shouts.

"Maybe you like bunny rabbits instead?" Theodore says as he begins making the shadow puppet of a rabbit.

Tim Collins puts the first slide on the overhead projector. "After your announcement to run, your overall approval among establishment Republicans is at 41 percent. Larry Richmond has a slight edge on you here. He polls at 47 percent. He edges you with higher approval among young Republicans, women in the party, and minority voters. The undecided voters in the state for the primary make 10 percent of the voters that we want to get. You have to get at least half of them to put you in a dead heat and be within the margin of error with Larry Richmond. Once we get your campaign even with his, we can win the primary in debates and in the media. Larry Richmond doesn't debate well, and he's not pleasant to see on television. The overhead I am using today was the polling data as of dinnertime last night, so that's pretty much where we stand. We do have some work to do, but with a good strategy, we should be able to squeak out of the primary with the win."

Tim finishes his presentation and takes the slide off the projector, and the lighted screen is still illuminated. Theodore makes the shadow puppet of a dog again.

"Arf! Arf! Arf! Arf! Burrrrrrrp!" Theodore says as he makes his shadow puppet speak. Gene quickly turns off the projector.

"Okay, Tim, good job with the polling data. We know where we stand. Russell, you can guide us through the strategy we need to follow."

Russell Dewitt stands and addresses the room. "If things are too difficult for you and your T-shirt to understand, Mr. Graham, just stop me and maybe I can explain the subject matter with puppets."

"Thanks, Mr. Dimwit, that's nice of you to be so willing to help me."

Russell grits his teeth and continues his presentation. "The strategy we have to take against Larry Richmond is to paint him as a Republican that is weak against Democrats. We can use the narrative that he won't stand up to liberal policies and the taxpayers will end up paying more if he is elected governor. We can tout the Douglas schools, the honors college and the community college, as proof of our commitment to education. We can use the publishing house to tout Gene Douglas as a successful business operator. Following this strategy, we will hold the voters we have, plus we will gain the support needed in the undecided group to put us in the dead heat. Once we are in the dead heat, we can beat him on the issues in the debates and media editorials. It's a simple, straightforward plan, and with super-PAC-funded advertising, there is no reason we can't win."

"That seems achievable. Teddy, do you have anything else to add here?"

"So, Russell, our strategy is to say that Larry Richmond will allow the Democrats to raise taxes and we won't?"

"Yes, Mr. Graham, it's that simple. But I guess that's a little difficult for the guy that can't tie a tie to understand."

Theodore stands up and takes one of the bottles of Heineken out of his backpack. He positions the neck of the bottle at the edge of the table and slams it down with his other hand to open it. Theodore throws the cap on the table and takes a sip of the beer.

"So by saying that Larry Richmond will raise our taxes, we will get the primary voters we need. Hmmm? Now I did a little research on Larry Richmond. Did you know he served six years in the state House? Did you know he served two years in the state Senate? When he was in the state House, he had a consistent record of voting against legislation with tax increases. When he was in the state Senate, he filibustered a transportation bill that would have increased local taxes for small communities and won. Also, when Mr. Richmond was in the Senate, he authored the Home Improvement Tax Reduction Bill that gave homeowners doing improvements to their homes a reduced, fixed tax rate that wouldn't increase for five years. I think if we went with your strategy, Mr. Dewitt, the Richmond campaign would counter with his actual record and the fact Gene Douglas never held public office," Theodore says and takes a sip of his beer.

"Is this correct, Tim?" Gene asks.

"Yes, Mr. Graham is right about Larry Richmond's record."

"Larry Richmond can also hit us on your business record if you are going to hit him falsely on taxes. The publishing house was near bankrupt, but then it started publishing religious books and it became a tax-exempt business. The school is tax-exempt, the community college is tax-exempt, and your house got tax-exempt status for its historical value to the community, yet it's not open to the public. I don't think handing your opponent the weapon to hit you with is a wise strategy," Theodore says.

"What do you propose, Teddy? Is there a better approach?" Gene asks.

Theodore takes another sip of the Heineken. "Tim said our polling data isn't that good with younger people, minorities, and women. I talked to Kevin Baker the other day. He's the coordinator for the Young Republicans Association in the state. He sets up the meetings and events for the group. I asked him why the association isn't more involved in the party itself. He told me it was because the candidates don't ask them to get involved until Election Day, and on Election Day, they are only asked to hand out campaign cards and stickers. I also talked to Demitri Smith, and I asked him why minorities are leaning toward Larry Richmond. He told me it's because Larry Richmond is from the city and the city has a minority population that knows his name. However, he also told me that Larry Richmond doesn't go into neighborhoods with higher minority populations. Women voters, they don't feel they are heard or respected by the party leaders or the candidates. I did a little research here on women. Twenty-seven of the counties in this state have women as chamber of commerce coordinators, but last gubernatorial election, only two of them were asked to host small business events."

"I'm hoping you are going to make a point that will help Mr. Graham. Maybe you can go back to doing shadow puppet shows. They seem more your speed," Russell says.

"Well, Russ, my point is that these groups within our party have been neglected by party advisers and the Republican Council for the last two gubernatorial elections. These voters within our own party are disenfranchised. They were encouraged to join the party and are expected to loyally vote for the party nominees, but they don't have a say in the direction it's heading. They don't have a forum to share their ideas or the opportunity to share their skills. Why are they ignored? You were the chairman of the Republican Council the last election and the vice-chairman the election before. Tell us why, Russ. Why?"

"These voters are only a small portion of the party. They won't make the difference we need to get us in the dead heat we need to be in before we start to debate. I don't expect you to be able to grasp that concept, Mr. Graham."

Theodore takes a sip of his beer. "Well, maybe you're right, Russ. My thought was, since it is so early in the race, why not take a stab at improving our numbers with women, minorities, and the young in our party? We can talk to the women that are county chamber of commerce coordinators and see if we can speak at some of their events, get to know some of their business participants, and hear what they have to say. For the Young Republicans, we can host a meeting and see if they want to run some ground operations in each of the counties. Give the young voters a chance to show us what they can do. A lot of times, all somebody wants is a chance to let their talents shine and they are less disenfranchised. With minority voters, let's go into the communities the party has neglected or ignored. The way I see it, if we can pick up 2 percent increases in each of these groups of voters, it will put us in a dead heat with Larry Richmond. It would put us both at 45 percent. I'm sure some of the undecided are women, minorities, and young, so we may even make out a little better and come out ahead in the next polling period. That's just my thoughts on getting us where we need to be."

"I don't think wasting time and the campaign's money on something that won't make a difference is in our best interest, Mr. Graham," Russell says.

The room is silent. Theodore returns to his seat and takes a few more sips of his beer. Robert stares at the wall and hopes not to get in an argument. Tim Collins begins writing some numbers and notes down on a page of polling data in front of him. Russell stares intimidatingly at Theodore.

"So what direction do we want to move in?" Gene asks.

Tim Collins stands up and moves toward Gene and shows him the notes he has jotted down. "Mr. Graham is right. If we can pull 2 percent from each of those groups, it will put us even with Larry Richmond. And 2 percent from each group is achievable. If there is a little momentum and possibly some media coverage, there is no reason we wouldn't pick up higher percentages."

"It really wouldn't cost the campaign all that much, some travel expenses and some minor administrative costs, but working with some of the chambers of commerce may fetch us some donors that will cover our expense. It's worth a shot," Robert Wermer adds.

"If Robert and Tim think it will work, then I am on board," Russell says.

Gene stands up. "This is the direction we will head. Teddy, you will make all the contacts and get us moving forward with this?"

"You bet, Gene. See, Mr. Dimwit, this is my lucky Monsters of Rock T-shirt. It brought me good luck and made me a better strategist than you."

"Russ, down the road, we may need your strategy ideas, but for now, I want you getting the super PAC in place. This is the first meeting, and we still have a long way to go, but it's a good start. Let's get to work and get these polling numbers where they need to be," Gene says, concluding the meeting.

"Any of you guys want a beer now that the meeting is over? We can make shadow puppets on the overhead projector. I know how to do a dog, a bunny, and a hawk, but that's about it," Teddy says.

Tim and Robert take a beer, and Russell leaves the room.

*   *   *

Gene Douglas walks across campus to Theodore's faculty house. As he approaches, he can hear electric guitars blaring from inside. At the front door, he knocks, but the guitar playing doesn't stop. He knocks again, louder and longer. The guitars still don't stop. He rings the doorbell, and that fails to get the attention of Theodore inside. He begins to repeatedly ring the doorbell and has no success. He sits on the stoop until the playing stops and then knocks and rings the doorbell again.

"Oh, hey, Gene-Bean, were you out here long? We were just playing guitar."

"The whole campus and half of the town know you were playing guitars."

"Did you come to hear us play?"

"No, Teddy, I came here to talk to you. Can I come in?"

Theodore opens the door and motions for Gene to enter. A few steps in the doorway, Gene begins shooing marijuana smoke away from his face.

"Were you just smoking weed?" Gene sarcastically asks.

"My glaucoma was acting up, so I was just taking my medicine. This here is my doctor and fellow guitarist, Wayne. He was just here helping me administer my treatment."

"Hello, Wayne, nice to meet you. You don't look like a doctor."

"I know. Damn Obamacare," Wayne responds.

"Come on in. Have a seat. Care for a bong rip?" Theodore offers.

Gene takes the bong and lighter out of Theodore's hand and begins to take a hit.

"No way, I got to get a picture of this! The next governor of our state is doing bong rips. You got my vote," Wayne says as he gets his smartphone out of his pocket.

Gene starts coughing out smoke and seems panicked by what Wayne has just said.

"No flash photography permitted, Wayne, you have to be cool," Theodore says.

Wayne puts his cell phone back in his pocket and says, "Yeah, I gotcha. You can't risk the whole blackmail thing. That's cool, we can just chill."

"Actually, Wayne, I would like to talk to Teddy alone for a bit. Can you please excuse us for a few minutes?"

"Oh, no problem. This is business, not pleasure. I gotcha. I will run to the store and get us the stuff to make tacos."

"Thanks, Wayne. Get me some rolling papers too. I'm almost out," Theodore says.

"Sure thing, Mr. G. You need anything, governor guy?"

"No, Wayne, thank you."

"Mr. Douglas, you got my vote if you legalize it. I want to be an entrepreneur. That will be a big help."

Gene makes sure Wayne has left and turns to Theodore. "He seems like a neat friend to have, or are you babysitting?"

"Don't let looks fool you, Gene. Wayne is a smart kid. He has a good business mind, the papers he writes for my English class at the community college are surprisingly good, and the kid works hard. Don't let the stoner stereotype fool you."

Teddy, the reason I am here is because of today's meeting. You got to lighten up on Russell Dewitt. He's from the party, and we need to get the party behind us."

Teddy gets out of his seat quickly. "Gene, come on! You heard his strategy at the meeting today. He was totally wrong. Russell Dewitt doesn't have a winning record. He was the party representative for the last two elections. His team, the Republicans, lost. Twice!"

"You righted the wrong, Teddy. That's why I have you, but I have Russell for his connections. We will let him focus on the super PAC liaison part of his job. Just don't make a dick out of him like you did today."

"I made a dick out of him because he is a dick. You want to fulfill your legacy, don't you? Why would you want somebody with a losing record? That's seems like a foolish bet. The party will get behind us because we will have the poll numbers and the financial backing. Russell Dewitt will then have to kiss our asses. I'm not going to kiss his ass because he is a shitty political strategist."

"Teddy, we have to play nice with him. His dad is Barton Dewitt, the fuel industry developer. He could invest a lot in the state and in my campaign."

"So the truth comes out. You're doing Barton a favor by hiring Russell. It's all about the money. I guess I should have connected the dots."

"Barton Dewitt's endorsement and investment in the state will be huge for my campaign and good for the state. It will create jobs. We need to have job creation as part of our platform."

"Investment in the state! Are you fucking kidding me? First, it's 'do old Bart a favor and hire his incompetent son.' Then after you're elected, it's 'do old Bart a favor and let him take advantage of a loophole so he doesn't have to pay taxes.' After that, it's 'do old Bart a favor and veto any environmental or EPA legislation.' Then after that, the next favor is that his public land use decisions get sealed by the courts so his environmental record is not open for public scrutiny under the right-to-know laws. Then he will bring in workers he already has trained from out of state, and you haven't created jobs for the people from your own state. Bart gets you to do a lot of favors for him, and you get nothing in the end. I bet you that old Bart has a history of buying politicians like this in other states."

"Russell Dewitt is a done deal. You got to learn to work with him. You're smart. I am sure you can figure out a way to be nice and have him work in our favor."

"Well, Gene, I guess I have no choice. I will have to play nice. You're the boss."

"Don't be like that, Teddy. You are the campaign manager. We don't do anything without your say, but work with Russell, don't embarrass the guy."

Theodore takes the bong off the table and has a hit of it. "I will do my best, but I'm not making any promises. All next week, we go out to the voters and work on getting the poll numbers in our favor. I'm sure your buddy Russell Dewitt is hoping I fail, but I promised not to let you down."

"Thanks, Teddy. All I ask is that you try with Russell. You are the only one I trust with getting me ready for this election. I will be ready to learn next week."

The door opens, and Wayne returns, holding a bag of groceries. "I guess I should have knocked first, in case you guys were having gay sex or something. Thank God you weren't. I got the stuff for tacos. You sticking around to eat, governor guy?"

"No, Wayne, I just had to talk some election business. We're done talking. You guys can go back to tacos and playing guitar."

"I wish life were that simple, Mr. Douglas, tacos and guitars. It couldn't get much better than that. Bummer you can't stick around."

"Yeah, it is a real bummer. I will let you guys get to it," Gene says and leaves.

Wayne waits until the door closes behind Gene. "That guy is kind of a stiff. I'm surprised he even hit the bong."

"That's what happens when you're born with a stick up your ass and carry a legacy on your shoulders. So what are we doing? Do we want to eat first or jam first?"

"How about this? We pack that bong, jam out a couple of tunes, and then cook tacos. That way, we can line ourselves up properly with the timing of the munchies."

"You are a heck of a planner. Did you ever think of becoming a political strategist?"

Wayne exhales after a hit from the bong. "Why, is Mr. Douglas hiring? I would work for him. We seemed to hit it off."

"I'll give you a reference, but I am not making any promises. Let's get our guitars on and start jamming. Let's rip it up."

CHAPTER 10

Monday

Theodore and Gene are riding in the back of Gene's limousine. Gene is polished, his expensive suit crisp and sharp, his red power necktie straight as a board, his shoes impeccably shined, and his hair perfectly stiff and still. Theodore is wearing casual slacks and a short-sleeved Oxford shirt with no tie and the collar unbuttoned. Gene appears nervous as he rereads notes and speech cues from his binder. Theodore appears relaxed as he watches the scenery outside the window and taps out a rhythm on his knee from a song in his head.

"Are you sure about this? This seems a little too simple, and I don't really get to say much or make much of a speech."

Theodore turns his focus from looking out the window to Gene. "Relax. Study that binder. It has this week's itinerary outlined. It tells you what speeches you have to make, it tells you what to say at each event, it tells you what small talk to make, what compliments to give, what lines you should repeat, what you should wear, and what photo ops to take advantage of. Follow the binder, and you will be fine."

"But you just gave me the binder yesterday afternoon. I can't remember all this after only one full day with it. Fulfilling my legacy depends on my performance."

"I put that binder together for you Saturday night. I couldn't get it to you any sooner than I did. The pages were still warm from the printer when I gave it to you. Focus on the first two pages—that's all you need for tonight. After we get through tonight, look at the pages for Tuesday. After we're done tomorrow, look at the pages for

Wednesday. You know the days of the week, right? We will take it one day at a time, and you will be fine."

"I don't know . . . these speech cues seem very general and vague. I feel as if I should fill in the gaps a little bit better and elaborate on the issues more. Don't you think I should be myself?"

"Whatever you do, Gene, don't be yourself. This is politics, and if the media is there when you are being yourself, there will be video and audio clips that will use your own words against you. I know how you are. What you are saying in your head never comes out of your mouth the same way you imagine it will. Most of the time, it is a word salad without a beginning or end and no points are made in between."

"I'm not that bad, am I?"

"Don't you remember the damage control I did after your announcement to run at Sandy's beauty pageant luncheon? Follow the binder, and you will be fine."

"But there are some gaps that are left open for question. Shouldn't I fill them in so people know where we stand?"

Theodore puts his hand on Gene's shoulder. "Gene, you made me your campaign manager because you trust me and think I am the best man for the job. You have to trust me. The gaps in the speech cues are intentional."

"What do you mean *intentional*? That makes us look unprepared."

Theodore holds up two fingers. "Two! There are two reasons the gaps are intentional. First, it shows you are a leader. When you are asked questions about the gaps, refer the people to other members of your staff. Strategy questions and anything you are unsure of, refer to me. Polling questions or statistics, refer them to Tim Collins. Financial questions, you refer them to Bob Wermer. Policy questions or suggestions, you refer them to Marty Price. This shows you have a well-trained staff that you command."

"That kind of makes sense. What's the second reason?"

"The second reason is that it's good to leave questions unanswered. If you leave questions unanswered, the press will always seek you out. If you answer all the questions right away, the media becomes complacent and reports on you in a dull and repetitive way. The newspapers can basically cut and paste their articles about you because you don't change. Readers get bored of the same scripted and sculpted lines. People will vote against you not because they don't like your policies but because they hate boredom. We got to make it so each press cycle has something new to say about you."

"How do you know these tricks, Teddy?"

"They're not too hard to figure out. You learn the players, get to know the fans, memorize the rules of the game, and bend them in your favor without breaking them."

"You certainly know the game, but I hope your plan works."

"You will be fine tonight, my friend. Wait for your introduction, make the speech I outlined for you, introduce me, and go sit down. When the presentation is over, engage with the people."

"What should I say when they ask me questions?"

"We just went over that. When they ask you questions, refer them to members of your staff. The people tonight are the Young Republicans, not the press. They want to know you care about them. You should ask them questions. People feel cared about when they are asked about themselves. People love to talk about themselves."

"What kind of questions do I ask them?"

Theodore takes a deep breath and looks Gene directly in the eyes. "You have to relax. People will sense your fear. When you ask people questions, ask them specific things. Don't be vague. You will only open yourself up for long philosophical conversations."

"What do you mean *specific* questions?"

"Questions that require a definitive answer. These are young Republicans. Most of them are in college or are starting at the ground floor of their careers. Ask them questions like, What's your major? Where are you working? Where are you from? How many people are in your family? Is your family a Republican family? How many years have you been with the Young Republicans? Questions that have a number for the answer are the best way to go. Just ask them simple questions."

"Shouldn't I ask them their thoughts on the issues and what I can do to serve them better? Isn't that why we're here tonight?"

Theodore shakes his head. "Buddy, you're making this harder than it has to be. People don't know their thoughts on the issues until the media tells them what to think. We have Tim Collins as our pollster and statistician. He reads and studies the media data and tells us what the people want. Marty Price reads the polling data and tailors our policy stances accordingly. The people don't tell it directly to you. If we let them tell you what they want directly, this would be a week-long event. We will only be here for three hours tops. I'm shooting for two hours. I got a new Victoria's Secret catalog in the mail today, and I would like to spend some alone time with it."

"I don't know . . . it just doesn't sound right."

"Let's role-play for a minute. I will be you engaging the people, and you will be a Young Republican, okay?"

"Okay, it's worth a try."

"What is your major at school?" Theodore asks.

"I am an accounting major."

"You can never have too many accountants. When you get done school, give me a call, maybe we can find a place for you."

"How about you? How many years have you been a Young Republican?" Theodore asks.

"Six years."

"Six years, that's fantastic! You will be an old Republican soon. Thanks for your dedication to the party."

"What kind of work do you do?"

"I'm a police officer, Mr. Douglas," Gene answers.

"You have a tough and dangerous job. Thank you for doing what you do. Stay safe out there and contact our office and let us know if there is any way we can help."

"Is it really that simple?" Gene asks.

"It *is* that simple. Ask a specific question, get a specific answer, compliment the answer, and move on to the next person. Try it tonight and you will see."

The chauffeur talks through the intercom. "We are pulling up to the place now, Mr. Douglas."

"Thank you, Ronny. Don't open the door for us until you hear us knock on the window," Gene instructs his driver.

"Yes, Mr. Douglas."

"Tim Collins and Sidney Hughes, our media coordinator, will meet us at the car and walk in with us. When we get out of the limo, engage with them briefly and then smile and wave to the people around us as we walk in. Shake a few hands, and if there is any press here, don't talk to them until after the event. I don't expect there to be any press here unless somebody from the Young Republicans notified them," Theodore instructs.

Gene checks his hair in the mirror, makes sure his tie is straight, and gives himself a quick look over to make sure nothing is out of place.

"Just so you know, Gene, we have a planted photographer working the room tonight, so always keep your composure and smile."

"Why do we have a planted photographer when Sidney is here?"

"You ask too many questions and worry too much. Sidney makes prepared statements from our campaign to the media, but a planted photographer leaks good stuff about us to the media and shares amateurish pictures and videos with them. It guarantees us some added free media coverage. There are Sidney and Tim now. Knock on the window for Ronny to open the door. Don't forget, smile and wave."

Gene and Theodore exit the limousine and exchange a few brief words with Tim and Sidney. They smile and wave to the few people gathered at the entrance of the restaurant that is hosting the Young Republicans event.

*   *   *

Gene and Theodore are seated at the head table in the large dining room with the rest of the officers and guests. From the back of the room, clinking glasses, rattling plates, and chiming silverware can be heard being cleared from the tables by the waitstaff. A few waiters are making their way around the room and filling the coffee mugs and water glasses of the people waiting for the program to begin. Kevin Baker, the Young Republicans senior coordinator, scans the room to make sure it is settled before he begins his presentation.

"Okay, folks, take your seats. We will begin in a few minutes," Kevin announces from the podium.

Theodore leans over to Gene. "Remember, stick to the basics from the binder. Keep the speech to the cues I gave you. Keep it brief and turn it over to me. You got this."

Kevin Baker bangs a gavel on the podium. "Okay, folks, let's settle down and get started." He waits until the shuffling and chatter stop and then begins his introduction. "Welcome, all of you, to the annual Young Republicans dinner. Thanks to the chefs, bartenders, and waitstaff of Admiral Barker's—you guys make this a delicious and wonderful atmosphere for this dinner each year. Before we get to the regular business at hand, our officer elections and making our mission statement for the coming year, we have a special guest that wants to talk to our group. Eugene Douglas, one of the Republican candidates seeking the party nomination to be governor of our great state, is here. He would like to say a few words to us tonight. Mr. Douglas, welcome. Come on up here to the podium, and let us hear what you have to say."

The young people sitting in their seats clap respectfully as Gene makes his way to the podium. He shakes Kevin Baker's hand and puts his hand on his shoulder and says a thank-you. Gene waves to the crowd as Kevin Baker takes his seat next to the podium.

"Thank you, Kevin. Thank you all for being here. Judging by the number of you here tonight, I can see that we have a strong Young Republican base. I, too, was a Young Republican. I attended this annual dinner for a good number of years. I even served a year as a trustee. Because of the Young Republicans, I learned a lot of my values and ethics. I met a lot of great leaders here. Mayor Mike Nardo, this town's four-term mayor, he was a Young Republican sitting in the same seats you are now when I was a Young Republican. I heard a speech at one of these annual dinners by Paul Bruni. I was so motivated by this man that I took a very active interest in politics. I got involved in his grassroots campaign. I knocked on hundreds of doors across the state and handed out thousands of campaign pamphlets. I had a lot of doors slammed in my face, but I believed in him. Paul Bruni got elected governor that year, and he went on to be one of the most successful two-term governors that this state has ever seen. I heard that man speak right here," Gene says and pauses for the applause. He is surprised by the big response from the room.

"This is why I am here tonight. There are a lot of you here, so there is obviously young people concerned about the future of the party. I just can't figure out why nobody is engaging you. There is nobody here asking you to get involved now. Right now! This is when the party needs you the most. I think it's wrong—and frankly, I find it offensive—that the party only calls on you a few days before elections and asks you to hand out candidate brochures, leaflets, and business cards at the polling places. What happened to the opportunity that came out of the Young Republicans? What leaders or what want-to-be leaders are giving you a chance to make a difference? What leaders are asking you to showcase your leadership skills, your organizational skills, and your talents? When I was here, I was here to make my government reflect my values. I was given opportunities to get involved. I took advantage of those opportunities. I made connections. I developed skills that helped me have the successes and good fortunes in my life. I made a good name for myself by getting involved here. Now, for some strange reason, the party is asking for your loyalty in exchange for nothing. I want to change that. I want to give you the opportunity to let yourselves shine. Show your leadership. Show the old party how to do things new ways. I want you to show me what you can do. I want to write reference letters for people who did good work here, just like Governor Paul Bruni did for me when I was a Young Republican."

There is louder and longer applause.

"I have opportunities for you if you want them. Opportunities require work. Good work gets noticed and leads to other opportunities. I'm offering a chance for the young in our party to be judged on their own good merit. Hard work now makes good fortunes later. When I talked to my staff about engaging the Young Republicans, they all shared my vision. They helped me come up with a plan and some ideas to bring back to the Young Republicans what I used to love about this organization. My campaign manager, Mr. Graham, is a details guy. He will explain the opportunities that I am offering you tonight. I hope you take advantage of them. I hope I can be a help in your success. Mr. Graham, come on up here and tell these folks what they can do."

The applause continues as Theodore makes his way to the podium. Gene waits and offers Theodore his hand to shake when he gets there. Theodore shakes Gene's hand and then offers up his fist for a fist bump. Gene bumps Theodore's fist and returns to his seat as the applause continues.

"Thank you, Gene. Thank you, Kevin, for allowing us to speak here this evening, and thank you all for listening. I hope the applause we are hearing here tonight is enthusiasm for opportunity. There are a couple of things the party has to do. First, we got to grow our party by getting people that share our values on our side. The only way to do that is to go out there, talk to the people, and get them behind our commitment of making the state a better place. Second, we have to grow opportunities in the state. You people are young and smart. You can see the difficulty you will have finding gainful employment when you get out of school. Those of you who have finished school and are just starting out in the workforce, you are seeing how hard it is to make ends meet. Some of you are working jobs that have nothing to do with your college major. Is that right? Is that how you envisioned your future when you chose your majors? I highly doubt it is. It's really sad to see when good people, Young Republicans, from our own state move to other states for better opportunities. Those opportunities should be here in our state. This brings me to my third point. Third, we have to get leaders in office that will listen to what the young people have to say. We need leaders that will understand what opportunities young people need. We need leaders that will get those opportunities for you. Now, Gene Douglas is my longtime friend. I know him better than anybody else. I took the job as his campaign manager because I believe he is one of those leaders that will take the cues from the people and get them what they need to succeed. That's what I believe. Gene is whom I believe in. You people here this evening will make up your own minds on whom you want to vote for, but I believe we can all agree that we need to take these three steps, grow the party, grow the opportunity, and elect the leaders that will listen and keep opportunities in our state."

The applause is louder and longer than before.

"This is where you come in. We need the leaders from this room. We need the idea people from this room. We need the planners, and we need the ones that can execute plans from this room. All the people we need to achieve these goals are sitting in this room. Let's not let the potential we have sitting in this room right now go to waste. The party lost the governor's race the last two elections because of wasted potential. Let's learn from those mistakes. Gene Douglas is the man that believes it's time to stop doing the same things we did wrong in the past and expecting them to be right this time around. We have to do things differently. We have to do things the right way in order to win. We have forty-one counties in this state, and we have to reach out to the people in all of them. We got to register voters. We have to find out what the people need. We have to provide them with the leaders and teams that will best satisfy those needs. In each of the counties, we need teams out there doing this work. It's important work. In this room are the people that will make up these teams. You spent lots of money on school, now you can show us what you've learned. Show us how valuable you are. If you have ability, show us, help us, and make a good name for yourself. If you help the party succeed, your work will not go unnoticed, not by Gene Douglas. When we grow the opportunities, you will be the ones that will have made it happen. You will be the ones that reap the rewards of your work."

Theodore pauses again for more applause.

"Our pollster and brilliant statistician, Tim Collins, is here tonight," Theodore says and points to Tim sitting at one of the tables in front of the stage. "He has information packets that will outline where our focus should be. It tells us the positions we need to fill, the jobs we need done, and where our teams of Young Republicans can be most effective. You are told all your life that to succeed, you have to start from the bottom and work your way to the top. This is the bottom. What we are offering you is a rung in the ladder to help you climb closer to the top. It's up to you to grab it. If you choose to grab it and make the most of the opportunity, I can guarantee you, if Gene Douglas is elected governor, there will be other rungs to help you climb to higher places. See Tim or your own Kevin Baker during the break or come talk to me or Mr. Douglas. Get those packets, see where you can be useful, and let's get to work. You can make the Young Republicans the group that changes the face of politics in our state. Thanks again for having us. I look forward to working with those of you that choose to make a difference and take advantage of the opportunity that Gene Douglas is offering you tonight."

Theodore finishes his speech to applause, and Kevin Baker returns to the podium.

"We're going to take a thirty-minute break, and then we will get to our meeting and the election of this year's Young Republican officers. Mr. Douglas and Mr. Graham will be here to talk and meet some of you. Tim Collins has those packets Mr. Graham mentioned. I have agreed to coordinate with Mr. Douglas's staff, and we can get the interested members of our group in the positions they want to be in. Let's try to keep the break as close to thirty minutes as we can."

The audience erupts into chatter, and people begin to move around the room. Gene and Theodore file into the crowd while Sidney, the media coordinator, takes photos of their interactions with the Young Republicans. Gene poses for selfies with some of the people, and Theodore talks to them about opportunities as they mingle.

A dark-haired young girl wearing glasses and dressed sharply in a business suit approaches Gene. "Mr. Douglas, my name is Marcy Gubreck. I am a law school graduate preparing to take the bar exam. I took an unpaid legal internship at a law firm. When I started the internship, it was a two-and-a-half-year internship. After two and a half years, I would have been considered for a paid position at the firm. I was three months away, and the law firm said that the unpaid internships are now five-year unpaid internships. They say it is due to the economy. It's highly unlikely that I can afford to feed and shelter myself while I work for free for nearly three more years. How does your plan stop businesses from taking advantage of young graduates? Does your plan guarantee employment, or are you just exploiting free young labor too?"

"Well, Ms. Gubreck, we need sharper legal minds like yours. Your predicament is all too common with other young graduates like you. Mr. Graham, my campaign manager, is also a brilliant legal mind. He can probably help you with this."

Theodore turns around and sees Gene with this attractive young girl and extends his hand to shake hers.

"Ms. Gubreck here was just telling me her law firm is changing the rules of her internship from two and a half years to five years unpaid. She asked how our plan would best help her if she chooses to get involved. I told her you are a lawyer and might be able to shed some light on this for her."

"Ms. Gubreck, is it?" Theodore asks.

"Marcy Gubreck, you can call me Marcy."

"Marcy, unfortunately, law firms do that. They exploit your time and talents for their profit. Who can afford to work a job where they don't get paid? What you got to do is get some legal credit and connections behind your name. Law firms will hire you for pay if you have some notoriety and are connected to good people. Working on a governor's campaign seems like a good place to get them."

"Can anything in one of your program packets or helping with the Gene Douglas campaign guarantee paid employment? Are you just another part of the system that's blowing smoke up my ass to get me to do something for nothing?"

"Well, Marcy, you have a lovely ass, and I would hate to do anything to it involving smoke, but if you are going to tolerate a bad deal from a law firm like that, I might question your legal skills. The Douglas campaign came here to ask people to show us their skills and help improve the voices of Young Republicans. I can't tell how valuable you are unless you share your skills. You can't tell how credible we are unless you get involved. There is the dilemma. We will need law students, legal research teams, copyright advisers, and good negotiators. You are welcome to join us and let us see your worth, or you can stay at an unpaid internship and try to make ends meet with a job that doesn't pay. We make our own choices, Marcy. I understand your hostility toward a political campaign, but I have a feeling you would be an asset to our team."

"I'm sorry, Mr. Graham, I'm just frustrated. My parents agreed to help me until I got a paying job at the firm, but I can't ask them to fund me for three more years."

"Marcy, I didn't mean to be so sharp with my response. I understand your frustration. You are obviously a brilliant young woman. I hope you will take a chance and get involved with the Douglas campaign. We need strong, brilliant women. Please forgive me. Here is my card. Whatever you decide to do, I understand. If I can help you or guide you, or if you just need some career advice, give me a call."

"You would do that for me?"

"Absolutely. I hate how the system is rigged, and I can picture you being a shark in a courtroom. You didn't even hesitate to ask if we were full of shit. That's what makes a good, no-nonsense, intimidating lawyer."

"I shouldn't have come on so strong, I'm sorry. Do your really think I have a lovely ass?" Marcy asks.

"Some of the statements made here tonight may raise some suspicion or questions, but my remark about your ass is 100 percent true. You can file a sexual harassment charge and prosecute me if you want. That might help get your legal career going."

"I would throw the book at you, Mr. Graham, but you're too cute to prosecute and send to prison. I think I may be calling you for career advice," she says as she runs her hand playfully up Theodore's arm and puts it on his chest.

"Very good, Ms. Gubreck. I look forward to hearing from you. It was a pleasure meeting you."

Gene carefully worked the room meeting people, shaking hands, taking selfies, and following Theodore's advice. He is surprised and pleased how well the night is going thus far. The break in the meeting goes beyond the thirty-minute mark. An hour passes. Kevin Baker is trying to get the attendants seated so he can begin the second half of the meeting. Tim Collins and Sidney hand all the opportunity packets out and are getting ready to leave.

"I think tonight went very well, Mr. Douglas," Tim Collins says.

"I think it did too. Thanks for helping us out. Hey, have you seen Teddy around? I lost track of him."

"He was talking to some people around the room, but I haven't seen him in a while."

"I'm sure he isn't far. Thanks again, Tim, and to you as well, Sidney. You guys travel safe. I guess I will see you both for the chamber of commerce lunch on Wednesday."

Gene makes it outside and sees Ronny, his limousine driver, standing by the car in the corner of the parking lot. Gene makes his way through the lot.

"Ronny, have you seen Mr. Graham?"

"Yes, Mr. Douglas. He is taking care of some business in the car right now."

Gene looks at Ronny with a puzzled expression. "What kind of business does he have to take care of? Makes no matter. Let's go home."

Gene opens the door to the limo, and inside he sees Theodore and Marcy Gubreck kissing and passionately groping. Marcy's hair is down, her skirt is partially lifted, her blouse is mostly undone, and a white lacy bra is exposed.

"Jesus Christ, Teddy. What the hell?"

"Oh, hey, Gene. You remember Ms. Gubreck? She decided to join our team. I think we can use her legal mind. Did you know she was eighth in her class at law school?" Theodore asks as Marcy begins to button her blouse and straighten her appearance.

"I remember her. I am glad you want to help us out. Thank you, Ms. Gubreck. You may want to get back inside. Mr. Baker is just about to get started."

"Okay, Mr. Douglas, thanks for the opportunity. I hope to see you again soon."

"You're welcome."

Theodore pops his head out of the limousine as Marcy slowly walks away tidying up. "Give me a call, Ms. Gubreck. We can work on that legal strategy later."

"See you soon, Furshizzle," she says and blows him a kiss.

Gene instructs Ronny to get the car started and ready to go as he gets in the back seat of the limousine with Theodore.

"What the hell are you thinking, Teddy? How can you be hooking up at one of my campaign events?"

"Gene, you turned her over to me to give her some answers and career advice. I was just doing my job."

"Since when does career advice and answers come from your penis?"

"You'd be surprised what you can find out from my penis. We just kind of hit it off. She seems like a nice girl. She came on to me, and you saw how sexy she is. Those glasses, that business suit, the confidence wrapped in brilliance—that's the type that gets my erotic thoughts going."

"She is pretty sexy, but do you really have to pull that kind of stuff on the campaign trail? Anyway, how do you think we did tonight?"

Theodore is buttoning his shirt and straightening himself out. "You did good tonight. You followed the speech cues, you handled the crowd well, and Tim handed all the packets out. We will have a good turnout of Young Republicans helping us out. I am certain. Marcy Gubreck may need to work a little closer with me so I can help her better."

"I'm sure she will. I'm glad you think it went well. I feel good about it too. What about tomorrow?"

"Read the binder. Do you have Sandy and Ernie all set for tomorrow?" Theodore asks.

"Yes, they'll be there. I'm not sure what we need them for, though."

"We need them with us, trust me. Now, don't forget to dress casual, and you and Ernie wear baseball hats. Make sure Sandy isn't dressed up flashy like she normally does, and have her put some type of hat on. Dress nice, but not too nice."

"What speeches do I have to make? Whom do I have to talk to? What group are we seeing?"

"You leave all that up to me, and I will pick all of you up around eight tomorrow morning. For now, let's raid the minibar in here. I have a joint in my wallet. Let's celebrate the good job you did."

"You know what, Teddy? I feel good about tonight. I think we can celebrate a little."

"That's my boy! You were awesome tonight. I have no doubt that you will be our next governor.

Tuesday

A big white van enters the gates of the Douglas mansion and speeds wildly up the driveway. Theodore is hiding inside so the Douglases don't see him. He wants them to see only the driver, Barnaby White, a nearly seven-foot-tall, 350-pound black man. Gene, Sandy, and Ernie Douglas are outside the front door, waiting for Theodore. Barnaby slams on the brakes and forcibly puts the van into park and gets out.

"How did you get past security?" Sandy Douglas shouts at the large black man.

"You can take what you want. Please don't hurt my family," Gene says.

Barnaby stands in front of them and stares without saying a word. In a quick motion, he turns to open the sliding side door of the van. Gene cowers because he thinks the large black man is going to hit him. Theodore jumps out of the van.

"You should see your faces. I think Gene may even have to change his underwear before we get going!" Theodore says.

"We thought . . . umm . . . I thought . . . umm, I didn't know what to think," Gene says.

Theodore laughs. "You were afraid of the big black man, you racist bastard! This is Barnaby White. He's the equipment maintenance man at the community college. He already works for you, Gene."

In a higher-pitched voice, a voice one won't expect to come out of a seven-foot, 350-pound black man, Barnaby speaks. "My name is Barnaby, but most people call me Sweet Barn. It's a pleasure to meet you and your beautiful family. I didn't mean to scare y'all, but my size and color have a tendency to scare people, not just white folks like y'all."

"It's a pleasure to meet you, Barnaby," Gene says and offers a handshake.

Barnaby takes Gene's hand; it looks tiny compared to his. "You can call me Sweet Barn, Mr. Douglas. It is very nice to meet you. Mrs. Douglas, you are prettier than Malibu Barbie, and, Ernie, I've heard you play guitar. You play blues almost as good as a Southern soul man."

"Sweet Barn is going to be our driver and security today. I see you all have hats like I told you to wear, so let's get rolling. The three of you will have to sit on the bench seat in the back. We will need all the space behind the cage divider later," Theodore says.

"Where are we going? And why are we dressed like the middle-class people that walk around the Hamptons?" Sandy asks.

"Upper-class snob much, Sandy?" Theodore says.

"We are going to Carter to do some shopping, Mrs. Douglas," Sweet Barn says.

"Carter? Isn't that the ghetto?" Gene asks.

"Well, Mr. Douglas, people that don't live there call it the ghetto, but I call it home."

Gene, embarrassed, shrugs his shoulders. "I didn't mean to offend you, Mr. White."

"You call me Sweet Barn, Mr. Douglas. It's okay, you didn't offend me. I'm happy for the opportunity to help you today. Teddy told me what y'all are going to do. It touched my heart."

Barnaby walks around the van to the driver's seat. Sandy and Ernie get in the back of the van while Gene pulls Theodore aside.

"Teddy, what the hell are we doing today?"

"We are getting the polling numbers in your favor. Just trust me and do what I tell you to do. Getting in the van is step 1."

Theodore rides shotgun, and as the Douglases sit side by side on the bench seat in front of the cargo cage, Barnaby drives the van out of the wealthy suburbs through the middle-class town and into Carter. They pass numerous boarded, graffiti-sprayed, and burned-out houses. They see sections of government housing from the sixties and seventies in desperate need of repair. They pass playgrounds with broken benches and equipment, fly-by-night pawn shops, cash-for-gold traders, Laundromats, and thrift shores. There isn't a white face seen as they travel the streets of Carter. Barnaby turns into a shopping plaza whose heyday has long since passed. He parks in front of Victoria's Grocery and Lotto. Barnaby exits the van and opens the sliding door to let the Douglases out. Theodore gets out and waits for them on the sidewalk. An elderly black woman exits the grocery store and greets them.

"It's such a nice thing what you are doing, Mr. Douglas. Thank you for doing it with the help of my store. I'm Victoria West," the woman says.

Gene looks very puzzled. "It's my pleasure to be doing this, Victoria. It's good to know you and be here with you on this special day. This is my wife, Sandy, and my son, Ernie."

"You stay here, Barnaby. Watch the van and help us load it when we come out. Do you think we can get everything in one trip, Victoria?" Theodore asks.

"I think so, Mr. Graham. We have some carts loaded in the stockroom. You can take a few shopping carts to load the baby formula. Don't worry about emptying the shelves. I have more coming this afternoon. Follow me, and we can get you on your way."

The Douglases take some empty shopping carts into the store. They load the empty carts with baby formula, bread, peanut butter, and other assorted groceries. They take the already-loaded carts out of the stockroom and push them to the front of the store, where Barnaby helps them load the van.

"This has to be a thousand dollars' worth of groceries. What are we going to do with all this?" Gene asks.

"It's ten thousand dollars' worth of groceries. The dollar doesn't stretch that far anymore. We are taking this van full of groceries over to help some people out," Theodore says.

"Why are we hauling groceries? Who is paying for all this?"

"You paid Victoria cash for all this, and you are doing some charity work."

"Ten thousand dollars of my campaign cash on groceries? What the hell, Teddy?"

"This is money well spent for a lot of reasons. Just roll with it."

"Do I have to make a speech or anything? There wasn't much in the binder about today's itinerary."

"Sometimes you have to let your actions and others' speak on your behalf. It will all make sense later. I promise."

"I don't even understand the point of our appearance at the Young Republican's dinner last night, but I am trusting you."

"I got some good news about that to share with you later, but for now, just get in the van."

"Are we ready to go, Teddy?" Sweet Barn asks. "These people are going to be so grateful, and you are helping so many. I am so very touched to be part of this."

"Yes, Sweet Barn, we are ready. Keep it together, big guy, dry those happy tears," Theodore says and pats him on the back.

Sweet Barn drives the van farther into the dilapidated Carter neighborhood. Theodore sits in the passenger seat and is sending a few texts. Gene and his family sit uncomfortably and quietly on the bench seat. The van pulls in front of an old bank no longer in operation. Hung on the front of the building is a white bedsheet with the black spray-painted words CARTER BAPTIST MISSION.

"I will go in and tell them we are here and get some of the fellows to help us unload," Sweet Barn says and exits the van.

Sandy leans forward to Teddy. "I've held my tongue long enough. I don't know what we are doing in this ghetto. I don't know what we are doing in this van with that strange black man. I don't know why we have to deliver groceries, but you are putting me and my family at risk by making us the only white people in this low-class neighborhood."

"Calm down, Mom. Teddy knows what he's doing, and Sweet Barn is a really good guy," Ernie says.

"Stay out of this, Ernie. Why are you letting Teddy put us at risk like this, Gene?"

"Honey, you have to trust him. He's been right about everything so far."

"We aren't people that blend in or belong in the ghetto. We will get stabbed or raped or shot or mugged!"

Teddy turns around. "Sandy, we are almost finished. Sweet Barn is going to come out with some people from the mission. They are going to unload these groceries, and we are going home. All you have to do here is shake a few hands, give some hugs, and say, 'You're welcome,' to a few people. Please just hang in there a little bit longer. It will all make sense later. I will explain it all at dinner tonight."

"What dinner? Where are we having dinner? I don't have any new outfits to wear out for a campaign dinner tonight."

"We can have dinner at your house. I will be your dinner guest."

"Are you inviting yourself for dinner at our place?"

"Calm down, Sandy. Teddy can come over for dinner. We have a lot of work to do, and I want to find out what this is all about too," Gene says.

"I have a couple of joints. I know how you like them."

"Teddy! Don't talk about joints in front of my son!" Sandy scolds.

"Oh, no. Now I am going to be one of those kids that use drugs because I have parents that use drugs. Children and youth might take me away from you," Ernie jokes.

"Don't make jokes, Ernie. Drugs are a very serious issue," Sandy warns.

"I know drugs are a very serious issue, Mom. I didn't want to say anything I wasn't supposed to. Teddy is coming over tonight for your intervention. He just mentioned the joints so he knew you would be there. I don't want to be the kid who has a mom that trades oral sex for weed."

"Ernie, quit playing mind games with your mother."

"Yeah, Ernie, knock it off. Your mom has given oral sex for a lot less than weed," Theodore jokes.

"Fuck you, Furshizzle!" Sandy yells.

"Don't use that kind of language in front of your son," Theodore jokes.

"You're an asshole, Teddy."

Theodore sees Sweet Barn and a few guys coming out of the building. "Let's get out of the van. Remember, shake some hands, give some hugs, and say, 'You're welcome,' and we will be done for the day."

Theodore and the Douglas family shake hands and talk with some of the people unloading the groceries from the van. They are very grateful. Sandy hugs a few of them. When the van is unloaded, they all get back inside. Theodore sends a few texts before they leave, and Sweet Barn drives them home and pulls in front of the Douglas mansion.

"Thanks, Sweet Barn. You were a big help today," Theodore says.

Sweet Barn, with tears in his eyes, leans over and hugs Theodore. "You're a good man, Teddy. Y'all are all good people. All of you know how to make a man's heart feel good."

"It's easy to tell why they call you Sweet Barn, big guy. You drive safe now."

*　　*　　*

Theodore is sitting in the living room with Gene and Sandy, waiting for the evening news to come on. Issac the butler walks into the room.

"Mr. Douglas, Grace Downwood of Channel 6 News called here three times this afternoon. They left this number for you to call when you get in," Issac says and holds a message slip out.

"Did they say what they wanted?"

"On the third call, Ms. Downwood asked if I knew if you went to Carter today. I told her I didn't know of your travel arrangements. Mr. Sidney Hughes, your media director, called and asked the same question."

"Thank you, Issac. I guess I should call them back."

"Very good, sir."

"Don't call them back yet. Wait until after the news. I got a few calls from Channel 6 as well. We'll see what it's all about in a few minutes," Theodore instructs.

"You're up to something, Teddy. I'm not sure if I like it or not yet."

"I'm certain you're going to like it."

"Hey, what was that good news from last night that you mentioned earlier?"

"Oh, yeah, I almost forgot. I have it in my briefcase. You made the *Scholarly Daily* this morning," Theodore says and hands Gene a college newspaper from his briefcase.

"What does it say about you?" Sandy asks.

"Well, let's see," Gene says and reads the article. *"Gubernatorial candidate Eugene Douglas spoke to Young Republicans during their annual dinner at Admiral Barker's in Beechwood last night. After hearing from the candidate and his campaign manager, Theodore Graham, it appears that there are political ears listening to the young in their party. Mr. Douglas spoke of his time in the Young Republicans and recalled being a Young Republican with Beechwood mayor Mike Nardo and spoke of the opportunities offered to the organization by former governor Paul Bruni. It appears Eugene Douglas wants to restore some of those opportunities to the Young Republicans. He is asking for young leaders, organizers, and idea people to help grow the party, bring opportunity to the state, and get good conservative leadership back into our state legislature. Eugene Douglas may be the inclusive candidate that can bring the young and old of the Republican Party together and take back the governor's mansion for the Republicans."*

"Oh my, Gene, that's great news!" Sandy says.

"It is great news. I just did what Teddy told me to do."

"You guys doubt me too much. You have to learn to trust me."

Gene hands the paper back to Theodore. "Is this going to bring up our poll numbers with the young people?"

"That's the idea. Oh! Put on the news. We can see if the fruits of our labor paid off for us today."

"There was no media there today, Teddy. We went to a grocery store and donated food to a mission in a ghetto. There were no cameras or reporters. I didn't do an interview or anything. I still don't understand what we did today."

"I don't know why we had to go to the ghetto either. I felt like a Mexican being smuggled across the border in that van. That Sweet Barn guy was weird, and why did we have to wear hats?" Sandy asks.

"Here it is, turn it up," Theodore says and points to the television.

"Is there a Good Samaritan seeking the governor's office? Channel 6 News may have uncovered reason to believe so. Channel 6 News received a tip earlier this morning that gubernatorial candidate Eugene Douglas and his family were seen buying groceries at Victoria's Grocery and Lotto in Carter today. Finding it unlikely that the Douglas family shops in Carter, Channel 6 investigated."

On the television screen are pictures of Gene, Sandy, and Ernie Douglas with their hats on, pushing grocery carts to the front of the store.

"Victoria West, owner of Victoria's Grocery and Lotto, said that she didn't know much about Eugene Douglas and wasn't sure what he looks like. She agreed to let us have access to store surveillance videos to investigate for ourselves. In the videos is a man resembling Mr. Douglas, a woman resembling Sandy Douglas, his wife, and a young man resembling their son, Ernie Douglas. We can see in the video that the three are being helped load the groceries into a white van at the front of the store by a tall African American man. Locals in Carter identified him as Sweet Barn White."

On the screen is video of the three loading groceries with Sweet Barn.

"A few minutes after we had investigated the store sighting, Channel 6 News tip line received another tip saying that the Douglas family was seen at the Carter Baptist Mission at the former Carter Savings and Loan. After last week's fire that destroyed the Carter mission's food pantry, it relocated to the former bank's building."

On the television screen is footage of the van parked outside the Carter Baptist Mission.

"Deborah Rang, the president of the mission, told Channel 6 News that there was a large donation of groceries, baby food, baby formula, diapers, and other merchandise donated today but said the mission respects the privacy of its donors. Channel 6 News placed calls to Eugene Douglas, his media director, and his campaign manager, but

none of those calls were returned. A closer analysis of surveillance video from the grocery store revealed the license plate of the van. Channel 6 News learned the van is registered to the maintenance department at the Douglas Community College. Our investigation led us to this man, Barnaby 'Sweet Barn' White, the man seen in the video helping load the van with the Douglas family."

Sweet Barn appears on the screen doing an interview with reporter Grace Downwood.

"Mr. White, store surveillance at Victoria's Grocery and Lotto in Carter shows a man resembling you loading a van owned by the community college with groceries. Were you there today with the Douglas family?" Grace Downwood asks Sweet Barn.

"There are cameras everywhere today. Nobody is safe from being on the TV. I was there with them, I can't lie. They didn't want y'all media and reporters and newspaper types to know about today. I hope I can keep my job at the community college, but I cannot tell a lie like that George Washington guy. The Douglas family asked me to drive them to Carter so we could pick up groceries and drop them off at the mission that burned down last week. I was so touched by their big hearts. They saw that story on the news and how the mission lost everything, and they wanted to help. It's tough out there today for many folks, and when the Carter mission burned down, it just made it tougher for people in Carter. The Douglas family did a wonderful thing. They supported a local business and a charity that helps local friends. I am so touched. Mr. Douglas is a sweet man. Mrs. Douglas is a beautiful woman inside and out, and their son, Ernie, is going to grow up to be a fine young man. Look at me, that kind family turned me into a big crying fool," Barnaby says in a high-pitched voice.

"There you have it, Channel 6 News investigative reporting uncovers the gubernatorial Good Samaritan. I'm Grace Downwood, reporting."

"Wow, you guys really made an impression on Sweet Barn. He said Sandy was beautiful inside and out. I would definitely have him drug-tested," Theodore jokes.

"Shut up, Teddy. Now I feel horrible for talking bad about him. Nobody has ever said something that nice about me."

"Don't get caught up in this, honey. Teddy staged all this."

"Yes, Sandy, you aren't beautiful inside and out. You are still a shallow, money-grubbing bitch that's made out of plastic and silicone, but we will keep that our secret."

"Fuck you, Teddy!"

"But how did you pull this off? Who called the Channel 6 tip line? Sweet Barn, was he in on this? How did you know Channel 6 News would report this like they did?"

"I just know how media and public opinion work. I sent the tips to Channel 6 News. Grace Downwood is a political reporter. She's investigative and wants to get beyond press releases from campaigns and expose what's behind them. I just put her skills to work for you. When I asked Sweet Barn to drive us into Carter, I told him you and your family were watching the news together and were so upset about the Carter mission burning down. I told him you felt an overwhelming need to do something to help those people. That big lug was so touched by it when I told him he broke into tears. I knew he would be perfect for the news. The viewers will embrace a giant with an even bigger heart. Victoria West was in on some of it. You spent ten grand in her store in the ghetto, so she was glad to play along. She told us where to park so the license number would be seen on the cameras and told me where to be so I didn't end up on the surveillance videos with you."

"Grace Downwood knows your cell phone number. Don't you think she figured out it was you?"

"I left my regular phone in my office. If she had it pinged, she would think I was in my office. I went to Walmart and bought a couple of pay-by-the-minute phones with untraceable numbers."

"I still don't understand."

"You wouldn't understand what Walmart is, you're rich. It's a store where the working poor shop for groceries and cheap foreign goods to get a taste of luxury for dirt-cheap prices. A good portion of their shoppers wear pajama pants to do their shopping because they realize that their life is as good as it gets and just don't care anymore."

"I know what Walmart is. I was never in one, but I know it's a store."

"Then maybe you don't know who the working poor are. They are the class of people that used to be the middle class. Stagnant wages, increased costs of living, lack of industry, lack of jobs, collapsed local economies, and the lack of access to education keeps them stuck in their place. In the next decade, the working poor will be the poor as more businesses close and jobs that people once held become mechanized."

"No, Teddy, what's an untraceable phone?"

"It's a phone I paid thirty dollars' cash for. It comes with calling and texting capabilities only. It's not a smartphone. There was no contract when I purchased it, and I paid cash for it so the number can't be traced to me. It's the preferred communication device of drug dealers, mob hit men, cheating husbands, cheating wives, and now, politicians like you playing the media."

"How do you know this stuff?"

"I am a man of the people that walks and talks among them. Plus, I watch a lot of *Law and Order* and *CSI* while stoned."

"So what does today do for the campaign?"

"We spent ten grand at a local business in a ghetto and donated ten grand to help people in the ghetto. It made it on the news. Tonight's news piece lets the people know you care about other people. The way that it was reported made it so it doesn't appear to be a publicity stunt. Sweet Barn is working poor, and he is black—that's two demographics we must appeal to. Next week, when the poll numbers come out, we will see how well we did."

"Sometimes, Teddy, I can't tell if you are an evil genius or a supernice guy."

"Sometimes I can't tell either. We do have to keep Sweet Barn in the picture, though. He and his brothers and a few of his friends run an event security company. They do security for concerts, sports events, and festival-type things. Your campaign is going to hire them."

"I was going to hire a security detail through the detective agency in town."

"Having Sweet Barn in the background of our media coverage throughout the campaign is going to keep our work today fresh in the minds of the voters. Plus, Sweet Barn is an adorable guy. It's hard not to love him. He is a tough giant with a heart of gold. He's almost like a Disney character."

"If you think it's what we have to do, we'll do it. I got to stop doubting you."

Sandy enters the room wearing nothing but a bra and panties. She is staggering and holding a big glass of rum and Coke.

"Why do you hate me so much, Teddy? I am so much better than that Claire Peterson twat that you fucked. I would have fucked you way better than her. Tell him how great my blow jobs are, Gene. Tell him, Gene!" Sandy says and plops herself in Theodore's lap. Some of her drink spills on him.

"How did you get so drunk and near naked so quickly?" Theodore asks.

"Sandy, you are making a fool of yourself! Go put some clothes on!" Gene yells.

Sandy gets off Teddy's lap and gets in Gene's face. "Sweet Barn said I am beautiful inside and out. Teddy Fur-fucking-Shizzle doesn't agree. I came here to show him," Sandy says and removes her bra and starts to take down her panties.

"Get a good look, Teddy. See how beautiful I am on the outside. I'm fucking gorgeous. If you want to see how beautiful I am on the inside, stick your pathetic little pecker inside me and you will see. I will rock your fucking world. Rock your fucking world!"

"Sandy, you're embarrassing yourself!" Gene shouts.

Theodore gets up and grabs his briefcase. "This is shit we have to keep out of the news. I am going to let you two have fun. I got her drunk and naked, Gene. It's now up to you to drive it home. I gotta go. Have fun with this."

"You promised there would be joints, Teddy. You said we would get high and have some fun!" Sandy slurs.

"I will see you tomorrow, Gene. Sandy, I did enjoy seeing you naked. You are beautiful on the outside. Your insides will be coming out soon enough when you vomit up all that rum. It won't be that beautiful."

Theodore passes Issac in the hallway. Issac is carrying a bath-robe for Sandy. They roll their eyes at each other over her behavior.

Theodore takes a joint out of his shirt pocket and tucks it in Issac's. Issac nods and winks at him and rushes into the parlor to cover the naked Sandy Douglas. Theodore lets himself out the front door.

Sandy Douglas can be heard shouting. "You said there would be joints! I want joints! Come back and get high with me, Teddy! I want joints!"

Wednesday

It's late morning. Theodore and Gene are in the back of Gene's limousine on their way to the Professional Women of Power's annual Power Lunch. Gene is reading through a binder and reviewing his speech. Theodore is staring out the window, as if to be in deep thought. He takes his cell phone out of his pocket and makes a call.

"Hello, Ann from Watkins, Fowler, and Baird. This is Theodore Graham from the Eugene Douglas for Governor campaign calling again. This is the third time I'm calling. I am trying to get a reference or talk to somebody about one of your staff, Marcy Gubreck."

Gene looks up from his binder and gives Theodore a puzzled look. Theodore sees the look on Gene's face and puts up one finger, asking for a minute.

"Is one of the partners there, Mr. Watkins, Mr. Fowler, or Mrs. Baird? If I could speak to one of them, that would be great," Theodore asks. "Sure, Ann, I will hold."

Gene looks again at Theodore. "Marcy Gubreck? Isn't that the girl from the Young Republicans I caught you making out with back here on Monday?"

"Yes, it is. I will explain," Theodore says and motions for Gene to be quiet.

Theodore returns to his phone conversation. "Good morning, Mr. Watkins. The reason I'm calling . . . well, I have to be honest with you. The Eugene Douglas campaign is looking to steal one of the brilliant members of your staff, Marcy Gubreck. We are looking for a young legal mind for our staff, and we want to scoop her up before she aces the bar exam and gets too expensive."

Gene puts his hands up and whispers, "What are you doing?"

Theodore puts his finger up to Gene and returns to his call. "No, we don't want to contract with a law firm. I am sure you can help us, but we want to hire Marcy Gubreck for our own team. She was eighth in her class at law school, she is an active member of the Young Republicans, and she is a perfect fit for our campaign. We want to make her an offer before she becomes unobtainable."

Gene shoots Theodore an irritated look as he overhears one end of the phone conversation.

"I'm also a lawyer, Mr. Watkins. I know how it works. I won't tell you what we are going to offer her just like you aren't going to tell me what you are paying her. We want her for us, and I am just calling to see if you can tell me anything about Marcy that may change our minds."

"Teddy, what the fuck?" Gene says.

Theodore puts his hand up to Gene's face to quiet him. "I don't think Mr. Douglas would be happy with me if I committed to a law firm that hasn't committed to his campaign. We want to work with Marcy Gubreck. She has a bright future ahead of her, and we want to make her a part of ours. I imagine an established law firm like Watkins, Fowler, and Baird wants her for the same reasons."

Theodore pauses to listen to Mr. Watkins for a moment and says, "Thanks, Mr. Watkins. I appreciate your time. I guess we will have to try to figure out what we need to offer Marcy to get her away from you. Okay, thanks again. Yes, you too. Goodbye."

"What the hell was that all about, Teddy? My campaign isn't hiring a slutty legal intern for you to fool around with. She is half your age!"

"No, we're not hiring her, but we are helping one of your young supporters. Don't worry about that now. Do you know what you are going to say today?" Theodore asks.

"I'm pretty sure I have it down."

"Good. Just don't piss Nancy Bradford off. She put this organization together and takes it very seriously. It's her baby. She is smart, tough as nails, and will rip you apart if she doesn't like you."

"Is there going to be any press here today?"

"There may be some local newspapers covering some of it, but there isn't going to be any television coverage. This organization doesn't get press coverage—the media isn't interested. You would know that if you reviewed your speech notes in the binder. That is the selling point of the speech. Are you sure you are ready for this? Do we need a quick review?"

"I'm ready, don't worry."

The limousine drops Theodore and Gene at the Gatesville Hotel and Conference Center, and they make their way into a medium-size ballroom. There are a few display tables featuring a variety of businesses at the rear of the room. The center of the room has tables that are set for the luncheon. At the front of the room, there is a platform stage with a podium at the center. Professionally dressed women are scattered throughout the room, talking and greeting one another and looking at the various displays. A polished woman in a sharp black business suit and a young girl with a clipboard come racing over to Theodore and Gene.

"You two, come with me," the polished woman commands.

Gene and Theodore follow the two women out of the ballroom to a hotel room that has been set up as a lounge with sofas and comfortable chairs. There are ice buckets with bottled water, juice, and a fruit-and-cheese tray on a hospitality table.

"Mr. Douglas, I am Nancy Bradford, the founder of Professional Women of Power, and this is my intern, Sheila. You two will wait in here. Sheila will come and get you when it is your turn to speak. I have arranged for the convention staff to bring your lunch here for you."

"It's nice to meet you, Nancy. Thanks for having us as your guests. Would you like us to be in the ballroom and meet some of your members?" Gene asks.

"No, you will have lunch in here, and my intern, Sheila, will come get you when it is your turn to speak, as I just told you."

"We would be glad to come in and meet with some of your members. This is my campaign manager, Theodore Graham, by the way."

"I gave you your instructions, Mr. Douglas. If you don't like my terms, you don't have to speak to my organization. I know who Mr. Graham is. He is the talented lawyer that gave up a prosperous law career to write trashy novels, adventure stories, and teach at your third-rate honors school and community college. He is a foolish man, and the only reason he was able to get you here is that you are the first politician that showed any interest in my group. You will have a chance to meet some of my members after you speak, but I don't want you in the ballroom before then. The women tend to get distracted from their purpose when there are unattended men in the room to compete over. Jealousy over attention distracts from the work we do."

"Yes, Mrs. Bradford, I will do as you instruct."

"It's nice to meet you, Nancy," Theodore says and offers a handshake.

"Yes, charmed, I'm sure, Mr. Graham." Nancy rolls her eyes and ignores his offer of a handshake. "Sheila will be in to get you when it's your turn to speak. Remain here until then."

The door closes behind Nancy and her intern. Gene turns to Theodore. "I never saw a woman cut you down to size like that before. I guess there are some women that can resist your charms."

"I don't even know what just happened here. I didn't even have to open my mouth to be hated by her. I felt like I was on an episode of *Designing Women*, being put in my place by Julia Sugarbaker. That really turned me on for some reason. Dixie Carter, that was one sexy woman."

"I have a better chance with Nancy Bradford than you do. That's a switch. That intern was like a well-trained robot. She's kind of scary."

"That is a switch, you suck with the ladies. We may have entered the bizzarro world when we came through the front doors of this old hotel. She did her homework on me and my work. I may have to rethink my life choices."

Theodore and Gene make themselves comfortable in the lounge. They are eating their lunch and waiting for Sheila the intern to come for Gene to make his speech. Theodore's cell phone rings.

"Hello. How are you, Marcy Gubreck? What can I do for you?" Theodore says. "That is great news! Mr. Douglas is here with me right now. You can tell him your good news and thank him yourself. Let me put my phone on speaker."

"Mr. Douglas, thank you so much. Mr. Watkins and the other partners in the law firm agreed to waive the waiting period of my internship after talking to Teddy this morning. They offered me a seventy-five-thousand-dollar salary with benefits, and once I pass the bar, I will be able to collect a percentage of the cases I work on. I guess they were afraid your campaign was going to steal me away. I will come work for your campaign if you can do better."

"I don't think we can afford you, Ms. Gubreck, but I hope you will still help us with the Young Republicans."

"You bet I will. I can't thank you enough. My parents are going to be so happy that they don't have to fund me for three more years while I work at an unpaid internship."

"Congratulations, Ms. Gubreck! I am happy we could help, but it was Mr. Graham who talked to your firm and made it all happen for you."

"I figured it was. I will thank him in person. Take me off speaker and let me speak to him."

"I like how you propose to give me thanks. Yes, tonight around eight sounds wonderful. I will pick up a nice bottle of wine. I will get some nice massage oil too. See you tonight, counselor."

Gene shakes his head and looks at Theodore with amazement. "You knew your phone call this morning would get her a job offer. I am glad you work for me and not against me."

"The internship policy at Watkins, Fowler, and Baird is bullshit. I had a feeling that one of the partners would give in to the fear of loss and offer her a job. They will probably donate to your campaign with the hopes that you will contract with their firm. Marcy Gubreck deserves a good-paying job, and we got it for her. She is going to be a good voice for your campaign. I look forward to her gratitude this evening."

"I bet you do. I would call you a dirty old man, but I would be a hypocrite because I am jealous."

There is a knock on the door, and Sheila the intern enters the room. "You will be speaking in five minutes, Mr. Douglas. Follow me, please."

Gene and Theodore follow the young intern to the wing of the ballroom stage.

"Ms. Bradford will introduce you, Mr. Douglas, and you can make your speech. After you speak, there is an empty seat in the front row. You can sit there until the program concludes, and you can meet some of our members."

"Where do you want me, Sheila?" Theodore asks.

"Mr. Graham, you may stay here to listen to Mr. Douglas speak, and when he is done speaking, you will return to the lounge. I will return to escort you back. Ms. Bradford doesn't want you in the ballroom meet-and-greet coaching Mr. Douglas. She wants the women of our group to judge Mr. Douglas on his own merit and not your snake-oil sales pitch."

"Yes, ma'am."

Gene looks at Theodore with a smile and laughs a little. "You don't really have a lot of fans here. I'm surprised you even got me the chance to speak. This Nancy Bradford woman sees right through you and your bullshit."

"Just do the speech from the binder. During the meet-and-greet, do like we practiced. Ask questions that require a specific answer and compliment. If one of the newspapers interview you, praise the organization and drop highlights and summaries of your speech. You'll be fine."

"I can handle this. Don't worry."

"Before we conclude our presentation and get to our meet-and-greet, I would like to introduce one more speaker. Eugene Douglas, who has recently announced his gubernatorial candidacy, has asked to speak with our group. In the ten-year history of our organization, there hasn't been one state representative, state senator, or governor that has taken an interest in us women or the work our group does. Mr. Douglas is the first politician to show any interest in our group. We should at least hear what he has to say. Please help me welcome our next guest, Mr. Eugene Douglas," Nancy Bradford says, introducing Gene. The group respectfully applauds.

Gene makes his way to the podium, waving to the group as they're applauding. Nancy Bradford shakes his hand and turns the podium over to him.

"Thank you, Nancy, for having me. It's quite an opportunity, and I am honored to be the first political hopeful to have the chance to speak to all of you. After Ms. Bradford's introduction, I feel fortunate that I have put together a smart campaign staff. I have a confession to make. I didn't know the Professional Women of Power organization existed until my first campaign staff meeting. We were going over some polling data and saw the approval rating of the Republican Party with women was low. I asked why that was. My campaign manager, Mr. Graham, told me that the party neglected women. He told me that nobody asked the women in the party what they thought about issues. Nobody asked them what issues were important to them. He also told me that in twenty-seven of our forty-one counties, women are heading their county and city chambers of commerce. Those twenty-seven women are members of this group, Professional Women of Power. This group is made up of leaders, entrepreneurs, professionals, hard workers, people who care, educators, and mothers. This group needs to be heard. In this room are the foot soldiers that build our communities better. I don't know why this group was ignored for so long, but I will tell you this, I am not going to ignore you. I can't let one of our state's greatest assets go unnoticed."

The group applauds. Gene pauses for a moment and looks over the room.

"This group has been putting small businesses in the vacant buildings of our downtowns. These small businesses are building our local economies. Stronger local economies are making better neighborhoods and creating more jobs. This group obviously knows what needs to be done. This group is doing what it can to get things done. I want to help this group get the resources and the backing it needs to continue the amazing things you are doing. I need the input of strong women for my campaign. I need women on my campaign staff to guide me to do the right thing for our state, our counties, our communities, and our neighborhoods. I am asking for the right people to come forward, and the right people are apparently right here in this ballroom."

There is a more enthusiastic applause from the crowd. Gene pauses and looks the crowd over once again.

"The election is a long way off. You have plenty of time to get to know me. You can decide whom you want to vote for when the polls are open. What I am asking for is your help. Show me how you do such great work. Tell me what you need to do it better. Let me help you get what you need. This is the first elected office I'm seeking. I would like to win, but I would like to win with the right people in my corner. I would like the Professional Women of Power to get on board and help me get things done. I am so thankful that my staff told me about this amazing group. I want to get you the recognition you deserve. Thank you for all your hard work and all that you do. Thank you for letting me speak here today. I hope we can work together and make this state a better place, build a better future, and turn something over to our children that we can be proud of," Gene finishes his speech to loud applause.

Gene turns the podium back over to Nancy Bradford and makes his way to the seat he was instructed to sit in. Sheila the intern makes sure Theodore returns to the lounge. Nancy concludes the program and opens the meet-and-greet session with the group's guests.

After the conclusion, Gene works the room talking to some of the women from the group. He asks specific questions and compliments the members, as Theodore trained him to do. The meet-and-greet session winds down, and he has shaken all the hands and made all the small talk he can. He makes his way out of the ballroom back to the lounge to get Theodore so they can leave.

Gene opens the door to the lounge. The odor and haze of marijuana smoke hangs in the air. He sees Theodore sitting back on one of the comfortable chairs. Nancy Bradford is mostly undressed on Theodore's lap, kissing him. He sees Gene and gives him a cheery wave while Nancy continues to make out with him. Gene makes a driving motion so Theodore knows to meet him in the car. Theodore gives him a smile and a thumbs-up.

Half an hour or so passes. Theodore makes his way to the limousine and gets in the back with Gene.

"What the hell happened?"

"Nancy Bradford was apologizing to me and thanking me."

"What happened to 'I'm sorry' and a plain old 'Thank you'? How did the hate she expressed for you this morning turn into a half naked make-out session?"

Theodore shrugs. "After the presentation, when the meet-and-greet began, she came into the lounge and told me she was sorry for insulting me when we arrived. She said she misjudged me and thought I was a shady political fabricator. She didn't think I knew what her group did or what it is all about. After your speech, she felt bad for being a bitch. We talked for a little bit, and I told her what else I knew about her organization and her work. Next thing I knew, she was taking clothes off and kissing me. It was intense and she was up for smoking a joint. Of course, I had to let her say thank you and accept her apology. It would have been impolite if I didn't."

"I make the speeches, you get laid. That doesn't seem fair. While you were getting horny and high, I was working the room. I think I did pretty well today. Hopefully, we can go up in the polls with women voters."

"You did do well, my blue-balled friend. You nailed the speech. They were loving what you had to say. Nancy said she will make a press release about working with our campaign. She is pretty influential, so I am sure we will improve our numbers with women voters. I'll tell you what, though, that Nancy Bradford sure knew how to get me to rise in the polls, if you know what I mean."

"I know what you mean. Your penis better not cost me this election."

"Maybe my penis can be your running mate. The title has a nice ring to it. I would have to address my penis as Lieutenant Governor."

Thursday

Sweet Barn, the nearly seven-foot-tall, 350-pound black man, sits in the driver's seat of a luxury minibus. In the back two seats are his similarly built brothers, Lizard Eddie and Funky Brian. The three men are all wearing black T-shirts with SECURITY written on them in bold white lettering. Theodore is sitting behind Sweet Barn, and Gene is sitting in the first seat behind the front door. Nobody is talking; the five men are just sitting in silence, waiting.

"I thought you said these guys were going to meet us at ten o'clock," Gene says to Theodore.

In his higher-pitched voice, Sweet Barn says, "We're waiting for black people, Mr. Douglas. We're twenty minutes late for everything."

"It's true, Gene. Black people live in a time zone twenty minutes behind us white folks. You should probably invest in another Rolex and wear two of them," Theodore chimes in.

Sweet Barn laughs. "That's silly, you don't need two watches. Don't listen to him, Mr. D. Just do the math."

"Here they are now," Theodore says and exits the bus to greet their guests.

"It's only fifteen minutes after. That Orlando French is half-white, he must have driven," Sweet Barn says and laughs.

Theodore gets back on the minibus, and Gene stands up to greet the men following him.

"Come on aboard, gentlemen. I would like you guys to meet Eugene Douglas, our gubernatorial hopeful. You can call him Gene," Theodore says. "Gene, this is Reverend Leroy Brubaker of the Carter Baptist Ministries. You probably know Fred Miles from television. He's always on the news and hosts *Our People* on Sunday morning, and this is the mayor of Carter, Orlando French. Last but not least is Black Voices president and writer, Everett Avery. Mr. Avery also publishes through your publishing house," Theodore introduces the guests to his boss, and the men shake hands.

Theodore points to the front of the bus. "Our driver and chief of security is Barnaby White. He likes to be called Sweet Barn. His brothers, Lizard Eddie and Funky Brian, make up the rest of our security detail. I don't believe they are going by their Christian names, but that's what I was told to call them. Make yourselves at home, and there is a minifridge with water and soft drinks. Help yourself."

"Are we ready to hit the road, Teddy?" Sweet Barn asks.

"Hit it, big guy."

Sweet Barn drives the minibus off the Douglas Youth Honors College campus, past the large well-kept and landscaped houses. He drives down the wide tree-lined Main Street of town, past the coffee shops, jewelry stores, boutiques, clothing stores, butcher shops, and theaters. The minibus passes a park with the lush green trees, stoic statues, a large fountain pond, and a dog park that's complete with K9 exercise equipment and poop-bag stations.

"Mr. Douglas, I know you didn't want a big deal made of it and you did your best to remain anonymous, but the media found you out. What you did for the Carter mission is very commendable. I offer my sincerest thanks to you and your family," Orlando French offers.

"My family and I saw the news story about the fire. It was tragic. My family talked about it and decided we had no choice but to do something for a place that helps so many."

"It was a wonderful thing you did, Mr. Douglas," Reverend Brubaker adds.

"We tried to do it under the radar of the media, but apparently, they are everywhere."

"The media is everywhere except where you need them to be," Everett Avery says as he enters the conversation.

"I guess there is some truth to that, Mr. Avery."

"There is a lot of truth to that, Mr. Douglas. Today is a perfect example. You ask to meet with black leaders so you can fake concern for our issues as you tour our neighborhood, and if we buy what you are selling, we go back to our people and tell them to vote for you. We vote for you, and come next election, our issues are the same and our neighborhood is worse. The mass media is a phone call away for you, but you didn't call them because you don't want to be held accountable for your empty promises. We get the attention of our own media, but the problem with that is, our people are the only ones listening, reading, and watching. We just keep preaching to the choir."

"Everett, enough," Fred Miles says.

Theodore slides forward in his seat. "I think that is an unfair assessment, Mr. Avery. We called you and asked you to give us a tour of your neighborhoods and to talk about the issues facing your people. You agreed to this. We are a campaign that is just starting, and we want to win on the issues. We asked you to make us less ignorant. Would you rather we be like Governor Harmon? He pledged thirty million dollars to the Black Caucus when he campaigned. Are the issues facing black people any different than they were seven years ago? Are things better? Are things worse? Has your community seen any of that money? Who endorsed that check? Was that money an empty campaign promise to get the black vote? We can turn the minibus around, call the media, and get our pictures taken with all of you. We can pledge a shitload of money that your communities will never see, but that phony pledge and the pictures with all of you will look awesome in the literature we mail to your neighborhoods. When your people vote for us and we don't deliver, we can turn it around and blame it on you because your pictures are in our literature. It would be easier for us to do things that way. We don't have to put a lot of time and effort into keeping things the same."

"Calm down, Teddy. You have to forgive Mr. Graham. He is very committed to doing the right thing and when his intentions are . . ." Gene says and pauses. A sour look comes over his face.

All the men on the minibus sniff and don sour expressions. Sweet Barn, also with an unpleasant expression, looks in the rearview mirror and sees his brother Brian with a sinister grin.

"Oh, no, you didn't, Funky Brian!" Sweet Barn says and gags a few times. "You promised you wouldn't eat eggs this morning. I can't"—he gags a few more times—"I can't . . . can't take this. The smell is awful. I can't—"

Sweet Barn gags a few more times and pulls the minibus over to the side of the road, opens the door, and runs out to vomit. His brother Lizard Eddie, laughing, runs out the door behind him.

Theodore is laughing at the situation, while Gene and their guests seem to have not yet comprehended what is happening. Outside the bus, Sweet Barn can be heard yelling in his high-pitched voice.

"I'm going to kill him, Lizard! He promised me, Lizard! Why did you let him eat eggs? He knows I can't handle that smell!" Sweet barn yells then vomits. "I'm going to kill him. He's going to blow this gig for us, Lizard. Our security business right down the toilet, because of his nasty ass."

Inside the bus, with a smile on his face, Theodore looks to the back of the bus. "Now we know why they call you Funky Brian."

The men on the bus all laugh.

Police sirens are heard getting closer, and tires screech on the side of the road behind the minibus.

"Put your hands where I could see them! I need backup! I need backup! Two large black males, possibly more inside. Send backup immediately!" a police officer shouts into his radio. He stands behind his car door with his gun drawn and pointed toward Lizard Eddie and Sweet Barn. More police sirens are instantly heard, and the minibus is quickly surrounded by police cruisers.

"Everybody in this bus, put your hands up. I have my gun drawn, and I will use it if you fail to cooperate," another police officer says as he boards the minibus. He notices Theodore and Gene.

"There are two white male hostages and five black males inside. All seem to be cooperating," the officer says into his radio. "Please keep your hands up and exit the bus and assume the position against it," he instructs the black men on the bus. "You two are safe now," the officer says to Gene and Theodore.

The black men exit the bus and line up alongside it with Sweet Barn and Lizard Eddie. Theodore and Gene exit the bus.

"Officer, this is all one big misunderstanding. We weren't being held hostage. Our driver fell ill after smelling his brother's fart. The men in SECURITY shirts are our security detail, and the other four men are guests of Mr. Douglas. You may have heard of him, he's running for governor," Theodore explains to the officer.

"Is this true, Mr. Douglas?"

"Yes, it is. This man is Reverend Brubaker, this man is Fred Miles, that man is the mayor of Carter, Orlando French, and that man is Everett Avery from Black Voices. The two men on the end, that man is Sweet Barn, our driver, and that man is his brother Eddie. The man on the end here is Funky Brian. They are all with us."

"Funky Brian White, you are in the wrong neighborhood. You are in violation of your parole. You're going to jail, son. Hands behind your back," the officer instructs.

"I have permission from my parole officer to be here. It's my work," Funky Brian explains to the officer as he is being handcuffed.

"He is an employee of the Douglas for Governor campaign, Officer," Theodore pleads.

"Don't tell me my job, sir. Funky Brian will sit in the back of that cruiser until we get this straightened out. All of you can get back on the bus."

All but two of the police cruisers leave the scene, and Funky Brian is placed inside the back of one of them. Two officers are talking on the side of the road as they wait to see if Brian's story checks out. The men on the bus watch out of the bus windows.

"I'm so, so, so sorry, Mr. Douglas. I'm so sorry, Teddy. I didn't mean for this to happen. Funky Brian eats half a dozen eggs every morning, and the smell that follows . . . it's very traumatic for me. It makes me sick, every time," Sweet Barn apologizes.

Theodore puts his hand on Sweet Barn's back. "It's okay, big guy. We just don't want anybody to get in trouble for the wrong reason. As long as Funky Brian called his PO, they will let him go and we can be on our way."

"I'm sure he did. He's been trying so hard to get himself together. Thanks for giving us a chance."

One of the officers can be seen talking on his radio. He goes to the police cruiser and lets Funky Brian out and removes his handcuffs. The other police cruiser leaves while Brian gets on the bus.

"Are you okay, Funky Brian?" Theodore asks.

"Yes, Mr. Graham, I'm fine. I'm sorry about all this."

The men on the bus quickly turn their attention to the police officer outside, who jumps out of his cruiser and is opening the other doors, fanning fresh air with his arms while gagging.

"Funky Brian, you farted in that cop car. Haha! You're a stinky motherfucker," Sweet Barn says as he is laughing.

The rest of the men on the bus start laughing too.

"Let's get this bus rolling before we get arrested for releasing toxic gas," Gene instructs Sweet Barn.

Sweet Barn situates himself behind the wheel. "Yes, sir, Mr. Douglas. Carter, here we come."

The bus pulls back onto the highway and makes its way into Carter. It passes abandoned strip malls, boarded-up houses, pawn shops, cash-for-gold traders, run-down government housing complexes built in the sixties and seventies, vandalized playgrounds, littered bus shelters, and homeless people pushing shopping carts.

"This is what you wanted us to show you, Mr. Douglas. There is almost no investment in our neighborhood. There hasn't been much since the seventies. There was some housing built, some parks and playgrounds, and a community center. After that, the clothing factory closed and moved to Panama. The bottling company sold out to a national company, and they shuttered our branch. The brewery, the same thing. The majority of people here lost their jobs. When Carter went from having twenty thousand jobs to having less than five thousand, the local economy tanked. The car dealers closed. The restaurants closed. The shopping centers and stores closed. We are down from seven grocery stores to one. Would you believe that our job situation is so bad that seven hundred people applied for a job opening at our McDonald's?" Orlando French says.

"What makes up your tax coffer?" Gene asks.

"The ones that are fortunate can get jobs in Gatesville stores, shops, restaurants, and hotels. Some of them get landscaping, contracting, and road construction jobs in your neighborhoods. When those people save enough money, they move away. Our taxpaying base gets smaller every year. It's hard to even keep the streetlights on at night," Mayor French says.

"We have to cut into basic service budgets every year. The average police-response time in our neighborhood is forty-two minutes. If a fire breaks out, the average response time of the firefighters is nineteen minutes. There is a ten-year waiting list for streets to get repaired. Every ten years, after the census, we get a bit of money from the state and the federal governments because we have such a high percentage of poverty and homeless persons. That money is quickly spent on Band-Aid fixes that get us by. The elderly that are still in town can live in price-fixed, government-approved housing. Carter Heights High-Rise has a toxic mold problem in the walls and in the ceilings because of the roof that was leaking for five years. The roof got repaired when the Board of Health investigated, but the mold problem still exists. The holding company of the building pays a guy to come in once a month to spray bathtub and shower mold remover in the crawlspaces and wall voids. It's a lot cheaper to buy a case of tub spray every month and call it mold remediation on paper than it is to do the right thing. I honestly don't know what the future of Carter is going to be. It doesn't look good," Fred Miles explains.

"I read in the paper about the drugs and violence here. Do you think that makes Carter look like a bad place to invest?" Gene asks.

Looking irritated, Everett Avery sits up in his seat. "Drugs and violence go hand in hand, Mr. Douglas. Drug dealers are territorial, and every gang wants control of the heroin, meth, and prescription-pill market. That's where violence enters the picture. The drugs come into Carter because there is almost no police coverage. In your white neighborhood, before we crossed the bridge, six police cars surrounded this luxury minibus on the side of the road because there were two black men next to it. They thought you and Mr. Graham were hostages because there were seven of us black folks. In Carter, the police patrol through here once or twice per shift, and the cops covering this area are rookie cops not yet getting paid enough, so they turn a blind eye to crime on the street. Meth junkies scrapped the metal from swing sets and sliding boards at the playgrounds. Carter can't afford new ones, so the parks become safe places for junkies to do drugs and prostitutes to do business. The Noah Carter statue in Founders Park and all the veterans' grave markers were stolen so the copper could be sold for drugs. There are good people and families that try to make this a better place—they volunteer and try to keep kids off the streets. Their efforts are noble, their intentions are good, but they are spread too thin. The kids that do well get out of Carter, and the ones that don't join gangs and destroy it a little more."

"This is why we asked to do this tour with all of you. I think we have a better chance at helping Carter if we know what the problems are," Gene says.

"We've had a lot of politicians that want to *help* Carter, but Carter never gets any help. Once the election is over, it will remain the wastebasket of rich white folks. You don't see homeless people on your streets. You don't have soup kitchens or shelters in your neighborhoods, because you don't want ugly, poor people lining up for help on your sidewalks. Junkies aren't looting your playgrounds, schools, and churches. You don't have abandoned factories, boarded businesses, and burned-down homes as the backdrop of your life for the last three decades. The stench of sewage and meth labs doesn't hang in your breathing air. If it's unpleasant, rich white folks send it across the river to us. When middle-class white folks feel the pinch of the rigged economy, you can guarantee our neighborhoods will only feel it more, but once you are poor, you can't fall much lower. Maybe to dirt poor, but that's not a far drop," Everett Avery says.

"We are guests, this is not the way we should be conducting ourselves, Mr. Avery," Reverend Brubaker scolds.

"Maybe Funky Brian can break up the tension with another fart," Theodore jokes.

"Yes, by all means, Mr. Graham, make jokes," Everett Avery says.

Theodore is irritated. "I don't want to joke, Mr. Avery, but if you are going to close your ears and close your mind, I might as well have some fun. You can't have it both ways, Mr. Avery. You can't say, 'Don't trust whitey,' out of one side of your mouth and ask him for help out of the other. If you don't trust our intentions, that's fine, don't vote for us. Vote for one of your own running against us. Where is a gubernatorial candidate from your neighborhood? Why aren't you running for governor against us? You seem to be winning the debate on this bus by casting shade on our intentions. Carter's problems didn't happen overnight, and they will not be fixed overnight. If you want to play the victim and make it about color, that's your choice. I don't see things getting better if we do it that way. I am white, and Gene Douglas is white, and that isn't going to change. If you want, we can go back to our rich white neighborhood and speculate what the problems are in poor neighborhoods, and you can go back to your neighborhood and blame us for not hearing your voice. That's how the racial divide has been handled for the last forty-five years. Look how well that worked out."

"Arguing isn't helping anything, gentlemen," Fred Miles warns. "What are you proposing, Mr. Douglas?"

"I'm not proposing anything now, nor am I in a position to offer anything today. I don't have all the facts. This week, I talked to young people and asked them to bring new ideas to our campaign. I met with business professionals and chamber of commerce leaders that have done wonderful things to rebuild communities. I'm not familiar with Carter, and that's why Mr. Graham contacted all of you. I am asking you to educate me. I'm asking for your input so I can run on a platform built by the concerns of the people I will be serving. There are obviously some problems, but if we busy our hands fixing problems instead of using them to point fingers, we might be able to do some good," Gene explains.

"That's beautiful, Mr. Douglas. You should put that on a T-shirt—I would wear one!" Sweet Barn says from the driver's seat.

"Thank you, Sweet Barn," Gene says and laughs. "Let's head to Victoria's so we can begin our walking portion of the tour."

"Yes, sir, Mr. Douglas."

"Mr. Douglas, I'm not sure a walking tour is a good idea. That may be a little dangerous," Mayor Orlando French protests.

"I'm not afraid. Sweet Barn will drop us at Victoria's, and we will walk four blocks down Main Street. You can point some things out to us, and we can make some notes. Once we get to Elm Street, we can go around the corner and have a nice lunch at Gloria's. We have Lizard Eddie and Funky Brian with us. I don't think we will be in any danger," Gene explains.

"How do you know about Gloria's?" Reverend Brubaker asks.

"Mr. Graham set up a late lunch at Gloria's for us. I have never been there. This will be my first time."

"One of my students from Carter completed his associate's degree, the first in the history of his family to hold a higher education degree. His family wanted to thank me for helping him stick with it and encouraging him to work hard. To show their gratitude, they took me to Gloria's for Sunday dinner with them. The smell of the place reminded me so much of the smell of my grandmother's house on Sundays after church when I was child. The smell triggered such good memories that tears welled up in my eyes. When I tasted the food, those tears rolled down my cheeks. Gloria saw my tears and gave me one of the most-needed and healing hugs of my life. Ever since then, I have dinner with Gloria's family and her staff on Sundays after she closes the restaurant. Besides Gene, they are the closest thing to family I have. I know she is usually closed on Thursday, but Gloria agreed to have a nice meal for the nine of us this afternoon," Theodore explains.

"Your security detail is eating with us?" Everett Avery asks.

"They are big boys, they have to eat too. They are welcome to break bread with us. We just have to remember not to let Funky Brian have eggs. We learned that lesson this morning. We may not agree on class, race, economics, and religion, but we can all agree on comfort food that tastes and feels good."

"True enough, Mr. Graham," Fred Miles agrees.

"I may have misjudged you, Mr. Graham, I'm sorry," Everett Avery offers.

Theodore shakes Everett's hand. "I get a little too wrapped up in what I feel passionate about, Mr. Avery. I apologize for being overly defensive and rude. I may have some good qualities, but if you want to find out how much of an asshole I am, just ask Gene's wife, Sandy."

"Oh, boy, does she hate Teddy!" Gene jokes.

"We do appreciate people who sincerely listen. Thank you, Mr. Douglas," Reverend Brubaker adds.

Sweet Barn pulls into the parking lot of Victoria's Grocery and Lotto. "Here we are, fellows. Enjoy your walk. I will meet y'all at Gloria's. Don't talk to the guy with the snake—he pees on people!"

Friday

"Welcome. Come in, Mr. Douglas. Come in, Mr. Graham. I have tea and coffee set up in the parlor," Georgette Lewis says as she opens her front door and lets the two men in.

"Thank you for inviting us in to talk with you today. You have a really beautiful home," Gene greets Georgette.

Theodore looks around at the wooden staircase and doorframes of the home. "The woodwork in this house is amazing, but whoever picked out the furniture and decor is a genius for complimenting it so well."

"Thank you, Mr. Graham, it is so kind of you to say. Interior decorating is a hobby of mine. My home is the first Victorian era project I attempted."

"For your first project, you really knocked this one out of the park! This place should be the centerpiece museum for the Victorian District. Your home is stunning, Mrs. Lewis," Theodore says as he continues to look around and admire the home.

"Thank you, Mr. Graham, thank you for noticing. Are you a fan of interior design?"

"I've always been a fan of Victorian homes. Sadly, so many people remodel and cover up the things that make these homes so charming. You found a way to showcase all this charm. I bet you are the most charming thing in the house, though."

"I may have been until I let you in, Mr. Graham. You are quite the charmer yourself. Please, gentlemen, have a seat," Georgette instructs Gene and Theodore.

Gene and Theodore each take an end of an antique sofa. Georgette sits in a Queen Ann chair adjacent to the sofa. Her elderly mother, Veronica, is sleeping in the chair opposite her.

"This is my mother, Veronica. She just had her medication, so she will be in and out of consciousness. Sometimes she wakes up sharp as a tack, and sometimes she wakes up very confused."

Gene starts, "Mrs. Lewis—"

"Call me Georgette."

"Georgette, we are in your neighborhood so I can introduce myself as a candidate with the hopes of being the next governor of our great state. Some of my staff is on your street, placing literature in mailboxes and doorways and telling people a little about me. A few people such as yourself agreed to invite me in for a chat and a chance to get to know me. I would like to learn a little bit about you and possibly exchange some ideas. Thank you for hosting us."

Out of a rolling snore, Georgette's mother, Veronica, becomes alert. "Are these guys from the insurance company?"

"No, Mom. This is Gene Douglas. He is running for governor, and this is his campaign manager, Mr. Graham."

"They look like insurance salesmen to me," Veronica says, slumps her head, and falls back to sleep.

Gene leans forward. "So, Georgette, tell me a little bit about you. What do you do? What's going on in your life?"

"Well, I am a regional manager at Simon and King, a food brokerage. We negotiate purchasing deals between the nation's top grocery retailers and manufacturers. I've been there for twenty-seven years."

"What does Mr. Lewis do?"

"Mr. Lewis chases after his twenty-four-year-old secretary and calls me to complain that my divorce attorney is treating him so unfairly."

"I'm sorry if I touched upon a sore subject."

"You didn't know, and it's okay. I made the choice to move on."

"What are some of the concerns that you have about the future, your future?"

Georgette adjusts herself in her seat and thinks for a moment. "My mother here has early-onset Alzheimer's. It started out with her forgetting little things and moments of confusion. The moments of confusion and forgetfulness got progressively worse and more frequent. I sold our family home last year and brought her here to live with me so I could keep an eye on her. Now she is starting to lose more of her capacities and needs constant attention. I'm fortunate my job allowed a three-month leave of absence to take care of her and I have some money in savings. Her Alzheimer's disqualifies her from being eligible for adult day care, and she doesn't have *enough* Alzheimer's to qualify for in-home care. I had to take leave and use all my vacation and sick time to care for her. I'm concerned that three months down the road, she will be worse and I will have to return to work. I can't afford to lose my career, my home, and everything I worked for to take care of my sick mother. Sometimes I feel selfish. I am well enough off to handle this, but what about other people with similar circumstances that don't have the same good fortunes I have? How do they manage? How do they get the help they need? Do they get help? Health care and care for our elderly . . . it just seems like the business end and the focus on the bottom line turned caring for others into something cruel and heartless."

"Health care is a huge issue. It is one of the big focuses of my campaign," Gene begins to explain as Georgette interrupts.

"Are you all right, Mr. Graham?" she asks Theodore after she notices his eyes glaze over and his expression turn to sadness.

"I'm sorry, Mrs. Lewis. Your story and your mother's Alzheimer's brought back a tough memory from my past," Theodore says, sounding a bit choked up.

"I'm sorry, Mr. Graham, and please call me Georgette. I didn't mean to upset you."

"It's okay. Your story and your struggle and Alzheimer's . . . I just didn't expect this memory to resurface so painfully today. I may not have properly made peace with it. It's such an unfair disease. It's such a misunderstood disease. It's such a sad disease."

"You have my curiosity, what are you remembering? I don't mean to pry, but maybe I can relate to some of the pain you are feeling. Sometimes it helps to talk about it," Georgette says in a nurturing tone.

"I feel pretty stupid. We came here to get to know about you and listen to your concerns. Gene, I apologize. Georgette, I apologize."

"It's okay, Teddy," Gene answers.

"Don't apologize, Mr. Graham. We're all human. Please tell me what's troubling you. Maybe we can lean on each other."

Theodore sits up in his seat, clears his throat, and takes a deep breath. "My mother passed away in a car accident when I was very young. After her passing, when school let out for the summer, my father would drop me at Mrs. Price's house when he left for work. Mrs. Price lost her husband in a car accident. She was widowed very young and was left to raise their children on her own. She had no skills, no education beyond high school, and her husband's insurance money didn't stretch that far. She had to find a way to make a living, pay for her home, feed her kids, and provide a future for her family. At the end of her road was a rock quarry that employed a fair number of people. Every morning, she sold fresh coffee and homemade baked goods for the men to take into work. Every afternoon, she sold hot lunches to the workers, and she served them at tables she set up in her basement. At the end of the day, she sold dinner platters to the bachelors and divorced guys so they had a decent supper to take home with them. Mrs. Price raised her children and put them through college on that income. Her children grew and moved away, so she offered to watch me during the summer. She didn't charge my father for babysitting or day care as long as I helped her serve breakfast and lunch to the quarry guys. I enjoyed working for her. It was something I looked forward to every summer. She was always a sharp, smart woman, but one year, I noticed her slipping a bit. She was getting forgetful. At first, it was little things. She would forget to turn on the coffeepots, she would forget to add things to her grocery list, she would forget to put vegetables and desserts on platters—simple things like that. By the middle of that summer, she was getting worse. She was forgetting names, and that was very unlike her. She knew the names of everybody that worked at the quarry, the names of their wives, the names of their children, and even the names of their dogs. She forgot my name one day. When I told my dad about it, he just told me she was a busy woman and people with a lot on their mind tend to forget. I was young, so I didn't question my father. One time, she forgot to shut off the gas for the stove, and after I told her I smelled the gas, she made it my job to turn off the gas. She told me to shut it off every day at half past three, when the quarry whistle blew. That summer ended, and I had to go back to school. After the first day of school, I was walking home with my friends when there was a loud boom that echoed all the way across town. Later that night, my father told me that it was Mrs. Price's house. It exploded because of a gas leak. She perished in the explosion. I went back to school—I wasn't there to shut the gas off. When we went to her funeral, her daughter told us that she had been diagnosed with Alzheimer's but she didn't know how bad it was affecting her mother because she lived far away. I felt so guilty. I felt responsible. If I had been there to shut the gas off, she might not have perished in a horrible explosion. If such a horrible disease wasn't ruining that amazing woman's mind and body, she would have remembered to shut the gas off. I'm sorry, this is such a trying memory for me . . . please . . . please excuse me a moment." Theodore leaves the parlor and goes into the hallway to regain his composure.

"Teddy, are you all right?" Gene asks.

"Mr. Douglas, if you will excuse me, I made him tell that story, and I see how difficult it was for him. I feel terrible, let me go check on him," Georgette says and leaves the room. "I'm so sorry I made you relive that memory, Mr. Graham. Let's go in the kitchen and get you a glass of water."

Gene remains in the parlor with Georgette's comatose mother, Veronica. He can hear Theodore and Georgette walk through the hallway into the kitchen. With a couple of snores, snorts, and grunts, Veronica wakes up.

"So what kind of insurance do you sell?" she asks.

"I'm not an insurance salesman. I am running for governor, and I came here to talk to you and your daughter about your concerns," Gene answers. "Georgette went to the kitchen with my campaign manager to get him a glass of water."

"Does he sell insurance too?"

"No, ma'am, neither one of us sells insurance."

"Then what the hell are you doing here dressed like that? You have to be selling something."

"I am running for governor, and I wanted you and Georgette to get to know me a little bit better so I can get your vote."

"I don't know if I can vote for you. Insurance salesmen are pretty slick. I don't know if I would trust one as our governor."

"What kind of governor would you like to see in office?"

"I've been around long enough to know that what comes out of a politician's mouth is usually the same thing that comes out of his bottom. If you are focused on being a good man instead of pleasing everybody, you will do fine."

Theodore and Georgette have been out of the room for some time. Gene is getting a little anxious and uncomfortable sitting alone in the parlor with the Alzheimer's-stricken Veronica. The parlor is quiet, but there is some noise and some moans coming from the kitchen that can be heard.

"Oh god. Oh god. Oh my god, it's been so long! Oh god, give it to me," Georgette can faintly be heard by Gene and Veronica in the parlor.

Gene becomes embarrassed. He tries to distract Veronica with more conversation.

"So who was your favorite governor?"

"Why do you need to know that to sell me insurance?"

"I'm not an insurance salesman, Mrs. Davis. I am running for governor."

"Oh, good for you, dear. Insurance is a dirty business," Veronica says, slumps her head, and falls back to sleep.

Georgette and Theodore return to the parlor looking a little flush and disheveled from their time in the kitchen. Georgette is glowing, and her hair is a little messed. Theodore has some lipstick on his collar and a big smile on his face.

"Sorry to keep you waiting, Mr. Douglas. I hope my mother was no bother while I was getting some water for Teddy."

"It was really good water, some of the best water I ever had. Thanks again," Theodore says and winks at Georgette.

"I hope we didn't take up too much of your time. I know you are busy. We did let Channel 6 News know whom we were visiting today. You may get a call from them, and they may ask you some of your thoughts about our visit. It's up to you. You don't have to talk to them if you don't want to," Gene explains as he and Theodore stand up to leave.

With a rolling snore and a quick jerk of her head, Veronica is awake again. "Who are these men? They better not be undertakers—I ain't dead yet!"

"Thanks for having us, Mrs. Lewis. I hope I can count on your support come election time."

"Yes, thank you, Georgette. I apologize for letting my emotions get the best of me. I appreciate the comforting and the really fine glass of water."

Georgette takes Theodore's hand. "You should come back again, Teddy. I would like to show you some more of the house. You seem to know and love your Victorian decor. You can have some more of that water too."

"I just may do that. That was fantastic water."

Gene and Theodore make their way out of the Lewis house and meet Sweet Barn, who is waiting with the luxury minibus at the corner. Gene appears angry.

"Take us home, Sweet Barn."

"Yes, sir, Mr. Douglas," Sweet Barn answers. "Was Mrs. Lewis a nice lady?"

"Mr. Graham got to know her very well," Gene answers. "What the fuck were you thinking, Teddy?"

"It went really well. I don't know why you're upset. Our visit there is going to be great for you. Don't worry."

"How is you having an emotional breakdown and then fucking Georgette Lewis going to be good for me? How does that happen, anyway? If your penis were running for governor, maybe it would help your dick get elected, but how the hell is it helping me?"

Sweet Barn breaks into hysterical laughter. "I don't mean to laugh, Mr. Douglas, but a funny picture popped into my head when you said that. I pictured a penis at a podium giving a governor's speech, and that made me laugh."

Theodore laughs. "I am Governor Dick Cock, and I will stand tall for the voters of this state."

"We have a long, hard road ahead of us, but we have balls, and we can face tough challenges," Sweet Barn adds.

Theodore laughs. "My penis would be a great governor as long as he doesn't piss away his relationship with the voters."

"Or as long he doesn't throw up from plunging in and out of hot, deep issues too soon," Sweet Barn adds and laughs.

"Even though I only have one eye, I have a vision for the future. It will be my pleasure to serve you. I can't let those special interests jerk me around, but I will penetrate the bureaucracy and come out on top," Theodore jokes.

Sweet Barn is laughing hysterically.

"Would you two stop making dick jokes? This isn't funny. I want to win the election, I need you to take this campaign seriously!"

"Gene, it's going to be fine. Watch Channel 6 News tonight, and when it's over, give me a call and thank me."

"How is it going to be fine?"

"Trust me. It's going to be great. You'll even want to take me out for a steak dinner after you see the news."

"We'll see, Teddy. You are full of surprises, but you scare the crap out of me."

Sweet Barn laughs again. "I don't think I could vote for a talking vagina. I pictured one giving a speech at the podium. It scared me a little."

"Having a vagina in charge could get a little hairy," Theodore jokes.

"You are funny, Teddy. Just as long as we don't get an asshole for a governor," Sweet Barn jokes.

"Oooh, that would stink," Theodore says.

Gene fails to see the humor.

* * *

Gene is sitting in the den, watching television and waiting for the six o'clock news to come on. Sandy comes into the room and sits next to him.

"How did door-to-door campaigning go?"

"I am waiting for the news so I could find out."

"That doesn't sound good. What did he do now?"

"It was just more of Teddy being Teddy. That's what scares me."

Sandy puts her hand on Gene's shoulder. "Why do you let him drive you crazy? You will have ulcers by the end of this campaign."

"I don't know, honey. He hasn't been wrong yet, but I have a bad feeling about today."

The evening news begins, and Sandy and Gene sit closely and watch it together. Grace Downwood's segment comes on after a commercial break.

"*Grace Downwood, our Channel 6 News 'Campaign Beat' reporter, was out on the trail following the Eugene Douglas campaign. She filed this report,*" the news anchor says as he introduces the segment.

"*I am Grace Downwood of Channel 6 News, and today we followed the Eugene Douglas for Governor campaign going door to door in the Shady Elm Grove area. Georgette Lewis and her mother, Veronica Davis, spoke with gubernatorial hopeful Douglas in their home and agreed to tell Channel 6 News about his visit,*" Grace Downwood says as she does a stand-in introduction with the Lewises' Victorian home as the backdrop. The picture cuts away to Georgette Lewis and her mother sitting in their parlor.

"*Mr. Douglas is a good man who takes the issues facing his constituents very seriously. I was very impressed by the sincerity of the Douglas campaign. Mr. Douglas and his campaign manager listened to me and empathized with my struggle to balance my career at Simon & King and maintain a home while caring for my mother, who has early-onset Alzheimer's. It gave me hope, and I know there are others out there that have more difficult struggles, working, raising children, caring for elderly parents, and making ends meet. It is refreshing to see a candidate that honestly and truly cares about the people he wants to serve. He made no promises. Instead, he took the time to listen.*"

"*How about you, Veronica? What did you think about Eugene Douglas?*"

"*Mr. Douglas seems like a decent man. I hope the usual game of politics doesn't ruin his good intentions. I have faith, though. His cam-*"

160

paign manager took Georgette into the kitchen, and I heard them pray-ing together."

"*There you have it. Some high praise from voters in the middle-class neighborhood of Shady Elm Grove. I'm Grace Downwood, reporting from the campaign trail for Channel 6 News.*"

"That was a really nice news segment. I never knew Teddy was religious."

"Teddy isn't religious, and they weren't praying," Gene says as he picks up his phone. He dials Theodore's number and puts it on speaker and sets it down.

"Hey, Gino-Bambino, the governor want-to-be-yo! How was the news? Where are you taking me out for my steak dinner tomor-row night? It better not be Applebee's—that place gives me the Hershey squirts."

"Sandy and I just got done watching. I don't know how you know how these things are going to turn out, but you did it again. I owe you a steak dinner. How about we celebrate at Angelo's Grille tomorrow night?"

"Angelo's sounds great. Tell Sandy to wear something that shows off those beautiful fake jugs of hers."

"Fuck you, Teddy. Since when did you get religious? How did you end up praying with that woman?"

"I've always been a devout parishioner at Saint Penelope the Pussy. You never give me credit, Sandy."

"I never even knew you went to church. Wait a minute. Penelope the Pussy? You didn't have sex with that lady, did you? Teddy, you're a pig."

"How did you know that news segment would go so well? I didn't talk about issues or answer any of her questions."

"Georgette Lewis wants the news cameras in her house filming. She doesn't care about the issues. Interior decorating is her passion. She wants to show off the work she did in her house. Why do you think I gushed over her home when she let us in? I was sucking up. That's probably why she sucked up to me and gushed on me a little bit in the kitchen."

"You're unbelievable, Teddy! You should be locked up," Sandy says.

"Saint Penelope the Pussy says, 'God bless you.' I will see you for dinner tomorrow night. Gene, I will see you at the festival. I will meet you there. Sweet Barn will pick you up around ten tomorrow morning. Later, Gene-Bean. Kisses, Sandy Sweet Tits."

Saturday

Sweet Barn escorts Gene from the parking lot and through the fairgrounds to meet up with Theodore. As they navigate through the crowd of tie-dye, short, and flip-flop-wearing attendees, random whiffs of marijuana and fried chicken fingers decorate the air. They pass a few dozen food trucks and make their way by vendor tents selling T-shirts, handmade glass paraphernalia, colorful tapestries, healing crystals, and polished stones. People stare with puzzled looks on their faces as the two mismatched men walk together. They arrive at the Rock the Vote tent and see Theodore and Ernie playing guitars and writing a set list. Theodore looks up, and a look of concern comes over his face.

"What are you doing dressed like that?" Theodore asks. "Didn't you look at the binder? I made a special note with bold-faced asterisks and everything. It tells you what to wear. This isn't the place for a suit and tie."

"This is my campaign, Teddy. I should be speaking for myself."

"You are trying to win the election, right?"

"I do want to win, but I want to win with my message. You made that binder, and it tells me what to wear, where to be, what to say, and how to act. I want people to hear from me, not the version of me that you created in that binder."

"Buddy, I understand you want to speak for yourself, but we are working on getting the polling numbers in your favor."

Ernie comes over to Theodore and Gene. "Dad, why are you wearing a suit? This isn't the place for suits."

"I am running for governor. Governors wear suits."

"You can't introduce my band looking like that."

"I have to dress for the part I want to play. I'm just going to tell the crowd a little bit about my campaign, touch on some of the issues that I feel strong about, and then introduce your band. It will be fine."

"Don't tell them you are my father when you introduce the band. Don't embarrass me. Please!"

"Come on, Gene. I know you want to speak for yourself, but today isn't the day. Lose the jacket and tie and deliver the speech from the binder."

"No, Teddy. I want the people to see me for me."

"They can see you for you after you get elected, but I'm afraid if the people here see you for you, you will get destroyed."

"Dad! Listen to Teddy. He knows what the fuck he is talking about."

"You don't talk to me with that language, Ernie. I am still your father. It will be fine. Teddy isn't the only one that knows how to talk to people."

A stagehand comes over to Ernie. "Your band's equipment is being rolled onstage now. You guys will be going on in about twenty minutes."

"Are you going to play some songs with us, Teddy?" Ernie asks.

"Hell yes! I'm going to jam with you guys."

"Good. Now please do something about my old man's speech."

Theodore puts his hand on Gene's shoulder. "Please, Gene. Follow the plan I put together for you. You've had a great week. Don't blow it now. I promise I will help you be you as the campaign progresses. Let's just get through today by sticking to the original plan."

"Trust me, I have a nice short speech to deliver, and it will appeal to the crowd. You'll see."

"Is this Sandy polluting your mind? Did she perform oral and fuck up your head again?"

"My wife says I need to be more assertive. She says I can't let you use my voice to speak for you."

"Of all the days you pick to listen to your plastic trophy wife! Are you sure I can't change your mind?"

"I will be fine. I just need me to be the center of my campaign."

Theodore shrugs his shoulders. "Suit yourself, big guy. Don't say I didn't warn you. Let's go up on the stage wing and wait for your introduction. You want a whack of this joint before you go up?"

"I can't be getting high in public on the campaign trail. You're my campaign manager. You shouldn't be getting high either."

Theodore lights his joint and takes a big drag off it. "Now we're even. You aren't going to listen to me, I'm not going to listen to you."

In the wing of the stage, Ernie's band is huddled in a circle, going over their set list. Gene appears out of place in his expensive suit as Theodore stands next to him in his khaki shorts, sandals, and black T-shirt that reads GUITARISTS ARE GOOD AT FINGERING. A long-haired man passes them and makes his way to the microphone at center stage.

"Hello, Friends and Fine Folks Festival! How about that last band? Did they rock or what? Give it up one more time for the Throaty Giraffes. Yeah! Let's hear it!" the festival's master of ceremonies says and pauses while the crowd cheers. "We got a ton of good music ahead of us, don't you worry, but first, the sponsor of the Rock the Vote tent wants to say a few words. Give it up for Mr. Eugene Douglas."

Gene walks onto the stage, and random shouts can be heard from the crowd.

"Nice suit, Narc!"

"Go back to the accounting firm, ya bean counter!"

"Fuck you and your shiny shoes!"

Gene smiles and takes the mic from the master of ceremonies. "Thank you for such a warm welcome! It's good to see you all of you out enjoying the rock-and-roll music on such a fine day."

There is a murmur of noise and chatter coming from the crowd. Some more random shouts can be heard.

"Way to ruin the festival, Suit!"

"You're not my real dad!"

"Make with the music, dingleberry!"

Gene ignores the shouts from the crowd and continues with his speech. "My name is Eugene Douglas, but you guys can call me Gene."

A few more shouts are heard from the crowd.

"How about we call you a cab and get you the fuck out of here?"

"We're here for music, not to buy insurance!"

Gene begins to speak a little louder. "I want to be your next governor, and I am here today to tell you a little bit about myself, and then I want to hear your voices."

The crowd begins to boo, and beach balls begin to bombard the stage. More random shouts can be heard over the boos.

"Our voices are saying, 'Shut the fuck up!'"

"Get off the stage!"

"No politics, no religion! No politics, no religion! No politics, no religion!"

The crowd then begins to chant in unison, "No politics, no religion! No politics, no religion!"

Gene tries to continue with his speech, but he can't be heard over the unruly chanting crowd. Theodore strolls onto the stage holding a bottle of beer. He kicks beach balls back into crowd and motions for them to quiet down as he approaches a microphone to the left of Gene. He taps on it a few times.

"Is this thing on? Is this thing on? Can't you hear me knockin'?"

The crowd hushes down slightly, and the chanting fades to a mumble.

"Who wants to get back to smoking weed and grooving to good music in this beautiful sunshine?" Theodore shouts into the microphone. The crowd loudly cheers. Theodore waits until the crowd calms a bit before continuing. "I'll take that as a yes. If that's what you want, shut your bong hit holes for a minute."

The crowd cheers loudly and then quiets down.

"This is my good friend Eugene Douglas, and I am his campaign manager, Theodore Graham."

There's a random shout from the crowd.

"Teddy Gram? Like the bear-shaped cookies?"

"Yes. Like the bear-shaped cookies, but spelled differently," Theodore answers. "My buddy Gene wants to be the governor of this great state. Governors wear suits. He is wearing his work uniform. He's never been to a festival like this before, and he looks out of place. He needs to learn to relax. Can all the good people here at the Friends and Fine Folks Festival give me a hand and help my buddy relax?"

Theodore walks over to Gene and tells him to unbutton his suit jacket and take it off. Theodore takes his jacket, goes to the edge of the stage, and throws it into the crowd. The crowd cheers. Theodore goes back to Gene and unties his tie. He takes the tie to the edge of the stage and throws it into the crowd.

"That's much better, isn't it?" Theodore shouts into the mic to the cheering crowd. "Now all Gene needs is a nice, cold adult beverage."

Theodore runs backstage and grabs another bottle of beer. He returns to the stage, uncaps the bottle, and puts it in Gene's hand. Theodore picks his beer up from the stage and clinks bottles with Gene. They both take a sip.

A chant can be heard building in the crowd. "Chug! Chug! Chug! Chug! Chug!"

Gene and Theodore clink bottles again and chug their beers. The crowd begins to roar.

"Gene seems to be starting to relax. There is only one more thing that will put my buddy at ease and make him feel at home here. How about the lovely ladies out there show my boy what festy love is all about?"

Another chant erupts in the crowd. "Tits! Tits! Tits! Tits! Tits!" A good number of women in the crowd lift their shirts and bikini tops to expose their breasts. Theodore goes to Gene and they high-five. The crowd is cheering loudly.

"All Gene wanted to say when he came out here today was that we are going to be hanging out after this next band at the Rock the Vote tent. Come on over, register to vote, and help Gene learn to relax a little more. Maybe you ladies can show him some more festy love. Who knows? You may be showing your breasts to the next governor of our great state! Come on over. Get registered. Talk to Gene. Vote for Gene. Don't vote for Gene. Doesn't matter. Just vote. Vote for somebody who will legalize it!"

"I couldn't have said it better, Teddy. Thank you. It gives me great pleasure to introduce this next band because my son is in it. I hope I didn't embarrass him too much in front of all his friends here today. Ernie, can you come out here?"

Ernie makes his way onto the stage carrying Theodore's guitar. He steps up to the microphone. "How many kids can say that their dad got a bunch of beautiful festy girls to show their breasts? I can. Thanks, Dad!"

The crowd cheers loudly and begins to chant again. "Tits! Tits! Tits! Tits! Tits!" Girls from the crowd again lift their shirts and bikini tops to show their breasts. The crowd is roaring with cheers.

"I look forward to playing for all of you here today, but I want to ask you all a favor. Teddy Graham, like the bear-shaped cookie, is a pretty decent guitarist. Help me get him to stay up here onstage and play a few songs with us."

"Teddy Grams! Teddy Grams! Teddy Grams!"

Theodore steps up to the microphone. "I don't know. Maybe if I saw some more breasts."

The crowd erupts with cheers, and some of the girls in the crowd show their breasts.

"Okay! I'll do it. Thank you, ladies! You're all beautiful people!" Theodore says and takes his guitar from Ernie. The crowd cheers.

"Without further delay, it gives me great pleasure to introduce my son's band, the Cover Hogs!" Gene says to loud applause from the crowd.

Theodore takes his place with the band, and they open the set with a ten-minute version of "Dancin' in the Streets." Theodore and Ernie fill the song with guitar jams Grateful Dead–style. At the end of the song, they fist-bump. The crowd erupts with loud cheering and whistling. They begin to chant the graham cracker cookie treat that is Theodore's namesake.

"Teddy Grams! Teddy Grams! Teddy Grams!"

After playing a few songs with the band, Theodore exits the stage and returns to Gene at the Rock the Vote tent. He is talking to some of the young festival attendees and encouraging them to register to vote.

"It looks like you are making some friends."

"You saved my ass again. That was nearly a disaster."

"Yes, I did. Next time Sandy wants you to rebel against my plans, run it by me first. I'll tell you if it's a good idea or not."

"Ernie's band sounds great. You guys really play well together. I never realized how much talent my son actually has. He has quite a fan base here."

"Indeed. In a few years, he will probably be in a band that headlines this event. How are you making out at the Rock the Vote tent?"

"There was a good number of people that registered to vote. There were people that dropped off beer and welcomed me to my first festival. One guy offered me weed because he wanted to get high with the governor. The offer was tempting, but I had to turn him down. I didn't have the heart to tell him that I have to get elected first."

An attractive young girl in a bikini top and a tie-dye skirt walks by the Rock the Vote tent and says, "Hey, Mr. Governor."

Gene and Theodore look over. She lifts her bikini top and exposes her breasts. She winks at Theodore before walking away.

"Thank you, young lady. Make sure you vote!"

"That was a nice gesture," Theodore jokes.

"That's been happening all afternoon. I have you to thank for that."

"You're welcome. It's the gift that keeps giving, and they come in pairs."

"How pissed off do you think Sandy would be if we skipped out on dinner tonight and stayed here drinking beer, getting baked, and looking at boobs?" Gene asks. "I could get into the festy lifestyle."

"I'm all in favor of sticking around. You had a good week. You deserve it. You're the one that has to deal with Sandy, and she's quite a handful when she's angry."

"I could say it is a campaign emergency."

Theodore laughs. "Wow. I'm surprised at you, Gino. You've loosened up. How many of those beers did you have?"

"I stopped counting after nine."

"That explains it. I better get Sweet Barn to take you home. It's after the tenth beer when good choices stop being made."

"Shit!" Gene slurs.

CHAPTER II

The smell of freshly brewed coffee hangs in the air of the conference room. A tray of fresh fruits and pastry occupies the center of the long dark-wood table. The Gene Douglas for Governor campaign staff is seated around the table, shuffling through legal pads and notebooks, putting the final touches on their reports before the morning meeting begins.

"Good morning, gentlemen. Today is the big day. I have a good feeling about today's official polling numbers," Theodore says when he enters the room.

"You're wearing slacks, a dress shirt, and carrying a brief case. Did you Google 'professional appearance' images?" Russ Dewitt asks.

Theodore places his briefcase on the table and reaches for a coffee mug. "Russ, I had a wake-and-bake this morning, and I'm in an awesome mood. I'm not going to let your snobbery and condescending comments steal my smiles."

"We'll see how much you're smiling when the poll numbers come in. I can't wait to see how far your circus act strategies set us back."

"You were wrong about everything so far. I have a feeling the polling numbers are going to prove that you're consistent," Theodore retorts.

Gene sits up in his seat. "There is no need for this. We're on the same team. Let's act like it."

"I'm sorry, Gene. You worked hard on improving these polling numbers. I don't think it is right for Russ to minimize and ridicule your efforts."

"I'm not minimizing your efforts. I just think you should stop following the advice of this idiot man-child and start running a serious campaign."

Gene, with an annoyed look on his face, turns to Russ. "This idiot man-child is one of the most intelligent people I know. He knows how to read people, and I believe he has made our campaign appeal to the people we need to. He is also one of the most loyal friends I have. You should watch your tone."

"I'm sorry, Gene," Russ concedes.

"Hahahahahaha, Russ got yelled at! Hahahahhaha," Theodore childishly chants.

"Teddy!" Gene shouts.

Theodore pours coffee from one of the pitchers into his mug. He opens his briefcase and removes a bottle of caramel-flavored vodka and pours some into his coffee. The others seated at the table turn their attention to him.

"Anybody want some caramel vodka for their coffee? It tastes like French vanilla, and nobody can tell you are drinking alcohol. It's win-win. It's what got me through my days as a teacher."

"I think you need to get out more often, Gene. If this clown is one of the most intelligent people you know, you got to change your social circle," Russ says.

"Enough, Russ."

"Yeah, fuck off, Russ."

Gene stands at the head of the table. "Let's get this meeting started. Tim Collins will be here a little bit later. The official polling data was just released this morning. He is putting some overheads and slides together so we can look at all the data. Sitting at the end of the table are two of the newest members of our team. Carl Michaels will be in charge of our ground operations, and sitting next to him, Kevin Baker, the Young Republicans coordinator. Kevin is going to be helping Carl staff some of our campaigning events with volunteers from the Young Republicans. Welcome to the team, fellows. We will be adding some more staff in the areas where we need improvement. We will figure that out after Tim briefs us with the polling research."

"I have a couple of suggestions for additional staff. Demitri Smith from the Black Caucus and Everett Avery of Black Voices should be hired as consultants. Nancy Bradford should also be hired to help Sidney. She will be a strong voice and a friendly face to help us with women voters," Theodore recommends.

"More clowns from Teddy's clown car," Russ Dewitt says.

"They're all good people. Let's table those suggestions for now until we see the numbers and determine what direction we need to be going in. Robert, how are we shaping up with finance?"

"The finances are looking good. The framework for the accounting is set up. We have accounts receivable set up for individual donors and for small-business contributions. We have accounts payable set up for expenses, and the assets of the campaign have all the necessary legal documentation, so they no longer appear to be the personal property of the Douglas family. We also have a tax-exempt number so we aren't on the hook for state and federal taxes in case the campaign has to become incorporated. The super PAC meeting tonight will shed some light on the larger finances and resources."

"There is a super PAC meeting tonight? How come nobody told me about it?" Theodore asks. "I'm playing with Ernie's band at the Karma Club tonight."

"It's okay, Teddy. Russ is coordinating with the super PAC. You don't have to be there."

"Do we even know who is in charge of our super PAC? I think Barry Newman would be great as the super PAC chairman."

"We don't want any more clowns from your clown car, Teddy. We got it covered," Russ adds.

"I wasn't aware we filled that position. Whom did we fill it with?" Theodore asks.

"We will talk about that later. Let's move on to Sidney Hughes and see where we are with media strategies," Gene says, changing the subject.

"I think you would tell your campaign manager whom you hired to run your super PAC."

"We're going to talk about that later. Let's move on. Sidney, go ahead."

Sidney stands and addresses the room. "We are waiting for the polling information before we craft our platform. Teddy agreed to help us sculpt the language for the mailers and internet media. There will be literature going out to individual households, small businesses, and civic organizations. Marty Price is setting up some focus groups in different areas of the state. Those groups will help us effectively target-market voters so we make the right policy statements to the right people. Marty is also doing some ratings research on the local news networks across the state to see where our political advertising will get us the most viewers and be cost-effective. The super PAC will almost certainly fund some advertising, and it will be up to Russ to make sure our message and the super PAC message are on the same page. We are going to have to make sure that the entire staff refers all media questions to my office. There should be no speaking off-the-cuff to reporters asking *gotcha* questions. This is important. We want our media presence to be on the offensive and not the defensive. We all have to stick to the same message. With each public appearance on the schedule, we will tailor answers in order to stick to the subjects we want to talk about. We will do briefings for each event to keep us all on the same page."

The door to the conference room opens, and Tim Collins enters.

"I think this is the man that we've all been waiting to see. I hope you are bringing good news," Gene says.

"I think you will be pleased, Mr. Douglas."

"If you are finished, Sidney, I will turn the room over to Tim."

"I'm finished for now and am just as anxious to look at the numbers as everybody else."

"Tim, once you get situated and get yourself a cup of coffee, the room is yours."

"Do you want some caramel-flavored vodka for your coffee?" Theodore asks.

With a puzzled look on his face, Tim says, "No, thanks, I'll pass for now." Tim turns on the overhead projector, and Theodore begins to make a shadow puppet of a dog on the screen.

"Woof, woof, woof!"

"Can't we have a serious meeting without this moron making shadow puppets?" Russ asks.

"Teddy should be able to make any shadow puppet he wants. His early campaign strategy seems to have paid off in the polling numbers," Tim says.

"Ruck Rou Russ," Theodore says as he makes his dog shadow puppet speak to Russ. He then changes the shadow puppet to the silhouette of his middle finger.

"Enough, Teddy. Tim, show us what you have," Gene says.

Tim places a slide on the projector. "This slide is where we were overall after your candidacy was announced. Larry Richmond edged you 47 percent to 41 percent. There was the 2 percent margin of error, and there was the 10 percent of undecided voters in play. At the bottom of the slide, you can see where we made some gains in the demographics. We're up 6 percent with young voters in the party. With women, we are up 4 percent. With minority voters, we are up 2 percent."

"This is great news. How about the overall data?" Gene asks.

"I'm saving the best news for last," Tim says as he places another slide on the overhead projector. "You can see that the margin of error is still at 2 percent, but the undecided voters in play have been reduced to 5 percent. You are leading Larry Richmond overall, 53 percent to 40 percent. Even if Larry Richmond gets all the undecideds and the entire margin of error goes to him, you still edge him by 6 percent."

"Let's hear it for the Republican nominee for our great state's gubernatorial election, Mr. Eugene Douglas!" Theodore proclaims. The campaign staff breaks into applause.

Gene waits for the room to quiet down. "Is this right? Are these the right numbers?"

"Yes, sir. The Larry Richmond campaign isn't having a very good morning. Unless some kind of disaster or scandal happens in our campaign, the nomination will be yours. The party and the financial investors are looking at these same numbers. You will start to see big money coming into the campaign."

"Teddy, where's that caramel vodka? I think we need to celebrate," Gene says.

Theodore opens his briefcase and pulls out the bottle and throws a handful of joints on the table. "We might as well get baked too."

"Let's not get carried away. Put them away."

Theodore gathers the joints from the table. "I threw nine joints on the table. I only picked up six. A couple people in this room are closet tokers, but that's okay. Keep the doobies. When you're ready to come out of the closet, come see me and we can party. Even if it's you, Russ."

"I didn't take your joints, but I have to admit, your strategy paid off. When we get to the general election, we'll see if your silliness is a fluke or not."

"What are the general election preliminary numbers?" Marty Price asks.

Tim Collins puts a new slide on the projector. "If it is us versus Sherman Jones, he leads us 50 percent to 47 percent. If it is Larry Richmond versus Sherman Jones, Jones leads him 52 percent to 45 percent. Those are early numbers and will change a lot until the next official polling results, but now we can focus on the general and not get dragged through the mud in the primary."

The conference room door opens, and a well-dressed man in an expensive suit walks in.

"Oh, fuck! This isn't the person that you are putting in charge of the super PAC?" Theodore says.

"Nice to see you too, Teddy, or are they still calling you Furshizzle like back in our college days?" the well-dressed man says. "For the rest of you, my name is Ray Whitney. Gene has asked me to head his super PAC. I'm sorry I'm late. Our flight was delayed."

"You can't be serious, Gene!" Theodore protests.

"Still shopping off-the-rack and sucking off the tit of the Douglas family, I see," Ray says to Theodore.

"I see you are still an obnoxious douche-nozzle."

"I don't know, Gene. How many times are you going to save Teddy 'Furshizzle' Graham? You and your family did it in college. He fucked up his career as a lawyer, and you gave him a job teaching at your schools. Your publishing house prints his white-trash fantasy novels, and now you have him working on your campaign."

"Teddy has done great work for me. We were just going over our numbers. His early strategy has won us some favorable numbers. We've all but won the primary, and the ballots aren't even printed yet."

"Well, isn't that special. That can be a chapter when he writes his rags-to-riches story. The Walmart crowd back in his poverty-stricken hick town will love it, I am sure."

"Enough, Ray. You have to forgive Ray. Teddy and I were friends with this guy back in college, and we used to bust balls all the time."

"What do you know about running a super PAC, Ray?" Theodore asks.

"I'm rich. I know about having lots of money. I know you have to have money to get things done. I know how money is politics. I know what Gene wants out of politics, and I know what I want out of politics. I don't believe I need to be any more qualified than that. I know the concept of money is hard for you to grasp, what with your food stamp upbringing."

"We can hash out all the super PAC details tonight at the meeting. This is Russell Dewitt. Once the ballots are officially out, he will be the super PAC liaison for the campaign," Gene says and introduces Russ to Ray.

Russ stands up and shakes Ray's hand. "It's a pleasure to meet you, Ray. It's nice to know there is somebody else that likes to give Mr. Graham a hard time."

"Excellent! We can compare notes and gang up on Teddy tonight. I can tell you some embarrassing stories about him."

"Teddy won't be able to make it tonight. He is playing with my son Ernie's band at a local club tonight."

Ray slams his hand off the table to pretend to be disappointed. "Well, that sucks. I was looking forward to busting his balls some more. I guess he is better off with the kids. Leave the business up to us adults. Hey, Gene, do you mind if my old man stops in for this evening's meeting? He would love to see you and meet your staff."

"Definitely. I would love to see old Mort."

"If you don't mind, Gene, I would like to get settled into my hotel. I will see everybody except for Teddy tonight," Ray says and leaves the conference room.

"Just when I thought Russ was the biggest asshole on the campaign staff, you bring in Ray Whitney," Theodore says. Just then, his cell phone rings. "Sorry, Gene, I think I should take this call."

Theodore stands up and goes to the corner of the room to take the call. "Hey, Larry, what can I do for you? We are having a staff meeting right now. I thought you would be doing the same? Okay. Call me back in five minutes. Give me a minute to clear the room."

Gene and the other staff members seated at the table overhear Theodore on the phone. They seem confused after hearing one side of his conversation.

"Gene, I need you to stay in the room. I need everybody else to clear the room."

"What's going on?"

"You and I are needed on conference call. It's an important call. You're going to want to take it. We can fill everyone else in after we have the details."

Gene stands at the head of the table. "We will end this meeting for today. The polling numbers are great news, go celebrate a little. Russ and Robert, I will see you tonight for the super PAC and finance meeting. We will meet here for a policy meeting tomorrow morning at nine."

The staff members pack up their laptops, legal pads, and notes and exit the room. Theodore's cell phone rings.

"Hey, Larry. It's just me and Gene in the room. Let me put you on speaker," Theodore says and places his cell phone on the table. "Go ahead, Larry, we can both hear you now."

"Good morning, Gene. This is Larry Richmond."

"How are you, Larry? What can I do for you this morning?"

"You have the polling numbers, Gene, you can probably figure out how I am doing. Congratulations. Look, I am calling you to let you know that I am dropping out of the gubernatorial race. I can't afford to put all my resources into fighting you. There is a senator's seat opening up in my district next year. I have a better chance of winning that seat than I do in the governor's race."

"That's surprising news! I'm glad you called. You made my staff's job a little easier. If there is anything I can do, don't hesitate to ask."

"Gene, I didn't go public with this yet. I will announce early tomorrow so it hits the morning news cycle. Please keep this phone call confidential until I announce. I will give you my full endorsement and encourage all my donors to do the same. In exchange, when I run for the Senate, I want your public endorsement and financial backers behind me."

"I can definitely do that for you, Larry. I will do everything I can for you. I appreciate you calling me first. I won't say a word until you announce."

"I will have a concession speech of sorts prepared, and I will announce my senatorial intentions. I will e-mail Teddy a copy, and you can have him prepare a response saying you support my senatorial intentions."

"I will gladly do that, Larry. Are we still on for Thursday night?" Theodore asks.

"Definitely. I scored a live Allman Brothers double album."

"Nice. I guess it's my turn to bring the pizza and beer."

"Yes, it's a double album, so bring a twelve-pack. Look, I gotta go. Congratulations, Gene! I will catch up with you guys later," Larry says and hangs up.

Gene has a big smile on his face. "This is the best news. I don't have to invest in a primary and can focus on the general election! Why did Larry call your phone and not the campaign office? What do you and Larry Richmond have going on Thursday night?"

"We are both avid collectors of vinyl records. I met him at a record store a few years ago, and since then, we get together one night a month and eat pizza, drink beer, and listen to records."

"There is so much I don't know about you."

"You never ask about me. Hey, why did you bring Ray Whitney into your campaign? You know my history with him. You know I can't stand the guy."

"His old man puts a lot of money into political campaigns and has a lot of influence over other donors. They follow his lead. He's a good guy to have in my corner."

"So it's about the Whitney money?"

"I know you don't like the money end of it. Once the super PAC is set up, you won't have to see or hear from Ray. That's why I put Russ in the liaison position. You won't have to deal with Ray and can concentrate on campaigning and public appearances. You're good at that. This morning's polling numbers proved that you are good at it."

"The less exposure I have to Ray Whitney, the better. I just wish you would be honest with me."

"I wasn't sure you would take the job if you knew. I need you to help me win this thing."

"I'm here for you, brother. Just be honest with me. I'm a big boy. I can handle honesty."

"You got it, Teddy. Have a good show tonight. Ernie is looking forward to you sitting in with his band. Sandy will be there. Don't let her get too drunk. I don't want to deal with one of her alcohol-induced meltdowns tonight."

"Hmmmm. Maybe that's how I will get back at you for bringing asshole Ray Whitney back into my life. I will get Sandy all liquored up and have sex with her in your limousine," Theodore jokes as he packs his briefcase and takes his cell phone off the conference room table.

"Fuck you, Furshizzle!"

"Rock and roll!" Theodore says and drops a joint in Gene's shirt pocket before leaving the room.

CHAPTER 12

Gene is sitting at the conference room table with Robert Wermer and Russ Dewitt. They are passing some financial reports back and forth across the table while they are waiting for Ray Whitney to arrive. Gene looks at his wristwatch.

"Ray should be here any minute now. Ever since I've known him, he's always been late. If he's not here in the next ten minutes, I will give him a call."

"I can easily forgive Mr. Whitney for being late. That's a guy that hates Teddy as much as I do, and he does a good job getting under his skin. He's better at it than me," Russ says.

Robert Wermer slides a paper across the table to Russ. "Compare this financial forecast from before the polling numbers to the financial forecast that I put together after the polling numbers this morning. You can say what you want about, Teddy, but the guy knows what he's doing. That new forecast shows a 44 percent gain, and that's just from a few weeks of campaign rollout events. He knows how to make the media work in our favor."

"Russ, you are going to have to learn to work with Teddy. I know he doesn't fit into the professional mold we want him to, but he is loyal and he delivers on promises. When you attack him like you do, he's going to come back at you. He is good at it," Gene says.

"Ray Whitney seems to be able to put Teddy in his place. I'm going to like working with that guy."

The conference room door opens. Ray Whitney walks in with his father, Morton Whitney, and another man. Ray is wearing slacks with a shirt and tie. The man is wearing a suit, and Morton is more relaxed, wearing a tracksuit.

Gene gets up to greet them. "I thought you forgot about us. I was just about to call you and see where you were. Mort, it's great to see you. You're looking well. How have you been?"

"Can the pleasantries. Small talk with you is the last thing I want to make. I don't have a lot of time, so I will make this brief. Sit down," Morton commands.

Gene says, "We were just about to—"

But Mort interrupts. "I don't give a fuck what you were about to do. I'm going to do what I'm going to do, and then the three of us are going to the titty bar up the road. You can go back to diddling your pricks like you were before we got here."

Russ stands up and extends his hand. "Mr. Whitney, I am Russ Dewitt, a strategist and the super PAC liaison for the campaign."

"I didn't give a shit about pleasantries with Gene, I certainly don't give a shit about pleasantries from you. Put that cock-stroker down. I don't shake hands. Just sit down and listen."

Russ sits back down. Ray and the other man take their seats at the table. Robert and Gene focus on Morton at the head of the table.

"Before I start, I want all the electronics out of this room. This meeting is totally confidential. Nothing is to be recorded, taped, or written down. If I see anybody with a pen in their hand when I am speaking, I will personally break their fingers. Collect all the mobile phones. Disconnect the wall phone. Remove this TV. That radio has got to go. Get all those computer and internet gadgets out of here. Don't just put them right outside the door either. Put them two or three rooms away," Morton orders.

"No problem, Mort, you got it," Gene says.

Russ and Robert collect the laptops and cell phones while Gene wheels the television cart out of the room. They return to the room later and take their seats. Mort waits for the shuffling and situating to stop before he starts speaking.

"I've been following your campaign since you announced. Your rollout at your wife's beauty pageant bullshit event almost put you out of the running before you even got in. I watched your pandering-to-the-people, dog-and-pony show. It might have been fun making people feel good about their politicians, but that's not how politics works."

"Our polling numbers say we did pretty well, and Larry Richmond will be announcing that he is dropping out of the race tomorrow morning," Gene interrupts.

"I thought I told you to shut the fuck up and listen to me? I know about Larry Richmond. I was the first phone call he made. You were the second. Since he is gone, you are the only pony in the race I can put my money on, but I do have some conditions. If you don't want to meet my conditions, I will take my money to the Sherman Jones campaign. The whole Democrats and Republicans thing doesn't mean shit to me. Politics does what the money tells it to do, and I am the money."

"We would be happy to have you on our team," Gene says.

"I don't want to be on your fucking team. I am offering to *buy* your team. Are you going to shut the fuck up and listen to me, or should we just leave for the titty bar now?"

"I'm sorry, Mort. Continue."

Morton rolls his eyes at Gene's apology and then continues. "I don't know what the fuck happened to you. Your father, grandfather, and great-grandfather were great men. They knew politics was a commodity that rich people could invest in, own, control, and prosper from. You, on the other hand, listen to that working-class Teddy Graham and his government-is-for-the-people bullshit. You should have kicked this dirt-farmer to the curb at Harvard, but no, your family took him in and helped him learn to mingle among us money folks. Karma takes care of the wealthy. That's probably why cancer got your mother and your old man is out of his skull senile and shitting in his adult diapers at that old folks' home."

"Those are my parents you are talking about. Teddy's done a lot for my family too. He did great for our community college, our youth honors college, our publishing house, and he took our debate team to the national debate finals this year. Teddy is grateful for what my family has done for him. He visits my father at the home regularly, more than I do."

Mort makes a masturbating motion. "How did you turn out to be such a cunt? You come from money, you could have purchased somebody else to do all that shit. I'm not trying to hurt your feelings when I talk about your parents, I'm just making the point that karma is controlled by money and the people who know how to use it. If you don't believe me, remember, I'm twenty-two years older than your father, and my health is perfect. Don't give me that only-the-good-die-young bullshit, because it's the poor and charitable that die young."

"I don't think that is a fair assessment, Mr. Whitney."

Morton motions for Ray and the other new man to follow him. "This is a waste of time, fellows. Let's go to the titty bar. Good luck with your legacy, Gene. Sherman Jones will be governor for the next eight years. You can try again then, but you might be shitting your adult diapers like your senile old man."

"No, no, no, Mort, I want to hear what you have to say, and I want Ray in charge of my super PAC."

"You can keep Ray. He's as useless as tits on a claw hammer. He's a load his mother should have swallowed, but she didn't, and I had to own up to the poor placement of my sperm. Are you going to interrupt me again, or are you going to hear me out?"

"I'm sorry, Mort. Please continue."

"I looked at your campaign, and I saw all the news clips. I guess maybe the working class and poor people are happy and singing 'Kumbaya' and thinking their voices matter, but that doesn't fly with me. Catering to women, niggers, time-clock punchers, and the retarded youth by including them as part of your campaign is a big mistake. That's not how politics works. You're supposed to scare the time-clock punchers by telling them the other guy is going to raise their taxes and give everything to the colored folks. The colored folks, you tell them you will only help them if they learn to behave. The retarded youth, you tell them to pull up their pants and get a job. The women, you make them feel guilty and blame the retarded youth on them for leaving the home and getting a career. Old people and middle-class folks, you tell them that you want to do more for them but you blame the poor for using up all the tax money on handouts.

Put on a flag pin, surround yourself with veterans, Christians, police officers, firefighters, athletes, puppies, and children. Give the voters a freedom boner. Craft a solid wall of rhetoric and learn how to fake empathy. The folks will vote you into office. It's been this way since the fifties, with a couple of equal-rights hiccups along the way. The equal-rights hiccups didn't work out so good for JFK, did they? My conditions are simple. I will put the money into your campaign and super PAC and you will get elected. Once you are elected, you do what my lobbyists tell you. Pass the legislation they tell you to. Veto the legislation they tell you to. Don't get cute and try to craft legislation—let the lobbyists do what I pay them for. They get paid shitloads of money to maintain the smoke and mirrors of politics. Don't bend to public opinion when problems arise, blame the problems on the failed policies of the opposition. I will also invest in the media so they lean toward your side while pretending to be fair. I will do all this for you if you fire that working-class wannabe hero of a campaign manager and hire that man sitting next to Ray. That is Dick Ratzinger. He will streamline your campaign to meet my conditions and put you in office. You can keep the other jackasses on your staff, but Teddy Graham has got to go."

Russ Dewitt begins clapping. "Finally, somebody is making some sense."

"I like this guy. He knows how it is. What's your name, Mr. Dipshit? Do you want to go to the titty bar with us and get suck-and-tug jobs from naked cocaine addicts and girls saving up for dental hygienist school?"

"It's Mr. Dewitt, but I would be honored to go with you, Mr. Whitney."

"I don't care what your name is, but you're welcome to come along. I'll even buy you a lap dance."

Gene's face is pale and has a worried expression. "I don't know, Mort. Teddy has been a loyal friend. I'm not sure if I can put his friendship aside."

"Don't be a fool, Gene! Mr. Whitney's investment in your campaign will guarantee you the win. I would rather see him on our side than have to face him behind Sherman Jones in the general election."

"I would listen to Mr. Dickdrip, he sees how harmful Teddy is."

"It's Dewitt."

"I don't care what your name is, and if you keep correcting me, I will disinvite you from going to the titty bar."

"Mort, can I think about this for a little bit?"

"You have until noon tomorrow. But while you're thinking, think about this. I will put twenty-five million dollars into your super PAC. The maximum contribution from an individual directly to your campaign is capped at ten thousand dollars. If you fire Teddy, you will get a check for ten thousand dollars from every member of my family—me, my wife, my three children, their spouses, and from the trust funds of all seven of my grandchildren. Plus, I will encourage some of my friends and neighbors and business colleagues to make some sizable donations. This shouldn't be a hard choice to make. But you have until noon tomorrow. If I don't hear from you by noon, I will know you didn't have the balls to fire your buddy. After noon, I will take a shit, maybe whack off, and then give Sherman Jones the same offer. He will jump at the opportunity, I am sure. Am I clear?"

"Yes, you are clear."

"Come on, fellows. You too, Mr. Dickspit. We have naked ladies at the titty bar to grope," Mort says. "I would invite you to come along, Gene, but you have some thinking to do."

Morton, Ray, Dick Ratzinger, and Russ all leave the room. Gene and Robert remain sitting at the table. Gene appears distraught.

"What do you think, Robert?"

"Politics is a dirty business, Gene. If I wanted to make decisions like the tough one you have, I would run for office. I don't like making those decisions. I will not be seeking elected office, and I will not comment or advise you either way."

"I understand completely. I guess I won't be sleeping tonight."

CHAPTER 13

Theodore enters the conference room. Each staff member is leafing through a red binder. Russ Dewitt is slumped in his chair with his binder open in front of him. It is obvious that his focus isn't on his binder. He seems to be in a great deal of discomfort.

"Good morning. Hello, new guy that I don't know yet. Russ, you look awful this morning," Theodore says as he greets the campaign staff.

Russ waves his hand to shoo Theodore away. He doesn't speak or lift his head from staring at his binder. Theodore puts his briefcase on the table. Russ cringes, as if the subtle thud of a briefcase being placed on the table were painful for him.

"Are you going to make it, Russ? It doesn't appear that you are up for today's meeting," Theodore says.

Russ again waves his hand as if to shoo him away.

Gene clears his throat. "Teddy, didn't you get my call this morning?"

"I was taking a dump and playing Angry Birds when you called. I was just about to complete a level, so I ignored the call. I figured it could wait until the meeting."

Gene gets out of his chair. "There is something I want to talk to you about. Let's go to my office."

"If it's about Larry Richmond, everybody here should already know. He was all over the news this morning."

"No, everybody knows about Larry. I wanted to run something by you before we began today."

"You got it, big guy."

Gene and Theodore leave the conference room, and Ray Whitney snickers as they exit the room. Theodore turns back and looks at him with a puzzled look. The two then enter Gene's office.

"Have a seat, Teddy."

Theodore takes a seat in the chair in front of Gene's desk. "Sitting down? I guess we're going to be here for a bit. You should have told me this was going to take some time. I would have grabbed a cup of coffee. It looks like you could use some coffee. Did you even sleep? Did Sandy come home from the gig last night and fuck your brains out?"

"No, she came in, mumbled something to me, and passed out."

"It was a great night. Ernie's band packed the Karma Club. It's a fun band to play with."

Gene wriggles uncomfortably in his seat. "That's great, but let me get straight to it. Since Larry Richmond dropped out of the race, we don't have a primary to run. That's because of you. You got us the polling numbers, and now the campaign can focus on the general election."

"You did good too. After we talked to Larry yesterday, I spent a good part of the afternoon starting a strategy plan. I have all the notes in my briefcase. I will share them at the meeting. Hey, why does Russ Dewitt look so rough this morning? Is he all right?"

"Russ went to a strip club with Ray Whitney and his old man last night. I think he overdid it and has a pretty nasty hangover."

"It looks like it's a doozy of a hangover. He can't even move his head. He's hurting. I almost feel bad for him. Is that why you look so rough today?"

"No, I didn't go with them. I had enough bad experiences at strip clubs with Sandy's mom. They don't really appeal to me anymore."

"What's in all those red binders, and who is that new guy in the room? Did you hire somebody to help Marty Price with research and campaign policy?"

Gene wriggles in his chair again. "Teddy, you told me yesterday you want me to be honest with you, so that's what I'm going to do. That new guy in there is my new campaign manager, and those red binders are the new campaign strategies."

"You're fucking with me!"

"No, Teddy, I'm not. With Larry Richmond gone, we need a whole new message. Dick Ratziner knows political strategy inside and out. He is more suited for politics. You were unsure about taking the job. Now you are off the hook."

"Morton Whitney came in here last night and waved a shitload of money in your face, didn't he?"

"It's not like that. Ray and Mort think I need somebody with a background in politics."

"Fuck you, Gene! If it involves the Whitneys, it's because of money. That's all it is with them, and you caved in when you saw dollar signs. It's not too late. We can go back in there, fire Ray and the new guy, and run the campaign we were running."

"I don't think the campaign we were running would get me into the governor's mansion. It was good enough for the primary election, but not for the general. This is the big leagues."

Theodore stands up. "It's not the big leagues, it's big bucks. I was hoping that together we could make politics about the people and doing the right thing."

"You can still have your job at the community college, the youth college, and you can still publish through the publishing house. It would be great to have you take the debate team to the nationals two years in a row. That would really help my campaign. You can help me best in that capacity. You would still get to live in the faculty house. You like that place."

"No, Gene. It's time for me to move on. It's time for me to do something new. I was planning on doing that, anyway, but I thought it would be great to help my friend become the next governor. Now I'm not even sure if you are my friend. If you can give me until next Saturday to be out of my place, that would be a huge help."

"You can take as long as you need. I'm still your friend."

"The sooner I put this all behind me, the better it will be. I just got to get my briefcase out of the conference room, and I will be on my way."

"Come over and have dinner with me and Sandy tonight. We can have some drinks and smoke some pot. Let's have some fun like we used to."

Theodore leans on Gene's desk and looks him directly in the eyes. "That sounds lovely, but I'm sorry, I can't make it. I have moving arrangements to make."

"Come on, Teddy, don't be like that."

Theodore ignores Gene as he leaves his office. He enters the conference room and makes his way to his briefcase on the table next to Russ. He still appears to be hurting from a horrible hangover.

"It is my sad duty to inform you all that I no longer work for the Eugene Douglas for Governor campaign. I wish you all the best of luck," Theodore addresses the room. "I understand you're the new campaign manager, and I understand your name is Dick. You look like a Dick, and, Ray, you are a dick." Theodore picks up his briefcase and is about to leave the room.

"Now you can go back to doing what poor people do, eating orange macaroni and cheese out of a box and tuna out of a can. Maybe some Spam too. You will once again be living the working-class dream," Ray says.

Theodore drops his briefcase to the floor and stares angrily at Ray.

"What are you going to do, Furshizzle? Hit me? Did I make you mad? Did I insult your lifetime of insufficient funds? Did I properly identify what's on your family's Thanksgiving dinner table?"

"Enough, Ray! There's no need to be like that," Gene says as he is coming back into the room.

Theodore stares at Ray and cups his hand. He places his cupped hand over his ass.

Frrrrrrrrrrrrrrrmmmmmrrrrrrrppp can be heard as Theodore farts into his hand.

"Russ doesn't look so good this morning, Ray. Maybe he can use a nice cup of fart," Theodore says as he places the cupped hand over Russ Dewitt's face.

Russ gets a whiff of the fart smell in Theodore's hand and begins to gag. After a few gags, Russ stands up and vomits across the table and all over Ray Whitney. Some vomit splashes on Gene's new campaign manager, Dick Ratzinger.

"Have a happy Thanksgiving, Ray," Theodore says. He picks up his briefcase, and as he is leaving, he hears the gags and groans of the others seated at the conference table.

Theodore exits the building and notices the Channel 6 News van parked out front. Reporter Grace Downwood approaches Theodore with her cameraman. When Theodore reaches the bottom step, she plants herself next to him.

"Mr. Graham, this is Grace Downwood of Channel 6 News. As campaign manager for Eugene Douglas, do you want to make a statement about Larry Richmond dropping out of the gubernatorial primary?"

Theodore stops next to the reporter so that her cameraman can get a clear still shot. "I am no longer working for the Douglas campaign, but I respect Larry Richmond's decision. I believe Larry will serve the people well and do an excellent job as a senator in Washington, DC. I look forward to hearing him outline his platform."

"Did the Douglas campaign terminate you?"

"*Terminate* is a harsh word, but it works. The Douglas campaign felt they needed a different strategy and brought in somebody they felt could do a better job for them in the general election."

"The polling data was just released yesterday morning. You were managing this campaign for the polling period. How can the Douglas campaign see those favorable numbers and decide to change strategy?"

"I don't know the reasons, and I wouldn't even venture a guess. You might want to interview the new campaign manager, Dick Ratzinger, or the super PAC trustee, Ray Whitney. They may not want to do an interview today, though. One of the strategists for the campaign came into this morning's meeting all hungover and vomited on Ray Whitney. I'm pretty sure some splashed on Dick Ratzinger too."

"Do you think with your departure, the polling numbers will become less favorable for Gene Douglas?"

"Gene Douglas is the one running for governor, not me. The polling numbers will depend on how well his new strategy registers with the voters of the state."

"Will you still vote for Gene Douglas?"

"I haven't heard the new strategy, so I can't answer that question now."

"Are you going to return to your position at the Douglas Youth Honors College as a teacher and debate coach? You did take the team to the national championship and won."

"The position was offered to me, but I turned it down. I'm going to move on to something new."

"What's next for Theodore Graham?"

"I haven't figured out the long-term plan yet. I was just told this morning that I was fired. The short-term plan is to get good and drunk. You and your cameraman are welcome to join me. After that, I may light some dog poop in a paper bag on fire, place it on Gene Douglas's doorstep, ring the doorbell, and run away. You got that, Issac? Don't answer the door tonight. Let Gene do it so he has to stomp out the flaming bag of poop."

"There you have it from Theodore Graham, the now-former campaign manager of the Eugene Douglas for Governor campaign. I'm Grace Downwood from Channel 6 News," the reporter says and motions for her cameraman to shut off the camera.

"Are you serious, or are you just messing with the media?"

"I am serious about being fired. I am serious about Russ Dewitt vomiting on the super PAC trustee and new campaign manager. I am serious about going to get drunk. I'm going to get high too, but I didn't want to incriminate myself on television. I wasn't serious about the dog poop in a bag thing, but if I get drunk enough, you never know. If you aren't going to get drunk with me, you and your camera guy can camp out in front of the Douglas mansion to see if I come through with the flaming bag of poo. Oooh, that rhymes."

"That sucks. I was looking forward to covering this campaign. It seemed different from the regular bullshit factory that politics has become."

"I was looking forward to working with you. You are one of the few investigative journalists left. You follow up on anonymous tips and you ask questions that are uncomfortable for people who are trying to hide something. I read your editorials in the *Weekly Beat*. You have quite a brain in your head. I admire your work. It's too bad the *Weekly Beat* is a four-day-a-week newspaper that only gets delivered on the days when nobody reads the paper. Thursday through Sunday is when the coupons come out. Got to get the masses shopping for useless crap. I guess advertising has to keep it afloat."

"I know. I don't know how much longer the paper will last, but at least I have the Channel 6 News gig."

"Yes, you do. Viewers must be informed who won the Cub Scout's Pinewood Derby and sailboat races and where the best basket bingo and bake sales are."

"Fuck you! This job keeps a roof over my head."

"Don't get offended. I'm sorry. It's early, and it's already been a bad day. I know you don't pick the stories you have to cover. I just hope you don't waste your talent. Your brilliance will serve you well on a bigger stage. If I can help you in any way, give me a call. Now, if you will excuse me, I'm going to get liquored up," Theodore says and walks away.

CHAPTER 14

Theodore is busying himself packing boxes with his memorabilia, his vinyl record collection, his books, and his marijuana smoking paraphernalia. He pulls a photo album off one of the shelves. He sets his bottle of beer on the coffee table and sits on the edge of his leather reading recliner. He leafs through the pages and looks at the photos and newspaper clippings from his time teaching at the youth honors college. He sees the picture of the debate team that he took to nationals. He sees pictures of some of the rich kids that he turned onto learning to occupy their time while they were waiting to come of age to collect their trust funds. He sees pictures of himself with Gene and Sandy at school events and dedication ceremonies. As he is looking at the nostalgia, the doorbell rings. He opens the door and sees Ernie Douglas.

"Ernie, what are you doing here? Come on in."

"I can't believe my father fired you. He also told me that I couldn't study at the musician's colony because I have to be on his campaign staff. After the election, I have to go to Harvard and begin to fulfill my part of the family legacy. I threatened to not obey him, but he threatened to cut me out of the family fortune."

"Sounds like first world problems to me."

"It's not funny, Teddy. He's stopping me from doing what I want to do."

"I don't mean to joke. I don't agree with what your father is doing, but he is your father. You should respect your parents. Your family legacy maps out a pretty nice life for you. Maybe you shouldn't knock it."

"That's not what I expected to hear from you. You're always the one who could make my parents listen to reason."

"I don't know if it was reason or if I was just bending them to my way of thinking. Whatever it was, I don't work for your family anymore. Your dad decided to hire a professional campaign manager."

"That professional dick-wad of a campaign manager gave me a red campaign-strategy binder, told me to study it, and said I would be training with a media coach starting next week."

"They are serious about getting you involved in the campaign. How much will you be doing?"

Ernie takes his backpack off and removes a red binder. "Here, see for yourself. I'm even getting paid for being on the campaign staff."

"That's not a bad deal. It's always good to get paid."

"He's only paying me so I can't do paid band gigs until after the election. That's over a year away. Then I will be going to college. The guys in the band are pretty much hating me right now. It's not fair."

"The guys in the band are pissed because they are untalented noise without you. You'll play in other bands. Do you mind if I make copies of this binder?"

"You can have that copy. I told my old man I threw the one he gave me in the river because he fired you. I didn't, though. The other one is in my dorm room. I had to meet with that Ratzinger guy this morning, and he gave me a new one. What do you want with it, anyway?"

"I really have no reason to have it, but I am just curious to see how close I came to putting a 'professional' campaign strategy together."

"You would have done way better than this new campaign manager. That binder reads more like a script of answers for FAQs."

"Are you talking in abbreviations now? When I see that abbreviation, I just think it's a politically correct way of saying fuck off. FA-Q, like, 'Fuck you.' Get it?"

"Yeah, fuck you too. But seriously, aren't you going to talk to my dad and get your job back? You can convince him. You always appeal to his sense of reason or guilt."

"I don't want my job back. I didn't accept his offer to keep teaching and coaching at the school. It's time for me to move on."

"What are you going to do? Where are you going? How are you going to make money?"

"Right now, I am going to go back to my old hometown to work at the musician's colony for a little bit. You forget that I am a lawyer and an author. I will have no problem making money. Besides, working for your family, I saved a lot of money. I didn't spend much of the money I earned working here. I lived rent-free in school housing and got invited to dinner at your place a lot. Most of what I spent my money on was weed, beer, vinyl records, and guitar strings. Growing up poor, I learned how to live on the cheap and squirrel money away."

"That's not what I wanted to hear. I can't believe you're giving up."

"Look, Ernie, I am not giving up. I was fired. I'm not going to talk to your father to get my job back so you can get to do what you want. You have to be the one to convince him. If you do, I can make sure you get a spot at the musician's colony. If you can't, call me when you go to college. I have some good contacts at Harvard, and I know a lot of club owners that will let you play there. He's your father, I'm not interfering with his parenting," Theodore says.

"That's bullshit, Teddy. I can't believe you are letting him get away with this."

"He's not getting away with anything. He's an adult making his own decisions. I understand your frustration, but I can't help you."

"Fuck you, Teddy! I thought you were cool," Ernie says and storms out of Theodore's place.

Theodore lets him go. He picks his beer off the table, takes a sip, and goes back to his packing. The front door opens.

"Yo, dingleberry, are you home?" his young friend Wayne hollers in the door.

"In here, Wayne."

"I saw you on the news yesterday. I can't believe mean Gene Douglas fired you," Wayne says. "You're moving out? Dude, that sucks."

"What brings you by?"

"I was just out delivering groceries for the store. I stopped in to see if you were really fired and if you wanted to smoke a bowl. Do you want to smoke a bowl?"

"Does the tinman have a sheet metal cock?"

"I never really thought about it. Maybe, but why would a robot need a cock? Robots don't really fuck. If they did, it would probably sound like garbage cans rolling around in the alley on a windy day."

"Yes, I want to smoke a bowl. The question was a joke, but I am glad that you put such serious thought into things."

"You taught me to ask questions and think analytically," Wayne says as he hands over a packed bowl and a BIC lighter.

Theodore lights the bowl and takes a long drag off it. "Thanks. I was going to smoke in a bit, anyway. It's nice to smoke in good company."

"When I pulled up, I saw Ernie Douglas storming out of here. I said hello to him, but he looked too pissed to talk."

"He's pretty pissed that his dad fired me. He tried to convince me to talk to his old man and get my job back. I told him I wouldn't, so now he isn't happy with me either."

"Aren't you pissed you got fired?"

"I'm more disappointed the way it went down. It ruined a long-time friendship. That's what upsets me the most. It wasn't really a job I wanted, but when I started doing it, I had fun. It was nice working with my friend."

"Where are you going now?"

"I'm going back to where I grew up, for a little while, anyway. I want to play music and relax my brain for a bit. I have another story idea, so I will do some writing too. I might even get back into law. I haven't decided on a definite direction yet."

"If you like working with friends and you want to stick around here, you can work with me."

"I don't think gathering shopping carts and delivering groceries and weed is something I am cut out for," Theodore says.

Wayne shakes his head. "No, not that. I have an idea. You would be the perfect guy to help me see this idea through."

"I'm almost afraid to ask."

"Remember those *Girls Gone Wild* videos from the eighties and nineties?"

"Yeah, I spent some alone time studying the art form."

"Ha, ha, whacking off is more like it. Anyway, all the girls in those videos are all grown up now. They're no longer slutty college girls, but they might have grown up to be slutty MILFs. I was thinking of finding some of the girls from those videos and making *MILFs Gone Wild* videos."

"I'm pretty sure the guy who made those *Girls Gone Wild* videos got in a shitload of trouble. Though it's tempting, count me out of that business venture."

"The offer is on the table. Think about it. I got to get back to the store, but do you want to hang out and play some guitar before you leave?"

"Definitely. How about Thursday night? We can go out drinking on Friday night. I'm probably leaving Saturday morning."

"Sounds good. I'm going to miss you, brother."

"I'm going to miss you, buddy. You're more than welcome to come down to the musician's colony. They can polish up your playing. Maybe they can make a rock-and-roll star out of you one day."

"I'm a better weed dealer than a musician. I just play to calm my mind like you do."

Theodore walks to the front door with him. "Thanks for the tokes."

"You got it," Wayne says as he walks down the front steps to his car.

As Wayne is pulling away, Teddy sees Sweet Barn making his way up the sidewalk, carrying an aluminum foil–covered plate. He waves to Theodore and walks up onto the porch.

"What's up, Sweet Barn?"

"When Mama saw on the news yesterday that you got fired, she started to cry. She liked how you looked out for me and my brothers. She wanted to do something for you, but she didn't know what, so she baked you a big plate of chocolate chip cookies. I ate four of them on the way over here. I hope you don't mind."

"I don't mind, big fellow. Your mom didn't have to go to all that trouble for me. Tell her I said thank you."

"I will, Teddy. I don't know why you are so special. Some Ratzinger guy called last night and told me that the Douglas campaign is letting our security company go. Mama didn't bake cookies for me and my brothers, so I ate a couple of yours."

"You guys got fired too? I'm sorry."

"I get to keep my job as maintenance at the community college, and Lizard Eddie gets to stay at the landscaping company, but Funky Brian needed this job. His probation depends on having a job. He's been so good lately and has been working so hard. I don't want to see him go back to jail or get on the crack again."

"I don't want that for your brother either. Are you still going to do the security business?"

"If we could find some work, we'll keep it. The Douglas campaign would have lasted well after Funky Brian's probation was over, but now that's not happening."

"I'll tell you what, I know the guy that owns the Bumpin' Club and the Riverside Band Shell. I can give him a call and see if he will hire you guys. It would be mostly Friday- and Saturday-night work, and you would have to put up with drunk rednecks and country music, but if he agrees, it would be a steady gig."

"You would do that for us?" Sweet Barn asks with tears welling up in his eyes.

"Of course I will. I love you guys, and I want to stay on your mom's good side. She is one tough lady. I want her to see her good boys doing good things," Theodore says.

Sweet Barn grabs Theodore and hugs him tightly. "Thank you. Thank you, Teddy. My whole family thanks you. We love you too. Mama is going to be saying a shitload of prayers for you in church this Sunday."

"You're welcome. It's the least I can do. I can't promise he will hire you, but he owes me a favor, and I will highly recommend you guys. You guys were good at security. Just don't let Funky Brian eat eggs before the job interview."

"I'll sew his mouth shut. I don't want his nasty fart-ass ruining our career," Sweet Barn says and hugs Theodore again. "I got to get going. I can't wait to tell them the news. Thank you, Teddy. You're one of the good white folks."

"You're welcome. I'll be in touch," Theodore says and returns inside to pack his things.

Theodore starts clearing more of his bookshelves and packing the books into milk crates. He climbs the stepladder and dusts the now-empty shelves. The doorbell rings.

"How the fuck am I ever going to get packed and move out of here if I am getting company all day?" he says to himself. He climbs down from the stepladder and answers the door.

When he opens the door, there is a balding overweight man with thick glasses staring back at him. The man is sweating profusely and wearing wide suspenders that are holding up pants that are pulled halfway over his large gut.

"Mr. Graham?" the man says, sounding out of breath.

"Who wants to know?"

"I'm Paul Hoptak. I'm the owner and operator of the *Weekly Beat*. I was wondering if I could have a few moments of your time. Can I come in?"

"I did my interview about getting fired from the Douglas campaign yesterday with Channel 6. I'm not doing any follow-ups or making any further comments."

"I'm not here to interview you. I was talking to Grace Downwood from Channel 6 about you at great length. I have a proposition for you."

Theodore opens the door. "Come on in, Mr. Hoptak. I am out of work, but I'm not desperate enough to start a paper route. Sit down. It looks like you can use a good sit."

Paul sits down on one of the antique parlor chairs. The leg of the chair cracks under his weight, and the chair topples over. Teddy helps him off the floor.

"I'm sorry about the chair, Mr. Graham. I'll pay for it."

"Don't worry about it. It came with the place. It belongs to Gene Douglas. Fuck him. Maybe the couch will support you a little better," Theodore says and guides him to the sofa.

"I'm not offering you a paper route, Mr. Graham, but I am offering you a feature writing and editor position at the *Weekly Beat*."

"As you can see, I am packing up and getting out of here. I'm not really interested in writing for a glorified Pennysaver paper."

"Mr. Graham, when my family took over this paper in '68, it was called *The Beat*. It put out eight papers per week. It had a Monday-morning edition to catch people up on news from the weekend sports and events. It had five evening editions and Saturday- and Sunday-morning editions. There were sixteen editorial contributors, thirty beat reporters, twelve editors, and over a hundred other employees that put it all together. It was a good paper. I want to make it a good paper again. Grace Downwood convinced me you can make it a good paper again."

"I don't know how she did that. I don't see how I can make it good again."

"You know people. People like you. Grace told me everything people liked about the Douglas campaign was your doing. She says if you were writing for the *Weekly Beat*, people would read it. You know how politics works. You know the players behind politics. You come from working-class roots and can relate to the people. She convinced me that my paper is the perfect platform for you to get people to pay attention to what they should."

"That sounds all well and good, and I don't want to offend you, but your paper is a coupon peddler that features fluff pieces about church events and ice cream socials. I subscribe so I can read Grace's editorials and keep up with local sports. I would imagine most of your subscribers get it to clip the coupons and see what's going on locally. It's a dying paper."

"All of what you are saying is true. I know all this, but this paper is all I know. My parents put everything they owned into this paper. It was their dream. They worked hard and did well with it. When they passed, they left it to me and my siblings. When the paper started dying, my siblings were smart enough to get out of the business. I bought all of them out so the paper could still be printed. Maybe it's for selfish reasons that I came here to talk to you. Grace convinced me that you could save this paper. I believe her. I know asking you to help me is a long shot, but it would be great to show my siblings that I made a wise business choice with the paper instead of hearing them say they told me so."

"I don't know. Grace is a brilliant woman, but I think she might be wrong about this one. I don't see me turning your paper around. Sometimes you just have to cut your losses, Mr. Hoptak."

"She did say that I would have to make some investments if I got you to come aboard. Here's what I am willing to do. I would invest in getting the *Weekly Beat* an online presence. You can write about what you want, but I want one feature editorial on local politics per week. I have a publishing shop. Most of the stuff that comes out of there is independently published books by people who think that they can write and church books. I will publish your books free of charge, but your editorials will be compiled and published every three months and sold by the paper. You would have to promote them. You won't have to do any sales, beat reporting, or fluff pieces, but you will have to work with the beat reporters and help them improve their writing. You would also be required to educate and inform the people that submit to the Saturday public commentary section. I read those submissions and cringe at how misinformed people are. Most of them just repeat what cable news tells them. You can write a fact-based piece on some of the hot topics. I am asking for a two-year commitment. If you agree to do this, you can come down for a tour of the place and we can talk about money then."

"As I mentioned before, and as you can see, I'm packing up. I don't have a place to live. You have to give me time to find a place to get settled."

"On the top floor of the newspaper is a newly remodeled apartment. It's a huge apartment, and the freight elevator goes right to it, so moving furniture in will be easy. My last tenant left because the printing press started too early in the morning on the weekends. It's yours if you take the job."

"I have to admit, I'm intrigued by your offer. I do love a good underdog story. How about I come down for a tour tomorrow and we can talk a little bit more?"

"Tomorrow will be great. Is noon okay?"

"Noon will be fine. You have my curiosity."

"Curiosity was all I wanted to create. Tomorrow I will sell it. Thank you, Mr. Graham," Paul says. "I will see you at lunchtime tomorrow."

CHAPTER 15

On a Sunday morning, Gene Douglas is relaxing poolside, reading his Sunday paper, and flipping from news network to news network to see if his campaign gets any mention. He settles on the local news channel because he has a better chance of being mentioned there.

"Good Sunday morning to you and welcome to State of the State This Week. I'm your host, Walter Carl, and joining me this hour are political analyst Brad Utes, journalist Joan Mowrey, and we welcome to the show once again Theodore Graham, the now former campaign manager for Eugene Douglas."

"Oh, shit. What the fuck is he doing?" Gene says to the himself as he watches.

Sandy is getting ready to spend her day sunbathing by the pool. She walks behind Gene and glances at the screen. "Is that Teddy? What's he doing on this show? I thought he went home after you fired him."

"So did I. This can't be good."

"Have you even talked to him since you fired him?"

"When he sent me the keys to his faculty house in the center of a bowl of Jell-O, I figured he was still pretty upset with me for firing him. I thought I should let him cool off for a while."

"It was a pretty shitty thing to do."

"Are you kidding me? When he was around, all you wanted me to do was get rid of him. You started a witch hunt against him and forced a termination hearing for him at the honors college. You didn't speak to me for three weeks when I voted against you. You told me not hire him as my campaign manager. I fired him. You got what you wanted. Now you are feeling sorry for him? For Christ's sake, Sandy, make up your damn mind!"

"He wasn't all bad. He was good for Ernie, and you weren't as miserable when he was around."

"I'll never figure you out, Sandy."

"Why is he on this show?"

"I don't know, but I have a feeling it isn't going to be good for me," Gene says and focuses his attention to the television.

"Welcome to the program. I want to start off with Mr. Graham. He's been a guest on our show before, but last time he joined us, he was the campaign manager for gubernatorial candidate Eugene Douglas. Today he joins us with a new title. Tell us about that," host Walter Carl says.

"Thanks for having me back, and yes, I have a new job. I am the new managing editor for the Weekly Beat. It's a local paper that's been in operation for over a century. It will be celebrating its 125th anniversary this year."

"I didn't realize the paper has been around that long. So how did you go from being a teacher, a debate coach, and a campaign manager to being the managing editor of a small newspaper? The Weekly Beat is very small. It seems like such a huge step-down from where you were."

"Some might say it's a step-down, but I look at it as a new chal-lenge. Paul Hoptak, the owner of the paper, came to me after I left the Douglas campaign and offered me the job. He asked me to help him relaunch his publication to make it relevant again. The Weekly Beat has been in his family since 1968, and he has watched the newspaper indus-try decline along with the size and quality of his paper. He didn't sell out to big media conglomerates to stay afloat. He still believes in the value of local news, local reporters writing about the things that local people are concerned about, and how national, state, and local events affect our own people. Mr. Hoptak told me his vision and convinced me to come aboard to help him make the relaunch happen."

"The Weekly Beat is basically just a beefed-up 'shopper's voice' paper. It's only one step above being offered for free at the front end of your local grocery store and in the entranceways of local diners. There is no real news in it. There is nothing really of substance in it," Brad Utes says.

"*Channel 6's own Grace Downwood contributes an editorial to it each week. She writes some really good pieces about her job covering local news as a female Native American journalist. They are brilliantly written articles that, sadly, not many people know about or take the time to read. That's why it needs a relaunch. It has to get with the times and do some things differently, and that's why I accepted Paul Hoptak's offer.*"

"*What are some of the things the Weekly Beat is doing to try to get readers back?*"

"*We have to get with the times. The Weekly Beat will have an online presence. There will be an online version of the paper put out seven days a week. The printed papers will still be delivered Thursdays through Sunday but will feature articles about local and state events and how the actions of politics affect the people. The nation and world section will feature articles from the Associated Press. The local sections will report on news from the four main towns in our area and feature articles from up-and-coming local journalists. The Sunday edition will have Harmon, Gatesville, Douglas Hills, and Carter sections, so each neighborhood is represented in our circulation area. There will also be local and national sports coverage, puzzles, the comics, and lifestyle sections. We will still have all the coupons and local sales inserts as well.*"

"*Do you think this is going to work to boost sales of the paper?*"

"*I hope it does. This is a unique area. The four main towns along the river are each different communities made up with people of different backgrounds. Harmon is made up of mostly working-class people that are working in the factories and mills in the area. Douglas Hills is the old-money section. It has the schools, the colleges, the quaint small businesses and is a bedroom community for people of wealth. Gatesville is a newer neighborhood, a sort of middle-class suburbia for the middle-management types. Carter is a borough that was an old industrial section of our area. It's in desperate need of some revitalization, but there are some leaders from Carter with ideas to rebuild their community. The relaunched Weekly Beat will bring the voices of these four boroughs together. The goal of the paper is to show the good, bad, and ugly of each neighborhood in one publication and get the readers of the paper to engage in open discourse to, hopefully, solve community issues instead of letting them fester and worsen.*"

"Those are some lofty goals being set by a struggling newspaper."

"I do enjoy a good underdog story. I am an underdog, so I tend to root for an underdog. I believe the efforts of the Weekly Beat to relaunch itself are noble. Why not inspire the readers to get behind working together to improve the neighborhoods they live in? I would just be happy to inspire more people to read a real newspaper," Theodore says.

"We have to go to a commercial break, but when we comeback, I'm sure Joan Mowrey of the Gatesville Courier, the Morning Sun Gazette, and the Harmon Herald has some questions for our guest, Theodore Graham. Stay tuned. We'll be back in a bit," Walter Carl says as he cuts to a commercial.

"What does Teddy know about newspapers? How did he end up there?" Sandy asks.

"I don't know how he got there, but Joan Mowrey is going to eat him alive after the commercial break. Dick Ratzinger promised her access to our campaign if she reports in our favor. She is our local news correspondent, and she actually knows how the news industry works. I almost feel bad for him," Gene says.

"Maybe you should talk to Teddy and get him to be a news correspondent. He can probably help you."

"Dick Ratzinger will never go for it. Besides, Teddy has no idea what he's doing. I think he may have completely lost it. Maybe he finally smoked too much weed and scrambled his brain."

"Teddy always has such good weed. You should invite him over. He always leaves a couple of joints as thanks for our hospitality."

"I'm not calling Teddy just to get you weed. You shouldn't be touching that stuff during the campaign. That could hurt our family values image."

"We're back with State of the State This Week. I'm Walter Carl. Good Sunday morning to you. If you are just joining us, before the break, we were talking with Theodore Graham, the new managing editor of the Weekly Beat, about the relaunch efforts of one of our oldest papers. Joining our guest today is political analyst Brad Utes and journalist Joan Mowrey. Now, Joan, I'm sure you have some questions for Mr. Graham. He will essentially be your competition with the relaunch of the Weekly Beat."

"I would hardly call the Weekly Beat the competition, but I do have some questions for Mr. Graham. Don't you think it's pretty easy for viewers and readers to figure out that you took this job just so you have a media outlet to bad-mouth and get back at the gubernatorial candidate that fired you for incompetence?"

"I don't believe it was incompetence that I was fired for. I don't think you believe I was fired for incompetence either. In fact, I knew you were going to be here today and I was going to ask you for your autograph on a well-written editorial you wrote the day before Larry Richmond dropped out of the gubernatorial race. I have it here in my jacket pocket," Theodore says and reaches in the jacket pocket of his sport coat and pulls out a newspaper clipping. "This article is from the Gatesville Courier, but you submitted the same article to the Harmon Herald and the Morning Sun Gazette. That's got to be a pretty sweet deal, getting paid three times for doing the work once. Anyway, the article is titled 'A Well-Managed Douglas Campaign Spells Doom for Richmond.' I wanted you to autograph it because you said such nice things about me in it. You praised Gene Douglas for making the right move by hiring his longtime friend, me, to run his campaign. In one line, you called me 'the magic man that knows how to play the polls.' I thought that was really nice of you to say, and I wanted to get you to sign it for my scrapbook. Joan, it breaks my heart that you are now calling me incompetent after you said such nice things."

"But you were fired from the Douglas campaign," Joan Mowrey says.

"You're right, Joan, I was fired from the campaign. I don't know why I was fired. I believe the Douglas campaign got rid of me so they could put together a team with more political experience. I did what I thought was right when I was there. I got fired. Getting fired is a learning part of any career. I'm certain you learned some good lessons when you were fired from the New York Times. I'm sure you learned that you are more suited for suburban and rural media outlets. I'm not bitter toward the Douglas campaign, and one of the stipulations for me taking on this job was that I wouldn't have to report on the gubernatorial race. Some of our other reporters may, but I won't."

"But you are the managing editor, you will be controlling what information about the governor's race gets put into the paper," Joan Mowrey says.

"Paul Hoptak is tasked with the governor's race and all articles dealing with it. I don't want to appear biased or phony. I only agreed to come to the Weekly Beat if it wasn't going to be more ice-cream-truck journalism."

"Ice-cream-truck journalism?"

"That's a term I like to pin on journalism today. It reminds me of when I was a troublemaking teenager. When the ice cream truck would come through our neighborhood, the kids and their housewife mothers would all flock to the truck to get cool, refreshing treats. Some of my neighborhood cronies and I would pay attention to which housewives were lined up and waiting for the ice cream truck with their kids. If they were outside, it meant nobody was in the house, so we would sneak in the back doors of their houses and raid their husbands' beer refrigerators."

"How is that like journalism?"

"A big story is like the ice cream truck, and the reporters are like the housewives that come out of the house to wait in line for the ice cream. All the reporters are focused on one story but aren't paying attention to all the other stories going on around them and miss the teenage hoodlums raiding their beer fridge. Last week, in two of the three papers you work for, I counted twenty-two articles on the governor's race from fourteen different reporters. Since Sherman Jones and Gene Douglas don't have primaries to run, there is nothing going on in the governor's race. Neither of them even did a campaign event. The articles talked about polling numbers and hypothetical, what-if questions about the race. It was basically reporting on news that didn't happen. That's not really journalism, is it? There was no coverage of the bills being voted on in the state House, the state Senate, or reporting on the cases coming out of the state Superior and Supreme Courts. You said you hardly think we are competition. Well, Joan, I guess we're not. You can follow the ice cream truck, and we are going to follow the thugs raiding the beer fridge. I can't tell the difference between your three papers. They're the same and don't totally reflect our local area. Maybe readers will see things like I do and want to read something different."

"I wish you luck with your four-days-per-week paper, but I will stick to my three seven- day- a- week papers," Joan Mowrey says.

"Quite a discussion we have on here on State of the State This Week. Speaking of the governor's race, when we come back from the next break, Joan, Brad, and I have lots to talk about, but before we say goodbye to Mr. Graham, where could we learn more about the relaunch of the Weekly Beat?" Walter Carl asks.

"This Wednesday, there will be a special free edition distributed in all four of our neighborhoods. Our website, thenewweeklybeat.com, goes online tomorrow and will feature the free edition. Subscription information can be learned on the web or by calling 1-800-the-beat. Like us on Facebook and follow us on Twitter," Theodore says.

"Thanks for being our guest today. Please come back and fill us in on the relaunch's progress. We wish you well. Stay tuned, folks, there is much more to come on State of the State This Week," Walter Carl says as he leads into commercial.

"It's like he almost knew what she was going to say. Amazing!" Gene says.

"Oh, honey, I think we should subscribe to Teddy's newspaper," Sandy says.

"We already do, and whose side are you on, anyway?"

"I'm on your side, but Teddy put Joan Mowrey in her place. I'm glad. She's a bitch. Did you see the shoes she is wearing? Who dresses that woman for television?"

"I hope all the voters are as bright as you and focused on her shoes instead of what Teddy was saying," Gene says.

"I know. Those cheap shoes with that expensive dress, it's like wearing flip-flops with a prom gown."

CHAPTER 16

The annual spring carnival has come to Gatesville, and the nice weather brings everybody out, even politicians. Gene Douglas is spending the late afternoon getting ready. He has been selected to be this year's carnival grand marshal. He is looking forward to being paraded around the fairgrounds in a shiny convertible, welcoming the crowd and using the ceremonial key to open the Gatesville Fairgrounds gate for eager carnival-goers. It's a happy occasion. There will be games, food, and rides for all to enjoy. He is looking forward to the softball fluff-piece press questions that are easy to answer cheerily and make his candidacy appealing to the carnival crowd. He is rehearsing the scripted answers in the mirror while he is shaving. His cell phone rings.

"What's up, Russ?"

"Gene, did you happen to get a chance to look at your buddy's article in the *Weekly Beat*?" Russ Dewitt asks.

"No, not yet. Nobody reads that paper."

"Do you have me on speaker?"

"Yes, only because I am shaving. Why, what's going on?"

"I have a feeling that I will get an unpleasant phone call from Ray or Mort Whitney very soon. You will probably be getting one from Dick Ratzinger. If you don't, make sure he reads tonight's *Weekly Beat* in the limousine before you guys get to the Gatesville carnival."

"You sound worried. Is it really that bad? What harm can an article in that little paper do? Teddy's article will be collecting bird shit and sunflower seed shells in the bottom of birdcages tomorrow. Nobody will put any stock into what he wrote."

"I hope you're right. Read it for yourself."

"Okay, I will. You worry too much."

"See for yourself. I will see you Monday morning. Have a good weekend."

Gene finishes shaving and goes to the parlor to read the paper. He picks up the *Weekly Beat* and sees the article that Russ was referring to on the editorial page.

A Look inside the Sausage Factory May Prove More Appealing

by Theodore Graham

It seems everyone else in our local media is covering the governor's race. That's boring to me. Neither candidate is doing anything exciting. Eugene Douglas will be opening the Gatesville carnival gates to the public this weekend, and Sherman Jones is hosting a golf tournament with local celebrities to raise funds for his campaign. They are hardly earth-shattering news events that will influence the elections or move the polling numbers. I find it fruitless to ask hypothetical questions and create what-if scenarios in order to report on news that isn't really happening. I will leave that to professional journalists at the bigger newspapers. I want to report on news that is actually happening.

The state legislature has one month of session left until they break for the summer, so I wanted to see what our state representatives and senators will be working on until they go on vacation. There is, of course, the budget bill. After a long slugfest along party lines, it is set to pass as a deficit budget in both chambers of Congress, and the governor is expected to sign it. There are a couple of bridges, parks, and memorial areas to get named after local folks of notoriety as a tribute to their good deeds. These won't be heated issues. There is the bill to update the schedule for the next fiscal year's legislative sessions. Nothing exciting there, only that the legislature will get an extra week of summer vacation and will leave a week earlier for the Christmas or winter holiday break. The one item I did find interesting is the Capitalist Ventures Protection Act.

I never heard mention of this bill. It wasn't on television news. I didn't read it in any of my local papers, but the Harmon *and* Gatesville *papers are owned by the same parent company and are nearly carbon copies of each other. The only difference in the two is whom their sports editorial writers are cheering for in the big games. The* Capital Beat *made no mention of it, but the Capitalist Venture Protection Act is in the public-and-media-scrutiny phase of the legislative process. It seemed that nobody looked into it. I think somebody would have on the basis of its title alone. Whom do capitalist ventures need protection from? Copies of the bill are open to public scrutiny, but they have to be viewed under supervision at the chamber library. I spent the earlier part of the week in the capitol building reading this document.*

Apparently, capitalist ventures are under attack from the public that the state government is tasked with protecting. There is a nice preamble to the bill that touts business interests that can bring jobs to our state but may balk at the opportunity because of government overreach and stringent regulations that deter entrepreneurs from conducting business in the state. The preamble to the bill actually reads like a politician's campaign rhetoric. It talks about creating jobs and bringing prosperity to the struggling state. However, it's the other paragraphs of the bill that raised my concern, but that's what I get for looking into how laws are made. Maybe some other people need to be grossed out too.

After the preamble, the Capitalist Ventures Protection Act reads like an all-encompassing permission slip for big business operations that use natural resources from both public and private land. The bill gives companies creating fifty or more jobs a five-year income tax freedom. The bill fast-tracks the permitting process and shortens the oversight period from governing bodies from 150 days to 30 days. Companies only have to make general disclosures of their activities and their intended uses of natural resources. Public scrutiny of these disclosures is only available with the written consent of the business conducting the operations, and all legal battles and litigation are guaranteed to be sealed in order to avoid being covered under public right-to-know laws. What I found most disturbing about this act was the total shift of liability from businesses to agencies and offices that grant permits.

Having a law degree and having some experience with the language of lobbyists, I will try to put into layman's terms what this bill means to the people of our state if it passes. The big news companies like to propose hypothetical situations, so I will do the same with my explanation.

Say that XYZ corporation comes to the state and they want to extract something from the ground. Under the current law, the EPA, the State Mining Commission, and the Water Mineral and Gas Extraction Commission would have ninety days to review the proposals and detailed reports of the extraction methods and all materials used in the process. All the governing bodies and public right-to-know laws grant an additional thirty days to ask questions and get more precise details on the propos-

als. *There is then an additional thirty days of review before any permits are granted.*

The state budget that is set to pass eliminates the State Mining Commission and Water Mineral and Gas Extraction Commission by defunding them. The EPA budget is cut by two-thirds. So under the new law, if the Capitalist Ventures Protection Act passes, the EPA, which has by then been cut by two-thirds, will have only thirty days to review general proposals and ask follow-up questions. Any further details released are at the discretion of the filing company. If the EPA does a fast-tracked review of a generalized proposal and grants a permit to the business to start their operation, the liability of any damages, hazards, or disasters caused by the company falls on the EPA or any other body issuing operating permits.

This means if the company spills a truckload of methyl-ethyl-harmful-bad-stuff on their work sites, they are not liable for its cleanup or the damages the spill causes. Instead, the liability and cost falls on the EPA and any other state or municipal body that grants a permit. That means the state and townships will be on the hook financially for any cleanups, investigations, and pending litigation. The company will also have the right to file lawsuits against any permitting body for lost profits incurred during investigations and environmental cleanup efforts. Plus, they're not paying income tax for the first five years of operation. It's a win-win for business. It's a dangerous slope for a state that is operating with a deficit budget and municipalities that are nearly bankrupt and having difficulty maintaining basic function of local government. Something seems off with this bill.

I decided to go right to the source of this bill and ask the senators that sponsored it. Democratic Senator Mark Maki answered my phone call straightaway. He touted the bill and said it would allow companies interested in conducting business in our state to be able to start operations quickly and efficiently while delivering much-needed jobs to our people. He basically highlighted the preamble of the bill. He seemed quite proud to tell me that the bill passed unanimously in committee and in test votes. It was likely to pass with a large majority. I asked him about the section on liability being placed on the government agencies that issue the permits. He told me he had to get back to me because he didn't have a chance to read the whole bill, the bill that he proudly sponsors.

I called Republican Senator Harry Flench. He also bragged about the bipartisan committee that supported the legislation and gave me the preamble summary to the pending legislation that is set to pass. When I asked him about the state agencies and municipal bodies absorbing all liabilities after the thirty-day reviewing period and permit granting, he told me he didn't read the whole bill. I asked him how he didn't know the details of a bill he was sponsoring, and he told me that a lobbyist company wrote the legislation and that he only had the chance to read the summary, which was the preamble of the bill.

I began to call some of the other thirteen senators on the bipartisan committee that passed the bill unanimously in test votes. The ones that returned my calls told me that they hadn't yet read the entire bill. So all these elected officials are excited about passing this bill in the last month before summer break but none that I spoke to read the whole thing or understood the details. This bill can become costly to taxpayers if they are going to be on the hook for the cost of government agencies that are assuming the liabilities of companies that have the potential to damage our land, water, and air. Taxes will go toward paying for cleanups, legal fees, studies, testing, and investigations. If those things interfere with business, the taxpayers will also have to cover the legal fees and lost profits of those companies losing money. That can get expensive. Townships will have to raise taxes just to cover their liabilities, and they won't even have enough left over to cover the cost of weekly trash pickups.

Being a legal mind, I decided to do a little research on the Capitalist Ventures Protection Act to see if there was any legal precedent set by similar legislation. What I did find in my research was that there are similar bills set to pass before the summer session in four other states. Some of the bills even have the same name. In one state, the exact same bill is called the Entrepreneurial Rights Act, and in another, it is called the Freedom of Capitalism Act. I also learned that these bills were penned for legislators in all five states by MRS Consultants. MRS stands for Mendelson, Ratzinger, and Smith. Ratzinger sounds familiar because Dick Ratzinger is who took my place as campaign manager for the Eugene Douglas for Governor campaign. I can't confirm the two are related. What I can confirm is that MW Investing and Developing company paid MRS Consultants three million dollars to pen this legislation and get it passed in all five states. MW stands for Morton Whitney, a multibillionaire investor in timber, petroleum, natural gas, mining, and plastics industries. He would definitely have an interest in doing business in all five of these states. He would also be very interested in not being liable for costs his operations do to the environment on private and public lands.

The Weekly Beat *is only a small newspaper with limited resources, but with only minor research and a few phone calls, I learned that our state and four other states may vote to give public protection away to private industry because elected officials failed to read proposed legislation. My paper is the only one covering this story, so I don't expect it to get much attention or public discourse. The larger media sources won't be looking either, though they have more resources to connect the dots of this story. They will speculate on how much Gene Douglas will improve his polling numbers with working-class voters based on how many fried Twinkies he consumes at the Gatesville Spring Carnival this evening. They will speculate on how far Sherman Jones can increase his lead by how much money he raises at his celebrity golf tournament. This was just my whim. I wanted to know more about how laws are made. I think I would have gagged less at the sausage factory.*

Gene throws the paper on the coffee table in front of him. "Nice try, Teddy, but nobody reads your shitty paper," he says to himself and returns to dressing for the day.

* * *

Gene is all smiles at the carnival parade as he waves to the crowd from the back of a classic convertible car. The crowd cheers him on as he waves his oversize gold key to the fairgrounds gate. At the gate, he welcomes the people to the carnival and opens it. The crowd rushes in to ride the rides, eat the fried foods, and play the games of chance. Gene steps over to the press area to comment on the event.

"It's a beautiful night and another great spring carnival here in Gatesville. The winter doldrums are behind us, and now friends and families can enjoy a night of fun. Next year, when I come to this carnival, I hope to be the governor of our great state," Gene says as he smiles for flashing cameras and local reporters.

"Mr. Douglas, I'm Grace Downwood of Channel 6 News. What are your thoughts on the Capitalist Ventures Protection Act?"

"Tonight is Gatesville's night, it's about fun," Gene responds.

"Is it true that your super PAC trustee is Ray Whitney, son of Mort Whitney, the billionaire who is paying lobbyists to get unfair legislation passed in our state?"

"Is your campaign manager related to the Ratzinger of MRS Consultants?"

"I'm not here to talk about a tiny article in a glorified grocery store paper. I'm here to have funnel cakes and maybe ride the tilt-a-whirl and bumper cars a few times," Gene answers.

"If the Capitalist Ventures Protection Act passes and you are elected governor, would you move to repeal it in order to protect taxpayers and municipalities that are struggling financially?"

Dick Ratzinger steps in front of Gene and moves him away from the microphone. "The Douglas campaign is here for the citizens of Gatesville tonight. We will take the inquiries of the press into consideration and issue a statement when we have more information."

Gene gets escorted through the crowd with Dick Ratzinger to the limousine by his security detail. Security gets both men in the back of the car and clears a path for the limousine to exit. Dick Ratzinger is furious with Gene.

"You know about this editorial in the *Weekly Beat* and didn't tell me," Dick says.

"I didn't think the press would be so familiar with the story already."

"They obviously are. We want to be on the offensive with the media and not the defensive. Your buddy Mr. Graham made sure he changed that. I will call essential campaign staff. We have to have an emergency meeting and draft a statement."

"Russ Dewitt told me about the article. I read it, but I didn't think it was that important. Do we really need to have a meeting about this?"

Dick Ratzinger holds up his iPad and shows Gene the video of them being escorted to the limousine from the press area at the carnival. The video shows the limousine leaving and cuts to video of Democratic gubernatorial candidate Sherman Jones making a statement to the press.

"Obviously, the editorial in the Weekly Beat raises a lot of questions. This small independent media source should be commended for bringing these questions into public light. The biggest concern is making sure that our legislators read and understand the entire legislation before taking a vote on it. I encourage legislators in our brother and sister states to do the same to protect the people from private companies that may not have their best interests at heart. I hope the Eugene Douglas campaign feels the same, though he may have some of the Whitney funding tied to their super PAC and campaign. My campaign staff will send a team first thing Monday morning to review the Capitalist Ventures Protection Act to ensure that the voters of this state are being protected from poor legislative practices."

"Mort Whitney just sent me a text. He will be at campaign headquarters around two o'clock in the morning. He obviously heard the news and is not happy," Dick says.

"I can't believe Teddy would write something like that."

Dick holds up his iPad again. "Believe it, and believe your friend's article will be talked about on CNN tomorrow. This involves five states that Mort invested heavily in."

CHAPTER 17

The conference room at the Douglas campaign headquarters begins to fill with staffers shortly after midnight. They are ready to do damage control. Tension can be felt in the room. Liquor breath and freshly brewed coffee can be smelled in air as well.

"If we craft the right statement to the press, this can blow over until the next polling period. We really don't start going head-to-head with Sherman Jones until after the next polling cycle," Gene says.

Tim Collins raises his head from his laptop. "Technically, you are right, but now we have to worry about independent polling. Each of the three local television networks have viewer polls on their websites that were posted just after midnight. My friend at Regent Marketing called to let me know they would be conducting a polling survey starting Monday morning after the early news cycle."

"Who is conducting that poll?"

"He couldn't say. That's client confidentiality. He can't risk his job."

Sidney Hughes enters the conference room with a phone log-book and legal pad in his hand. "The media office is having quite a busy night. I've received calls from every local news outlet. All of them want your official statement to be their exclusive. I also got a call from Governor Harmon's office. They aren't happy. They are pulling an all-nighter at the capital, making copies of the Capitalist Ventures Protection Act, because of overwhelming media request to scrutinize the bill. They will now be open to the public tomorrow morning. Marty, I suggest you take somebody with you and go out and get a look at the bill."

"Right. I'll take Kevin Baker with me first thing in the morning."

"Kevin Baker decided that he doesn't want the Young Republicans wrapped up in this. He resigned from the campaign. Take Russ with you," Gene says.

"I called you and warned you about Teddy's article before the carnival. Your buddy caused this mess, I'm not spending a Saturday fixing it," Russ says.

"If you want to keep your job on this campaign, you will go with Marty," Gene says.

Sidney Hughes slams a book on the table. "We can't come apart now. We have to come up with a press statement for tomorrow morning. The campaign obviously has to come out against the Capitalist Ventures Protection Act and has to downplay our ties to Whitney money, MRS Consultants, and any legislator that sponsors the bill. We will have to spin it so Gene Douglas appears to be the candidate that will stop this type of legislation from passing."

"This campaign will do what Mort Whitney tells you to do. He is on his way now," Dick Ratzinger says.

Morton Whitney arrives with his son, Ray. They enter the conference room, and the focus of everyone goes to them.

"Good morning, Mort. I'm sorry you had—" Gene says before Mort cuts him off.

"You're a retard. Shut the fuck up. It's because of your stupid friend that I am here in the middle of the night. I want all electronics, recording devices, cell phones, and internet doodads out of this room before I say another word."

"Ray shouldn't be here. The super PAC isn't allowed to communicate directly with the campaign, only with the liaison. If the media sees him here, we're in violation," Russ says.

"Ray shouldn't blah blah waaa. Ray will be wherever the fuck I tell him to be. If the media sees him here, you will go on the news and tell them you are coming out of the closet and want to have dirty-ass sex with him. They'll believe that, Mr. Dipshit."

"My name is Mr. Dewitt, and I am not gay."

"With a name like that and those cocksucking lips, nobody would believe you. Now shut the fuck up."

Gene comes back into the conference room. "All the electronics are out of the room. Now we can figure this out."

"I already figured it out. You're just going to shut up and listen. This little stunt could cost me billions. We are going to turn this whole thing back on Theodore Graham and the piece-of-shit newspaper he is working for. I already have calls to Senator Maki and Senator Flench. They are going to play along. You are going to make this statement to the press tomorrow," Morton says and slides a piece of paper across the table.

Gene looks over the paper. "Are you sure this will work? It seems like it leaves a lot of questions unanswered."

"Were you born stupid, or do you just have a monthly subscription? Unanswered questions will keep the media occupied asking them. This buys time for my lobbyists to redraft new legislation. Thanks to your friend, the legislation I wanted to pass won't pass before the summer session. Hopefully, we can get it to squeak through in the fall. Your job is to scare the people back onto your side."

"Will the new legislation be better for the people?"

"The new legislation will be better for me. If it's better for me, it's better for you. I'm not in it for the people, and I am investing a lot of money in you to fool the people into believing that you're for the people. I'm beginning to regret putting my money behind you and not Sherman Jones. I wouldn't be dealing with this shit if I went with him."

"What if Teddy writes other things that make us look bad?"

"You worry about making your press statement. Make sure you sound convincing. We'll figure out how to deal with Mr. Graham later. Ratzinger, a lot of this is on you. You should have been paying attention, but you let this slip under your radar. You make sure this dumbass delivers the press statement perfectly."

"Yes, Mr. Whitney."

"I called Gene when the article came out and warned him that it would be trouble," Russ says.

"Well, laddy-fucking-dah, Mr. Dickspit. It's three in the morning, and where the fuck am I? I am correcting problems because the warning that you gave was ineffective. I don't give pats on the back or reward brownnosers by letting them keep their booger lockers in my asshole a little longer when they don't get the job done. Grow a set and get the job done. Now if you whistle-dicks will excuse me, I have damage control to do in four other states. Come on, Ray. Hopefully, I can blame some of this on my retarded son," Mort says and leaves with his son.

The Douglas campaign staff prepares Gene for the morning press conference. They spend the night making sure the speech is flawless and his delivery is perfect. Dick Ratzinger reminds him to make his statement and not to take questions from the press.

*   *   *

Paul Hoptak is sitting in his office at the *Weekly Beat*. He sees Theodore coming up from the printing room. As he is walking by his office window, he taps on the window and motions for Theodore to come inside.

"Good morning, Paul. You look exceptionally bald and fat this morning, but you are smiling."

"You're pretty baked this morning. Should I institute an employee drug policy?"

"You wouldn't if you want me to continue to work here."

"I would be a fool to have you pee in a cup. Three days into the relaunch of my newspaper, you already have national attention. CNN is reporting on the crooked lobbyist legislation across five states. I have nearly every paper in the state offering to pay me to reprint your editorial in their Monday editions alongside their follow-up articles to the story you broke. The state assembly library building is open on a Saturday morning, and reporters are lined up to have an hour with one of the two hundred copies of the Capitalist Ventures Protection Act. I have calls from papers and television stations in other states offering to pay us if we forward your notes and resources to them. The circulation office doesn't open until eight o'clock, but every time I walked by there this morning, I heard the phone ringing. That's good news for me. I don't feel bad about being this bald and fat if you keep making me smile like this."

"Glad I can help, boss. You have a nice smile."

"You were down in the print room early. Do you have an article going in the Sunday edition?" Paul asks.

"Yes. I was just down there making sure they leave me some space. I will get it to them this afternoon."

"Anything good?"

"Just a fluff piece about one of our carriers having his bike stolen."

"Which carrier?"

"My old carrier from Douglas Hills, Kenny McMacy."

"He's been delivering for us for a long time. Does he use his bike to deliver papers? Should I buy him a new bike?"

"You already did. You can read about it in tomorrow's paper," Theodore says.

"When was it stolen?"

"Sometime last night. Kenny was late picking up his bundle of papers this morning because his bike was stolen. I got him a ride and helped him deliver his papers. After that, we stopped by the Douglas Youth College security office to see if there was anything on their video surveillance, but we didn't see anything, so I decided to write the piece for tomorrow's paper."

"It should be an interesting read. You aren't required to write fluff pieces, though."

"I know, but I felt compelled, and I didn't think you would mind."

Paul flips on the television in his office. "I said you could write what you want. Hey, you want to stick around? Your buddy Gene Douglas is about to make his statement to the press about your editorial."

"This should be interesting," Theodore says and turns his focus to television.

"I'm Grace Downwood of Channel 6 News, reporting from the Eugene Douglas for Governor headquarters in Douglas Hills. The gubernatorial candidate is expected to make a statement about the Capitalist

Ventures Protection Act that was exposed as being a questionable piece of legislation. It was exposed by his former campaign manager, Theodore Graham, who now works for the Weekly Beat. Mr. Douglas is coming to the podium now. Let's listen."

"It's unfortunate that I have to be here this morning to make this statement. An editorial written by Theodore Graham, the campaign manager that I was forced to terminate because of his lack of experience, has caused this media frenzy. I see that his lack of experience as a journalist is going to be problematic for my campaign as well. Since my opponent in this gubernatorial race issued an official statement on this attempted political smear from the failing Weekly Beat, the media expects me to make a statement also. The Douglas campaign is no way in favor of legislation that hurts the taxpayers, municipalities, and voters of our state. I spoke early this morning with the none-too-happy sponsors of the Capitalists Ventures Act, Senator Mark Maki and Senator Harry Flench. Both Senators are unhappy with Mr. Graham and the Weekly Beat. They have prepared amendments to this incomplete bill that fix the issues of the false controversy that was created by Mr. Graham and his newspaper. Those amendments were to be presented during debate in a future legislative session. Mr. Graham failed to report that fact. Thanks to the Weekly Beat and Mr. Graham, that bill won't pass before the summer recess and it will further delay jobs being created in our state.

"My campaign is in favor of creating jobs. Morton Whitney is a job creator, not only in our state, but in others as well. It's no coincidence that Morton Whitney supports my campaign. He wants a governor that is in favor of creating jobs with him. His son, Ray, chairs a super PAC that wants to put the right resources behind a candidate that wants to create good-paying jobs for the hardworking people. That candidate is me. If my opponent wants to believe a false editorial from a failing four-day newspaper, written by a former employee of mine, that's his choice. My choice is to find ways to provide good-paying jobs for the people that I want to serve. I only hope this editorial doesn't stop the half-million jobs that could be created in the next four years in five states. Thank you for coming out this morning," Gene concludes his speech.

Sidney Hughes can be seen escorting Gene away from the crowd as the press continues to shout questions. Dick Ratzinger steps to the podium.

"Candidate Douglas will take no further questions. The campaign feels there is no need to comment further on this irrelevant story, and he wants to return to strengthening his platform as a job creator for the citizens of our state. Thank you."

Paul shuts off the television. "How could you do this to my paper? What the fuck were you thinking when you wrote that piece?"

"What? You were the one that approved it. Of course they're going to attack me and the paper."

"I'm just fucking with you. There is no such thing as bad publicity. I'm going to keep the circulation office open until five today even if I have to work the phones myself. This is going to sell a shit-load of subscriptions!"

"I thought you were really mad."

"I can't be mad. This is the best day this paper has seen in years. Obviously, Gene Douglas didn't read this morning's paper either."

"I didn't write anything for today's issue."

"You didn't, but *State of the State This Week* now advertises their Sunday show and their guests on the front page of the Saturday edition. You're on the show tomorrow, and I'm sure they aren't just going to talk to you about the weather."

"Oh, shit, I forgot. I better get tomorrow's editorial written and then prepare for that shit storm."

"I'm sure it will be entertaining television. Make sure you mention our little paper."

"I'm sure some of the guests will be mentioning our little paper, but maybe not in such a flattering light," Theodore says as he leaves Paul's office.

Chapter 18

Gene is about to enjoy his Sunday ritual reading the newspapers and enjoying a late-morning cup of coffee by the pool. He is still a little tired from his all-night campaign meeting and early-morning press conference on Saturday. He wants to make the most of his relaxation time before he is too busy with the campaign. From the pile of papers, he chooses the *Weekly Beat* over the *Gatesville Courier* and the *Harmon Herald*. He flips to the editorial page and finds Theodore's article.

Our Boy Kenny and His Bike
by Theodore Graham

The presses stopped after the early Saturday-morning print. The printers were sweeping up the shop and prepping the machines so they were ready for the Sunday edition. The delivery vans were returning from their drop-offs, but there was still a bundle of 150 papers sitting on the loading dock. The distribution dispatcher stood angrily by them, waiting to scold the late carrier.

"You're really late picking these up. We're going to get a lot of angry phone calls from your customers if they aren't on their doorsteps by 7:00 a.m.," he said to the young man arriving on the loading dock.

"I'm sorry I'm late. My bike was stolen last night. I'll get them delivered as soon as I can," the young man said.

That voice was familiar. It was Kenny, my old paperboy from Douglas Hills. All the time I lived there, this boy was never late. He's been a paperboy for the Weekly Beat *since he was twelve years old. Now at the age of seventeen, he is readying himself for college in the fall. He was awarded an athletic scholarship to play baseball at the state university. He was also offered a scholastic scholarship to another out-of-state school but chose to stay closer to home and lessen travel expenses back and forth for him and his widowed mother. This wasn't some ordinary teenager acting irresponsibly. His work record and his academic record show that this young man is dependable and motivated. There was no reason to doubt his bike was stolen. There was no reason to scold this young man. His morning was already started off on the wrong foot. I didn't want to see this kid's day get worse.*

I yelled to the distribution dispatcher, "Grab one of the vans! We'll help Kenny get his papers delivered on time."

The distribution dispatcher gave me a look like he didn't think I was serious, but once he saw my face, he knew I wasn't kidding and grabbed the keys to a van. Kenny loaded his bundle of papers in the van, and the three of us headed to Douglas Hills to cover his route. We worked together as a team and got all the papers delivered, and 11 of the 150 papers were delivered after the 7:00 a.m. time goal. Not too bad. The three of us worked well together, and it was kind of fun, but what was going to happen with Kenny's route for Sunday's delivery? He still didn't have his bike.

Before we dropped Kenny off at home, we stopped by the Douglas Hills Police Department and reported his bike missing. The friendly desk sergeant told us that there had been a rash of stolen bicycles and there had been a dozen reports last week. Kenny lives at the west end of Douglas Hills, just off the Douglas Youth Honors College campus. If his bike was stolen from his back porch, either the thief fled through the woods behind his house or took off through campus. The woods back there are very swampy and would be difficult to navigate in the dark, so it made more sense for the thief to take off across campus. We stopped by the campus security office. Campus security agreed to let us review some of the surveillance video around campus during the night, but there wasn't much activity on campus. On the tapes, we saw a few late-night dog walkers, a few drunks crossing the campus as they were heading back to Harmon, and Ray and Morton Whitney coming out of the Douglas campaign headquarters and getting into their limousine shortly after 3:00 a.m. We weren't concerned with an early-morning or late-night campaign meeting, and we weren't concerned with a super PAC trustee violating campaign finance laws by communicating directly with a candidate. We wanted to find Kenny's bike so he could make his Sunday deliveries on time. We had no luck, but we thanked security for their help. They were very professional and accommodating. I felt terrible for Kenny when we dropped him off at baseball practice. I told him I would pick him up after lunch and we would get him a new bike. With his five years of dedicated and dependable service to the Weekly Beat, *it was only right that we help Kenny continue to serve our subscribers. A new bike was needed, but I knew how much that old bike meant to him.*

The bike was not only a means for Kenny to make his deliveries and earn money; it had senti-

mental value. He won that bike at a father-and-son fishing derby at the Gatesville Dam when he was eleven years old. A few short weeks after that derby, Kenny lost his father to a sudden heart attack. His father's passing left him and his mother to fend for themselves. His mother, Angela, works three jobs to pay for their Douglas Hills home and keep them afloat. Angela works as the housekeeping and laundry manager at the country club. She is a waitress at the Route 12 Diner and works the night shift doing housekeeping at Sunny Acres Retirement Community. Even with three jobs, she couldn't afford to have him attend the Douglas Youth Honors College, but she didn't want to take Kenny out of the Harmon School District since he was doing so well there and it is one of the better-performing public schools. For some, a bike is just a bike, but for Kenny, that bike is his livelihood.

Thursday and Friday afternoons, Kenny pedals his bike from school to the Weekly Beat *loading dock and picks up his papers. From there he pedals his bike to Douglas Hills and does his deliveries, making sure all the papers are delivered by 5:00 p.m. From there he pedals back to the school for baseball practice, and after practice, he is a math and science tutor for struggling students. After tutoring, he pedals home to concentrate on his own studies. On Saturday and Sunday mornings, he is at the paper's loading dock at 5:15 a.m. sharp. He picks up his papers and pedals his bike through his route and then to the school for baseball practice. From practice, he pedals to the country club and picks up some caddy work at the golf course or buses tables in the clubhouse for some extra cash. He is saving for the expensive college years ahead of him. Kenny isn't a lazy kid that is afraid of hard work. Without that bike, he would struggle that much harder, but knowing him, I doubt he would give up. That bike carries that boy everywhere he needs to be so he can be the respectable man that he is becoming.*

The Weekly Beat *is a small paper serving small towns. It's only suiting that we celebrate the good people that live in our communities. Kenny is one of the many small-town heroes that we should celebrate. He is one of the good people that I have the good fortune of knowing. He has a bright future ahead of him. I find it only right to make people aware of his hard work and determination to do well. I know there are others like him. Kenny's story, his stolen bike, and our adventures of yesterday have inspired me to hopefully be able to write about other talented and dedicated people. I would like to make a regular Sunday feature in the* Weekly Beat *highlighting other good friends and neighbors. If my readers know of others like Kenny and would like to see their story told, please contact us so we can showcase the people that make our communities great. As for the bike thieves, knock it off and consider a path of hard work like our boy Kenny.*

Gene slams the paper down on the coffee table in front of him. "That dirty son of a bitch had to find a way to get a dig in! Unbelievable!"

Sandy is sunbathing by the pool. "Why do you read his paper if it's going to upset you so much? You like to relax on Sundays. Why do you irritate yourself like that?"

"I just wanted to see what he is up to. He wrote a fluff piece about the paperboy having his bike stolen. Nobody is going to read it, but he had to make mention of our late-night campaign meeting that his last article initiated."

"You didn't think anybody was going to read his last article, but look what happened. They probably won't read a fluff piece, though. Maybe he will talk about it on that local Sunday show this morning."

"He was on *State of the State This Week* last Sunday. He's not going to be on again."

"It was on the front page of his paper yesterday that he was going to be on the show today. Maybe I read it wrong."

Gene picks his copy of the *Weekly Beat* and sees the advertisement. "Oh, for fuck's sake! Why is he on again? Why do they put him on that show?"

"Is he going to be on today?"

"Yes, but I have no idea why."

Sandy gets off her sunbathing chair and wraps a towel around herself. "He probably gets the show good ratings. He is an interesting guest. He's a good-looking guy, and people relate to him."

"Since when did you become so in favor of Teddy?"

"I miss having him around."

"If he were still hanging around, you would be telling me to get rid of him. I don't understand you."

"Do you think he'll come over for dinner tonight if we invite him? I'm sure Ernie would skip eating on campus to see Teddy."

"No, dammit, we're not having the guy that's trying to ruin me over for dinner!"

"You're the one that fired him. Don't yell at me. Can we at least watch him on television?"

"I pretty much have to watch so I can see how much damage control I have to do tomorrow."

"*Good Sunday morning to you. I'm Walter Carl, host of State of the State This Week. This week I welcome my guests, political analyst Brad Utes; senior political correspondent of the Capital Register, Jimmy Jenner; and managing editor of the newly relaunched the Weekly Beat, Theodore Graham. Welcome to our show.*

"*Good morning, fellows, and welcome to the show. The big topic coming in this weekend was the story from the Weekly Beat that shed some light on the Capitalist Ventures Protection Bill that was scheduled to pass in the state assembly before the summer recess. It looks like that bill will not pass because of one of our guests today. Theodore Graham wrote the article, and it caused quite a stir, not just in our state, but also in four other states that had similar pending legislation. What's going on here, Mr. Graham?"*

"Well, all the other papers and news outlets are covering the governor's race, but there isn't much going on there. There was no primary race and no major events or announcements by the candidates. I'm sure the staff of Sherman Jones and Gene Douglas are getting their candidates ready for the general election push from August until November. There is no real news in the race, just a lot of media speculation on the polling numbers. There is, however, a lot going on in the state assembly. I went to the capital with the hopes of writing an article about the deficit budget that was set to pass, but I saw the Capitalist Ventures Protection Act was coming up for a vote. I'd never heard of the bill, so I took advantage of the public-scrutiny period and read it. What I found was very disturbing. The preamble of the bill talked about creating jobs and prosperity for the state, but after the preamble, it went into detail of how the permitting bodies of state and local governments will assume all the liability of companies in the event of environmental hazards, chemical spills, and contaminated natural lands or resources. It's almost criminal how this bill was written."

"One of the biggest problems that you cited in your article is that the senators sponsoring this bill didn't read it. Is that right?"

"I think it's pretty important that the senators read the bills that they are sponsoring. There was even a test vote on the bill conducted, and it was set to pass by a large margin. I talked to the sponsors of the bill. They touted the preamble but knew nothing else about the bill they were proud of."

"In reality, Mr. Graham, your editorial was an exercise in poor journalism. You failed to mention that Senator Maki and Senator Flench were set to offer amendments to the bill before the vote," panelist Jimmy Jenner says.

"Well, Jimmy, both senators had every opportunity to mention the amendments to the bill when I interviewed them. They were both happy to go on the record to praise the bill they were sponsoring. When I asked them questions about the details of the bill, that would have been the per-

fect opportunity for them to tell me they had amendments to fix the discrepancies. Instead, both Senators Maki and Flench told me they didn't read it and that a lobbyist group penned it. My notes and conversations with the senators reflect the truth in what I reported. You're welcome to contact the Weekly Beat and do a follow-up article using my research."

"The only reason you wrote that article was to smear your former boss, gubernatorial candidate Gene Douglas," Jimmy Jenner retorts.

"The reason I wrote the article was to expose a bill that had the potential to hurt our state, municipalities, and taxpayers. Maybe you didn't read my article or your reading comprehension skills are poor, but the article wasn't about the governor's race at all. It's not my fault that the other media outlets chased down both candidates for a statement as soon as the article came out. Neither candidate had anything to do with writing or passing the legislation. I would hope that both candidates would come out against poor legislation. That should be common sense. I didn't expect either candidate to have to answer for something they had nothing to do with. How come your paper didn't go after the senators for a statement? Your paper is right there in the capital. How come the Capital Register didn't write anything about the Capitalist Ventures Protection Act? Your paper didn't even write about the deficit budget that's supposed to pass. I read your article this week about the sandwiches and beer that each candidate is most likely to eat in each county on the campaign trail. I can see why you are the senior political correspondent for your paper. You tackle the tough issues."

"I guess it's just convenient that you tied the lobbyist group and the holding company that paid the lobbyists to write the bill to your former boss. Even your fluff piece about the stolen bicycle this morning made mention of the Whitneys leaving the Douglas campaign headquarters at three on Saturday morning."

"I didn't connect the Whitney and MRS Consultants dots to the Douglas campaign, but obviously, you did. My article this morning was about finding one of our carrier's stolen bike. We saw Mort and Ray Whitney on the security cameras coming out of the campaign headquarters. We were looking for a stolen bicycle. If you are interested in why the Whitneys were there, maybe you could do some investigative journalism. Maybe you can find out why a super PAC trustee is meeting directly with *a candidate at 3:00 a.m. Maybe you can find out why the guy who hired MRS Consultants to write the Capitalist Venture Act was attending that meeting. You insult my paper for not being good journalism, but why aren't you looking into these stories? You're the big-newspaper guy. Do your job, or are you busy writing articles about which pizza topping the candidates would prefer?"*

"We have some heated discussion on State of the State This Week, but it is time for us to take a break. We will return with more from our guests when we come back," host Walter Carl says and leads into a commercial break.

"Teddy looks really good in that suit. That red tie makes him look powerful," Sandy says.

"I don't care how Teddy looks! Did you hear what he was saying? He's not making me look good in the eyes of my financial backers."

"Well, that Jimmy Jenner guy is being a jerk to Teddy. He's just standing up for himself."

"We're back with State of the State This Week. I'm Walter Carl, and my guests today are Jimmy Jenner of the Capitalist Register, Theodore Graham of the Weekly Beat, and political analyst Brad Utes. Welcome back. We haven't heard from Brad this morning. What have you got to say today?"

"Theodore and Jimmy brought up MRS Consultants. In some of the other states, there has been discussion over the weekend about investigating their dealings in state governments. Some elected officials are even moving to revisit legislation penned by them. Are they going to be carefully looked at in our state?" Brad Utes asks.

"That's up to our elected officials. Our state government has a Legislative Oversight Commission that's made up of lawyers that are tasked with investigating the legality and fairness of legislation. Where were they on the Capitalist Ventures Protection Act? They're also tasked with advising on the budget, but I haven't heard much from them. I did find in my initial budget research that MRS Consultants were hired to advise on the budget. I didn't understand why consultants were hired to advise on a deficit budget. It didn't make sense. That's why we have auditors," Theodore responds.

"That's a good point. We already have a commission of legal minds to advise on the budget. Why would the State pay outsiders to come in? I'm sure come Monday, the budget talks will be revisited. There's going to be a lot of unhappy voters when they learn there are possible cuts to education, public transportation, health and human services and increases in subsidies to companies like Morton Whitney's. Theodore, you may work for a small paper, but you uncovered a hot mess in our state. At least you got people thinking."

"Let's be realistic. Theodore Graham is a failed campaign manager that was hired by the Weekly Beat so he can sell papers to the conspiracy theorists and gossip hounds while taking jabs at the candidate that fired him. After the campaign, nobody will be interested in what he has to say," Jimmy Jenner says.

"Gentlemen, let's not make this morning's discussion personal," Walter Carl says.

"It's okay, Walter. Jimmy has a right to his opinion. He can accuse me of going after my former boss with the Weekly Beat. So far, I have written two stories, neither involving Gene Douglas. One was about poor legislation being sent through the state assembly by lobbyists, and the other was about one of our carriers having his bike stolen. I believe the Weekly Beat hired me for the same reasons that Gene Douglas hired me at his schools and publishing house. Gene hired me to improve his businesses. The Douglas Youth Honors College is the national scholastic debate champions, and the national GPA for the honors college is third in the nation. The Douglas Community College increased its enrollment by 43 percent, and the publishing house is not facing bankruptcy protection and is set to show a profit this year. Gene is a good friend of mine and hired me to do a good job for him. He hired me to do the same as a campaign manager. I did the best I could but was let go due to my lack of political experience. I accept that. My hope is that his new campaign strategy is still for upholding the values he hired me to bring to his family's business ventures. I believe Paul Hoptak of the Weekly Beat came to me because he saw an opportunity where Gene Douglas let one go. Mr. Jenner, you can bad-mouth me and my paper because you are upset that I raise political issues you ignored, or you can act like a senior political correspondent at a major capital city news organization and write jour-

nalistic pieces to inform the people. Your subscribers, or lack of subscribers, will let you know how well you're doing."

"And that brings us to our next break. We'll be back with more State of the State This Week after a few words from our sponsors."

Gene shuts off the television. "Sometimes I forget how much Teddy actually did for us, but then I see the shit storm he just made for me."

"He said nice things about you and called you his friend."

"His friendship is half of the problem," Gene says and goes to patio bar and pours himself a glass of scotch.

CHAPTER 19

The sound of breaking glass and the banging of a door from the alleyway three floors below wakes Theodore from his sound sleep. He smells smoke. Once full consciousness takes control of his mind, he jumps out of bed and runs to the window. He sees smoke rising from the smashed windows of his 1972 Buick Skylark. In an instant, an orange flash of light appears in the interior. Theodore grabs the fire extinguisher, exits the window, and climbs onto the fire escape. He makes his way to street level.

At the bottom of the fire escape, he notices a beat-up IROC-Z idling at the end of the alleyway with the trunk open. When he turns around, he sees the double doors to the press room are pried open. He drops the fire extinguisher and runs to the idling car and removes the keys from the ignition. He ignores his burning Buick and approaches the open doors. In the doorway, the crowbar used to pry the steel doors open rests on the stoop. Theodore picks it up.

The smell of kerosene is strong when he enters the building. He sees the silhouette of a man emptying a fuel can in the press operator's office. There are three full fuel cans by the entrance to the printing press room. Quietly he crosses the corridor and backs himself against the wall next to the doorway. When the intruder exits the office, Theodore swings the crowbar as hard as he can and smashes it against the back of the intruder and knocks him to the floor. Theodore quickly makes his way to the light switch and flips it on.

"Mr. Graham?" the man on the floor says, and Theodore stands over him with the crowbar.

"Cy Marino. What the fuck are you doing?"

Cy sits up. "I thought that looked like your Skylark out there. What are you doing here? I think you broke my back."

"I live upstairs. I work for the newspaper. Do you have a gun, and do you have a cell phone on you?"

Cy reaches in his jacket pocket and pulls out a cell phone. "Yeah, here's my phone. I left my gun on the front seat of the car."

"Dial 911 and report a vehicle fire at the *Weekly Beat* and have them send the police to pick up an arsonist."

"Dude, I'm not calling the cops on myself. I thought you were cool. I'm sorry about your car. If I had known it was yours, I would have left it alone."

"Do you want me to hit you with the crowbar again?" Theodore asks.

"No, man, you really hurt my back. Thank God my uncle is a chiropractor."

"Call 911, or I will you hit you again and call them myself."

Cy dials 911 and places his phone up to his ear. "Yeah, I like to report a car fire by the newspaper building." He looks up at Theodore. "What's the name of this place again?"

Theodore shakes his head. "It's the *Weekly Beat!*"

Cy returns to the call. "Yeah, it's the *Weekly Beat.*" He covers his phone so the operator can't hear him. "Do I have to tell them the arsonist part?"

Theodore takes the phone out of his hand. "This is Theodore Graham. There is a car fire outside the *Weekly Beat* building. Send the police too. I caught an arsonist. Yes. It was the guy you were talking to first. No, I'm not kidding. Thank you." Theodore ends the call and throws the cell phone back at Cy. "I can't believe you torched my car."

"I'm sorry, dude. You mind if I have a cigarette while we wait for the police?"

"Let's go outside. I don't think it's a smart idea to smoke with all the kerosene fumes in here."

"Good thinking," Cy says and can barely straighten his back as he stands.

"Don't get any bright ideas about trying to run, or I will hit you with the crowbar again. Besides, I took the keys out of your ignition and threw them down the storm drain."

"Why did you do that? Now I'm going to have to wake up my girlfriend and have her bring the spare key."

Theodore walks outside of the building with Cy. "Don't worry, I think the cops will give you a ride to wherever you need to go."

"Do you have a light, Mr. G?"

"Are you serious? I'm barefoot, wearing boxer shorts and a T-shirt. Where would I have a lighter? What kind of arsonist are you, anyway?"

"Yeah, I left my lighter on the front seat of the car next to my pistol."

"How did you light my car on fire?"

"Oh, that was easy. I just smashed the window with the crowbar and threw a lit road flare under the front seat."

"How were you going to light the building on fire?"

"Oh, shit. I guess I would have had to go back and get more flares out of my trunk."

"You're probably the dumbest criminal ever. Why would you light my car on fire outside and then go in the building to pour the kerosene? The fire outside would draw attention, and you would have been caught fleeing."

"You know, I never thought of that. Hey, you should help us plan these jobs. You're pretty smart. I knew you were smart when I took your class at the community college."

"Thanks, Cy. I thought you showed a lot of potential. I was kind of bummed when you dropped out. How come you dropped out?"

"When I was working the loading dock at the warehouse, while I was waiting for trucks, I would do my homework. The other guys would call me egghead and nerd and shit like that. I hated that. Hey, man, my back is sore from where you hit me. Would you mind going to my car and getting my lighter for me?"

"I don't have shoes on. I'm not doing that."

"Aw, man. Come on."

"Who put you up to this, anyway?"

"I don't know who. Some guy in a suit came by the shop. He gave Mario an envelope with five grand in it and said to burn this building down early Tuesday morning. This week is dragging. It feels like it should be Wednesday already. Don't you think?"

"I thought the week was going fast. Who was this guy in a suit?"

"I don't know who he was. Mario was supposed to do the job himself, but he has to take my niece to the orthodontist early this morning. She tried to bite the head off of one of her dolls and got a bunch of doll hair tangled in her braces."

"I'm pretty lucky it was you that did the job, then."

"Me too. I owe my bookie a shitload of money. Final four kicked my ass this year. I needed this job."

Theodore sees the police car pulling in front of the building and hears the sirens of the fire engine coming down the street. "Well, Cy, it was good seeing you again, and it was nice to catch up. It looks like your ride is here," Theodore says and pats Cy on the back. "Back here, Officer!"

"I can't believe you wouldn't let me go. Mario is going to be pissed," Cy says.

The police handcuff Cy and load him into the police car. Theodore watches as the firefighters extinguish his burning car. That Buick was the last brand-new thing his father owned. He remembers how proud he was of that vehicle when he brought it home from the showroom of the dealership. He remembers his father handing him the keys to it when he got his acceptance letter from Harvard. Never again would he rev the motor and enjoy the warble of its big powerful engine.

He has his suspicions about who is behind this.

"Hey, we got to get a report and some information from you," a police officer says.

"No problem. I'll tell you what I know. You might want to call Paul Hoptak, the owner of the building, and have him come down here," Theodore says.

"Do you know the guy that you caught doing this?"

"Yeah. He was a former student of mine at the community college."

"I guess you aren't getting a Teacher of the Year award. That guy is as dumb as a fucking post. Whoever hired him to do this can't be that bright either. Any idea who would want to burn this building down?"

"I have a partial list in my head."

"Oh, yeah, you're that fired campaign manager that works for this paper now. You made some powerful enemies. At least you only lost a car tonight. If your former student had gotten this lit, this old building would have gone up in no time," the officer says. "I'm going to take a look around and write some notes for the report. Don't go too far. I might have some questions."

"I'll be right here," Theodore says as he notices the Channel 6 News van pull in front of the building.

"Get some shots of the smoking car and then get some shots of the firefighters packing up the hose. I'll ask if I can get some shots of the double doors that were pried to get into the building. Ask the engine captain if he would give us an interview," Grace Downwood could be heard giving instructions to her cameraman. "Theodore Graham, is that you?"

"Yes, Grace, it's me."

"Can I get an interview?"

"Can I put pants and shoes on first?"

"What fun would that be? We already have footage of you talking to the police officer in your boxer shorts. We don't want continuity errors raising questions about our journalistic integrity, do we?"

"I guess not. Go ahead, I'll do your interview."

Grace tells her cameraman where to stand. "Shoot him from the waist up. I don't want to get an R rating for what might start to fall out of the button fly of his boxers."

"Thanks for the heads-up," Theodore says and adjusts the contents of his boxers.

"This is Grace Downwood of Channel 6 News, reporting from the *Weekly Beat* building in Harmon. Standing with me is managing editor of the *Weekly Beat* and resident of one of the apartments in the building, Theodore Graham. Can you tell me what happened here this morning?"

"I woke up to the sound of smashing glass and a slamming door. When I looked out the window, I saw my car was on fire. I came down the fire escape and heard the IROC-Z idling at the end of the alley. I turned the car off and dropped the keys in the storm drain. I noticed the double doors to the press room were open. I went inside, and there was a man pouring kerosene on the floor. With the crowbar he used to pry the door open, I took him down when he walked by me in the dark."

"Any idea who the man who did this is?"

"The police have the man in custody and are conducting an investigation. I'm just glad nobody was hurt, and I am thankful for the quick response of the police and volunteer firefighters."

"Do you think this arson attempt has anything to do with recent articles and controversy surrounding the relaunch of the *Weekly Beat*."

"I don't want to make any accusations or guess who is behind this. I trust the police will do a full investigation, a thorough interview of the suspect, and get to the bottom of it."

"Were you injured in this incident?"

"Not physically, but my '72 Buick Skylark is just a burned chunk of metal. My father gave me that car. There was a lot of sentimental value wrapped up in that car. I guess I will mend from my hurt feelings."

"Grace Downwood, Channel 6 News, reporting from an arson attempt early this morning in Harmon," the reporter says and motions for her cameraman to cut. "Go over and get some more footage of the burned car, the IROC-Z, get the license plate in the frame, and go out front and get a shot of the *Weekly Beat* sign."

"Don't you want to stick around for coffee?"

"We got to hurry back to the station and put this together for the six o'clock news. Our female viewers will see you in your T-shirt with your bedhead and will rewatch this story all the way up until *Good Morning America* comes on. Hopefully for the news at noon or the nightly news, we will have more information. If we don't get any more info, we will run your interview again. You get the housewife ratings for us."

"I'm glad my tragedy is your ratings treasure."

"A girl's got to shoot for those local news awards if she wants to get on the national news. I'm sorry about your car, and I'm glad you're not hurt."

"Thanks. I'll make sure you get my vote for a daytime Emmy."

CHAPTER 20

The Eugene Douglas for Governor campaign staff sits eagerly around the conference room table, waiting for Tim Collins to arrive with the midsummer polling numbers. Laptops, legal pads, and research printouts sit in front of each staff member. Shuffling papers, turning pages, the sound of coffee being poured, and the occasional stirring spoon are the only noises heard. Tension and fear of the polling results after the shortcomings in the previous weeks keep chatter in the room to a minimum.

"I know it's been a rough couple of weeks. Teddy Graham, the *Weekly Beat*, the Capitalist Ventures Protection Act, and all the other scandal-hungry media haven't been kind. The weeks leading up to today were supposed to be filled with fluff publicity and fund-raising. It didn't work out that way, but we have to play the hand we're dealt. Once we get the numbers, we will see where we stand and craft our platform and our message. Mort will be joining us a little later. Let's start the meeting with Robert. He can tell us where we stand with finance," Dick Ratzinger says as he opens the meeting.

"We have a pretty solid financial base. The fund-raising we hoped to do in the weeks after the primary leading up to the general election push fell well below what we projected. That's for obvious reasons, and I'm not going to throw salt in that wound. We do have the party loyalist contributions coming in. The State Republican Committee is pushing members to support our campaign, but the chairman reached out and said we better get our shit together and get in a favorable light with the media. We will have to raise some money along with campaigning. It's going to be a little more work than we anticipated, but we can brainstorm fund-raising ideas after we see the polling numbers. I'm sure the super PAC will push some money our way."

"That's not horrible news. We can make up some ground. I'm going to work a little harder and a little bit longer. I'm not afraid of hard work," Gene says.

"Sidney, what media opportunities do you have for us right now? Are there any interviews worth taking? Are there any easy issues to make statements on?" Dick Ratzinger asks.

"Most of the newspapers and television reporters are asking us to make a statement on the arson attempt at the *Weekly Beat*. There are a few reporters calling and asking for our thoughts on lobbyist influence in the government and want comments on the extended legislative session to renegotiate the budget without using lobbyists. You can probably make a blanket statement about the state Congress mending their ways and choosing a better path forward," Sidney says.

"That's a trap. My son's name is attached to that lobbying firm. If the regular newspapers don't catch on to that, Teddy Graham surely will. I am sure we will be at the mercy of the *Weekly Beat*," Dick Ratzinger says.

"*State of the State This Week* calls the media office almost every day and asks us if Gene would sit in on the panel with Teddy."

"I could do that. I can let the people know that he isn't getting the best of me or the campaign," Gene says.

"Are you kidding me, Dad? Teddy would destroy you. He knows how to turn your words against you, and he is brilliant at it. Do any of you pay attention to the social media and blogs about your campaign? Do you know what people are saying?"

"It's the social media. Nobody is paying attention."

"That's probably why you will lose the election," Ernie says.

"Ernie, you are part of this team, and our goal is to win this election. We will not have any member of this staff concede defeat or even hint of it."

"Then pay attention to what I am telling you."

"I'm sorry. Let's hear what you have to say."

Ernie grabs his laptop and places it at the head of the conference table. He goes over to a cabinet and pulls out a projector and hooks it to his computer and begins clicking and typing a few things. A blog site comes up on the screen.

"Is that the internet? How did you get that on the overhead?" Gene asks.

"I hope Sherman Jones is less familiar with technology than you are. But I'm positive we will win, because we can't concede defeat while being inherently ignorant," Ernie says.

"Don't be smart."

"All right, I gather most of you are unfamiliar with Eric's Open Forum. It is a page operated by a political science major at a local college. His blog has nearly half a million followers, and all he does is ask people to comment on political topics. He doesn't write articles and doesn't offer his opinion. I'm pretty sure it's a sociology project of some sort, but it's popular. People can comment anonymously. Let's look at this week's topic," Ernie says and clicks a few more things on his computer. "Here it is."

The staff around the conference table focus their attention on the screen at the front of the room.

Eric's Open Forum

The general election push is about to begin. Each campaign anxiously awaits the midsummer polling numbers to craft their rhetoric and platforms to appeal to the voters. Before the mass media plasters poll numbers all over the papers and newscasts in order to blind the people with meaningless math, I want to hear what real people think before blind statistics cloud our judgment.

The Governor's Race: Sherman Jones vs. Eugene Douglas Voice your opinion, but remember, no arguing *with the opinions of others.*

"That's this week's topic. If everybody saw that. I will open the comments section. There are a lot of idiots who comment, but there are people who make good points too," Ernie says and clicks on the comment section.

> This is going to be another election of picking the lesser of two evils. I was going to go with Gene Douglas until he jumped in bed with big money and special interests. Sherman Jones is the lesser of two evils, but I am still forced to choose evil.
>
> Gene Douglas has a hotter wife. I would love for Sandy Douglas to sit on my face and leave beer farts. Douglas got my vote.
>
> When you surround yourself with pieces of shit, you turn into a piece of shit. Morton Whitney is trying to purchase the government, and it breaks my heart that Gene Douglas is helping him.
>
> Ratzinger is a suiting name for Gene's campaign manager. With those beady, dead eyes, he looks like a rat. That guy seems shadier than Chris Chritie's shadow.
>
> Gene Douglas is almost as fake as his wife's tits, but if he wins, I will be able to brag that the first lady of my state is a regular in my spank bank.
>
> I thought this governor's race would be different after Gene Douglas announced. He seemed to be about the people. Something changed. I think somebody showed him dollar signs.
>
> I wish Teddy Graham were running for governor. Neither one of these clowns has a clue.
>
> Sherman Jones is just another liberal fucktard that is going to pander to minorities welfare scum and the vagina vote. He's going to promise a lot of free shit to lazy people and get elected. Our taxes are going to go through the roof. Save your pennies, folks. People who don't work for a living are counting on you.

I didn't grow up in the Douglas mansion, so I can't relate to the trust fund candidate. Gene Douglas can suck it.

I shit out things that would do a better job than these two idiots.

It's too early to say whom I am voting for. I want to know where they stand on education, women issues, gun violence, and campaign finance.

Sherman Jones wasn't always rich. Gene Douglas was. It doesn't take a genius to figure out who is going to be better for the middle class.

The Gene Douglas that donated to the Carter Food Bank and the Gene Douglas we have now are two different people. He's fake, like his phony trophy wife.

Anybody know where I can purchase a pair of Sandy Douglas's panties?

Tax-and-spend liberals like Sherman Jones are killing our country and our state. Gene Douglas will bring jobs, lower taxes, and a more efficient government. Best thing he ever did was get rid of that pretty boy Teddy Graham. He would have managed Gene Douglas right into defeat.

"This is just first page of the comments. There are thirty-eight more. I will e-mail all of you the link to this page, and you can look at the rest of them yourselves. People aren't reading newspapers and watching the news. People are reading and commenting on sites like this. They can look at this page on their phones when they're taking a shit, riding a bus, waiting in a doctor's office, or just looking for ways to get out of thinking for themselves. As you can see, there aren't a lot of positive comments about our campaign, and there are a lot of people that think my mother is hot. Robert, if you are looking for fund-raising ideas, maybe you can auction off a blow job from my mother or sell calendars of her posing in stages of undress."

"That's your mother you are talking about."

"That *is* my mother. The same woman who risked a dangerous breech birth for me so she wouldn't have a scar for her beauty pageant body. My point is, all of you have to get familiar with this type of media and change what these people are saying about you."

"He makes a good point. We're going to have to get some staff to follow this type of media, and we are going to have to get some of our people commenting on this page. Does this Eric guy really have a half-million followers?" Sidney asks.

"Yes. He gets more every day. He will be over two million subscribers by the election. I am almost certain of that."

"Can't we go on this page and defend ourselves?" Gene asks.

"Nope. People who argue or offer counterpoints to the statements of others are kicked off the page. The best way to do it is to go on the page and offer good opinions about the campaign without sounding like you work for the campaign."

"Good job, son. You shed light on something important. Oh, here comes Tim Collins. He has what we're waiting for."

Tim comes into the conference room. "Good morning. I don't think I am going to be the man of the hour this morning," Tim says as he flips on the overhead projector.

"I miss Teddy's shadow puppets on the screen," Robert Wermer jokes.

"I don't. That idiot is the reason for all the problems we're having now," Russ Dewitt says.

"We could use Teddy's comic relief. I've seen the numbers. You'll see we have lots of work ahead of us and lots of catching up to do."

"They can't be that bad," Dick Ratzinger says.

"See for yourself," Tim says as he places a slide on the projector. "I'm not going to beat around the bush. Sherman Jones is beating us by double digits in the most recent polls. He has 54 percent to our 44 percent with a 2 percent margin of error. Our overall approval rating is at 51 percent."

"That's not too bad. We can improve on that," Gene says.

"We better, but we are at 51 percent, down from 60 percent. Sherman Jones is at 56 percent, up 4 percent from 52. Some of the survey answers list the following reasons for your lowered approval:

change of personnel, lobbyist and special interest affiliation, lack of political experience, being out of touch with the middle class, inability to run your own campaign."

"How did we do across the demographics?" Dick Ratzinger asks.

"Everything we gained for the last polling cycle we lost. With women, we're down 5 percent. With minorities, we lost the 2 percent we gained and went down an additional 5 percent. We're down 7 percent with minorities. With young voters, we're down 8 percent. Kevin Baker called and told me that attendance at Young Republican meetings is down and presidents in three of his chapters across the state have resigned. It looks like we went backward instead of forward. If we had a stronger opponent, I would say we're done, but Sherman Jones isn't out of our reach. It's going to take a lot of work, though. I know this isn't going to be a popular opinion, but I believe we should revisit some of Teddy's strategies with voters."

"That's not going to happen. Teddy Graham was a circus act. His approach to politics doesn't work, and we will not take the campaign I'm managing down that road again," Dick Ratzinger says.

"That's not what the numbers say, Dick," Tim answers.

"If you have a problem with the way I'm running things, you're more than welcome to resign."

"If it's that easy, I resign," Ernie says.

"You can't resign, you're my son. Tim isn't resigning either, he's the best statistician in the state. Dick, you're the campaign manager. You saw the numbers. It's your job to get us the numbers we need to win," Gene says and then turns his attention to a noise outside the conference room. "Who is that in the hallway?"

"It looks like a UPS guy," Russ says.

The conference room door opens. It is Morton Whitney dressed in a UPS uniform. He is dragging a cart with a large box strapped to it.

"Mort? What are you doing dressed like that?" Gene asks.

"I had to dress like a UPS guy because the last time I was here, your security cameras caught me coming in and out of the building. I had to rent a UPS truck to come here. Anyway, I don't have a lot of time to explain complex issues to your monkey brain. You know the drill. I want all the electronic gadgets out of here. None of this gets recorded. Let's go, get 'em out. I don't have a lot of time."

"Everything is out, Mort. We just looked at the poll numbers, and they aren't that great."

"I had the poll numbers four days ago. I'm rich, and I know how to spend my money on the right things. Of course the poll numbers are shit. Your rags-to-riches friend Teddy made them shit. Your horse's ass personality didn't help us either."

"Now that I know there are no recording devices in here. I think I should mention something," Russ says.

"Nobody cares that you got your period and you are blossoming into a woman, Mr. Dicktits."

"All I wanted was to let you know that the media is pressuring the campaign finance commission to investigate the super PAC communicating directly with the campaign. Ray was seen on surveillance video with you last time, Mort. They threatened to freeze the super PAC's finance and assets if they have to investigate."

"Oh, for fuck's sake. I hate this damn electronic age. What happened to the good old days when you could get away with shit? Look at me. I'm dressed like a UPS guy! I look like a fucking turd with my name sewn on my shirt. Fine! Ray will resign from the super PAC and announce before the six o'clock news. I will put a less-retarded idiot in charge of your super PAC. Maybe I can find a good nigger or some cunt to fill the position and improve the poll numbers with those demographics."

"What's in the box?" Dick Ratzinger asks.

"Since I had the poll numbers early, I had a couple of days to make a new campaign strategy. These are your new binders. If it wouldn't hurt the campaign, Dick, I would fire your pathetic ass. It would look bad if we were on a third campaign manager. You better get your act together and take care of Teddy Graham. He made you his bitch."

"What about the polling numbers?" Gene asks.

"What about the blah blah waa? Don't you worry. Let the media report this morning's poll numbers. On Wednesday, you will have a press conference and you will tell them that you had an independent poll done across the state and you question the accuracy of today's poll and think the liberal media has biased the numbers."

"Won't the media ask to see the results of this independent poll?"

"What the fuck? Do you think I'm as dumb as you? I had the polling done. Getting good polling numbers is easy if you can control whom the automatic dialers are calling. Don't worry, everything checks out. Any reporter can get the answers he needs right down to the phone numbers called to the name of the company that conducted the study. The press will go apeshit over the discrepancies, and this morning's numbers no longer matter."

"Which media do we want to announce on?" Sidney Hughes asks.

"Barry Barnhardt of Channel 3 News is desperate for a good story. He knows you will be calling, and he will set up the interview. You will be on his show before the lunchtime news, and by dinnertime, you will own the local media cycle. In the next week, I will have editorials in newspapers across the state to help improve your demographics. The papers and internet media that women read will make you appealing to women. The papers that blacks read will have a free fried chicken coupon. There will even be an editorial written in Mexican so all the spicaricans will like you. We will turn this all around."

"What about young voters? Ernie showed us some really interesting stuff on social media that young people read."

"Your son and his band are going to host a three-day music festival at the Gatesville Fairgrounds. His band will be the headliner all three days, and there will be some other shit bands playing their shit music. It's not about the music. For young people, it's about finger-banging insecure girls and smoking pot. In order to get into the festival, people will have to purchase a DOUGLAS FOR GOVERNOR T-shirt and hat for twenty dollars and wear it. The media and internet will make the event go viral, plus these young kids can't take a shit without telling the world where they are, whom they are with, and what they are doing. Wi-Fi at the event will be free, but every social media post will say that they are at the Douglas for Governor Music Festival. The young voters will see that, and their whole view of your campaign will change."

"I don't have a band anymore. My band broke up when I came to work for the campaign."

"I'm sure if you talk to your little friends and tell them they will be getting paid five grand to play, they will get back together."

"I don't think they will be interested in selling out their music for crooked politics."

"You would be surprised what people sell out for. Musicians can't wait to sell out. It's the untalented ones that say that sellout bullshit. Don't be a cunt like your old man. Make it happen if you want to have a bright future."

"Hey, Mort, that's my son you're talking to."

"That's unfortunate for him. Ratzinger, I'm counting on you to get this all done. I expect regular reports. This is all I have time for. I got to get out of this turd suit."

"I want no part of this. Gene, I resign," Tim Collins says.

"Tim, you can't quit."

"This is fraud. I'm done here."

"You signed a confidentiality agreement. Not a word about this campaign leaves this room," Dick Ratzinger says.

"The voters will figure out what went on here. I don't have to say a word. Fuck you, Dick," Tim says and packs up his notes and puts them in his briefcase.

"Don't be like that. Come on, Tim," Gene says.

"I resign too," Ernie says.

"No, you don't. You have a pretty nice trust fund and inheritance to lose if you do."

"Fuck!"

CHAPTER 21

Theodore is in his office, working on his editorial for Thursday's paper. Paul Hoptak walks by his office and taps on the window. Theodore motions for him to come in.

"Hey, troublemaker, what are you working on?"

"Troublemaker? Don't you mean moneymaker? This paper's circulation is up by nine thousand."

"Sorry, Mr. Moneymaker. What scandal will you cause this week?"

"I'm working on a piece about how the state budget will now balance since the elected people looked and talked about what they are actually passing. I think both gubernatorial candidates can come out in favor of that. I don't foresee a scandal, but you know how trouble follows me."

"Your former boss is going to be on TV in a couple of minutes. You want to come over to my office and watch?"

"Let me save this file, and I'll be right over. Open the windows, though. Your office always smells like Swiss Miss, Fritos, and shame. I can account for two of the odors, but I'm afraid to ask about your internet porn viewing habits."

"The windows are open. I got the Frito smell out, but there is some Swiss Miss and shame lingering. I like a cup of cocoa with my bondage porn."

"I knew you were a freak. What show is Gene going to be on?"

"*Our Town*, with Barry Barnhardt."

"I never understood why that guy gets a daily half-hour show before the noon news comes on. I guess they are rewarding him for years of service. Now he's too out of shape to chase real news stories.

He tried to interview me after Gene announced his candidacy, but he couldn't catch his breath to get a question out."

"It's a shame. He used to be good. I think the only reason Channel 3 keeps him around and gives him a show is that he owns most of the shares of the station. If they treat him badly, he will sell out to a big news conglomerate," Paul says and clicks on the television. "It's just about to start."

"You got any of those Fritos left?"

"Good morning and welcome to Our Town. I'm your host, Channel 3's own Barry Barnhardt. Thank you for joining us and making Our Town your town. Today, our guests are gubernatorial candidate Eugene Douglas, and joining us for the second half is award-winning gardener Mary Misner, who will be telling us how to prune our summer plants and keep those pesky ants away.

"My first guest is Eugene Douglas. He has high hopes to occupy the governor's mansion next year, but he's having a tough week. The polling numbers came out on Monday, and they are favoring his opponent. Also on Monday, the chairman of his super PAC resigned for violating campaign finance rules. Tell us a little bit about your tough week."

"Ray Whitney did resign from the super PAC on Monday. The media raised a lot of controversy about him communicating directly with the campaign. The campaign finance laws are vague, but since the media witch hunt put pressure on the campaign finance commission to act on one of their vague rules, the super PAC had to act. Ray supports my campaign and its values. He did the right thing, and he actually did me a favor. Now the media can call off the scandal hounds and actually report on how the candidates feel about the issues and how they will serve the people."

"Ray Whitney, isn't he the son of industrialist Morton Whitney, a generous financial contributor to your campaign? There is also some controversy surrounding him and his influence on legislation."

"Morton is jobs creator, not just in our state, but in many other states as well. The lobbyist company he hired poorly penned some legislative proposals. Of course the media wants to put a bounty on his head, because it's easier to paint one man as a bad guy. Even with a phony scandal, there hasn't been charges brought against him or MRS Consultants.

No laws were found to be broken. Sadly, all this scandal did was further delay the creation of jobs that our state and other states desperately need. Morton supports my campaign because I am the candidate that wants to bring good-paying jobs to our hardworking citizens."

"What about the polling numbers released this week? They are a lot less favorable than they were before the primary. Some of the gains that you made, you lost this quarter. It looks like Sherman Jones has a huge advantage over you. What's going on there?"

"Our pollster was studying the polling data from previous elections and comparing it with the news cycle when the data was released. We found it pretty interesting that the polling follows the favorites in the media. Because of this, we funded our own study. I'm glad we did, because our study tells a whole different story than the so-called unbiased state polling data."

"So your independent study produced different results?"

"Yes, and what world of difference. In our study, we lead Sherman Jones overall, 57 percent to 41 percent. There is still a 2 percent margin of error. It wasn't all good news either. We did lose some ground with women voters and minorities, but I plan to get them back when they hear my platform and what I want to bring to the residents of our state."

"Doesn't a study that you funded appear biased in your favor?"

"We didn't just go to a statistics firm and say, 'We're the Douglas for Governor campaign and want a study done to make us look good.' The statistics firm was hired to do the exact same study the state conducts to get election data. Our study asked the same questions with the same wording. Our study polled areas from all across the state. It is the exact same study with way different results."

"Why is there such a huge difference in the results?"

"I would like to find that out as well. I'm sure the media hounds will be calling my polling data biased, but any reporter that contacts my press office can get a copy of the study. It's very detailed. It says how it was conducted, what questions were asked, how many women took the survey, how many men took the survey, age ranges, and income levels of those polled."

"It sounds like it was a well-conducted study."

"I believe it was well done. I encourage any reporter who is tempted to call my polling biased to get a copy of the study from my press office and, if the state will release their data, get a copy of that. Compare the two and see for themselves which one they think is more accurate."

"As a media guy, I know the state study. You can get a copy of it under right-to-know laws, but you have to fill out a written request complete with details of who you are and why you want it. The requests take five business days to get reviewed, and the state still has the right to seal any data that it feels like sealing. It could take up to ten days sometimes."

"If you want a copy of my polling study, all you have to do is show your press credentials, and my press office will hand you a copy. I hope this stops this media circus so the candidates can actually talk about the issues and have reporters write about what we are saying instead of talking about numbers that aren't accurate."

"Hopefully, good journalists will make that happen. They owe it to the voters. I am part of the media. I hope you can say that I interviewed you fairly."

"You asked me some tough questions and I gave you straight answers. You didn't ask me gotcha questions like some media people do. You treated me fairly, and I thank you and Our Town for having me on today."

"Before I let you go, I understand that your son, Ernie, is helping the campaign."

"Thank you for reminding me. Ernie has been working really hard for the campaign, and he is such a talented musician. His band, the Cover Hogs, is headlining a three-day music festival at the Gatesville Fairgrounds this weekend. There will be food and merchandise vendors and thirteen different bands playing over the course of the three days. Admission is free if you purchase a DOUGLAS FOR GOVERNOR T-shirt and hat for twenty dollars. Parking is free if you place a Douglas for Governor magnetic bumper sticker on your car. There are a limited number of camping passes available, but they are going fast. Part of the of the proceeds go to the Gatesville Fairgrounds, a third goes to our state's veteran hospitals, and the other third goes to our grassroots campaign."

"Those are great causes to come out for. Are you going to be there as well?"

"*Unfortunately, I can't be there on Friday night and Sunday after-noon because of separate campaign events. My son and I should have coordinated better on our schedules, but I will be there all day Saturday to talk to voters and eat some good festival food. Saturday night, my wife and I want to sit and enjoy the talents of my son and his band.*"

"*There you have it from Gene Douglas himself. Get out there this weekend for good music and support our local fairgrounds and veterans hospitals. When we come back for the second half of our show, Mary Misner will be here with some great gardening tips for those of us striving for a green thumb. Stay tuned! There is a lot more Our Town to come.*"

Paul Hoptak turns off the television in his office. "I smell something fishy going on here."

"Why did you turn the television off? I wanted to see Mary Misner. I have a fantasy about gardening naked with her and then making sweet love to her on a bed of soft ferns. I bet she has a nice pussy willow," Theodore says.

"You can make that happen. Set up an interview with her. She's a media whore and will take any attention she can get."

"Hmmm, I just may do that."

"What do you think about Gene's interview?"

"There's definitely something fishy going on there. I think the key is in that polling data that Gene is offering up. It's definitely an attempt to take attention off Monday's polling numbers."

"Maybe you should get a copy and write an editorial for Sunday's edition."

"You know if I cover this story, we are feeding right into Gene's media bias narrative, but this would be a huge break if Grace Downwood can expose what's really going on here."

"True that. I will give her a call and have her get a copy of his polling."

"Besides, I have a music festival in Gatesville to go to this weekend."

"Are you really going to that?"

"Sure. I can use a new T-shirt and hat and bumper sticker. It's twenty bucks well spent. I played with that band a few times. I wonder if they would let me sit in on Saturday night."

"I don't think Gene Douglas had a solid bowel movement since you joined my little paper. Your antics may put him in adult diapers this weekend."

"It's about the music, not the politics."

"Rock on, Furshizzle."

Chapter 22

Since the announcement of his independent polling results, it appears as though the Eugene Douglas for Governor campaign has turned a corner. The free-fall-from-favor ability has seemed to stop, and steps in a positive direction are the next logical motion. In the three days that follow Gene's guest appearance on *Our Town* with Barry Barnhardt, all the media is abuzz with hints of scandal. Conspiracy theorists gloat since proof exists the media is trying to pull the wool over their eyes. Commentators on social media curse the liberal media for biasing polling data and praise Gene's independent study. Local television news alludes to Sherman Jones exploiting polling data that is inaccurate. Newspapers print articles praising the now-level playing field for candidates to play politics on. Gene has some relief from doing damage control and can enjoy being viewed in a good light.

On Saturday afternoon, Gene arrives at the sold-out Gatesville Fairgrounds. People come out en masse for the music festival that his son, Ernie, and his band, the Cover Hogs, are headlining. From the vendor area to the food court and all across the field in front of the main stage, crowds of people can be seen wearing DOUGLAS FOR GOVERNOR T-shirts and hats.

Gene is overlooking a sea of his supporters as he heads to the press area.

"Good afternoon, ladies and gentleman of the press. Candidate Douglas will make a brief statement and take a few questions. Please welcome to the podium the next governor of our great state, Eugene Douglas," Dick Ratzinger announces.

Gene is all smiles and waves as he makes his way to the podium littered with microphones. "Good afternoon and welcome to Gatesville! I couldn't have asked for a better day or better weather to be here. This festival is an honor for me. It's an honor because my one and only son, Ernie, put his band back together and organized this festival. It will help raise much-needed funding for veterans hospitals across the state and support the beautiful Gatesville Fairgrounds so they can continue to host great events. Being a proud father, I know nothing beats that feeling. I've been blessed with a loving family, and the values I learned as a family man, I will carry with me everywhere I go. I am confident I will get to carry these values with me to the governor's mansion so I can use them to serve the people of our great state. The outpouring of support that I see here today, it's overwhelming. Before I take questions, I would like to bring my son out here to say a few words. Ernie, come on out here."

Ernie makes his way to the podium. He shakes his father's hand and gets a pat on the shoulder from him. "Thank you. Talking to the press is something new to me, so please be kind. I love my family, and I love music. When my dad and Mr. Ratzinger gave me the green light to do this festival with the campaign's blessing, I was able to combine two of my loves for good causes. I never dreamed that it would sell out. I can't thank everybody enough for coming out. I just want everyone to enjoy the day, visit our food, merchandise, and craft vendors, and listen to the talented musicians gathered here this weekend. The Cover Hogs go on tonight at eight, and I promise that we are going to do a great show. Thanks again, everybody!"

"I have an amazing son, don't I? I wouldn't have this amazing son without an amazing wife. Sandy, come on out here so I can show off my wonderful family to the press gathered here."

Sandy joins Gene and Ernie onstage. The three take advantage of the photo opportunity and smile and wave for the snapping cameras.

"Come on, Sandy, say a few words to these fine folks."

"I just want to say that I love my family and I am grateful for all the support for us today. Today is supposed to be fun, so let's go enjoy ourselves!" Sandy says as she smiles and poses for the cameras.

Gene returns to the podium and hugs his wife. "Isn't she beautiful?" he says as she walks away. "Okay, now I will take some questions from the press."

"Did your son get his musical ability from his parents?"

"I don't know where Ernie gets his musical talent. It's not from me. I have difficulty playing the radio. He may have gotten it from Sandy. She sings beautifully in the shower."

"How did you decide on the charities you are supporting with this event?"

"Veterans hospitals in our state was kind of a no-brainer. Our veterans hospitals provide care for the men and women who bravely put on uniforms to protect our freedom. Sadly, the hospitals have to wait for the federal and state governments to get their acts together and get them the funding they need. We will do what we can today to help them, and when I get elected governor, I will get our state's act together and get our veterans the support they need and the care they deserve. Supporting the Gatesville Fairgrounds is also important. This is a beautiful plot of land and a wonderful event venue. It's been a place that has made fond memories for me for all my life. I want to see this local treasure making those same fond memories for future generations."

"What about the other third of the proceeds going to your campaign?"

"I wish campaigning were free and I didn't have to raise money, but unfortunately, that's not the way it is. If you are unhappy with campaigns having to raise money to get elected to serve the people, vote for me in November. I will fight for campaign finance reform. I want your vote to be your voice, not what money can buy."

"What do you have to say about the two sets of polling data?"

"I was hoping I wouldn't have to talk shop today, but you asked. I felt horrible about Monday's polling results. I felt wonderful on Wednesday when I received our independent polling results. This only raises questions about how polling data is gathered. Until the polling system is fixed, my opponent and I can share a level playing field and you folks in the media can write about where we stand on the issues and how we propose to deal with them. That's what matters most."

"What about your ties to Morton and Ray Whitney? Ray Whitney resigned as head of your super PAC, and Morton is tied to MRS Consultants, the lobby firm under investigation in our state and three others."

"Ray did the right thing by resigning. He didn't want my campaign to have to focus on campaign finance laws and violations of vague rules. His father, Morton, is a jobs creator. There's an old saying, 'You have to spend money to make money.' Morton Whitney is investing in my campaign because I will eliminate the red tape and constraining regulations that prevent businesses that want to create jobs in our state. What's wrong with creating jobs and making money? That's how capitalism is supposed to work. Ray and Mort will be joining my wife and me this evening to watch my son's band play. Their family has been friends with my family for many years. Maybe you guys in the media can write about our friendship and not turn it into a scandal."

"What kind of food are you going to eat at the festival today?"

"Good, an easy question. I am going to enjoy one of Iggy's Italian sausage sandwiches and follow it up with a funnel cake later on. I am going to see if I can sneak in some other treats throughout the day, but Sandy keeps a close watch over my calories and cholesterol. While we watch Ernie's band tonight, we are all going to have a few cold beers and enjoy some great music."

Dick Ratzinger approaches the podium. "That's all the questions Mr. Douglas has time for. Thanks for coming out. Make sure you take some time to enjoy all this festival has to offer."

Dick joins Gene and Sandy as they are escorted out of the press area. Gene and Sandy greet the crowd with friendly small talk and handshakes. The press follows eagerly along behind them as they meet up with the Whitneys. Morton is there with his wife. Ray is there with his wife and their two teenage sons. The nine of them move through the crowd to the VIP deck overlooking the stage to enjoy some of the bands playing before Ernie's. They eat dinner together and are enjoying a few beers. Sandy looks out into the crowd.

"How come some people are wearing different campaign shirts and hats?"

"We only have one kind. They're all the same."

"No, they aren't. Look out into the crowd."

Gene notices there are people with something added to the shirts. He makes his way to the deck railing to get a closer look. He notices the added item to the shirts are stickers of urinating Calvins from the popular cartoon series *Calvin and Hobbes*. The small stickers on the hats and large stickers on the T-shirts make it appear that Calvin is peeing on the Douglas for Governor campaign logo. Gene tries to make it over to Dick Ratzinger without catching Morton's attention.

"Where are the people getting the pissing Calvin stickers? They don't look good for us."

"Come on, we'll go find out," Dick says. He and Gene make their way down the steps and away from the VIP deck.

There is a crowd of college-age kids with the stickers on their shirts and hats passing by. Dick grabs one of them by the arm and pulls him over.

"Dude, what's your problem?" the unsuspecting twenty-something asks.

"Where did you get those stickers? Where are they coming from?"

"Oh, dude, you gotta go get one for your shirts. They are giving them away for free by the vendor tents if you post an 'It's About Music, Not Politics' selfie on your social media page."

"What kind of selfie?" Dick asks.

The kid pulls out his cell phone and shows him a picture of himself with some of his friends posing with the urinating Calvins on their shirts. The picture is captioned "It's About Music, Not Politics."

"That's all you got to do, and they will give you a sticker. That's how we fight the system. The Wi-Fi is free, but they put their campaign bullshit on our posts. We don't let anybody steal our freedom of speech. We're here to hear good music and have a good time, not be part of a campaign."

Dick lets the kid go and turns around to Gene. "This is bad. We have to hope Morton doesn't see this, or he will snap."

"Let's just go back on the deck and keep his beer mug full. We can try to keep him drunk and distracted so he won't look into the crowd."

They go back to the VIP deck with the others. Ray's eldest son is looking at his cell phone and checking his Facebook page.

"Hey, Grandpa, can we go get some pissing stickers before the show starts?"

"What kind of sticker? What's a pissing sticker?"

"This is a pissing sticker," the boy says and shows Mort a Facebook post with one of his friends wearing one.

Morton stands up and looks out into the crowd. He sees the majority of the crowd is wearing the stickers. He notices there are a few news reporters and television cameras around some of the festival attendees.

"Ratzinger!"

"Yes, Mr. Whitney?"

"Look around this crowd. Look at the stickers they are putting on our campaign shirts. It's a fucking cartoon character pissing on our campaign logo. How could you let this happen?"

"Sir, I had no idea people were going to do this."

"I trusted you to put this together and not fuck it up. It's all over social media! There are reporters out there talking to these long-haired, lazy dopeheads. You got to do something about this."

"How do you propose I do that?"

"Get that retard candidate over here."

Dick gets Gene's attention. "What's up, Mort?"

"Don't what's-up me, you fucking moron! Look at these stickers. Those pissing stickers are literally pissing all over your campaign. Why in the fuck did I pick your campaign to support? Tell your son to tell this crowd that his band won't play unless they take off those stickers."

"I can't tell him to say that. This crowd will riot. It would make things worse."

"Ratzinger!"

"Yes, Mr. Whitney?"

"Gene is useless too. You got to go over and get the free Wi-Fi shut down so no more of these potheads can post shit on social media with their cell phones and electronic doo-dads."

"I'll see what I can do."

"Get it the fuck done if you want to work for me ever again. And find those pud strokers that are handing out these stickers and have them thrown out or shot."

"Yes, sir!"

Gene goes over to Morton. "Let's sit down and have another beer. The band is about to start. We can figure out how to handle this later. It might not be that bad."

"Everything that involves you is a disaster. Who would go out of their way to pull off this sabotage?"

Gene hands Morton a full mug of beer and sits down between him and Sandy. The stage lights shine on the center of the stage. The festival announcer makes his way to the microphone.

"Hello, Gatesville. How is everybody doing tonight?" the announcer says as he fires up the crowd. "It's time to get to tonight's main event. Is everybody feeling all right?" he says, and the crowd erupts with loud cheers. "All right, you folks sound ready for a good time. Please welcome to the stage, your hometown musical heroes, the Cover Hogs!"

Ernie's band makes their way onto the stage. They are wearing plain white T-shirts with the logo IT'S ABOUT THE MUSIC written in black across the front of them. Another man joins the band onstage. He is wearing a Steve Urkel shirt with the catchphrase DID I DO THAT? across the front of it. The man joining the band is Theodore Graham. The crowd goes wild, and the band opens up with a cover of the Allman Brothers song "Whipping Post."

"That cocksucker! Now I know who the piece of shit behind all this is!" Morton yells.

"Calm down, Mort. Don't make a scene."

"This is your friend. He is ruining your campaign!"

"Teddy has been working with Ernie on guitar for a long time. He's played with the band before. I probably should have told the guys not to invite him."

"Gee, you think? Even retards think you're retarded."

After a twelve-minute version of "Whipping Post," the crowd roars with delight. Theodore goes to the center microphone.

"Thank you, Gatesville, for having us here tonight. This crowd is awesome! The Calvin stickers on your shirts and hats are great. You guys are hilarious. Before we get back to the music, I do want to raise my beer and say hello to my good friend Gene Douglas. The media has been putting the two of us at odds lately, but I just want to let him know that I still love him as my friend. You too, Sandy, I love you both!"

Gene and Sandy stand up and raise their beer mugs up as a spotlight shines on them. The crowd cheers and holds up their drinks.

"There is another guy over there sitting with them, Ray Whitney. He was a douchebag in college when I knew him, and he just had to resign from his job because he is still a douchebag. Please help me welcome him."

The crowd begins to chant. "Douchebag! Douchebag! Douchebag! Douchebag!"

"You guys are great. Fuck you, Ray! Now let's get back to some music!"

The crowd cheers loudly, and the band rips into a cover of the James Gang hit "Walk Away."

CHAPTER 23

After he has tossed and turned all night, Sunday morning arrives. The events of the music festival swirl in Gene's mind. What started out as a perfect event to boost his campaign ended with his financial backers becoming furious with him. Gene is dreading the coming days.

Sandy comes out of the bathroom in her bikini. She is ready for her Sunday ritual of sunbathing by the pool. "Aren't you going to get out of bed today?"

"Eventually, but I am lacking the motivation right now. I didn't sleep well."

"I know you didn't. You were rolling around and sighing most of the night. The fresh air will do you good. You can have some coffee, read your papers, get some sun. Later on, we can go to Gatesville to see Ernie play. He told me that Teddy is going to play with them again."

"I don't want to hear his name. I'm not too happy with Ernie either. My son betrayed me. He had to have a hand in last night's disaster. I can't be seen in public today. I can't handle any press."

"Teddy toasted you as his friend. Can you blame him for not liking Ray or Mort? They have been putting him down since you guys were in college. I was glad he made a fool of Ray in front of all those people. He finally got his revenge for the whole Furshizzle nickname and the embarrassment it caused him. It took him thirty years, but he finally did it."

"His revenge on the Whitneys is tearing me down. It's tearing us down."

"You brought the Whitneys in and pushed Teddy out. I don't care for the Whitneys either. Did you see what Mort's and Ray's wives were wearing? They are ten times richer than us, but they look like they shop off the rack at Walmart."

"What they're wearing doesn't mean a goddamn thing! I don't know where your brain is sometimes."

"You don't have to yell at me. I make sure I look good for you. I'm going down by the pool for a little bit, and then I am going to Gatesville to see our son's band play. You can join me if you want, or you can stay in bed and mope all day."

"I'm going to stay here a bit. Can you have Issac bring up the newspapers, some coffee, and toast?"

"I'll tell him, Mr. Grouchy Pants."

Gene turns on the television and flips around the local news stations. All of them seem to be featuring the festival. Video clips of the crowd wearing urinating Calvin stickers on his campaign hats and shirts are lead-in shots to Theodore coming onstage with Ernie's band. They show the toast he made to Gene and Sandy, and there are pictures of them raising their drinks to one another. The news then shows the crowd chanting "Douchebag" toward Ray Whitney. Disgusted, Gene turns off the television.

Issac comes in the bedroom with orange juice, coffee, and a stack of newspapers on a serving tray. "Good morning, sir," he says.

"I'm not sure how good it is. Do I even want to read the papers?"

"Not unless you like to see piles of bullshit in written form, Mr. Douglas."

"With the campaign, I kind of have to look at them."

"If it's at the cost of your happiness, I wouldn't bother, sir."

Gene laughs a little at what Issac says and begins leafing through the papers. On the front page of the *Gatesville Courier* is a picture of Teddy, Gene, and Sandy raising their drinks to one another. The *Harmon Herald* has the headline ART TELLS POLITICS WHAT IT THINKS and has a picture of a young guy with long hair proudly displaying his DOUGLAS FOR GOVERNOR shirt with the urinating Calvin sticker. The *Capital Register* has the headline THEODORE GRAHAM, WORST FRIEND EVER and has a picture of Theodore in his Steve Urkel shirt raising his beer to Gene. On the bottom of the stack is the *Weekly Beat* with the headline SOLD-OUT FESTIVAL HELPS VETERANS HOSPITALS AND LOCAL FAIRGROUND.

"Wow, Teddy's paper spins the positive," Gene says to himself.

Gene skims through the rest of the *Weekly Beat* and comes to the editorial page. He looks for an editorial by Teddy, but there is none on the page. One editorial jumps out at him instead.

Polling Data and Hiding in Plain Sight
by Grace Downwood

After Our Town *with Barry Barnhardt on Wednesday morning, I took Gene Douglas up on his offer of transparency. His independent polling data was offered up to anybody with press credentials. It was touted as totally legit, unbiased, and on the level. I swung by Douglas campaign headquarters showed my press credentials and picked up my copy.*

At first glance, everything seems to be in order. The first page consists of the polling results that are in favor of Gene Douglas. The results say everything the gubernatorial candidate said on television. The second page lists the company that compiled that data, Langley Statistics and Logistics, and offers a toll-free number to call. Under the company name and toll-free number is a list of the automatic dialing machines being used and their state certification numbers. The third page is a copy of the polling questions. Those questions match the State Elections Bureau study. The next fifty pages is a list of the phone numbers called, the day they were called, the time they were called, and the duration of the call. Everything seems to be in order and appears to be on the level. For a journalist, there is nothing worse than wasting time doing research on a nonstory and finding out it is actually a nonstory.

When I was a little girl getting enthusiastic about reading and learning, I remember sitting in the front seat of my grandfather's Pontiac station wagon and reading the words on the side-view mirror, "Objects in the mirror may be closer than they appear." From that day forward, I knew there existed a distorted reality and it was up to me to ask questions. Even on Let's Make a Deal, *contestants did their best to make an informed decision before picking door number 1, 2, or 3. As a journalist, it's up to me to ask questions. The easiest place to start to ask questions about the polling was the 1-800 number. I figured I could call it, find out everything checks out, and move on to another story.*

I called the number. A lovely girl, Samantha, pleasantly answered the phone, Langley Statistics and Logistics. I asked her if it was the same company that conducted the study for the Douglas for Governor campaign. She told me that their client list is confidential. I asked her whom I could talk to if I wanted to conduct a study of my own. Samantha offered to take my number and have somebody get back to me. I asked her if I could mail the information to their company to see if they would be able to conduct a media study for me. She again told me she could have somebody call me back. I agreed to leave my number, but I asked her for a mailing address so I could send my information to them. She hesitated but then gave me an address. It was a Capital City address in a building owned by MW Investments. MW stands for Morton Whitney. That raised suspicion, so I went online and looked up the building and the directory of businesses operating in it. There was no listing for Langley Statistics and Logistics.

I did a Google search of Langley Statistics and Logistics and found nothing, not a phone number, not a website, and not an address. I contacted the Capital City Chamber of Commerce and asked if there was a business license listed for the company. The chamber secretary couldn't locate one on her computer but took my number and offered to have the director call me back. I found it very odd that there was no record of a company that just completed such a large undertaking.

After some suspicion was raised, the next logical step was to look at the automatic dialing machines that were used. The make and models of the machine with their certification numbers were listed in the study. I called the Weights, Measures, and Certification Commission. They are the state department that oversees and issues certification approvals for scales, consumer quality control assurances, and the approvals for these type of automatic dialing machines. I told the man who answered the phone that I wanted some information on the certification numbers from the study. When I told him the numbers, he told me it might take a while to get the information because those certification numbers are over twenty years old. I asked him how often automatic dialers have to be recertified. He told me ones that are used internally for private organizations don't have to be recertified but ones used to call the general public for telemarketing, consumer surveys, and polling have to be done every four years. He told me most are done in our state the year before a presidential election. It appeared the machines used in this independent poll were in violation of the rules of the Consumer Telecommunications and Marketing Act.

After I found another piece of information that didn't check out, I looked at the call log. Automatic dialers don't log time in measurements of p.m. or a.m.; they go by a twenty-four-hour clock, commonly known as military time. As I scanned through the list, I noticed some of these calls were made at odd hours of the day, 2:00 a.m., 3:00 a.m., and 4:00 a.m. or 0200 hours, 0300 hours, and 0400 hours. Who gives positive answers to a telemarketer at those odd hours? That is another violation of the Consumer Telecommunications and Marketing Act. The act clearly states that telemarketing in our state can only be conducted between the hours of 9:00 a.m. and 9:00 p.m., or 0900 hours and 2100 hours. Fines can be issued to polling companies for every call made outside of those hours. Another thing I found odd was that this polling was done in four days. The State Elections Bureau study takes about four business weeks or twenty days to complete. It seems like Langley Statistics and Logistics are a bunch of hardworking go-getters. They must be so busy that they didn't even have time to start a website, file a business license with the Capital City Chamber of Commerce, or establish a mailing address. I guess the people at MW Investments drop off their mail for them.

I didn't have time to dig any further into the independent study paperwork that the Gene Douglas campaign handed me. Working two jobs is time-consuming. I'm sure some of my journalistic colleagues at other news and media outlets have done some of the same research and fact-checking on this as well. I'm sure some other reporters are always on the lookout for things that are hiding in plain sight. They say the devil is in the details, and after studying this independent polling data, I believe I may have been pretty close to hell.

Gene crumbles the newspaper and throws it to the floor. "Fuck! Fuck! Fuck! Mother fuck!"

"Are you all right in there, Mr. Douglas?" Issac says and knocks on the bedroom door.

"I'm okay. I am just a little stumped with the crossword puzzle."

"Okay, Mr. Douglas. I find I get less frustrated if I do the word finds. Sunday is too nice a day to be thinking too hard."

"Thanks, Issac."

"Can I get you anything else? Would you like another cup of coffee?"

"I'm fine. Thank you, Issac."

Sandy comes busting into the bedroom. "Gene, quick, put on the television. Ernie just called me. Somebody called in a bomb threat at the Gatesville Fairgrounds. He said he is okay but they canceled the rest of the festival and are evacuating the fairgrounds now."

Gene turns on the television and finds the news report. Sandy watches with him and sees news helicopters are showing the festival campers tearing down their tents, the vendors packing up, traffic being directed out, and the bomb squad sweeping the buildings. His cell phone rings. He sees that it is Dick Ratzinger. Gene throws his phone on the floor and darts into the bathroom to vomit.

CHAPTER 24

Dreading the day ahead of him, tired, nervous, and stressed, Gene gets in his limousine. What is supposed to be a good Monday morning after a weekend of positive momentum for his campaign is now a morning filled with scandal, pestering reporters, and damage control. The limo goes through the front gates of the Douglas mansion past a herd of reporters shouting questions. It goes up the wide tree-lined streets of Douglas Hills and past a gathering of protesters on the youth honors college campus. Security has reporters barricaded at the end of the driveway at the campaign headquarters. Gene exits the limousine and makes his way inside the building without turning around to acknowledge the barrage of inquiries from the reporters. Inside the conference room, the staff is brainstorming how to handle the mess.

"Normally, I would say 'Good morning,' but it doesn't feel that good. Ernie, I didn't expect to see you here after your stunt this weekend," Gene says.

"I'm still a paid member of your campaign staff. I'm showing up for work."

"Ray, what are you doing here? You're not on my staff."

"Since your buddy and his little newspaper got me fired from the super PAC, I am now your assistant campaign manager."

Gene puts his briefcase on the table and pours himself a cup of coffee. "Ray, get out. You're not my assistant campaign manager, and you are not a member of my staff."

"My dad is funding your campaign and wants me here to make sure that you and Ratzinger stop fucking it up."

"Well, my dad doesn't need you here. You have enough trouble keeping yourself from fucking up."

Ray stands up and gets in Ernie's face. "Listen here, you little piece of shit. We are in the predicament we're in now because of your little protest. Consider yourself fired."

"The chanting crowd on Saturday night was right. You are a douchebag." Ernie holds up his cell phone and plays a video of the crowd at the festival chanting, "Douchebag!" to Ray.

"Don't be cocky with me, you piece of shit. I will choke you!"

Gene stands up. "That's enough out of you, douchebag. Get out of my building!"

"You will be hearing from my dad. Kiss your funding goodbye."

"I'll be hearing from your dad either way. Now get out!"

"You're just our puppet, Gene. We will put our money behind Sherman Jones, and you will lose this election. You will lose big. We will make sure he destroys you. You won't even be able to run for dog catcher in Carter. You've fucked up your legacy."

"Sherman Jones doesn't want a douchebag on his staff," Gene says as he opens the door of the conference room. "Security. Come in here for a minute."

A tall, broad, and well-built security agent enters the conference room. "Yes, Mr. Douglas."

"Mr. Whitney is an unwelcome guest at this headquarters. Escort him out of the building and make sure you do it in front of the reporters and television cameras. He can tell the press why he is being escorted out himself."

"Yes, Mr. Douglas," the security agent says and grabs Ray.

"You'll be sorry, Gene. I'll make sure of it. You're finished. I will end you!"

"I don't think that was a good idea," Dick Ratzinger says.

"You can either follow him out or stay here and do your job. Your choice, Dick."

"It's about time you grew a set. Way to go, Dad."

"That's enough out of you," Gene says. "Sidney, release a press statement that says Ray Whitney is not a member of our staff. Though we appreciate his support and are counting on his vote, he is not welcome in private meetings conducted by the Douglas for Governor campaign staff."

"I'll do that right away, Gene."

"Marty, what are this morning's issues? Let's get them out in the open and figure this hot mess out. Let's address them one at a time."

"We are still getting questions about the arson attempt at the *Weekly Beat.*"

"That one is the least of our concerns. The response for that one . . . We commend the police for quickly taking the suspect into custody. We have no reason to believe the police won't do a full and thorough investigation, and we are glad that no one was injured and damages were minimal," Dick says.

"We have the—" Marty starts and is interrupted by a commotion outside in the hallway.

"Now who is here?" Gene asks.

The door of the conference room flies open. It's Morton Whitney dressed as a priest complete with collar, robe, and rosary beads. "I'm really sick and tired of having to come here in costume. The press are everywhere, my driveway, my Capital City building, your driveway, and outside of this shithole!"

"What are we going to tell the press when they ask what a priest is doing here?" Russ asks.

"We can tell them a priest was here to give you last rites after I choke you to death, Mr. PoopLips."

"My name is Russ Dewitt!"

"Who the fuck would name their daughter Russ? Just tell the goddamn press you had a priest here for some protection of religious freedom policy talks. They'll believe that."

"They're going to want the name of the priest and the parish or organization," Russ says.

"The urge to kill you grows stronger every time you open your mouth. Tell them Father Nunfucker was here and he was collecting money for Saint Peter the Pillow-Biter's Fart Festival. You mean to tell me that none of you mouth-breathers can make up a believable story to tell the press?"

"The press is outside today because of your independent polling lie. You didn't cover your tracks too well with that one, did you, Mort?" Ernie says as he looks up from his cell phone screen.

"Look, you little leg-humper. It was the wiseass nonsense you pulled at the festival over the weekend that made this campaign look like a bunch of booger-eating short bus riders. How could you let that middle-class mutt Teddy Graham play you like such a fool? You're lucky I called in that bomb threat. God only knows how much more damage he could have done to my campaign," Morton says.

"That's my son, and this is my campaign. I'm not going to stand by and let you talk to him like that!"

"I thought my son's only victory in life was being the sperm that got to the egg first. I see that was your son's only life victory too. We have so much in common, don't we? Where is my idiot son, anyway?"

"I kicked him out. He is not on my campaign staff."

"He is what I tell you he is. I'm funding this shit show. I sent him here to keep Ratzinger and the rest of you clowns from fucking up. I have a lot of money invested in this campaign, and if you lose, I lose billions. I have to make this government work for me."

"Mr. Whitney," Ernie asks.

"What do you want? It better not be permission to go to the bathroom, because I'm not helping you wipe your ass."

"Did you really call in that bomb threat yesterday?"

"Of course I did. I couldn't let that sardine-slurping class Teddy Graham do any more damage."

"Were you ever diagnosed with Alzheimer's?"

"Gene, you are going to have to tell your wife you had to have a late-term abortion seventeen years after the fact, because I am going to kill that little wiseass of yours. What kind of fucking question is that?"

"I only asked because normally when you come in, you usually ask us to get rid of all recording devices and electronics. You didn't do that today, and I was able to get a video of you in your priest outfit saying you called in yesterday's bomb threat. You just seem a little forgetful. That's why I asked. I'm just looking out for your health," Ernie says.

"You little son of a bitch! Give me that phone. Give it to me right fucking now! Get that phone off your son, or I swear I will kill him!"

"I'm still recording your death threats. They sound funnier because you're wearing a priest costume."

Mort lunges at Ernie, but other staffers at the table grab him.

"Security!" Gene yells.

The large security guard comes running in the room. "Yes, Mr. Douglas?"

"Please detain Mr. Whitney until the police arrive. Marty, call the police."

"Let me go. I will destroy you! I will destroy everybody in this room! None of you will ever work in politics again. Money controls politics, and I'm the money! I am the money!" Morton shouts as he tries to wriggle his way out of the security agent's grip.

"Still recording, Mr. Whitney," Ernie says.

"I'm going to kill you, you little puke stain."

"Mr. Whitney, we can do this the easy way or the hard way. I will put you on the ground with my knee in your back if I have to. Now, are you going to be still and quiet?" the security agent calmly says.

"Quick, turn on the news. The next shit storm is about to hit," Sidney Hughes says, looking up from his phone.

Gene turns on the television, and the staffers focus their attention on the TV at the front of the conference room. The security agent holding Mort turns toward the television. Mort is mumbling and cursing under his breath.

"Channel 6 News interrupts this program to bring you this special report," an announcer says as *News Anchor Silvia Sleuth is seen behind the news desk.*

"We have some late breaking news this morning on the arson attempt at the Weekly Beat. The suspect in custody, Cy Marino, unable to make bail, awaits trial in county lockup. In a statement from the defendant's lawyer, claims are made that there are more powerful entities at

work in this case and it wasn't simply just a case of a small-time arsonist attempting to burn a building down. We join Channel 6 reporter Cindy Shannahan live at the law office of Watkins, Fowler, and Baird."

"Thank you, Silvia. I'm here at the law firm Watkins, Fowler, and Baird with Attorney Marcy Gubreck, defendant Cy Marino's lawyer in this arson case. New details of this case have emerged. Can you tell us about them?"

"Yes. This morning, the defendant's brother, Mario Marino, brought surveillance footage from his auto body and collision repair shop to the law firm with the hopes of getting reduced charges or a possible plea deal for his differently abled brother. The video surveillance shows a man handing an envelope to Mario Marino, who then turned the envelope over to his brother, Cy. The police were called to our law firm. Mario Marino is in police custody, being interviewed, and may face charges as an accomplice," Marcy Gubreck says.

"Has the man in the surveillance footage been positively identified?"

"Yes, the man has been positively identified, and the district judge has issued a warrant for his arrest. The man has been identified as Richard 'Dick' Ratzinger, campaign manager for gubernatorial candidate Eugene Douglas. Police are going to his home and his place of employment and hope to have him in custody for questioning within the hour."

The screen becomes a split screen, with Sylvia Sleuth at the anchor's desk and Cindy Shannahan doing her stand-in with Marcy Gubreck.

"Cindy, we just received word that police have been called by the Douglas campaign headquarters. A patrol car is on its way. Is this the reason?" Silvia Sleuth asks.

"We have no information on that here. The Douglas campaign has not been contacted by the law firm."

The screen goes back to a full shot of Silvia at the anchor's desk. "We will have more coverage of this story as more information comes in. Reporter Grace Downwood is already at the Douglas campaign head-quarters, waiting for a press conference. We will check in with her soon. For now, we will rejoin this morning's programming already in progress."

"I knew you would fuck that up too, Ratzinger!" Mort says.

"Dick, you should make a break for it now so we can watch an O. J. Simpson–like police chase on live television. Too bad you drive a BMW and not a white Ford Bronco," Ernie jokes.

"Ernie, enough. Dick, do yourself a favor, call your wife and family now and cooperate with the police when they get here," Gene says.

"I will, and I will tell them where the cash came from," Dick says. His voice is weak, and his face has lost all color.

"You lawyer up and shut the fuck up if you even want to work for me again!" Morton yells.

Two police officers are escorted into the conference room by another security agent. Gene explains the situation to them, and they radio for another squad car. Dick Ratzinger is being handcuffed and read his rights while Ernie shows the other officer the video recording of Morton admitting to making the bomb threat to the Gatesville festival.

"You're going to have to come to the station with us so we can get a copy of the video," the police officer tells Ernie.

Two more police officers enter the conference room.

"Place handcuffs on Mr. Whitney and read him his rights. Is there a back door out of here? There is a lot of press outside," the police officer asks.

"I would consider it personal favor to the Douglas for Governor campaign if you took these two gentlemen out in front of the press. Can you do me that favor?" Gene asks.

"I gotcha. Sherman Jones only wishes he could get this much press coverage," the officer says. "Okay, fellows, make sure you make the department look good for the cameras, and let's get these two out of here."

"You'll pay. All of you will pay for this!" Morton shouts as he is led out of the room.

Gene turns on the television. "We might as well watch it on television. We can figure out how to put a shine on this shit later."

The staff watches as police escort Dick and Morton out of the building. Dick has his head down and is silent as he is taken to a waiting police car. The press snaps photographs and shouts random questions at

Ernie, the police officers, and the suspects in custody. Morton didn't go so quietly.

"I was framed! Gene Douglas and his son are crooks. They did this to me. I'm a jobs creator! Vote for Sherman Jones! Vote for Sherman Jones!"

The stand-in reporter appears on the television screen.

"I'm Grace Downwood of Channel 6 News, reporting live from the Douglas campaign headquarters in Douglas Hills. What we just witnessed here was campaign manager Dick Ratzinger and multibillionaire businessman Morton Whitney being led out of the building in handcuffs by police officers. With the police officers was Ernie Douglas, but he wasn't in restraints. From what we are seeing here, we believe that Ernie Douglas is acting as a participating witness. For what, we are unsure. From earlier reports, we know that there is a warrant out for Mr. Ratzinger's arrest for his involvement in the attempted arson investigation at the Weekly Beat building in Harmon. We are unsure of why Morton Whitney is being arrested. Earlier today, we witnessed Ray Whitney being escorted out of the building by the Douglas campaign security but have no further details on his removal at this time. Quite a busy morning here at this campaign headquarters. We will try to get all the details and a statement from police and the Douglas campaign soon. I'm going to turn it back over to you in the studio, Silvia."

"Thank you, Grace. We will check in with you throughout the day as more details come in. Pretty exciting morning. We will return you to programming already in progress and update you as more details emerge. Make sure to tune in for the news at noon and get the latest."

Gene turns off the television. "Okay, folks. If anybody wants to quit, do it now. If not, stick around, pour some fresh coffee, and let's craft a press statement to separate ourselves from these people and figure out how to move forward."

CHAPTER 25

Theodore is sitting at the desk in his apartment, writing an editorial for Thursday's edition of the *Weekly Beat*. A half-empty beer bottle sits on the desk's corner, there is a joint burning in the ashtray, and the classic rock station is blaring ZZ Top in the background. The door buzzer sounds.

"Paul, what's up? What brings you upstairs?"

"The elevator."

"Yeah, you get winded combing what remains of your hair. The stairs would have killed you. It looks like you worked up a sweat pushing the button to the top floor."

"If there weren't an elevator, I would have called. I haven't been up here since you moved in. Looks like you made yourself comfortable, and it smells like Willie Nelson's tour bus."

"I call it home. What's going on?"

"I came to see if you were watching the Gene Douglas campaign fall apart."

"I haven't even turned on the television today. I was working in the office with some of the writers and editing some of their articles for the online edition. Now I'm working on my piece for Thursday."

"Anything good?"

"Just a piece about wasted potential and opportunities in some of our communities."

"So you know nothing about this morning's events? You haven't seen Gene's press conference?"

"I haven't had the television on since last week, and that was only to watch *Jeopardy* and *Happy Days* reruns. Are they still talking about the festival?"

"How can you be a newsman at my paper if you don't follow the news? The news is talking about the festival, Grace Downwood's editorial, Ray Whitney being escorted out of the Douglas campaign headquarters by security, Dick Ratzinger paying the Marino brothers to burn this building down, and Mort Whitney being arrested for making the bomb threat to the Gatesville Fairgrounds yesterday. This is the busiest news day in decades, and you're missing it. You're a part of it, for Christ's sake."

"Holy shit! Did Gene make a statement to the press?"

"Yes, earlier this afternoon. Channel 6 has it on their website. You should watch it."

Theodore invites Paul to sit down and opens his laptop. He logs onto the Channel 6 News website and clicks on Gene's press conference, and they watch.

Russ Dewitt comes to the podium in front of the campaign headquarters. "Candidate Douglas would like to make a brief statement before taking any questions from the press. Please hold your questions until the end. Written copies of the press release statements are available. See Sidney Hughes, our media coordinator, for an official copy. Without further delay, here is gubernatorial candidate Eugene Douglas."

Gene makes his way to the podium, his expression humble, and he appears to have aged since Theodore saw him last.

"Good afternoon. I owe the voters of this state an apology. I am truly sorry. I deeply regret the point where my campaign began listening to wealthy donors and special interests that were attempting to purchase my candidacy for their own personal gain and legislative influence. Their voices weren't the voices of the people that I want to serve. I beg for forgiveness, and I vow that I will do everything in my power to regain the trust of my constituents.

"After the events of this morning and reviewing the media discoveries made about my personal associations in the past weeks, my campaign staff was forced to do some deep soul searching. We had to seriously consider our options. One option was suspending our campaign and dropping out of this race. There have been many people that worked hard to get us to this point. I couldn't, in good conscience, let their hard work be in vain. I choose to stay in the race and earn back the trust of the people.

It's an uphill battle that I am willing to fight. It's a fight for the future of our state. It's a fight to restore prosperity to the people. It's a fight to build a better tomorrow for the children of today. It's a fight for freedom. It's a fight for those wanting change for the better. I ask you to join me so I can fight for the voices of every voter in this great state. Thank you. I will now take a few questions from the press."

"Did you have any knowledge that your campaign manager hired arsonists to burn down the Weekly Beat?" a reporter asks.

"I had no knowledge of Dick Ratzinger's involvement in the arson attempt. Police are thoroughly investigating the case. The campaign is fully cooperating with investigators and providing any information that we can."

"Did you have any knowledge of Morton Whitney calling in the bomb threat to the Gatesville Fairgrounds yesterday morning?"

"I had no idea that Mort Whitney made that threat until he admitted to making it in front of my staff this morning. I'm happy for my son's quick thinking to record Mr. Whitney's statements. Ernie has turned all video over to the police, and we are cooperating fully with any investigation."

"Have you appointed a new campaign manager?"

"The campaign is taking a look at our staffing needs. There will be some changes made. I'm sure there will be some new faces joining our team. There will be some familiar faces taking on additional duties. We will be meeting tomorrow to determine our personnel makeup, and I will announce my new team then."

"Are you planning to ask Teddy Graham to rejoin your team?"

"We will decide on our staffing needs in tomorrow's meeting."

"The past three months have been littered with controversy surrounding your campaign. Your biggest financial backer calls in a bomb threat at one of your campaign events, and your campaign manager contracted criminals to burn down the building of a newspaper giving you bad press. How do you plan on earning the trust of the people back? Can you earn it back?"

"I am ashamed of myself for associating with Morton Whitney, Ray Whitney, and Dick Ratzinger. I should have paid more attention to those that advised me against working with them. I regret that I didn't. I hope

I can earn the trust of the people back. I am going to try to do it by going back out and talking to the people. It worked for me when I started this campaign. I see no reason it can't work again."

"How can the people believe that you had no involvement with the criminal activity that went on around your campaign?"

"As I said earlier, I had no knowledge of the activity and we are cooperating fully with law enforcement."

"How are you going to reinvent your campaign in such a short time?"

"First, I have to make it up to the Gatesville Fairgrounds. My son has offered the service of his band to headline another festival there. This time, none of the proceeds will benefit the campaign. All proceeds will benefit veterans hospitals, the Gatesville Fairgrounds, and local law enforcement. Local law enforcement had to conduct a mass evacuation of the fairgrounds yesterday because of the actions of Morton Whitney. They did it quickly, safely, and efficiently. Sadly, to the taxpayers, it was a costly undertaking. I have to make it up to them. We're talking to the fairground staff now and hopefully can have this new festival in two weeks."

"Do you think a festival will win back the trust of the people?"

"No. I have a lot of work ahead of me. I have doors to knock on, neighborhoods to visit, a platform to communicate to voters, voices to listen to, and ideas for our future to develop. I'm not expecting an easy road ahead of me. It's going to be hard work, but I am willing to do it."

"The Sherman Jones campaign made a statement earlier saying that your associations have cost you this election. Is your campaign a lost cause at this point?"

"My opponent is welcome to his opinion. I look forward to debating him. The voters will see that our platform is better than his. It is better for working people. It is better for taxpayers. It is better for property owners. It is better for the future of our state. He has to prove himself a better candidate on the issues than I am and not simply win by exploiting the missteps of my campaign."

Russ Dewitt makes his way back to the podium, and Gene leaves. "I'm sorry, that's all the time candidate Douglas has for questions right now. Don't forget to get a copy of the press release from Sidney Hughes. It has some more details that we didn't get to elaborate on in this Q-and-A session. Thank you, members of the press."

The video of the press conference ends, and Theodore looks up from the computer screen. "I would have loved to have been a fly on the wall at the Douglas headquarters to see how all this went down today."

"You should look at the footage of Dick Ratzinger and Mort Whitney being brought out of the building."

Theodore finds those clips on the website. He watches security bring Ray Whitney out of the campaign headquarters in front of the press. Ray is seen running to his car to get away from reporters. He sees Dick Ratzinger with his head down being led to the police car. He sees Mort Whitney in handcuffs dressed as a priest and yelling at the press as police escort him to a squad car.

"Why was Mort dressed like a priest?"

"I'm curious about that myself."

"They could sync up Benny Hill montage music to those clips and make it hilarious."

"Yakety Sax, yeah, that would be funny. I'm surprised nobody from the press attempted to call you for comment on any of this."

"I turned my cell phone off on Saturday before the festival and haven't turned it back on yet."

"What if I needed you? What if there was an emergency?"

"You're sitting in my apartment now. You found me. Is there an emergency you have to tell me about?"

"No, but don't you think you should check in periodically? It's been nearly three days."

Theodore takes his phone off the desk and turns it on. "I was busy playing guitar and writing over the weekend. I didn't want to cloud my head with the nonsense that comes through on this device." The phone starts beeping, pinging, and vibrating as it boots itself. "One hundred and forty-four texts, sixty-eight missed calls, and thirty-four voice mails. I should probably check on some of these."

"Well, I'm going to let you get to that. I think I got the weed munchies just by being in your apartment. I'm going to find some dinner. Will I see you at the staff meeting tomorrow?"

"You get the munchies just by hearing words that rhyme with foods. Don't blame my glaucoma medication for your hunger."

"You don't have glaucoma."

"That's because of the medicine. Duh. I will see you at the meeting tomorrow. Do you have good news for us?"

"I do. Advertising revenue is up by a lot. We may be able to print more than four days a week. We can talk about it then."

"This glorified grocery store paper is turning into something, after all," Theodore says as the elevator door shuts on Paul.

Theodore sits on the sofa and begins to delete text messages and check voice mails on his phone. Most of his calls were from reporters seeking comments and trying to get interviews about the Douglas campaign. The door buzzer sounds again. Theodore opens the door. It's Gene.

"Eugene Douglas! Well, I'll be damned! You look like shit, my friend. Come in."

"Hi, Teddy. The new place looks great. Ernie told me you had a pretty good setup here."

"Yeah, it's not bad at all. The apartment is as long as the building, so I have plenty of room. That end is acoustically set up for guitar practices and jam sessions. The middle is where I work, write, and entertain, and that end is the kitchen, bedrooms, and bathroom. I call it home," Theodore says and leads Gene to the living room.

"Not a bad setup at all. It's like the ultimate bachelor pad."

"Your limo wasn't followed here by a bunch of press, was it?"

"No. I had enough press for today, and I didn't want to create another story. I had one of my security team drive me over in his car so I wouldn't draw attention."

"So what brings you by? You want to smoke a joint? Drink a beer?"

"No. I can't be getting baked right now, but I will take a beer. I suppose you saw the news today."

Theodore goes to the minifridge in his guitar area and gets two beers out. "My goal was to be media-free until tomorrow. My cell phone was off. I didn't turn on the television. I didn't pick up a newspaper. I tried to avoid the nonsense, but Paul Hoptak was just up here to make sure I saw today's news. I just got done watching it online. You had quite a day."

"It was a day from hell, and I think it's going to launch the week from hell. There is a ton of damage control to do, but it's for the right reasons. I guess you know that I am done with Ray and Mort Whitney. Dick Ratzinger is fired too. You were right about them, Teddy."

"I'm not one to say I told you so. You learned the hard way, but you can move on from there," Theodore says. "Why was Mort dressed like a priest? Watching him yell and scream at the press as they put him in the police car was hilarious."

"He was paranoid about being seen by the press since you exposed him on security cameras, so he came in disguise. Last time, he was dressed as a UPS guy."

"How did he end up getting arrested for making the bomb threat?"

"Usually, he would come in and make us get rid of all the electronic devices, but this morning, he was so frazzled that he forgot. Ernie recorded him admitting it with his cell phone. The media will be releasing those videos once they are processed into evidence. Mort may have been preoccupied with the thought of facing fraud charges for the phony independent polling that Grace Downwood exposed."

"She is a good investigative reporter, plus she has a knack at looking for things hiding in plain sight."

"I know you helped her uncover the fraud."

"It wasn't that hard to uncover. I thought you would be smart enough to check into it before you offered it up to the press. You practically dared the press to look into it. Grace was the reporter who took the dare. I'm sure the other news outlets and regulatory bodies are looking into it today."

"I should have looked into it. I should have listened to you from the beginning. I should have done a lot of things. Your articles and appearances on *State of the State This Week* didn't help either. Couldn't you have left well enough alone?"

"I could have, but you are my friend, and I was looking out for you."

"How was stirring up trouble for me, my financiers, my super PAC, and my campaign looking out for me?"

"If I didn't expose that stuff now, some other reporter from a bigger paper might expose it later. What if they did it after you got elected governor? How do you think being a governor arrested for fraud would look? How would that let Ernie fulfill his legacy with a fraudulent former governor for a father? You could have been easily sent to jail. I just hope for your sake that the investigation doesn't incriminate you in any way. It's possible you will be implicated."

"No. They acted all on their own. We took a close look at everything today. The campaign didn't pay for the phony polling. The bomb threat was Mort acting alone. Dick Ratzinger was on surveillance video paying cash to a guy to burn down this building, but I think Mort ordered him to do it. None of that came from me or the staff. None of us were aware of any of it."

"I'm glad you're not involved, but I could have been killed if that arson attempt had succeeded. I was up here sleeping. I lost my Skylark in the incident. I'm not happy about that. I loved that car."

"I know you did. I'm sorry. I will replace it or purchase another one for you. I'm sure you can find one for sale in those auto locators."

"It wouldn't be the same, but if I find one, I am holding you to that promise."

"You find one, I will pay for it. That's a promise."

"So what brings you here, anyway? I don't think you answered that question."

"I should have listened to you from the beginning. You got me the good polling numbers for the primary, and I am sure you would have improved them for the next polling cycle. I didn't listen, and I know I made a mistake letting you go. I'm here today to ask you to come back to my campaign."

"I have a job at the *Weekly Beat* now. I signed a two-year agreement with Paul Hoptak."

"I'm sure we can talk to Paul and work something out. You can give his paper exclusive reports in exchange for flexibility. I'm sure if he is any kind of businessman, he will see the value in that."

"Maybe, but I'm not really interested in coming back."

"There is nobody better than you who could get me out of this negative rut and make me look good to the voters again. You know how to turn things around. I need you back. I want my friend back in charge of my team."

Theodore stands up and paces around the living room as he thinks about Gene's offer. "No. I'm sorry, Gene, but my answer is no. I don't want to do it."

"Come on, Teddy, I need you. I need my friend behind me again."

"Our friendship doesn't change. We can hang out, have dinners, go places, do things, get baked, and just call each other to shoot the shit, but I am not at all interested it managing your campaign again, and I'm not giving you tips to get you out of the trouble you're in now."

"If you come back to my campaign, I will win and you can get baked in the governor's mansion with me. You would like to add to your list of the famous places where you got high, wouldn't you?"

"I would like that, but if you win, I'm sure you'll invite your friend over anyway, right?"

"You're right. Look, Teddy, I really need you. I'm in a deep hole now, and I need your help to get out of it. I'm begging you to come back."

"No, Gene, I won't do it. I don't want to do it."

"Why not? What can I do to get you to come back? More money? Final say? What will it take?"

"I just don't feel like coming back into that environment. I moved here to work at your schools. I had to mingle among your wealthy, elite friends. I never fit in. The committee and staff at the youth college made me feel bad about growing up lower middle class. They only tolerated me because I improved the school's ranking and took the debate team to nationals and won. My father worked hard to make sure my future wasn't in the lower middle class. He made me work hard to use my brain to get ahead. He made sure I got into an Ivy League school so I could do better than him and have a great future and have the things he never could. I made it to where my father dreamed of me going. I did it only to find out that people that come from money still look down on those that didn't always have it."

"I never looked down on you."

"You haven't, and your family never has. That's why we're friends. But your rich circle of friends, I put up with them for nearly four years and did a good job for you, but when the Whitneys and big money came knocking at your campaign door, you found it easy to let me go. That hurt. I'm not putting myself in that position again."

"I promise, if you come back, that you are running the show and have the final say."

"No, Gene. I like it here. I like the challenge. I like the people I get to work with, and they never try to make me feel bad about where I came from. You're going to have to find somebody else."

"Will you at least think about it? How about you sleep on it and call me tomorrow?"

"No is my answer. I will call you tomorrow and say no, but I will take you up on your offer to come over for dinner and drinks with you and Sandy. We can get high. I will bring joints, but I won't work for your campaign."

"We would love to have you over for dinner. Sandy even asked if I would invite you over a few weeks ago. We can talk more about getting you back then."

"I'm not coming back. That's a guarantee. Who prepped you for the press conference today? You did really well, considering the circumstances."

"Sidney helped with the press statement, and Russ prepped me for the questions."

"Promote one of those guys. I don't want the job."

"Think about it," Gene says as he stands up to leave.

"You want some joints to take home with you? I'm sure Sandy would like some. She was probably bummed about not being able to get baked at the festival," Theodore says and goes over to the cookie jar and removes a handful of already-rolled doobies.

"She was a little bummed about that, but we have to be careful in the public eye," Gene says and takes the left-handed cigarettes from Theodore and puts them in his jacket pocket.

"What time is dinner?"

"How does seven sound?"

"Perfect! I'll see you then. I will bring the bong to toke for the special occasion."

CHAPTER 26

Gene enters the conference room looking rested and ready to work. The events leading up to this morning's staff meeting have been unpleasant and damaging to his campaign, but Gene has a look of confidence about him. He has spent the early morning hours pumping himself up with determination and positive thoughts. Sandy having sex with him has only added to the spring in his step.

"Good morning. I hope all of you are ready for a long day. We have a lot of work to do. I am counting on all of you to help me bring this team back and take it all the way to the governor's mansion. Shall we get started?"

"Is Teddy going to come back?" Ernie asks.

"No, he's not, and neither is Tim Collins. We have to work with who we have in this room."

"Who is going to be the new campaign manager?" Russ Dewitt asks.

"Well, I gave this a little thought last night. I even looked at some résumés. Russ, yours is quite impressive. You have worked for a lot of campaigns with only moderate success. You are a due for a big win. Is managing this campaign something you would be interested in?"

"Yes, of course I'm interested."

"No fucking way! Russ has done nothing but suck up to Mort Whitney and Dick Ratzinger, and those two are going to jail. They are the reason we're in this mess. I'll talk to Teddy," Ernie says.

"Teddy is not coming back. He has a contract with the *Weekly Beat* that he can't break. He's not an option. Let's put it all on the table and brainstorm. If Russ is half as good as his résumé says he is, he will emerge as a leader and be able to manage this campaign. If not, we will see where we are at the end of the day. We will do what we have to do."

"I can handle it. I won't let you down," Russ says.

"Show me you will, don't tell me you will. Okay, let's get started. Sidney, what's in the media?"

"Sherman Jones made a statement to the press. Do you want me to play it for you?"

"Yes, we have to hear what our opponent is saying."

Sidney connects his laptop to the projector, scrolls, and clicks a few keys. "This was his press statement from last night."

"It's unfortunate that my opponent had poor associations. Associates like those of Mr. Douglas are what gives politics a bad name. People that can use their money to influence government take the people out of a government of the people. Candidates that sell government influence only hurt the people whose vote they seek. It's wrong. It is my hope that Mr. Douglas has seen the error of his ways and learned valuable lessons. Was he selling government influence to the Whitneys? Can Gene Douglas be trusted? That's up to the voters to decide. Should Republicans risk damaging the chances of good candidates seeking House and Senate seats by endorsing a gubernatorial candidate with such untrustworthy affiliations? That's up to the party leadership. My campaign is focused on the issues. My staff is made up of members that have the needs of the people as their number one priority. I will face any candidate that challenges me, and I am confident I will win. My platform is for the people. My people are for the people. Special interests can look elsewhere to purchase influence. Sherman Jones isn't selling any. Sherman Jones isn't for sale."

"He landed some punches with that. He likes to refer to himself in the third person too. We did give him the boxing gloves to hit us with. I expected him to take advantage of our missteps. How do we respond?" Gene asks.

"We don't respond. We should come out strong on important issues in public appearances and in news conferences. Meanwhile, we should take a look at his donor disclosures, his super PAC backers, and be ready to hit back. Our super PAC can have some negative ads made if we need them when it's closer to the election. Sherman Jones is going to keep hitting us with our missteps as long as the media is interested. We have to change their interests," Russ says.

"That sounds like a good plan. Marty, I will put you on that research. Did the party leadership make any statements?"

"Mark Winters, the party chairman, made a brief statement to the press. He called me last night to make an off-the-record statement telling us we better get our shit together and that they are looking for another candidate just in case the investigations implicate you in anything. I'll read what he said to the press," Sidney says.

"The party has no reason to believe that Eugene Douglas had any knowledge or involvement in the activities of Dick Ratzinger or Morton Whitney. We trust investigators to be thorough and are confident that our candidate will be free and clear of any wrongdoing."

"Mark could have hammered us if he wanted to, but he didn't. He left the door open for us to be redeemed. What about the papers? What are the headlines saying?"

"They're not as nice. Most of the papers feature pictures of Mort and Dick being arrested with pictures of you next to them. The *Gatesville Courier* headline reads, DOUGLAS A DUD? HOW DEEP DOES THE FRAUD RUN? The *Harmon Herald* headline is, EVERYTHING'S COMING UP SHERMAN! DOUGLAS FALLOUT A GIFT. The *Capital Register* headline reads, DIRTY MONEY = DIRTY POLITICS; TEAM DOUGLAS A FRAUD. That's what the big papers are saying."

"Did the *Weekly Beat* put anything out?"

"The *Weekly Beat* online edition for today has a small piece written by Teddy. The headline is, DOUGLAS CHASES THE WOLVES OUT OF HIS HENHOUSE. It doesn't say anything terrible. Teddy wrote that you rid your campaign of bad influences and it's up to you to make a comeback."

"I expected that jackass to tear us down with this," Russ says.

"If that jackass were here, you wouldn't have the chance to be campaign manager," Gene snaps back.

"I'm sorry, Gene, force of habit."

"What appearances can we make this week?"

"All the news networks would love to get an interview. Maybe we can start with something easy, like *Our Town* with Barry Barnhardt, to fine-tune our narrative and work up to tougher interviews on Channel 6 and Channel 4. All the papers expressed an interest in an exclusive interview."

"I recommend that we avoid doing the interviews and press conferences and go right to the public. We can schedule some speaking engagements for different organizations and events. We will leave some time open for press Q and A, but we can defer all questions about scandal to the investigators and stick to the issues," Russ says.

"Russ, when did you get a brain? That's the smartest statement that you made since you've been here," Ernie says.

"Ernie, that's enough. If we are going to go right to the public, we should know what the public is saying. Ernie, how about you hook your laptop up to the projector and get that social media page up on the screen so we can look at some of the comments from the public?"

Ernie moves to the front of the room and hooks his laptop to the projector. With a few short clicks, he has the comments section of a social media blog on the screen. "See for yourself. Winning back the trust of the people isn't going to be easy."

I find it hard to believe that Gene Douglas was ignorant of the criminal activity surrounding his campaign. This means one of two things. One, Gene Douglas is a moron and is too dumb to lead. Two, Gene Douglas knew what was going on and was smart enough not to get caught. Either way, he can't be trusted to be our governor.

I hope Gene Douglas goes to jail so I can go over to the Douglas mansion and take care of the sexy Sandy Douglas personally.

Teddy Graham wouldn't have let this happen.

I hope Mort Whitney and Dick Ratzinger get ass-raped in prison. Karma will make Gene Douglas the losing candidate on Election Day.

The only thing more crooked than the Douglas campaign is an Arkansas dental x-ray.

Politics has always been about the money. Maybe the Douglas campaign will shed some light on this fact and the people will finally embrace change and take the government that belongs to them back. We can hope, but I have my doubts. People are dumb enough to eat Hot Pockets.

I wonder if Sandy Douglas's farts smell like burned Legos because of all the plastic surgery.

Just wait. I'm sure the investigation will find that Gene Douglas had a hand in everything. It is, after all, the Douglas for Governor campaign.

America is about second chances. Let's see how Gene Douglas redeems himself before we judge him.

Why the fuck was Morton Whitney dressed like a priest?

Our choice for governor is between Sherman Jones and Gene Douglas. I think I'm going to start doing meth.

I think it is nice that Gene Douglas is going to have another music festival to raise money for veterans, law enforcement, and the fairgrounds. I think his apology is sincere. I will keep an open mind about him until election day.

If Sandy Douglas shows us her tits at the next press conference, all will be forgiven.

A crooked political campaign—who didn't see this coming? Really!

Gene Douglas is guilty by association. He should just disappear and become a sad footnote in our state's history.

Fuck you, Gene Douglas! You're not innocent. I wouldn't mind becoming Ernie's stepfather, though. Sandy D, please do me.

We liked Gene Douglas better when Teddy Graham was running his campaign. Maybe Teddy Graham should run for governor.

The rats are the first ones to leave a sinking ship. Dick Ratzinger, Ray Whitney, and Mort Whitney left the ship yesterday. Captain Douglas is going down with his ship.

Gene Douglas messed up big time, but Sherman Jones didn't have to be such a dick about it. Let's see what they do from here.

"Have we seen enough?" Ernie asks.

"Yes, that's plenty," Gene says.

"Hey, Robert, how much did the Whitneys give directly to the campaign?" Russ Dewitt asks.

Robert Wermer flips through a few pages of ledger. "A little over 150,000. I have no idea how much he put into the super PAC."

"The super PAC money isn't my concern. They can help us with political ads closer to the election, but I have an idea how to change public opinion," Russ says.

"What's your idea?"

"All campaign donations are nonrefundable donations, so the Whitneys aren't getting their money back, but how much would it hurt us financially to spend 150,000 this week?" Russ asks.

"It would hurt. It would leave a lump for sure. With the recent events, I can't guarantee that there will be more coming in. We may have to cut some expenses."

"What's your idea, Russ?"

"If we can swing it, we can separate ourselves from Whitney money. You can say publicly that the Whitney family donated 150,000 to your campaign and you don't want anything to do with their dirty money. You want to put that money to good use. The head of the State Firefighters Commission is looking for funding so they can improve emergency response times across the state. You can donate the Whitney money for a good cause, and you can make it in a statement in front of the press. I think if we do that first, we will change public opinion. The general public is a bunch of fickle mush-heads that changes their mind when the media tells them. After our announcement, we will own the press cycle and can turn their attention to our side of the issues."

"That's a great idea. It's like Teddy is speaking through you."

"Even Teddy isn't this brilliant," Russ jokes.

"I think we can afford to donate the money. It will probably bring some contributions in as well. Spend bad money to make good money," Robert Wermer says.

"Sidney, see if you can set this up with the fire commissioner and the press. The sooner, the better. Tomorrow would be great."

"I'm sure it can be done. This is a great idea. It may turn some things around. Good job, Russ."

"We can work on my speech once Sidney gets everything set up. Now, we should work on strategy. We have three different strategy binders, one from Teddy and two from Mort. There are some good points in all of them. Let's take what we can use from each of them, create a new one, and get this campaign back on course for the governor's mansion. We can do this, folks," Gene says with renewed enthusiasm for his campaign.

CHAPTER 27

It has been a grueling week for Gene, but by the week's end, he is feeling pretty good about how things are turning in his favor. On Monday, evil influences left his campaign in police custody. Tuesday, he reorganized his staff and put together a new strategy. On Wednesday, a well-planned publicity stunt won him media attention. Thursday, Friday, and Saturday were filled with speaking engagements across the state where he talked about the issues concerning the voters. Everything was falling in line with the new plan. He still has a long road ahead of him, but for the first time in a long time, things are moving in the right direction. The campaign is gearing up for the heart of the battle. Free time is a waning luxury for Gene. This is one of the last Sunday mornings he will have the luxury of relaxing on the patio by the pool and catching up on the news of the week.

Sandy comes out of the house in her bikini with a towel thrown over her shoulders. She sees Gene sitting in the patio lounge reading his newspapers and enjoying his coffee. "What's good in the news today?"

"Nothing, really. I'm being raked over the coals for associating with the Whitneys. I'm being praised for my donation to the State Firefighters Association. I'm being criticized for my donation to the State Firefighters Association. I talked about the issues for the last three days, and the media still isn't reporting about it. They're reporting about the reformation of my campaign staff but tell me it's a bad move for not bringing Teddy back."

"We had such a good time the other night when he came over for dinner. It was nice to hang out like friends again. You weren't his boss. He wasn't your employee. It was just friends enjoying good company."

"I did have a good time. I didn't realize how much I missed that. I wish he would come back to my campaign, though, but I respect his decision not to."

"You should give him a call and see if he wants to come over tonight. We can barbecue by the pool, have some drinks, and pass a joint or two like we used to do."

"You just want him to bring more weed for you."

"I am out of joints, and he always leaves a few as a gift."

"He sent me home with a dozen joints on Monday and left a bunch here after dinner on Tuesday. You couldn't have smoked them all already."

"You were busy most of the week, so I got high and listened to music by the pool. If you become the governor, I'm not going to be able to enjoy being high."

"Yes, we're going to have to be careful from now until the election. There are a lot of campaign events coming up. We're going to have to maintain the wholesome family image. You won't be able to get drunk and slutty."

"Fuck you! That only happened a few times."

"That's true, I'm sorry. Usually, it only happens when you're drinking."

"You better be sorry. Wait, what? I can handle my alcohol."

"I'm only kidding, honey."

"You better be. Are you going to call Teddy and invite him over tonight?"

"He's not going to answer now. I'll call him later. He's going to be on TV in about five minutes."

"How come he is on television more than you? You're the one running for governor."

"I will be on television a lot in the coming weeks. This is the calm before the storm. Let's enjoy it while we still can," Gene says and turns on the television. Sandy gets a wine cooler from the patio bar and sits next to him on the glider. They focus their attention on the television.

"Good Sunday morning to you and welcome to State of the State This Week. I am your host, Walter Carl. It was a busy week in local news. Joining me to talk about it today are Jimmy Jenner of the Capital Register and Capital Beat, Joan Mowery of the Gatesville Courier and the Harmon Herald, and Theodore Graham of the Weekly Beat.

"We have a lot to discuss today, but first, I want to congratulate our guest Theodore Graham. His paper, the Weekly Beat, is going from a four-days-per-week newspaper to a six-days-per-week newspaper. The Weekly Beat, only a short time ago, was near extinction, and now it's adding two additional print days. Tell us a little bit about that."

"Let me just start by saying we are a seven-day-per-week newspaper online, but yes, the Weekly Beat has added Tuesday and Wednesday to its print schedule. Monday, the online version will be a recap and highlight edition of the weekend events."

"Most newspapers are getting smaller, relying on online circulation or going out of business. How did your paper buck the trend?"

"I think the Weekly Beat bucked the trend by being different. We have a lot of young writers that are up-and-coming. They are following the basics of journalism and asking the questions, who, what, when, where, why, how much, and how many. We ask those questions and let the readers form their own opinion on facts. Our editorial pages feature writers with many different points of view on a variety of topics. There is open discourse between our writers and our readers, daily, online, and in our Saturday print edition. The reporters aren't getting in line to chase the stories that all the other newspapers are covering. The editorialists aren't writing similar articles with the same opinion. The diversity in our news coverage is what I credit with our newfound success. We aren't owned by a big company telling us what to write, and we aren't writing to please advertisers. The Weekly Beat is refreshing to read when you compare it to other mass-produced newspapers."

"You're not being very clever at disguising your contempt for our newspapers, Mr. Graham," Joan Mowrey says.

"I don't consider it contempt, and I wasn't disguising it. All three of the papers you write for, Joan, are basically carbon copies of one another. Whatever you write for the Harmon Herald is printed in the Gatesville Courier and the Morning Sun Gazette. Your company has one set of

reporters writing for three newspapers. It's cost-effective from a printing standpoint, but who wants to subscribe to both of your newspapers if they are pretty much exactly the same?"

"That's not really a fair assessment. We are writing about the issues that the people are concerned about and not just what our writers feel like writing. We are professional journalists at acclaimed newspapers, not a glorified high school newspaper like the Weekly Beat," Jimmy Jenner says.

"Our circulation numbers doubled and continue to increase. Our advertising revenue followed suit. Are your papers doing as well? We may not be the professional journalists that you claim to be, but your papers and Joan's papers cover stories that the Weekly Beat uncovers. Your papers didn't cover the Capitalist Venture and Protection Act until my paper wrote about it. Your papers didn't cover Ray Whitney, a super PAC trustee, violating campaign finance laws until after we covered it. Your papers didn't even check into Morton Whitney's fraudulent polling data until Grace Downwood highlighted the discrepancies in her editorial last week. Maybe our success is because we are leading journalists and not professional journalists like you say you are."

"Well, we have a very heated discussion between professional colleagues this week, but we have a lot to talk about, so let's move on to another subject. The governor's race, what do you think about the events of this week? Joan?"

"I think this was the beginning of the end of the Eugene Douglas campaign. Two of his staff members were brought out of his headquarters in handcuffs on Monday. Another one that was suspected of violating campaign finance laws was escorted out by security. Gene Douglas was attacking the media with independent polling data that turned out to be fraudulent. He associated himself with people that were buying government to serve their interests. The voters notice these kinds of things, and I think Mr. Douglas is foolish to continue his campaign. I think it is foolish for the Republican Party in our state to continue to back him."

"He is definitely finished in this race. Sherman Jones is going to be the next governor. The stunt on Wednesday with his donation to the State Firefighters Association is a desperate attempt to get voters back on his side. I don't think it's going to work. You probably agree with me on

this, Mr. Graham. I don't even think you could save his campaign if you went back to your old job as his campaign manager," Jimmy Jenner says.

"You were the first Douglas campaign manager when he had favorable polling numbers in the primary quarter. Were you asked to return?" Walter Carl asks.

"I have a new job now, and no, I wasn't asked to return. I was let go from the campaign because of my lack of political experience. I accept that and respect his decision to let me go."

"Did you respect his decision to associate with Morton Whitney?" Joan Mowrey asks.

"It wasn't my decision to make, but Gene Douglas made the decision, and he regrets it. I think his reformation this week is a step in the right direction."

"Russ Dewitt has been very critical about your methods. He even called you an overgrown man-child that accidentally wandered his way to the adult table in one of his editorials that he submitted to our paper. Are you now praising the failing Douglas campaign?" Jimmy Jenner asks.

"I'm not even going to try to hide the fact that there is a personal tension and mutual dislike between myself and Russ Dewitt. I do, however, have to admit his political résumé is better and broader than mine. He should have been made the campaign manager after I was let go. He probably should have been made the manager from day one. He's done a pretty good job as head of the campaign this week."

"You can sit on this show and tell me he is doing a good job. You don't think Wednesday's donation to the State Firefighters Association was a huge publicity stunt?"

"Donating 5,000 or 10,000 dollars, I would have agreed that it was a publicity stunt, but this was a donation of 150,000 dollars. That's a lot of money for a campaign to spend, especially with all the negativity surrounding it. Gene Douglas spent that money knowing full well, with the negativity surrounding his campaign, that he risked not making up that financial loss. I'm sure the campaign staff is making some deep spending and salary cuts."

"Do you think after this week, he is doing too little too late to save his campaign? Do you think he has a chance against Sherman Jones?

"Don't get me wrong, I'm not saying all is well for Gene Douglas. If he were running against a stronger opponent, I would recommend he drop out of the race and let his party scramble to find a new candidate. Sherman Jones is not that strong of a candidate. He is a decent guy. He doesn't have a bad record in political office, but he doesn't have a good record either. He voted along party lines as he was told by senior staff when he was in the House of Representatives. He didn't introduce any legislation of his own and brought very little success home to his constituents. When he was the mayor of his hometown, he kept the budget balanced and the garbage trucks picking up the trash on time, but he didn't make any improvements or any noteworthy changes. Gene Douglas is fortunate to be running against an opponent that is no more exciting than oatmeal."

"How is Gene Douglas going to get past the criminals that he associated himself with? Will the public ever trust him again?" Jimmy Jenner asks.

"That's going to depend on two things, how hard Gene Douglas is willing to work to earn the trust of the people back and how the media covers his campaign."

"Are you saying the media should ignore what happened and try to make him look good?" Joan Mowery asks.

"No, not at all. But the media should cover what Gene Douglas is actually doing. He made the donation to the State Firefighters Association on Wednesday. The news has covered nothing other than that story since it happened on Wednesday. Thursday, Gene spoke to veterans organizations about getting better medical care through the state hospital system. He listened to ideas from veterans about preventing veteran homelessness and investing in 'patriot housing' for those that served. On Friday, he did a three-hundred-mile round-trip tour of vacant and blighted industrial and retail properties with business leaders, developers, and investors. On Saturday, he listened to a community organization in Harmon with ideas to fight a growing heroin problem. He also listened to teachers with ideas to better education and improve our student state ranking in the country. That evening, he attended the State Police Officer's Annual Ball and was able to talk to law enforcement officials and hear about their needs when it comes to protecting our citizens. There was no coverage

of any of that by big media outlets. The big newspapers spent three days arguing over if the Douglas campaign event on Wednesday was a stunt or not."

"Maybe those events would be covered if the media knew about them."

"Every evening and every morning, the Douglas campaign releases an updated schedule to all the media outlets via e-mail and posts it on the press release page on the website. This week, the campaign announced that members of the press can reserve seats in the media caravan that follows Gene Douglas to these events. The Weekly Beat was able to get three reporters on that van because the only other newspapers that took advantage of this service were the Smithdale Weekly and the Greendale Times."

"I wasn't aware this was available," Joan Mowrey says.

"Reading is fundamental, Joan. The information is there if you look, and there is more than one story going on at a time."

"We're running a little over this morning. This has been a really good discussion about our state's gubernatorial race. Unfortunately, we have to take a quick break but will return with more after some words from our sponsors," Walter Carl says and cuts to a commercial.

"Wow! Teddy put those people in their place. He should have told that skank Joan Mowrey that her fuck-me pumps don't go with her pants suit," Sandy says.

"Next time you see Teddy, you will have to tell him to be more vocal about poor choices in footwear."

"Don't make fun of me. Shoes can make or break an outfit. I bet other women watching this show that have half-decent taste in shoes dismissed everything she said when they saw what she was wearing."

"I'm just happy that Teddy talked about our press caravan. They will be fighting over seats on the van after today, and more people will be writing about what we are saying about the issues."

"Teddy did good for you today. I hope he comes over for dinner tonight."

State of the State This Week comes back on. Host Walter Carl is sitting at the host desk all by himself. The guest chairs are all empty.

"Welcome back to State of the State This Week. We have just received some breaking news. Gubernatorial candidate Sherman Jones died of a

massive heart attack early this morning. We will be ending the show early and turning it over to the Channel 6 news desk. I would like to thank my guests, Theodore Graham, Joan Mowrey, and Jimmy Jenner. All of us here at State of the State This Week send our thoughts and prayers to the Jones family and the Sherman Jones for Governor campaign staff. I will now turn you over to Silvia Sleuth at the Channel 6 news desk, who has more details on this story."

"Oh my god, honey, that's terrible! It's good for you, though. You will win now."

Gene's cell phone rings. "Hello? Yes, Sidney, I just heard. Round everybody up, and we will meet at headquarters in an hour. Okay. I will see you in bit."

"Do you have to go?"

"Yes, I have to go. I'm not sure when I'll be back."

"Are you still going to invite Teddy over for dinner."

"Really, Sandy?" Gene says and leaves the patio to get ready for the emergency meeting.

CHAPTER 28

The writer's room at the *Weekly Beat* begins to fill up with young reporters early on a Monday morning. Attendees purchase coffee and snacks from the vending machines along the wall and find a seat at the table. Notepads, voice recorders, and cell phones litter the table as eager reporters wait for instructions and assignments.

"Morning," Theodore says as he enters the room. "Notice I didn't say *good* in front of *morning*. Seven o'clock Monday morning is a bitch, but we are going to have to get used to it. We are now a for-real newspaper and must figure out what to fill our pages with."

Theodore inches between the back of the chairs and wall and makes his way to the head of the table. He removes his laptop and a legal pad from his briefcase and sets them on the table.

"Is Paul coming? Is he attending this meeting?" Theodore asks.

"He is in the print shop. The printers are cleaning and doing maintenance on the presses and getting them ready for our first Tuesday edition. He should be here any minute," Mary Brimmer says.

"Okay, I guess we can get started. What's everybody working on? Mary, we will start with you."

"I am planning on going to the Douglas campaign to find out their strategy since Sherman Jones passed away yesterday."

"How about you, Tyler?"

"I am going to put a piece together about the possible candidates the Democrats may run in Sherman Jones's place."

"Jerry, what are your intentions?"

"I am going to get in contact with the Sherman Jones headquarters and see what the—" Jerry McCreed says but is interrupted by the commotion of Paul Hoptak entering the room.

"Sorry I'm late. Don't mind me, keep the meeting going," Paul says as he tries to wiggle his chubby body behind the chairs and the wall of the room. He doesn't fit. Reporters seated stand up and push their chairs in so Paul can make his way to a chair next to Theodore at the head of the table.

"I'm sorry for the interruption, but since I have everybody's attention, I feel I should mark this occasion with a few words. Tomorrow, our paper, the *Weekly Beat*, will be printing a Tuesday edition. It will be the first printed Tuesday edition in thirteen years—" Paul says and is interrupted as one of the printing staff enters the room.

"The coffee machine in the printers' lunchroom is out of order. I just came in here to grab a coffee. Don't let me interrupt."

"I was saying that tomorrow will be the first time we printed on a Tuesday in thirteen years. We stopped printing because the paper was losing money and couldn't—"

Paul is interrupted again. "This machine won't take my dollar. Does anybody have a different dollar?"

Everybody at the table searches their pockets, wallets, and purses for a dollar bill to exchange with the man so he can get his coffee. Brent hands him a fresh dollar bill and takes the wrinkled, beat-up dollar.

Paul waits for the commotion to quiet. "As I was saying, thirteen years ago, I had to make the tough decision to stop printing seven days per week to cut costs so I could stay in business today—"

"What's the trick to this machine? The cup didn't come down the chute."

"Bang on the right side of the machine."

Boom boom boom!

"No, you have to bang on it more toward the middle."

Boom boom boom!

"I have better luck when I bang on the front of the machine right below the buttons," Mary says.

Boom boom boom!

"Sometimes you have to grab the top of the machine and shake it, and the cup will fall down."

Rattle rattle rattle! Boom boom boom!

"Oh, there we go," the printer says as the cup falls down and begins to fill with coffee. "Sorry again for interrupting."

"Back to what I was saying. Thirteen years ago, I had to stop printing every day. I did my best to keep this paper running. I had to reduce the staff. I had to let go of talented writers, and I had—"

Paul is interrupted again by a different man entering the room.

"This machine has better cupcakes than the one in our lunchroom."

"Anyway, because of Teddy here, the paper has doubled in circulation—"

Paul is interrupted again.

"This machine won't take a five. Does anybody have five ones for a five?"

"You got to be fucking kidding me! It's going to be thirteen more years until we get this meeting started. Maybe we can do an article about the tricks, techniques, and pointers to make the most of a vending machine experience," Theodore says.

"My dad owns a vending machine company. I could probably write a good article about that."

"I was kidding, Brent. Can't we lock that door when we have meetings? These constant interruptions are counterproductive to what we want to accomplish."

"Maybe we should have writer's meetings in the conference room upstairs," Paul suggests.

"There's a conference room upstairs?"

"Yes. There's a nice big table with leather high-back chairs, a dry erase board, a projection screen, a small reference library, and we should be able to get the Wi-Fi up there."

"Why haven't we been using it?"

"It's two flights of stairs to get up there."

"The building has an elevator."

"But the elevator is on the opposite side of the building, and you have to walk all the way across the length of the building."

"Holy shit, Paul, you are the laziest person I know. Maybe some exertion would do you some good. Let's go up there. Where is it?" Theodore asks.

"Go out the door, make a right, go up the steps to the next floor, and it is the first two doors on your right. The placards on the door say CONFERENCE ROOM."

"Everybody grab your stuff, and let's go up there so we can conduct a meeting and not have to compete with the popularity of the snack machines."

"Take my keys so you can open the doors. I will meet you up there in a little bit. I'm going to get a bag of Fritos out of the machine, and I will come up in the elevator," Paul says.

Theodore shakes his head in disbelief as he leaves the room. The five young writers follow him, and they make their way to the conference room upstairs. Theodore opens the door with Paul's keys and flips on the light switch.

"This is more like it. Now we won't have to compete with Twinkie sales. Go ahead in and get yourself settled. We have to wait for Paul, anyway."

"Do I have time to run back downstairs to get another cup of coffee?"

"Unbe-fuckin-lievable! You didn't think to get one when we were down there? This is a newspaper, not a kindergarten class," Theodore says.

Paul enters the room with a bag of Fritos in his hand. Sweat is beading on his forehead, and he is trying to catch his breath. "Whew, I made it. Teddy, you got to calm down. We'll get these writers out there. Don't worry. Let me catch my breath, and I will finish what I was saying downstairs."

"If Paul is going to regularly attend our Monday meetings, some of you may want to take a CPR class. Paul, did you get your wind back yet?"

"Yes. The point I wanted to make downstairs was the *Weekly Beat* was near bankrupt and almost put out of business. I tried to keep it afloat as best as I could. At the beginning of this year, I decided if I couldn't turn this paper around by the beginning of next year, I was going to sell out or just shut it down and sell the building. Teddy was a heaven-sent opportunity that I took a chance on. Because of him, we are here today. He turned my paper around. He gave new life back to the dream I didn't give up on. Because of him, I could tell my siblings, the ones who made me buy their shares of the *Weekly Beat* twelve years ago, to fuck off. Our circulation has doubled, our advertising revenue is up, our sales team expanded, our senior reporters and editorial writers are busy, and I added you five aspiring journalists to our regular staff. Teddy, he's going to be in charge. Listen to him. Let him guide you. Take his advice. If you do that, I have no doubt you will be feature writers here in no time. I expect all of you will do a good job, so I just want to say thanks in advance. Teddy, the room is yours. Work your magic."

"I didn't do anything special for this paper. I got a dictionary and looked up the definition of a *journalist*. I Googled what a journalist does and tried to do that. To my surprise, it worked. The five of you are recent graduates with degrees in communications or journalism. If college didn't teach what journalism was all about, I suggest you do what I did and find out what your job is. Just a show of hands, how many of you planned on writing about Gene Douglas, Sherman Jones, or the gubernatorial race?"

Theodore looks around the room and sees that all five reporters raised their hand.

"Okay. You all raised your hands. That's the problem with journalism today. Everybody chases one story. This is the Sherman Jones story. He's dead, and he won't be running for governor, end of story. By the time *America's Funniest Videos* came on last night, most of the people across the state knew he was dead. This morning, every paper and news channel reported on this fact. Our online version has his obituary and a nice article following his life and career. He's not coming back to life. He's not coming back as a zombie candidate, and he's not going to contribute any commentary to the news cycle. The Democrats aren't going to announce anything about who is going to run in his place until after Sherman Jones is put in the ground.

Any talk about who will run in his place is speculation. You are journalists, not speculators. I won't put news that isn't really happening in this paper, so don't write any. The Gene Douglas campaign isn't going to comment on the race until next week's news cycle begins. They don't want to risk getting accused of exploiting the tragedy of their deceased opponent. The governor's race is basically a nonstory this week. Next week, when it is a story, our senior staff will cover it."

"What are we supposed to write about?" Mary Brimmer asks.

"You *are* the journalists. Our paper covers four towns. Get out there and find the stories. Write about the issues facing these towns."

"I thought you said we couldn't write about the governor's race," Sasha Monet says.

"The issues aren't the governor's race. The issues are what the candidates say they are focused on, but they will never talk about in detail unless the press asks them to. Spend this week writing about the issues, and next week, the issues can be brought to the people running for elected office."

"What are the issues?"

"The issues are the things that face the voters—taxes, education, government-funded services, pollution, jobs, pay rates, women issues, infrastructure, race relations, health, and safety. There are organizations and advocates for all the issues. Find them. You are the journalists. Go out there and ask people who, what, when, where, why, how much, and how many. I'm not going to hand out regular assignments. I expect all of you to go out there to find stories and write about them. I will help you with them, but I'm not going to spoon-feed you," Theodore says.

"How are we going to know where to go?"

"Okay, I will assign you areas. Mary, you are from Harmon, go there. Jerry, you cover Carter. Sasha, you cover Douglas Hills, and, Brent, you cover Gatesville. Tyler, you live close to the capital, so go to the state assembly building, talk to state senators and representatives and their staff. Find the stories. Write the stories. If they are good, your work will be put in the paper and you will advance."

"You young folks don't know how refreshing it is to hear Teddy say these things. This is the way journalism is supposed to work.

It's why this paper is doing so well today," Paul says. "If any special assignments come in, I will assign them to you. Until then, go out and be journalists and write. That's what you went to school for. I expect my reporters to raise the level of discourse. If you want to write what everybody else is writing about, start a blog or write long comments on Facebook."

"Thanks, Paul. I will go out on the road with some of you this week. We can get you some contacts in your areas, and I will show you the places you want to poke around. I hired you because all of you have the talent needed to succeed. It's up to you to make it work for you. If you don't have any questions, go to your areas, familiarize yourselves, and find a story. Let's meet back here this evening at five and see what you came up with."

The young reporters pack up their things and leave the conference room. Theodore and Paul remain in the conference room so they can talk.

"What do you think of the conference room?"

"This is a great room. I can't believe you didn't tell me about it. You let me have cramped meetings in my office and in the writers' room downstairs."

"You know how I feel about exercise and exerting myself."

"Anybody can look at you and easily recognize that you are against it."

"What's going to happen with this governor's race?"

"I think Gene Douglas was handed the biggest gift from God. Sherman Jones was the best the Democrats could come up with, and now he is dead. I'm sure they will come up with some empty suit to give it a last-ditch effort, but they will basically punt and try again in four years."

"Do you think the conspiracy theorists will be coming out of the woodwork?"

"They always do. Last night on some social media page, I saw some Chicken Little saying Gene Douglas paid somebody to poison Sherman Jones and cause his heart attack."

"He might be right. We should have one of the new reporters look into it," Paul jokes.

"Sure. I will send one of them over to interview some forty-something guy with Cheetos-stained fingers that still lives in his parents' basement. He can tell us how the social media and the brilliant mind of Ted Nugent taught him how the world works."

"Who knows, they might be on to something."

"For all I know, you might be one of those guys. You live in your parents' old house. You are rapidly balding. You are overweight and unmarried. You don't have Cheetos-stained fingers, but your fingerprints and the underneath of your fingernails are filled with Frito salt. Did you ever see a for-real vagina?"

"I have, but sadly, it was back when they had hair. Because of World Wide Web pornography, I know there have been advances in genital landscaping."

"Yes, there have been advances in that area, but you got to be careful. *Statutory rape* is a term that gets thrown around loosely and a lot these days. The young ones aren't worth the risk."

"You are a worldly man, Teddy Graham, a wealth of knowledge by way of acquired wisdom."

"We'll have to see if we can't get you laid. Having you live vicariously through me is kind of creepy."

"I have that effect on people."

Chapter 29

Theodore sits behind his desk in his office, writing. His office door is open because he loves the sound of the commotion of the busy office. The noise doesn't seem to be a distraction for him. There's a knock on the door.

"You're up and at it early," Paul says.

"I had dinner with Gene and Sandy Douglas last night and didn't get a chance to finish my editorial for today's edition."

"I hope you got me some inside scoop on the governor's race. What are you working on?"

"It was dinner with friends, we didn't talk politics. I am, however, going to piss the state assembly off. They only accomplished 19 percent of what was on the docket at the beginning of the last session but voted to extend the summer recess by two weeks and voted to convene the current session three days early to beat the weekend traffic in the capital."

"Shame is one hell of a motivator."

"It's too bad that it motivates them to call the paper and complain that we published the article instead of changing their behavior, but that's politics. Anyway, what brings your Frito-munching ass to the doorway of my office?"

Paul reaches into his jacket pocket, pulls out a snack-size bag of Fritos, and waves it in the air. "They're the breakfast of champions. I like Fritos with my morning coffee. I like to dip them."

"It's not even half past seven. How can your stomach handle all that grease and salt?"

"I don't have a problem, not anymore, anyway. In the nineties, they used to put that manufactured oil chemical olestra in them.

They were supposed to be low calorie, low fat, and better for you, but the fake oil didn't digest well and gave me greasy farts and my bowel movements resembled a can of silly string being discharged. I ruined a lot of underwear in those days."

"I bet that story would be a hit with the ladies."

"You think? Maybe I should put it on my E-Harmony profile."

"It's worth a shot. I would love to hear you wax nostalgic about your feces of past decades, but I have an article to finish. What's on your mind?"

"Sasha Monet, one of our rookie writers, she hasn't submitted anything worth publishing. She's struggling. When she came back to the office yesterday, she seemed very frustrated. I told her you would meet with her this morning before she went out on the road."

"Yeah, no problem. I think she might be struggling with disciplining herself and being assertive in the field. I will talk to her."

"I knew you would. I just wanted to give you a heads-up. I'll let you get back to work. How can you concentrate on your writing with your office door open?"

"Actually, the mornings here are music to my ears. At six thirty, there is the banging and clanging of the guys in the print shop getting the machines ready. At seven, there is the sound of the shuffle of reporters and editors filing in. They go in their offices and check their answering machines and voice mail, and you can hear the mumble of messages and beeps and hang-up dial tones. About seven thirty, you can hear some of the writers and editors arguing over commas, cuts, and rejected articles. At eight, the commotion calms down. Everybody has their coffee and snacks. When you listen closely between eight and nine, you can hear the clicks of keyboards as the writers do their revisions. At nine o'clock, the commotion could be heard again as the reporters and the sales team gets ready to go out on the road. At nine fifteen, the printers run the test print. After that, the building gets quiet. The only things that interrupt the silence are the ringing phones in the circulation office, Jill the receptionist talking on the phone or to the walk-ins that come into the front office. It's the same every day, and I find the routine calming."

"I can tell why you are a musician. You put a lot of deep thought into the noise here. Now I will be keying my ears into those sounds. I will let you listen to your work-time music. Talk to Sasha and get her on the right track. Here's a noise that I will leave to ponder," Paul says as he turns around and farts. He leaves the doorway and goes down the hall.

"You're a gross man, Paul!"

"I'm just happy olestra is no longer a problem!"

Theodore returns to his writing until there is another knock on his door. It's Sasha Monet. She is wearing a gray blouse with the buttons down to her breasts unbuttoned. She is also wearing a snug-fitting black skirt that is a little on the short side. She stands in the doorway to Theodore's office, appearing taller from red high-heel shoes. Her makeup is meticulously done, and her black hair is shiny and carefully styled.

"Come on in, Sasha. Paul told me you would be in to talk to me this morning. Close the door and have a seat."

Sasha enters the office and grabs the doorknob. She twirls on her heels and bends forward when she shuts the door. The top of her stockings show slightly from beneath the bottom of her short skirt. She playfully struts to the chair in front of Theodore's desk and pulls it back closer to the center of the room. She carefully sits down and exposes the tops of her stockings and a glimpse of her red panties as she slowly crosses her legs.

Theodore pauses for a minute as his mind processes her entrance. "Paul tells me you are struggling a bit. What seems to be the problem?"

Sasha leans into Theodore's desks so the top line of her red bra and cleavage is exposed. "Well, you assigned me to Douglas Hills, and there is nothing going on there. I can't find anything to write about. There are no stories there. Can't you give me some leads? I am desperate. I need a good story to write about. I would do anything if you would point me in the right direction," she asks and leans back in the chair and uncrosses and crosses her legs.

"There's a lot going on in Douglas Hills. The youth campus has a lot of new staff coming in this year. There is a new debate coach. Go to a Douglas Hills council meeting and see what they talk about. Harmon performs a lot of the basic services for Douglas Hills. Harmon is looking at a deficit city budget. Douglas Hills is operating on a surplus budget. Douglas Hills has a part-time police department, so Harmon police have to cover that area during evenings, nights, and weekends. There are a hundred story possibilities that come to mind."

"Teddy, you're so smart. How do you think of all these things? You are a really good journalist. Can you please help me become as good as you?" Sasha asks and leans on the front of the desk and pushes her cleavage a little higher up in the open part of her blouse.

Theodore clears a lump from his throat. "Whom did you talk to when you were out there for the past few days?"

"I talked to the guy who is remodeling the diner. That might be a story. I talked to the lady at the bookstore. I left a message with Wendy Uher to see if she wanted to do an interview with me and talk about the beauty pageants," Sasha says as she twirls her finger in her hair and smiles.

"Those are good story ideas. That diner has a neat history, so it's going to be good to see it open again. Wendy Uher will call you back. She loves free press coverage of the beauty pageants. If she doesn't call you back soon, I can probably talk to Sandy Douglas. She founded the organization, and she likes to talk about herself."

"That would be great! You would do that for me? I wouldn't know how to thank you," Sasha says with the hint of playfulness.

"I forgot, I have a contact list of the who's who in Douglas Hills. Let me open that file and print you a copy," Theodore says and begins clicking a few keys and scrolling his mouse.

Sasha stands up and struts around Theodore's desk and stands next to him sitting in his chair. She leans down and casually brushes against him. She places her cheek close to his. Theodore can smell her strong perfume. She places her hand on his back and begins to rub it gently in a circle.

"Go back and sit down. I know what you're trying to do."

"I just wanted to see what contacts you had there."

"Sasha, I'm not stupid. You are flirting with me. The open buttons of your blouse, the shortness of your skirt, and the choreographed way you show me your cleavage, your red lacy bra, your stockings, and the peeks at your panties."

Sasha sits back down and slowly crosses her legs again. "I didn't know I was doing that."

"The fuck you didn't. You don't normally dress like that. Are you planning on walking the streets of Douglas Hills looking for a story in those heels?" Theodore asks. "I have a reputation for thinking with my penis, and you have given it a lot to think about it. Sasha, you're too smart to be the girl that sleeps her way to the top. I hired you for your writing instincts and ability, not because you are an attractive girl I want to have my way with."

"I just don't know what to write. I don't know how to find these stories."

"I fault your education and generation for that. I'm betting, in high school and college, the head of the school newspapers told you what to write about and you did it. You did it very well, but they did you a great disservice. They never forced you to think. Thinking is a lost art these days. The essays and articles you turned in with your résumé, that's what got you in the door here. I know you can write about Douglas Hills just as well, but you have to learn to uncover the stories yourself. I know you can do it."

"I don't know if I can. I just want to get some leads."

"You're too good for that. If you want leads, I will send you over to the lifestyle and community department. They will give you assignments. You can cover Cub Scout graduations and Pinewood Derby Races. You can cover the exciting world of Girl Scout cookie sales. You can cover the church rummage sales, bake sales, and ice cream socials. If that's what you want, I can make that happen for you, but I think it would be such a waste."

"I don't want to cover those things. Can't you help me get started?"

"I'll tell you what. Go home, change into sensible clothes, wash that sweet perfume off, and head to Douglas Hills. I will meet you at Bruno's Deli for lunch, and then I will show you some good places to find your stories. I will try to introduce you to some of the contacts. How does that sound?"

"That sounds good. Thank you, Teddy."

The intercom on Theodore's desk beeps. "Good morning, Jill. What can I do for you?"

"There is a condescending woman out here named Delores Daniels. She ordered me to let her speak to you. Should I throat-punch her and send her on her way, or should I send her to your office?"

"Don't throat-punch her. That will only make her angrier. Send her in."

"Okay, Teddy, it's your funeral."

"So, Sasha, you will get out of your flirtatious wear and I will see you for lunch. We can help you find your groove."

"Thank you, Teddy. I'm sorry for coming in here like I did this morning."

"It's okay. It would be so much easier if I just took you up on your sexual advances in exchange for assignments, but it would make lesser people out of both of us."

"I didn't take it totally off the table," Sasha says and playfully winks as she leaves his office. She passes Delores Daniels in the hallway. Both women look each other over and exchange judgmental expressions.

"Delores Daniels, did you come here because you missed reprimanding me for my questionable behavior?"

Delores enters the office and closes the door behind her. "I do not miss you in the least, Mr. Graham. You also may want to find a receptionist that conducts herself in a more professional manner."

"Jill probably didn't realize your icy persona is your polite side. Please, Mrs. D, have a seat."

"You can call me Delores or Ms. Daniels."

"Yes, Ms. Delores."

"You haven't changed a bit, Mr. Graham," Delores says.

"You can call me, Grandmaster T Funkadelic G, and I will call you, Double D?"

"I will not, and you will not. Who was that courtesan that I saw leaving your office? Her harlot perfume hangs heavy in the air."

"That was Sasha, one of our young reporters. She covers Douglas Hills for our paper. Maybe you two could have lunch sometime."

"How did I know she would have a pole dancer's name? I'm sorry, I don't see the two of us acquainting ourselves."

"You two already did in my mind, and this evening, I will spend some alone time thinking about it."

"I'm so glad that I don't have to encounter your barroom antics on a daily basis any longer."

"Well, Delores, I miss you. That young girl Sasha, she came in dressed like that this morning and teased and flirted with me. She offered herself to me in exchange for story leads so she could get ahead. The temptation with that twenty-something was so strong, but I was professional and turned her advances down. I corrected her behavior and offered to show her how to succeed without having to sleep her way to the top. If you did that, Delores, I wouldn't turn your advances down. I would be all over you like a sweater on a chubby chick. You still know how to drive me wild. I used to get in trouble at the school just so you would call me to your office and berate my professionalism."

"You may think I would be flattered by your charm, but the urge to vomit is surfacing. Where is your wastebasket in case you choose to make more advances toward my cunning?"

"Enough with the pleasantries. What brings you to my newspaper? You could have placed a personal ad looking for love over the phone or online."

"Don't waste your A-list humor on me. I don't know if you knew or not, but I have a seat on the State Democrats Committee."

"Oh my goodness. I didn't know that. Does Gene Douglas know that he has a Democrat superintendent in his Republican henhouse?"

"He does not, and I would appreciate you keeping that to yourself."

"I should ask you to show me your tits in exchange for my silence, but I am trying to impress you with my manners as a gentleman. Your secret is safe with me."

"Your improved, slightly-above-swine manners are noted. We are now only light-years away from a warm embrace."

"So what does the Democratic Committee want with me?"

"As you know, Sherman Jones has passed away. The Democrats have to come up with a candidate to run against Gene Douglas in this fall's election. The committee has been scrambling to come up with a short list of candidates to endorse. Your name made the short list."

"I don't know how you compile your lists. I'm sorry to waste your time, but I am not a registered Democrat."

"No, you are registered as an independent, which, by our party rules, makes you an eligible candidate."

"I have no interest in—" Theodore says and is interrupted.

"No! I don't want to hear your reasoning, Mr. Graham."

"But Gene is my—"

"No! I am not here to hear you reject the idea. I am here to let you know that there is a committee meeting tomorrow afternoon at two o'clock. You will come in then and talk to that committee for a little while. I'm sure after a few words from you, they will agree with me that you are the worst possible candidate for governor in the history of our state."

"Why would I even waste my time going to that meeting?"

"I know you well enough to know that you will humor us."

"What's in it for me?"

"It will be an opportunity for you to put on your crass man-child routine for wealthy figures of authority and challenge the system. It's your burlesque house demeanor—you can't resist an opportunity."

"You know, Delores, I have things to do at a job I love. I don't feel like doing dog-and-pony shows for the rich and power-clinging class anymore. I'm not going to be there."

"I told the committee that I would ask you personally. There is a mutual hatred between us, but I swallowed my pride to ask you. Can you at least acknowledge the personal pride I had to swallow to come here to ask you this and do me this favor?"

"That hurts. I don't hate you. I'm sad that you hate me. Why should I do you a favor? Is there anything else you are willing to swallow?"

"No. *No!* You are a pig. I didn't want to play the 'you owe me one' card, but it was I who voted against my better judgment, but with my conscience, to keep you on at the school. I did so because deep down I know you are a highly intelligent man."

"That's the nicest thing you ever said about me. I will be there if you do one thing for me."

"I am afraid to ask the conditions of your ultimatum, Mr. Graham, but I must. What is it?"

"Tonight, when I'm alone and am thinking about you and Sasha, my young reporter, I want to accurately picture your undergarments. Sasha had on a lacy red bra and panties with stockings. Yours, I can't see. If you describe yours to me, I will be there. If you show them to me, I will show up on time instead of forty-five minutes late."

"You are a foul man. I'm not doing that."

"Thanks for stopping by. It was good to see you, Ms. Daniels. Good luck with your committee meeting."

Delores stands up, ready to leave. "I wish you would do me this favor, Mr. Graham."

"Good day to you, Ms. Daniels."

Delores makes her way to the doorway and stops. "My bra is lacy and purple with panties that match. I am wearing pantyhose, not stockings."

"I will see you tomorrow and in my dreams tonight. Purple is way hotter than I expected. Thank you, Ms. Daniels."

"Fuck you, Theodore. Be there, and be on time," Delores says and hands him a business card with the address of the meeting on it. She storms out of the office.

Paul Hoptak is walking down the hallway as Delores leaves Theodore's office. He pokes his head in the door. "Who was that fine-looking woman that just left your office?"

"Some lady that wants me to run for governor."

"That's nice. You would be good at it. I'd vote for you. Good for you, buddy," Paul says and continues on his way

CHAPTER 30

Theodore enters a downtown office building in Greendale. He is wearing cargo shorts, sandals, and an NWA concert T-shirt from the early nineties. In the lobby, he passes people in business suits carrying briefcases and having professional-sounding conversations on their cell phones. He boards the elevator, and a well-dressed business-woman gets in behind him. He pushes the button for the ninth floor.

"Nine, please," the woman says.

"I'm going to nine too. How awesome is that?"

The woman looks him over. "Are you lost?"

"No, I have an interview in this building today."

"It was nice of you to get dressed up for it."

"I don't want the job. I'm only showing up for the interview as a favor."

"Well, you're well on your way to not getting it. You can take pride in the fact you are a successful failure. Good for you."

"Thanks, I think."

"What booming enterprise will be fraught with disappointment when they learn they cannot acquire your services?"

"Some people want me to run for governor."

"Oh, shit! You're Teddy Graham."

"You would be surprised how often I get that reaction."

"I'm Pamela Eynon. I'm chairing that committee you are here to see."

"It's nice to meet you, Pamela. This saves us both a bunch of time. No sense doing the interview. You know I don't want the job, and you got a look at me and aren't going to hire me. Since we both freed up our afternoon, do you want to go get tacos? There is a taco truck down by the parking garage. Maybe we can make out afterward."

"No, I don't want tacos, and you're not getting off that easily," Pamela says.

"Is making out off the table too?"

The elevator door opens at the ninth floor. "You are entertaining. Come on, let's go talk to the rest of the committee."

Theodore follows Pamela through a reception area down a hallway into a large conference room. There are five other people sitting around a large oval table.

"I had the opportunity to meet Mr. Graham in the elevator on the way here," Pamela says.

"Yes, we hit it off. I think there's a good chance we'll make out. Not sure about tacos, though. They might be a deal breaker."

"Have a seat at the end of the table, Mr. Graham," Pamela orders.

"Can't I sit next to you? We've grown so close lately."

Pamela stands at the head of the table. "Let me start off by telling you this meeting is confidential. We would appreciate your discretion. Let me introduce you to this committee. You already know Delores Daniels. Tim Collins, you also know from the Douglas campaign. Gary Brown does policy and strategy research for the Democratic Committee. Ned Gibson is a political adviser and works as a consultant for our current governor. Ed Reese is a publicist that works for us."

"Nice to meet all of you. Tim, it's good to see you again. I knew you left the Douglas campaign, but I didn't think know you went over to the Democrats."

"A statistician has to work, Teddy. I provide the numbers. The ones that I worked for tried to change them."

"I gotcha, buddy. I'm not faulting you. You're the best at what you do. These people are lucky to have you doing it for them."

"Mr. Graham, I am sure that you are aware by now that you have made a short list of possible candidates that we came up with to run against Gene Douglas."

"I'm not sure how I did that. I'm not a registered Democrat. I'm not interested in being the governor. I'm not going to run against my friend. Cross my name of this short list so I can take you out for tacos by the parking garage. Delores, you are welcome to join us too. Tacos are on me. You guys just have to pony up the making out part."

"I told you he wouldn't take this seriously," Delores says.

"I tried to tell you yesterday I wouldn't take this seriously. I don't understand why I'm even being considered. Delores knows me and doesn't like me. Tim's worked with me. He knows my problem with authority and my issues with conformity. Pamela, you took one look at me in the elevator and made a decision about me. That's three out of the six of you that have a less-than-favorable view of me. I'm sure you could have told these other guys, Ed, Ned, and Gary, that I am not what you are looking for."

"I have worked with you. I didn't like you when I first encountered you, but then I saw you work. You are a very calculated man. You know how the system works. You know how to work it for you. You're a guy that knows how to get things done," Tim Collins says.

"Thanks, but running for governor isn't something I would even consider. I don't want to fill a dead man's shoes, and I especially don't want to run against my friend. How did my name even come to be in this discussion?"

Ned Gibson stands up and moves to the screen at the front of the room. "Mr. Graham, we didn't want you either. The thought of you running in Sherman Jones's place started off as a joke. We saw some yokels on social media mentioning your name amid the scandals and fallout with the Whitneys and the Douglas campaign. We all had a good, hearty laugh. Ms. Daniels looked up your voting registration and saw you were an independent. According to the bylaws of our party, in such events as these, the party can select candidates from within the party or an unaffiliated candidate that share similar values. In the sad time of Sherman Jones's passing, we needed some more laughs. Just for shits and giggles, we ran your name through some polling, surveys, and scenarios."

"If you wanted some shits and giggles, you could have just called me to come down here and hang out. I would have brought some joints for the giggles, and we could have played the pull-my-finger game for the shits. I have a book of dirty limericks. I could have read it aloud to boost your spirits. You didn't have to come up with this running-for-governor nonsense to get me to chill with you guys."

"Tim, turn on the projector," Ned says. The screen shows a list of names with a bunch of polling statistics. "Pamela, do you want to explain this to Mr. Graham?"

"As you can see, we had a short list of five people. Because we saw your name dropped a few times on social media sites, we decided, just for fun, to vet you through our polling criteria. As you can see, you polled better than the five people from our own party. With women, minorities, young voters, and swing voters, you came out ahead of all of them. The overall margin of error is at 5 percent, but in a general election, if it were to take place now, Gene Douglas would beat you. He is at 55 percent, you are at 40 percent. Even if you covered the entire margin of error, he would beat you by at least 5 percent."

"Why would you even have me here if the polling says that I'm going to lose?"

"Because your numbers are better than the five best people we could put forward."

"Can't you find better people? Even you people don't like me."

"We don't expect you to win. You won't win. We've conceded that we will lose the governor race, but we are looking at the bigger picture," Pamela says.

"I'm not seeing the bigger picture that you are."

"Can I take this, Pam?" Tim Collins asks.

"Please do. You are the numbers guy."

Tim stands up and moves to the front of the room and stands by the screen. "If we run any of the five people we came up with, it would be like running a dial tone against Gene Douglas. Just look at the numbers here. Nobody knows any of these people, and there isn't enough time until the election to get people excited about them. The base would most likely stay home and not vote at all. With you, on the other hand, people know about you. You took the Douglas Youth Honors College to the National Debate and won. Your record as a professor at the school, as an author, as a campaign manager, as a lawyer, and now as the man who turned the *Weekly Beat* around made you a known man. You exposed the corruption with the Whitneys and would have been a casualty if the arson attempt on your newspaper were successful. You put the other media people in their place and shame them for their practices. You would motivate our base, and that's what we are looking for."

"Okay, I motivate the Democratic base, but you just said not enough to win. Why bother?"

"It's the bigger picture. We have a lot of close races across the state in the assembly. There are a lot of House seats that are close races, and there are five Senate seats within our reach. If you motivate the base, they will come out to vote for you. While they are voting, they will vote along party lines in those races and we will take the majority in the assembly," Tim explains.

"But Gene Douglas will win, and he will have veto power over any legislation put forward by Democrats. It will be another do-nothing state assembly."

"If he threatens a veto, we accuse him of catering to special interests in the media. His association with the Whitneys is proof that he associates with corrupt people, and we don't let the people forget it unless he helps pass some progressive legislation. If Gene works with us, he gets a second term. If he doesn't, we take the governor's mansion back in four years."

"I don't fully support the Democrats' platform. The battle between conservatives and liberals is media-made. The Republicans hate liberals so much they get more conservative, and the Democrats hate the Republicans so much they get more liberal. It keeps the people divided, and the drama that exists between the two sides is what keeps the media going. If you look at the history of this country, the liberals weren't always right and the conservatives weren't always right. It's the right application of both sets of values that finds progress. I'm not putting myself in play so overreaching liberal policies can be moved forward."

"This is why you appeal to our base, Mr. Graham. You keep yourself grounded with logic and reason," Ned Gibson says.

"Thanks for noticing, but this doesn't sit right with me. I don't want to be a puppet in the party's master plan. I don't want to get down in the muck of a campaign, especially against a longtime friend."

"We understand that. So if you will run as our candidate, your campaign is yours. You fill your staff with the people you want. You will run on the platform you want and make the appearances you want. The party will provide the start-up money for your campaign. The estate of Sherman Jones owns all his campaign funds and has all rights to his super PAC money, so you will have to do your own fund-raising. That is going to be part of your appeal, a real grassroots campaign with little funding. There is the possibility that somebody may start a super PAC for you, and after the election, that money is yours."

"Look, Mr. Graham, we're not 100 percent sold on you either. You obviously need time to think about this. Time isn't something we have a lot of. Sherman Jones gets buried tomorrow. The weekend news cycle belongs to him. We are going to announce our candidate first thing on Monday morning. Whoever our candidate is will make their first public appearance on Wednesday. We will meet with you again tomorrow afternoon. You can give us your answer, your demands, and your ideas then. You have tonight to think about it," Pamela says.

"I already told you that I—" Theodore begins but is interrupted by Pamela.

"You have until tomorrow afternoon at three o'clock to think about it. Run this through your mind. Use this time to examine the possibilities."

"But I—"

"But nothing. We brought you in because you have a calculating and logical mind. At least give us the courtesy of putting our proposal through your thought process."

"You ruined my weekend. I was going to finish my work for the *Weekly Beat* this evening and enjoy a good weekend of weed, beer, and practicing guitar with Ernie Douglas's band."

"You'll have plenty of time for bong hits and jam sessions after we talk tomorrow."

"What if I don't show up?"

"You'll be here, Mr. Graham. You are not the type of person that lets others down."

"Are you the type of person that lets people down?" Theodore asks.

"I do my best not to," Pamela says.

"I will think about this and be here tomorrow and honor your request if you honor mine."

"What request is that?"

"I asked you to have some tacos with me. Have some tacos with me, let me pick your brain, and let me decide how I feel about you. The making out part, we can keep that in the back of our minds and see where tacos lead."

"Fair enough, Mr. Graham. I will join you for tacos if you're buying. They are really good tacos. The making out, not going to happen today."

"Now we're talking. I can float the making-out part again tomorrow. Pamela, I will wait for you in the lobby. I'm sure the committee wants to talk shit about me. Delores, the invitation for you to join us for tacos is still on the table. I will see the rest of you losers tomorrow," Theodore says and leaves the meeting.

CHAPTER 31

Friday Night

Theodore sits behind the desk in his apartment, looking up state assembly races. He is researching each candidate, looking at their records, browsing their websites, reading their platforms, and checking into their financial backing. He prints pages that he wants to spend a little more time studying and places them in manila folders spread out on the floor. The afternoon meeting with the Democratic Committee occupies his mind. He is weighing the pros and cons. The option of running for governor against his friend Gene taunts him. He hears the elevator reach his floor, and the buzzer for his apartment sounds. Theodore opens the door and finds Delores Daniels. She is wearing blue jeans and a casual black blouse and is carrying a six-pack of beer.

"Delores Daniels, for what do I owe the honor of your appearance? And why are you dressed like that?"

"I'm not working. I do own comfortable clothes. I brought you a present," Delores says and hands him the beer.

"Thank you. Come on in. What are you doing here?"

"I want to talk to you about the decision you have to make," Delores says as she enters the apartment. She sees the folders, clippings, and articles spread all over the floor. "I can see you are putting some serious thought into it."

"I've been cursing your name and regretting your visit to my office. This isn't what I wanted occupying my mind this weekend. I'm half-tempted to blow off the meeting with the committee tomorrow afternoon."

"You're only half-tempted—that's a good sign."

"You show up here on a Friday night dressed casually and gift me a six-pack of beer. You are totally out of character. I don't know the Delores Daniels standing in front of me this evening. You usually look at me with disgust and disappointment. Tonight, you show up at my door and greet me with a smile. Am I being duped?"

"I'm not here to deceive you. I know you have a lot of questions and your mind is tormented with making this decision. I've worked with you. I've seen how you work. I know how you suffer with overthinking about things. I don't want you to do that with this decision."

"If you didn't, you wouldn't have visited my office with this proposal. Don't bullshit me. Maybe this is revenge for all the stress I caused you. I guess karma is doing its due diligence."

"Revenge isn't my motive. This is something I believe strongly in. You are the advocate for change our state needs. Off-the-rack politics is killing this country. We chase profits instead of progress. The ones at the top are insecure, so they close the doors of opportunity for others so they can remain at the top."

"The possibility of me running for governor was brought up by your committee as a joke. I don't want to agree to this and be a punch line. I'm a clown, but I don't want to be the joke."

"It was a joke until we ran the numbers. Then it became serious."

"I don't get you. On a normal day, my mere existence offends you. What changed? Are you setting me up for a fall?"

"I already told you that revenge isn't my motive. I'm here because I believe you are here at the right time and in the right place to do the right thing."

"Being a tool for the Democrats to game the system and taking the opportunity for Republicans to game the system away isn't what I believe to be the right thing."

"That's not it. Getting a stagnant system to work again is what it's about."

"If I did this according to the committee's plan, the Democrats would have the majority in both Houses of the assembly and you would get to blackmail a Republican governor into pushing your agenda forward."

"We will be pushing progress forward, not politics."

"If I don't run, according to your numbers, the assembly would remain in Republican hands and Gene Douglas would win. What's to say they won't move an agenda forward?"

"Look at the information you have in the research you have scattered all over your floor. You're smart enough to follow the money. You know who the affiliations are, religious organizations with money, industrial war profiteers, highly paid lobbyists with agendas, and divisive media that takes sides. I know you recognize all this. You called Gene Douglas out on his affiliation with Mort Whitney. I am certain you are the guy that can go to the people and change this."

"You know what, Delores? You're never this nice to me. I'm not used to compliments from you. I've never seen you dressed this way. You brought me beer. Your shape-shifting made my decision. This is way too good to be true. I will be at that meeting tomorrow out of respect for Pam Eynon and the rest of the committee, but I am not going to run. I feel like I am being played. I thank you for the beer, but I think it's time for you to leave."

"You know what, Teddy Graham? Fuck you! I've always been in a position of what seemed to be authority over you, and you always felt threatened by it. You're not the only one to come from poor beginnings. My family owned a farm for four generations. Corporate farming came in with their lobbyists and their purchased politicians and took away what my family built for two centuries. My father spent his remaining years fixing farm equipment for the people who took all he knew away."

"I'm sorry. I didn't know."

"Stick your sorry up your ass. I also had to overcome odds to get where I am. I had to eat the same shit from these rich assholes that you did. The only difference between me and you is that I conformed and didn't upset the powers that be. Maybe I'm not as good as you because I did, but that was my choice. I sucked up to the wealthy. I did what they expected me to do. I changed my persona and became the bitch that you had to deal with. I was hired at Douglas school to maintain their standards. I kept my views to myself. I kept opinions to myself. I lost friends and family because they didn't recognize what I had become. I threw myself into my work and spent much of my adult life alone because I chose to play the bitch role. I thought the big paychecks were the reward for trading away who I was. You came into my world and made me feel my hollow existence. I'm jealous of you."

"Why would you be jealous of me?"

"Because you have the balls to stick to your guns. You have the brains to work the system in your favor. People like you. People don't like me. I'm viewed as a cold, unfeeling bitch. I chose to play the role because I don't have the confidence you have. My life is an unhappy existence. I got involved with the Democratic Committee with the hopes of changing the system that I compromised myself for. I believed that you can set the needed change in motion."

"I don't think I am what you think I am."

"When you first came to the Douglas school, I hated your guts. It was my goal to destroy you to protect my rich bosses and the image of the school. You fought my authority at every turn, and you beat me every time. That school became better because of you. The students looked up to you, and they actually wanted to learn. The trust-fund kids were actually applying themselves. That was when I became jealous of you. You made the things I wanted to happen actually happen. You showed no regard for authority, did things your way, and succeeded in the process. I could never do that. Since I met you, I wished I were more like you."

"I had no idea you felt that way."

"No worries, I don't anymore. I dropped my authoritarian persona tonight and came here with the hopes of talking like friends and discussing your options. You talk to your friends over drinks and marijuana. I brought beer. I don't know where to get marijuana. I thought talking with you would help and you wouldn't have to agonize alone with this decision. I was fooling myself. We're not friends! I was silly to think I could relate to you in a different way. I'll be leaving now," Delores says and gets up from the couch.

"I didn't know—"

DANIEL URBAN

"No worries. You don't have to make this decision anymore. Don't show up for the meeting tomorrow. I will let the committee know we are going to go with plan B. You weren't interested from the beginning. I should have left you alone. The idea of your candidacy started as a joke. The joke's on us. We wasted our time on silliness. Enjoy the beer and have a nice life, Teddy Graham. Sorry to bother you," Delores says and hurries out of the apartment.

Theodore opens the door and sees the elevator doors closing. "Delores, wait! Don't go!"

"There's nothing else to say," Delores says as the elevator doors close. She disappears out of Theodore's view.

Theodore goes back into his apartment and slams the door behind him. "Fuck! Fuck! Fuck!" Theodore kicks the research folders on the floor. "Son of a bitch! Why do I have to be such an asshole?"

Saturday Afternoon

Theodore gets out of the elevator on the ninth floor and makes his way down the hall to the reception area of the Democratic Party headquarters. He is wearing a suit and carrying his briefcase.

"Good afternoon, how can I help you?" a receptionist says as she greets him.

"I'm Theodore Graham, I have a three o'clock meeting with the committee."

"Your appointment was canceled, Mr. Graham."

"There may have been some misunderstanding, but I am here now, so the appointment isn't canceled. I'll just go in and talk to them now."

"They're in there with someone else now. I can take your information and see if we can reschedule your meeting for Monday or Tuesday of next week."

"Just call Pamela Eynon and tell her that Theodore Graham is out here. She will want to see me."

"She's in the middle of a meeting right now and does not want to be disturbed."

"Interrupt her. If she finds out I was here and was told to leave by you, she isn't going to be happy with you. She may fire you."

"Hold on, Mr. Graham," the receptionist says and presses the intercom button. "Pam, I'm sorry to bother you. Theodore Graham is here for the three o'clock appointment you canceled."

"Tell Mr. Graham that we are sorry for the misunderstanding. We didn't think he was going to show, but we no longer need to meet with him. We are sorry for taking up his time."

"You heard her, Mr. Graham. You aren't needed here. I apologize for the inconvenience."

"I'm just going to go in there. This is important," Theodore says and busts into the conference room.

"I'm sorry, Pam. He just walked in," the receptionist says as she follows behind Theodore.

"It's okay, Cindy. Mr. Graham has problems with authority. I'll handle this. You can go back to your desk."

"I came here to give you my—" Theodore begins and is interrupted.

"You're only here as a courtesy to us. I appreciate that, but Delores already made your intentions known to us. We decided to go a different way. Sorry for wasting your time."

"Who is this guy? Is this plan B?" Theodore asks and points to a man sitting at the opposite end of the table.

The man stands up. "I'm Nathan Winters. I'm a big fan of your writing, Mr. Graham."

"Thank you. I appreciate that. Thanks for reading."

"We shouldn't have bothered you to begin with. We found a better solution, and we are going to go that route," Pamela says.

"Is Nathan Winters your better solution?"

"Yes, and he actually wants the job."

"Okay. I just came down to give you my demands and criteria to see if the committee was willing to meet them and work with me. I even wore a suit. You know what? Never mind. I'm better off. I'm glad you found somebody with better polling numbers. I'm sorry to interrupt your meeting. Good luck, Nathan."

"Thank you, Mr. Graham. I will be counting on your vote on election day."

"We'll see how you do, bro. Give it hell," Theodore says and walks out of the conference room.

Theodore walks to the reception desk. "Cindy, I am sorry for treating you the way I did when I came in here."

"It's okay, Mr. Graham. I'll chalk it up to a big misunderstanding."

"Mr. Graham, stop!" Pamela yells. "Don't leave yet. Come on in and talk."

Theodore stops. "Are you sure? I don't want to hold you up. I know how critical time is for you."

"Come back to the conference room."

Theodore turns around and sees Nathan Winters sitting in the waiting area across the reception desk.

"We'll only be a few minutes, Mr. Winters. Thank you for understanding," Pamela says as she goes back into the conference room. "Have a seat, Mr. Graham."

"You look like shit in a suit, Teddy. Did you even sleep? Why did you put a suit on today?" Tim Collins asks.

"I didn't sleep. This meeting kept me up. I have a suit on because I am dressing for the job I want to pretend I want."

"You made your answer clear from the beginning, Mr. Graham. You were crystal clear about your decision last night when we spoke," Delores Daniels says.

"Delores, I owe you an apology. I didn't hear you out and jumped to conclusions."

"Time is ticking for us, Mr. Graham. I know you like to play your mind games, but we don't have time for them. Can you get to your point, if you have one?" Ned Gibson says.

"Yesterday, you told me of this offer and you told me I had the night to think about it. It did take the whole night to think about it. You also told me you would hear my criteria if I would seriously consider running. I have my criteria."

"Are you seriously considering running?" Pamela asks.

"Yes. I did some homework last night and looked into what you said. If you think I am the one that can help you achieve your goal,

I will run, but I have a few conditions. If you can't or don't want to meet them, we can part company and there will be no hard feelings."

"Let's hear your demands," Ned Gibson says.

"You said I would get to pick my own campaign staff. Is that correct?"

"Yes, we did say that. As long as no member is a danger to the party."

"I am the one that is a danger to the party, but you asked me to run. That's on you. My number one criteria is that Delores Daniels would be my campaign manager."

"Absolutely not!" Delores says.

"Please listen to me, Delores. For the longest time, there existed a big misunderstanding between us. We've always been put on opposing sides of arguments. We pushed back at each other because circumstances dictated we had to. After we spoke last night, I thought about the potential for the success we could have if we were on the same team and working for the same goals. I've always respected your intelligence and admired how much you focused on the details of your work. The Douglas Youth Honors College's success is to your credit."

"What are your other criteria?" Pamela asks.

"If number one isn't met, we're done here. If number one is met, number two is Tim Collins is my pollster. I also want to try to get Nancy Bradford, the founder of Professional Women of Power, on my staff. Everett Avery and Fred Miles from the Black Caucus would also be good players to have on my team. I would like to get Kevin Baker of the Young Republicans on my team if he is willing. I think he switched parties after the Douglas campaign fallout. I would also like to hire my own security team."

"These aren't unreasonable requests, Mr. Graham. Why the change of heart?" Ned Gibson asks.

"I don't like stagnant politics, useless Congress, or special interest control of government. If I am the advocate for change that you think I am and I didn't at least try, I believe regret would forever swirl in my head."

"I don't see any of the people that you want on your staff being a problem, if they are willing to sign on. Tim, are you willing to be on Mr. Graham's team?" Ned Gibson asks.

"I'm in. This is the direction we need to go. I'm on board."

"We can even put that Nathan Winters guy on my staff as an adviser. He seems like a nice guy, and I feel bad for shattering his high hopes today."

"Oh, shit. He's still waiting in the reception area. He's an accountant. If his feelings aren't too hurt, maybe he will handle your finance," Pamela says.

"Delores, Ms. Daniels, what do you say we work on the same team for once?" Theodore asks.

"Is this because I made you feel guilty?"

"You did make me feel guilty, but I feel guilty because of my own ignorance. I don't think there is anybody that can put this team together in the short amount of time we have like you could. It will be a disorganized embarrassment if you aren't on this team."

"Will you behave if I say yes?"

"I will be myself. Being myself is what got me the positive polling numbers. I'm not going to win anyway, so I'm not going to change. We don't have time for me to have a metamorphosis. You will just keep the team running and put me in the right places at the right time."

"I will have to quit my job at the school."

"You can take a sabbatical and return after the election."

"Before we jump the gun, does anybody on this committee object to Theodore's demands or his candidacy?" Pamela asks. "Nobody has their hand up. Now's the time to speak. We won't have time to hear unvoiced dissent moving forward."

"I'll do it," Delores says.

"Thank you, Delores. I'm your candidate. I am running for governor. There's just one other thing—two, actually."

"I knew there was a catch. Okay, let's hear them," Pamela says.

"I want to talk to Paul Hoptak and Gene Douglas and let them know. I owe my friend and my boss that courtesy. I will make sure neither of them leak it to the media before the committee announces on Monday morning."

"That seems like a reasonable request we can honor."

"I would also like the Democratic Committee to make the announcement in the *Weekly Beat* exclusively in the Monday online edition."

"We can't just make an announcement in an online paper."

"Consider it a cold open. Make the official announcement in the online paper. Make a press release to the other papers that you made an exclusive announcement in the *Weekly Beat* online edition. After that, we won't say anything until Wednesday, when I hold my first press conference."

"I don't think that's going to work. There will be a media uproar."

"I signed a two-year contract with Paul Hoptak. He will not let me break that contract or allow any flexibility unless I kick something back to him. If there is a media uproar, it will draw attention to the campaign. If we announce online and go silent until Wednesday, we build suspense."

"This actually sounds like a good idea. We would build interest, attention, and on Wednesday, we would have momentum moving forward," Ned Gibson says.

"I now see the value in announcing this way. Let's do it. This is the birth of the Theodore Graham for Governor campaign," Pamela says.

"Lord help us," Theodore says.

Sunday Morning

Theodore walks along North Elm Street in Harmon. The street is lined with seventy-year-old maple and oak trees with wide trunks. Sidewalk tiles are uneven, raised, and cracked from far-reaching tree roots under them. There is a mailbox on opposite corners of each block, and CHILDREN PLAYING signs are hung opposite the mailboxes.

He makes his way to the tiny single home of his boss, Paul Hoptak, and knocks on the wooden screen door.

"Teddy, what brings you to my home on a beautiful Sunday morning?"

"I have to talk to you about a time-sensitive issue, before you find out from somebody else."

"It can't wait until the Monday morning staff meeting?"

"No, because it's going to be in the online edition at six o'clock tomorrow morning."

"I can't wait to hear this. Did you have coffee yet? Come on in for coffee and tell me about this news. I have a feeling that I'm going to need to be sitting down to hear this. I'm old and fat with a poor diet and do minimal exercise. I must warn you, big news is not always good for my heart."

Theodore follows Paul in the front door, through the living room, through the dining room, and into the kitchen to a breakfast nook with a big window that overlooks a big grassy yard with a tall oak tree in the center.

"I expected you to live like a slob. Walking through your house, I see I was wrong. You keep a lovely home."

"It's obviously not me that keeps the house tidy. I have a housekeeper that comes in to clean and cook a few days a week. This was the home my parents bought after they purchased the *Weekly Beat*. This is where they built their dream. I couldn't disrespect them and live like the slob that I am."

"You are a sentimental man. You surprise me."

"I am. My dad worked for the *Pittsburgh Gazette*. He started out as a printer and worked his way up to a feature writer and then to chief editor. That was where he met my mother. She was in charge of the community pages. They both hated working there because the paper wouldn't print articles that upset advertisers and local politicians. They both believed in the media's role to tell the truth and dreamed of owning their own newspaper. They chased a dream and put everything they had into the *Weekly Beat*. I loved their dream, and I loved their romantic story."

"You have a heart. You're actually a sweet guy."

"Maybe I am, but that's why I'm so fond of my paper. You saved my parents' dream, Teddy. I can't thank you enough for that," Paul says and places cups and saucers on the table.

"You approached me and convinced me to work for you. The credit is all yours. I'm sure your parents are proud of how you carried on their dream."

"I hope so. I was always amazed by their vision. I was the eldest of four children, so I vividly remember making the move here. I saw the struggling, sacrificing, scrimping, and saving they had to do to make their dream come true. They did it against tough odds, but they always did it together. I guess I appreciated their sacrifice more than my siblings. They bought this house because it was affordable and just adequate enough for our family to get by. Money was tight until they got the paper going and made it profitable. They walked the ten blocks to and from work every day. They didn't want to waste money on gas. My mom was a beat reporter that took the bus to get stories. It was the good old days, I guess."

"They were good old days. People actually worked toward dreams. Dreams today are mostly about obtaining material goods that leave people feeling empty and still wanting more."

"That's so true. You make some profound observations," Paul says as he pours coffee into the cups and sits down. "Okay, so tell me about this time-sensitive news."

"I'm going to run for governor."

"You joked about that at the office the other day. You need to get some new material. Some funny material would be nice."

"I'm serious. The lady at the office the other day was Delores Daniels. She is now my campaign manager."

"Quit fucking around. What's really the news you came here to tell me?"

"*That* is the news. I am going to run for governor. The Democratic Committee is going to announce it tomorrow."

"You have officially smoked too much marijuana. Your medical benefits cover thirty days in a substance-abuse rehabilitation center if you go voluntarily. I will give you a ride if you are ready to admit you have a problem," Paul jokes.

"No, Paul, I am really running for governor."

"Why in God's name would you do that? You can't do that. You signed a two-year contract with me."

"I am well aware of our contract. I don't plan on leaving the paper. I'm going to keep writing and working for you, but I will need some flexibility."

"This is unacceptable! We just went to six-days-a-week, and I'm considering adding the seventh day to the print schedule. I can't afford to be flexible."

"Well, here's the deal. Tomorrow, the Democratic committee is going to announce to all media that they made a special announcement in the *Weekly Beat* Monday online edition. They're not going to release any more information until my press conference on Wednesday afternoon. You will own the exclusive story that goes online at six o'clock tomorrow morning. The *Weekly Beat* will have exclusive access to the campaign, and Grace Downwood will be our local television correspondent."

"How did you get the Democratic Committee to agree to that? Never mind. I forgot whom I was talking to. What happens when you win the election? You can't be governor and work for the paper."

"I'm not going to win. We looked at a bunch of different polling data. Even if I do everything right and cover the margin of error, Gene Douglas beats me. It's late in the race, and I only have enough financing behind me to fund a skeleton crew for a campaign staff. I can't afford to buy media time or run political ads."

"Why would you do this if you can't win?"

"I have no interest in being the governor, but the Democrats don't want to appear like they rolled over and died. They want somebody that's going to fire up the base and get them into voting booths."

"You're a Republican. Isn't that just going to piss off the base?"

"I'm actually an independent. Most people assume I'm a Republican because I worked for Gene Douglas, but I'm not affiliated with a party."

"Does Gene know about this yet?"

"I'm going to tell him tonight."

"Can I go with you? I always wanted to know what it sounds like when somebody's asshole falls out. He's not going to be happy."

"He'll be fine with it when he knows I won't win."

"There is a chance you might win."

"There is, but it's miniscule."

"Well, Teddy, I tell you what. I'm okay with this. Your loyalty to my paper was part of your conditions with the Democrats. I know you are a stand-up guy. This is going to be one of the most entertaining gubernatorial elections in the history of this state, and I have exclusive access. This might make me rich. I might be able to afford one of those cleaning ladies that clean in a bikini or topless. You have my blessing."

"Thank you, Paul. That means a lot."

"You can count on my vote."

"No! I don't want the job, don't vote for me."

"Oh, yeah."

Sunday Night

The chandelier in the dining room overlooking the pool and patio of the Douglas mansion is brightly lit. Issac clears the coffee cups and dessert plates from the table. Theodore, Gene, and Sandy are still sitting around the table, talking and laughing after their meal.

"I'm glad things worked out like they did. I missed hanging out and simply enjoying our friendship. There was too much friction between us with the school and politics. I like having you around, Teddy," Sandy says.

"You're too sober to be saying nice things, Sandy," Theodore says.

"I can't be getting drunk tonight. I have to meet Wendy Uher later and work on some of the plans for the beauty pageants."

"You mean Gene and I will be smoking a joint and having some drinks on the patio without your company?"

"Sadly, yes, but if you guys are still there when I get back, I will join you. Save me some of the good stuff."

"I'm a newspaper man now. I have a staff meeting at seven o'clock tomorrow morning. I don't have the luxury of staying up late and partying anymore. I need my beauty sleep."

"You don't need beauty sleep when you have a good plastic surgeon."

"You don't even need the floatation device supplied by an airline in the event of a crash. Those breasts of yours will keep you afloat."

"Yes, they are practical and fun. I married a smart woman," Gene says.

"Aw, didn't I marry a sweet man?"

"He's okay, I guess," Theodore jokes.

"I should probably get going. I will leave you two to have fun without me," Sandy says and throws the napkin from her lap on the table and stands up. She goes over and hugs Theodore in his chair. "Thanks for coming over. We will see you next weekend for the Gatesville festival." Sandy gives him a peck on the cheek.

"Yeah, that's right. I'm looking forward to it. Playing with Ernie's band is always a fun time," Theodore says. "Since I probably won't be here when you get home, I made you a little present to enjoy when you get back." Theodore reaches in his shirt pocket and removes a joint.

Sandy takes the joint from his hand and gives Theodore another peck on the cheek. "You know how to spoil a lady. Why don't you spoil me like that, Gene?"

"I guess being a multimillionaire, living in this mansion, and all the plastic surgery you want don't compare to nicely rolled joints."

"You got to try harder, Gene," Theodore jokes.

"I love ya anyway, honey," Sandy says and gives Gene a kiss. "I'll see you when I get home."

"What do you say we go out on the patio and have a drink and look at the stars?" Gene asks.

"That's a fine idea, my friend. It's a gorgeous night."

"You said you had something to talk to me about when I talked to you yesterday. What's going on?" Gene asks as he hands Theodore a beer from the minifridge.

"I was trying to figure out the best way to tell you what I have to tell you. There is no best way, so I'm just going to tell you," Theodore says and pulls a joint out of his shirt pocket and lights it. He takes a long puff off it and hands it to Gene.

"I'm almost afraid to hear it. Go ahead, say what you have to say."

"I am going to be your opponent in the governor's race."

Gene chokes on the marijuana smoke as he exhales. He goes into a coughing fit. "You can't joke with me like that when I'm smoking this shit. I nearly coughed myself to death."

"You don't cough, you don't get off, right? Gene, I wasn't joking."

"Cut it out. You can't run as a Democrat, you're a Republican!"

"I'm not, actually. I'm an unaffiliated independent."

"Get the fuck out of here! You're not an independent, you worked for my campaign."

"You didn't require me to be a Republican, and you never checked."

"I guess I should have checked, but you're just screwing with me. You're not running against me. What did you really need to tell me?"

"That is what I came here to tell you. The Democratic Committee asked me to run in place of Sherman Jones. They will announce in the online edition of my paper tomorrow. Wednesday, I will be making my official announcement and holding a press conference."

"All right, where is this joke going?"

Theodore takes a drag off the joint. As he exhales, he says, "This isn't a joke, Gene."

"It has to be a joke. There is no possible way you could run. There is no possible way you would run."

"It's not a joke!" Theodore shouts. "The committee approached me, and they made some good points. I thought about it a bit and decided to do it."

"How could you do this? This is my legacy. You know that. I've been waiting for my whole life to fulfill it. You can't do this. You're supposed to be my friend."

"Our friendship doesn't change."

"The fuck it doesn't! This doesn't even make sense. Teddy, you truly are an asshole!"

"Relax, I'm not going to win the election. The pollsters ran the numbers. If I do everything right and cover the entire margin of error, you beat me by no less than 5 percent of the vote. You can check the numbers with your pollsters."

"If you are going to lose, then why do it? Why would they even ask you to do it?"

"The Democrats have nobody to run. Anybody that showed an interest polled so low that the Democrats probably wouldn't even bother to come out and vote. I'm a known name lately, and it would get some of the base to come out. Not enough will come out for me to beat you. You have no worries. I'm doing it because it helps the *Weekly Beat*."

"How am I going to campaign against you? You know it's going to get nasty."

"I'm not going to get nasty. You don't have to get nasty. Our friendship will be one of the most redeeming things about this campaign."

"You know Russ Dewitt is going to want to come at you hard."

"Don't let him. It's your campaign. You can come at me for not being a native of the state and my lack of seriousness."

"People tend to like you better than they like me."

"In social situations, yes. I am a clown. That's a lot of fun. As their governor, no. You are serious and successful. I've had four jobs in the last three years that I didn't keep. You can hit me for not being able to handle the pressure of being a successful lawyer. It doesn't have to get nasty."

"Are you sure about these polling numbers?"

"Yes. Check them with your staff tomorrow. You are going to win. When I come out on an issue, you come out with a better alternative. This will be the most memorable election in state history, and you will be the winner."

"Who is going to run this losing campaign?"

"Delores Daniels."

"No way! She is the superintendent of my school. I can't afford to lose her. She hates your guts. She won't manage your campaign."

"Her being my campaign manager was one of my conditions. I need somebody intelligent that I respect to keep me grounded. It's better if she doesn't like me. She won't worry about hurting my feelings when she disagrees with me."

"If I refuse to let her have the time off, she couldn't be your campaign manager and you wouldn't run. Right?"

"Her contract clearly states she can take sabbatical once every five years for personal reasons. If you refuse it, she would leave and file a lawsuit against you. It would look bad for you in the campaign, and then I might win. If I win, I would appoint her to head the Department of Education."

"You have this pretty well figured out. You love upsetting my world. I just started shitting solid and sleeping at night. Now you drop this in my lap. Were you put on this earth to taunt me?"

"I'm not taunting you. I'm more like a sparring partner. I will keep you on your toes. You will be sharp and in shape until election day. If I didn't enter the race and they put some unknown against you, the race would get stale. People would get sick of you and vote against you out of spite. Spite is a one heck of a motivator."

Gene takes the joint from Theodore. "This one of the shadiest things you could do to me. I hope you're right about all this. What about this weekend in Gatesville when you are playing with my son's band?"

"That will be the perfect opportunity to showcase the strength of our friendship and put politics aside. We can be all laughs and hugs and handshakes. It would be a great photo op if Russ Dewitt and I can be seen laughing together. We don't have to make political speeches, and I will publicly commend you for putting the festival together and supporting the charities you are."

"You know what? I didn't trust you when you were my campaign manager. I should have. I did a shitty thing by firing you. The Whitneys waved a shitload of money in my face and guaranteed me a victory if I played nice with them. I turned my back on a friend, but you never turned your back on me. I'm going to trust you on this."

"There's no reason not to. I know your legacy. You've been whining to me about it since college. Now, whom does a whore have to blow to get another beer around here?"

Gene goes to the minifridge behind the patio bar and gets another beer out. "Normally, I would say I have a better chance of getting some from you than my wife, but Sandy has been putting out pretty regularly lately."

"That's a good thing. It's about time she treats you right."

"Oh, believe me, I'm not complaining. I paid for all the plastic decorations. It's about time I get to enjoy the holidays."

"Yeah, buddy! Merry Christmas to you. Get what you paid for."

Wednesday Afternoon

There is a crowd of reporters and politically interested people gathered at the bottom of the marble steps of the Harmon City Hall. The Theodore Graham for Governor campaign is assembled with his campaign staff in a small meeting room just inside the glass doors of the building. Theodore paces around in the room and practices his speech and answers for the press in his head.

"You have about ten minutes until you go on. Are you ready?" Delores asks.

Theodore stops pacing. "I'm as ready as I'm going to be. How do I look? Is my tie straight? Do I have boogers?" Theodore asks and shows his nostrils to her.

"Gross. No, you don't have boogers," Delores says and straightens Theodore's tie.

"All right. Delores, you will assemble the staff on the landing next to the podium and announce me. Sweet Barn, you will walk down the steps with me and stand to the left of me. Are Lizard Eddie and Funky Brian in position? I don't want anybody getting hit by a car while they are listening to my speech. It wouldn't look good for the campaign."

"Teddy, calm down. Everybody is where they are supposed to be. I made sure of it. This is why you made me your manager. I got this."

"I'm sorry. I'm not used to having a team supporting me."

"I'm happy to be on your team, Teddy. My mama is so thankful you hired us to be your security guards. She is here to see your speech today. She wants you to come over for dinner so she can thank you with a nice meal," Sweet Barn says.

"I would be happy to come over for dinner. Before I go out there, go down and make sure your mom has a spot right up front to see my speech. Better yet, take another chair down and seat her next to my staff."

"She's not on staff. We don't want the press to look into her," Delores says.

"I'm putting her on my staff as an adviser."

"We don't know anything about her. What is she going to advise us on?"

"Yeah, Teddy, Mama doesn't know about politics. She just likes you because you are nice to her boys."

"You listen to your mama, right?"

"Yeah. I don't want to let her down or get on her bad side."

"Good. I am appointing her 'official mom' of my campaign. My mom passed away, so I don't have a mom to give me good advice and help me listen to my heart. I don't want to let your mama down or get on her bad side."

Tears begin to well up in Sweet Barn's eyes. "You are the nicest man I know. You're gonna make Mama so happy." He grabs Theodore and gives him a big hug.

"Keep it together, big guy. You can't be crying in front of the press. I need you strong out there. Ask your mom if she would like to bake her goodies for our staff meetings too. Her chocolate chip cookies are the best."

"I'll get it together. I'll ask her about baking for you too. Let me take a chair down and bring her up front. She's going to be so excited."

Theodore looks at Delores and sees tears welling in her eyes. "Why are you crying? I can't have my giant security chief and campaign manager crying out there."

"That was a sweet thing you did for Sweet Barn's mother. I'm so busy not liking you that I forget that you have big heart."

"Hurry up and start hating me again. We only have a few minutes until we go out there. I want you on my staff because you think I'm a piece of shit. Don't get distracted by my sweet side," Theodore says. "Here, pull my finger. That will disgust you enough to stop your tears."

"I'm not pulling your finger."

"Good, because I don't have a fart at the surface, and I don't want to push. It would suck if I shit myself right before I announce that I am running for governor."

"There you are. That's the Teddy I know and can't stand."

"Okay, is everybody ready? Ed, you go down to the bottom of the steps and help Sweet Barn's mom up to her seat. Ms. Daniels, go do your thing. We have a campaign to launch. Let's do this!"

Theodore and Sweet Barn watch through the glass doors as the staff makes their way to their seats on the landing of the marble steps. Delores stands behind the podium and waits for the murmur of the waiting crowd to settle.

"Good afternoon, members of the press and concerned citizens. The new Democratic gubernatorial candidate will be making the official announcement of his intentions momentarily. He will make a brief statement and take questions from members of the press. Members of the press can obtain a written copy of the briefing as well as the contact and staffing information after the conclusion of the press conference. Thank you. May I now introduce to you, Mr. Theodore Graham," Delores says and begins to clap as Theodore and Sweet Barn make their way down the marble steps.

Theodore waves at the crowd and waits for the dull round of clapping to stop. "Good afternoon, everybody. I stand before you today in a moment of mourning and loss. The man originally set to be walking this path was sadly taken from us. Sherman Jones dedicated himself to serving the people of this state. From a city councilman to a mayor to a member of the House of Representatives, Mr. Jones put the voice of the people in his platforms and tirelessly served to preserve the will of the people. It is only because of his passing that I stand in front of you today. I am the next best thing, and far from as good as him. I only hope that I am good enough to carry the torch that Sherman Jones carried for the people of this state. My name is Theodore Graham, and I am announcing my candidacy for governor of this great state."

Theodore waits for a brief round of applause to fade.

"I'm not standing in front of you and telling you that I am carrying on the Sherman Jones campaign. I have my own platform, values, and ideals. I have a hand-picked staff to help me voice my message and put together a campaign that is focused on serving the interests of the citizens of this state. The election is a little over two months away. I have a lot of work to do. This hand-picked staff is the best of the best, and they will help me help the people in my role as the next governor of our state."

The crowd applauds politely.

"The campaign website will be launched later this evening, and you will all be able to learn about my platform and my staff. My staff is the team that is going to take us all the way to the governor's office. We are a team. Teamwork will be the centerpiece of my campaign. We all have to work together as a team to make our future prosperous and something we can proudly pass on to future generations that will carry this great state beyond what our imaginations believe to be possible.

"I would also like to introduce you to the newest member of my campaign staff. She was just added this morning, and I believe she will be filling the most important role of my campaign. Mrs. Sophia White, seated with my staff, will fill the role of my campaign mom. I lost my mom many years ago. That loss left a hole where that special bond used to exist. Through my friendships with her sons, my security team, I met Sophia. Sophia is a strong woman that has raised a family through times of struggle and loss but somehow manages to keep her faith, a welcoming home, and generous heart that shares kindness with others. No matter where I am, what job I hold, or what choices are in front of me, Sophia seems to know when I am struggling and boosts my spirits. She sends a plate of cookies with a note of encouraging words. When she does that, the feeling of 'everything is going to be all right' comes to ease my mind. It's the kind of encouragement that only a mother can give. I welcome Sophia as my campaign mom. She will give me the encouragement I need to move forward. She will give me the kick in the ass I need when I am slacking. She will give me love from her heart so I can be the best me I can be. Where would any of us be without a mom in their corner?"

The applause from the crowd is loud and enthusiastic. Theodore walks to the end of his seated staff and greets Sophia. The tiny woman reaches up to Theodore. He leans down to hug her, and she hugs him back and gives him a peck on the cheek. He turns to face the crowd with Sophia. The crowd claps louder. The two wave to the crowd. Theodore gives her a peck on the cheek and returns to the podium and waits for the cheers to calm.

"I will take some questions from the press."

"How come you decided to run for governor?" a reporter shouts.

"Short answer, to meet women. Long answer, I watched election after election where the issues are no different from the last. I've watched politician after politician promise to do something about those issues, yet the issues remain the same. I get the impression that nothing is getting done, and I want to take a chance on my ideas and get things done."

"You are a Republican. How can the Democrats trust that you won't apply your Republican values to your policies if you get elected?"

"You are a journalist, you should be doing your homework before you come to these events. My voter registration and the rules of the party are open and available for press and public scrutiny. It's your job as a reporter to look these things up. If I were Republican, I wouldn't be eligible to run on the Democratic ticket, according to party rules. The Democrats, according to those rules, can, however, run a Democrat or a nonaffiliated independent. I'm a nonaffiliated independent."

"If you are elected, will you register as a Democrat?"

"No. The two-party system is part of the problem. It makes issues appear to have only two sides. Many issues are complex and have many sides. As an independent, I can look at all sides and not have to be loyal to a side to spite the opposition."

"Why is the Democratic Party backing you?"

"At first, I thought it was because I was as cute as a button, but I've come to find that they want to put a progressive agenda forward so we can put an end to stagnant government."

"When you say *progressive agenda*, don't you mean a liberal agenda where you will cater to minority voters and show a blatant disregard for the majority?"

"You are also a journalist. I encourage your newspaper to supply you with a dictionary. *Progressive* and *liberal* are two different words with two different meanings. If I were catering to the minority and disregarding the majority, wouldn't that defeat the purpose of hoping to get a majority vote? When you get your dictionary, look up *progressive*, *liberal*, *majority*, and *minority*. Once you know the language, come at me with more questions."

"By looking at the members of your staff, it does appear you are catering to minorities. Aren't you?"

"Maybe if we stop calling them minorities and start calling them people, we would no longer need these types of questions. I have women on my staff because I am a man and don't know what concerns women voters. I have black and Hispanic members on my staff because I am white and I don't know what concerns black and Hispanic members of my constituency. It's just easier to have them on my staff so I can ask them directly. I can't consider myself informed by the people if I am man-splaining women issues and white-splaining nonwhite issues. If you want to look a little deeper into my staffing choices, I have Catholics, Jewish people, Baptists, and Protestants on my staff. I also have a financial adviser because I am not an accountant and political strategist because I am not a politician."

"You never held or ran for political office. Do you think your lack of political experience will hurt you in the election?"

"Correction, I did run for political office. I ran for student council in fifth grade and lost to a girl with pigtails named Susan. If a voter thinks my lack of political experience will make me a poor choice, it is their right not to vote for me. I meet all the requirements needed to run for governor. It's my choice to run, just like it is the voter's choice to pick the candidate that they feel is the best for them."

"Aren't you entering this race to get back at Gene Douglas for firing you as his campaign manager?"

"Gene Douglas has been a friend of mine since our first day of college. Our friendship hasn't changed. I will be hanging out with the Gene Douglas and his beautiful wife, Sandy, this weekend at his fundraiser for veterans hospitals, law enforcement officials, emergency responders, and the Gatesville Fairgrounds. I will be playing with the band of his son, Ernie, there on Friday and Saturday night. I encourage everybody to come out and support all these good causes."

"Do the financial sponsors of your campaign have an agenda that you will move forward on if you are elected?"

"I received enough money from the Democratic Party to meet the basic financial needs of this campaign. I haven't even had chance to do any fund-raising or send mailers out looking for donors. So I basically don't have a lucrative source of funding that I have to cater to. The voters are the ones with the agenda I want to move on. I am here to serve them, not the highest bidder."

"Aren't you just in this race to promote your newspaper, the *Weekly Beat*? Aren't their reporters just going to move your campaign forward by writing positive articles in your favor?"

"I work for the *Weekly Beat*. I'm loyal to my employer and coworkers. I will give them interviews and quotes and statements out of loyalty to my professional friendships, but they are professional journalists. I expect them to be reporting the facts, good, bad, or indifferent."

"Aren't your policies going to be costly for the taxpayers? Won't you be just another tax-and-spend Democrat that pushes forward programs that don't work?"

"What newspaper are you from?"

"The *Capital Register*," the reporter answers.

"I guess the *Capital Register* is a speculating media and not a journalistic enterprise. In my original statement, I said that our website with my policies and platform will be launched later this evening. I have not spoken about my platform or policies, so your question is based on assumptions and speculation. I can't tell the media how to do its job, but it would do their readers and viewers a disservice if they continue to report on information that is not yet available."

"What are your feelings on taxes?"

"I hate paying them like everybody else, but they are a necessary evil. I would like to see taxes come down, but there has been a trend for over two centuries that clearly shows that operating costs continue to rise. If I get elected governor, I would like to better manage how those tax dollars are spent. I can't promise to cut taxes and then have to gut services that benefit the citizens of our state."

"In what areas would you cut spending to reduce taxes?"

"I can't get into the specifics until I look at where the money is going. Ideally, I would like to see the taxes be effectively spent where the benefits are better for the greater good and not just a few special interests."

"Isn't what you are proposing communism?"

"Great, another reporter that needs a dictionary. What I just stated about tax spending is more like socialism than communism. Those are two different words with two different meanings. Do yourself a favor and look them up. If you have a job to inform the public, you better inform yourself first."

"Are you saying you are a socialist?"

"No, I didn't say that. But when you look up the meaning of *socialist*, you will see that we have a socialist infrastructure. We have firefighters that protect the greater good of their communities. We have police forces that do the same. We have garbage trucks that pick up everybody's trash. We have public schools to educate all children. We have public highways. We have a military that protects the whole nation. It's a system that protects the greater good. It is a form of socialism, but that doesn't make me a socialist. I didn't invent the system. I am running for governor to improve the system.

"That's all the questions I have time for today. I will be hitting the campaign trail, and there will be plenty of opportunities to ask questions. My press secretary, Pam Eynon, will be handing out my itinerary and information to make it easier for the press to stalk me. After my platform is made public this evening, I expect more in-depth questions that I will be happy to answer. Please learn a little bit more about me before you decide which way to vote. Thank you all for coming out today," Theodore says and leaves the podium. He walks up the marble steps and back into the city hall building. Sweet Barn and Delores follow him.

The three get in the building and into the small meeting room. "Did you have to be so insulting to the members of the press? They are just going to call the campaign office and complain about you treating them unfairly," Delores says.

"When they call, tell them to improve their methods instead of complaining when they get called out for doing their job poorly."

"I don't care what those reporters do. They're not nice to you. I haven't seen my mama's smile that bright for years. You made that woman the happiest woman in the world today. Thank you, Teddy," Sweet Barn says.

"You're welcome, buddy. Go back out there and bring her up with the rest of the staff. I would like her to join us for lunch."

"I will. I'll go get her now. You're a wonderful man, Teddy Graham."

"Am I the only one that wants to hug you and throat-punch you at the same time?" Delores asks.

CHAPTER 32

Sweet Barn is behind the wheel of the conversion van, driving Theodore, Delores, and Nancy Bradford to their first major campaign event. Theodore is sitting quietly, going over some notes for his speech. Nancy and Delores are sitting at the small table in the back, talking and going over the headlines in the morning papers to see how the press is treating his campaign announcement.

"I don't know how he does it. The newspaper reporters that he insulted with his answers yesterday have written surprisingly fair articles about the campaign," Delores says.

"Most of those reporters either signed up for a seat in the press van or asked for campaign credentials in our press area for events," Nancy says.

"They should be raking him over the coals. They should hate him for being the wiseass man-child that spews nothing but condescension and snark. I'll never understand his appeal."

"I hated him before I got to really know him. At the beginning of the Gene Douglas campaign, when he was his campaign manager, they attended one of my events. I didn't want Teddy undermining my plan, so I had my intern keep him away from the crowd. I thought he was going to play his powerful mind games with the women there. I wasn't having any part of it. When I heard Gene Douglas speak, I knew the speech was written by Teddy. I was surprised by how much he knew about and respected my organization. I went back to the room where I made him wait for Gene to thank him, and before I knew it, I was all over him. I can't explain it, but I just wanted to be held by him and be close to him. Never in my life was I that kind of girl, but that night, I kind of was."

"Are you telling me you and Teddy were intimate?"

"That night I was. I can't really explain what came over me. I was always so focused on my work, and I put all my efforts into Professional Women of Power. Most of the local politicians I dealt with gave me a lot of hollow praise for my work, and when they spoke about my group, they talked down to it. I was tired of being talked down to, so I became a bitch. You know how the male mind works. If they perceive you as a threat to them or as a bitch in general, they just assume you are a lesbian. Not Teddy. He took my bitchiness in stride, followed my criteria, and had Gene highlight the efforts and success of my work in his speech. I was thrown off by it. It showed me how complacent I was in my thinking toward men in general," Nancy says.

"How did a nice speech turn into intimacy?"

"It just felt good to have a man recognize, understand, and appreciate what I was working hard for. I found comfort in him. I felt respected. That feeling made him attractive to me, because he made me feel good about myself. I succumbed to his charm, I guess, but I don't regret it."

"I didn't know there was something between the two of you. I would have never guessed. Now I know why you're on the staff," Delores says.

"Oh, no, you didn't just say that. It's not like that at all, Delores, and I don't appreciate you wrongly assuming it is. I came to this campaign because I believe Teddy is the real deal, not because I have a crush on him like a schoolgirl. I don't appreciate what you are insinuating. You are off base and way out of line."

"I know you ladies are talking low, but this van isn't that big. I heard every word you were saying after the word *lesbian* was mentioned. Lesbian was what captured my interest. You know this is a conversion van. That table folds up and the back seat folds down into a bed. We have forty minutes until we get to Cannonsburg. If you two want to get some lesbian stuff out of the way, don't let me stop you. If you want me to join you two, then I will have Sweet Barn drive around a little bit longer."

"I knew it was only a matter of time before the man-child part of you showed up," Delores says.

"Yes, Delores, Nancy and I shared a moment of intimacy, and it was great. I don't regret it, and we are both consenting adults. Nancy is not on this staff because we hooked up. She is on this staff because her business sense fits well with my vision of building local economies. You are on this staff because I know you're meticulous and principled in your management skills. You balanced business, education, the student curriculum, met state regulations, and kept the wealthy figureheads of the board happy. You ran that honors college, and it only did as well as it did because of you. I only did as well as I did there because of you. For both of you, it's your commitment to success that I want to surround myself with."

"I'm sorry. I didn't mean to insinuate anything sinister," Delores says.

"Well, you did. This isn't high school, Ms. Daniels. There's no need to fight over boys. I guess Nancy, Sweet Barn, and I are the only mature ones in this conversion van."

"Don't worry, Ms. Daniels, I'm not that mature. When somebody says *titmouse*, I still giggle. It's a funny word," Sweet Barn says from the driver's seat.

Theodore laughs. "I laughed when he said *titmouse*, so I guess Nancy is the only mature one here."

"All of you better grow the fuck up," Nancy jokes.

"I need all of you on my side. We have a lot of work to do, and we can't do it well if we make it about the adventures of my penis."

"If I so much as see that white trouser snake near my big black ass, I'm quitting," Sweet Barn jokes.

"You have no worries, Sweet Barn. I'm keeping it zipped up. Now, if you two ladies are done talking about me, tell me what the press is saying. How did our announcement go over?"

"I will read you some of the headlines, and you can decide for yourself," Delores says. "The *Gatesville Courier* says, GUBERNATORIAL RACE IS A BATTLE OF BUDDIES. The *Harmon Herald* says, DEMOCRATS OPT FOR CIRCUS ACT CANDIDATE. The *Capital Register* says, TEDDY GRAHAM: WILL WE CHOKE ON THIS BREATH OF FRESH AIR? The *Capital*

Beat says, WILL PEOPLE LISTEN TO NEW IDEAS? DEMOCRATS HOPE. The *Morning Sun Gazette* says, RIP, SHERMAN JONES; HELLO, TEDDY GRAHAM. Your paper says, JOURNALIST BASHING MAY HURT GRAHAM'S CHANCES. Would you like me to continue?"

"No, I thought I would have done better than that. What are the people saying?"

Nancy reaches into her briefcase and pulls out some papers. "I printed the comments section of a social media page this morning. Have a look."

Theodore takes the page from Nancy and begins to read the comments.

Teddy Graham—at least he's not a politician.

He has no money behind his campaign, so we can't accuse him of being corrupt.

Somebody with new ideas is always the object of ridicule. Godspeed, Theodore Graham.

I don't know how good he would be at being a governor, but I wouldn't mind seeing what's inside that suit. He's a hottie.

It's a shame. Most people won't take the time to go to his website and read his platform. There are some good ideas there.

Theodore is just another liberal fuck-tard that wants us all to sing "Kumbaya!" while he gives our rights away to minorities and taxes the shit out of the people for programs that will fail. They will fail because he listens to the bossy women on his staff that don't know how the real world works.

The campaign trail can be very stressful. I would volunteer to have tension-breaking sex with Teddy so he could stay focused on winning. Mmmmmmmmmm, he's dreamy.

It's about time a candidate calls the media out for being the idiots they are. How many bad politi-

cians did we end up with because media is too busy speculating instead of relaying the facts?

Teddy Graham, too little, too late for the Democrats.

Oh, how short memories are! Have most of you forgotten the crooked money and criminal activity associated with the Douglas campaign? John Q. Public will again be too stupid to vote the right man in office this election, but when the egg is on their faces, they will want Theodore Graham. Please try again in four years, Mr. Graham.

The only jobs that Teddy Graham will create is hand jobs and blow jobs for himself, and those positions will be filled by the MILFs and cougars on his staff. I'm jealous, but I'm not voting for this conman.

Teddy Graham, I believe, can work with anybody as long as success is the goal they are working for. I believe he is the uniter we need.

Teddy Graham better hurry the fuck up and convince me to vote for him. If not, I'm staying home on election day and having some alone time with internet porn.

How can we trust a man that would turn on his friend and run against him in the election?

Theodore Graham is what this state needs. We've had a stagnant state assembly for sixteen years and governors that couldn't get things moving forward. Where did that get us? Higher taxes, shittier schools, bankrupt boroughs and townships, and our elected officials sold our government and resources to the special interests that bid the highest.

His inclusion of Mrs. White on his staff for motherly advice only makes me believe there is a moral heart that beats in his chest. He's too sweet for politics.

*I saw him on the news last night and was like,
"No, shit!" I got high with that dude in the parking
lot of a Who concert. He had some fucking kick-ass
weed and is funny as shit too. He got my vote. Hope
he legalizes it!*

"It's not all bad. You got mixed reviews," Nancy says.

"Yeah, it could have been a lot worse, I guess," Theodore says.

"Let me take a look at that," Delores says and takes the paper away from Theodore and begins to read it.

"We're here, Teddy. Where do you want me to park?"

"Park on the side of building. Have Lizard Eddie and Funky Brian park the press van on the other side of the stage. It looks like most of the local television stations are set up already."

Sweet Barn parks the van on the side of the building. He gets out of the van to show his brothers where to park. They show the members of the press where to set up for the press conference.

"The crowd seems to be mostly press. There are not too many onlookers from the public," Nancy says.

"I see a couple of campaign signs waving. Our volunteers did their job handing out the campaign posters, pins, and bumper stickers," Delores says.

"We will get more handed out this weekend. Kevin Baker has a lot of his reformed Young Republicans going all over the state to events, festivals, and shows this weekend."

"Teddy, are you ready? This event is where you outline your platform. Make it good and change those headlines and minds."

"You got this, Teddy."

"I will go out and announce you. You make your speech and take a couple of questions from the press. After that, go mingle with some of the people. Grace Downwood and her cameraman will be following you as you meet and greet the public. You will do a stand-in interview with her at the end. Got it?"

"Yes, I got it. Let's do it."

"Nancy, we will be by the podium with Teddy. He is going to mention your organization, so you will probably be asked to talk to the press afterward."

"Okay, I brought some handouts about the projects of Professional Women of Power to pass along to them."

"Perfect. Here goes nothing," Delores says and makes her way toward the stage.

"Good afternoon, ladies and gentlemen. Our candidate will make a brief statement about his platform and will then take a few questions from the press. Members of the press who weren't passengers on our media caravan can obtain a detailed copy of the press release from Carrie, who is standing by the Channel 6 News van. Ladies and gentlemen, members of the press, it is my privilege to introduce the Democratic candidate for governor of our great state. Please welcome, Mr. Theodore Graham."

Theodore waves to the people as he approaches the stage. He takes a moment to go out and shake some hands with people gathered at the side of the stage. He walks up the three steps to the stage and makes his way to the podium. A young woman standing in front lifts her top and exposes her breasts.

Theodore sees this woman and points to her. "Thank you, very nice, thank you. Hello, Cannonsburg! I'm happy to be here with you all today. It's such a beautiful day to be in such a beautiful town. The young lady up front here, I appreciate the special welcome. Thank you."

The woman lifts her top again as Theodore waits for the applause to stop and the crowd to settle.

He looks around the crowd again and then takes his note cards from his front pocket and places them on the podium in from of him.

"Economics. Economics is the number one issue of my platform. When an economy is good, people do well. When and economy is bad, people do poorly. A good economy brings jobs, opportunity, growth, and prosperity to a community. A bad economy brings unemployment, scarcity, stagnation, and blight. We can look around at many of our communities and see the effects of a poor local economy. When I travel across the state, I see public schools, hospitals, community centers, high-rise centers, public housing, and highways that were built in the sixties and the seventies. At the time of their construction, the state and these communities were prosperous. There was industry. People had jobs. Families were sending their kids to college. It was possible to save money. Those are the kinds of things that happen in a good economy."

Theodore pauses and scans the crowd. He glances at his notes and returns his focus to the people in front of him.

"Something has happened in the last forty years. These communities aren't as prosperous as they once were. What's missing? Industry, jobs, and a progressive vision. Communities are a work in progress. Progress is ongoing. We can't continue to beat our chest and celebrate victories of the past while they crumble around us. Time doesn't stand still, and progress doesn't happen without a deep commitment. I want to make that commitment and invest in the potential of our communities. I want to celebrate victories of today. In order to celebrate victories of today, we have to listen to those with ideas and vision. I stand in front of this vacant strip mall because I listened to people with ideas and vision."

Theodore pauses. Some in the crowd begin to clap.

"If I look back six months, this abandoned strip mall seemed destined to remain an eyesore in Cannonsburg. When I look ahead six months, this strip mall will house two restaurants, a day care center, a youth activity center, and seven shops that make and sell their own locally made products. And 235 jobs will be created. The building as a whole will be incorporated so the employees that work here will have access to affordable health benefits. The merchants in this newly refurbished plaza will hire local people. The newly incorporated center will have a one-year tax exemption and a four-year fixed tax rate if they purchase materials and services from local retailers and contractors. Tax breaks are available to local retailers and contractors if they help the project meet budget and completion deadlines. This is going to be a boost to the local economy, and when local economies do well, local people do well."

Theodore pauses for more applause.

"This isn't my idea. This wasn't my vision. It was the collective brainpower of the members of the Professional Women of Power organization. The founder of this organization, Nancy Bradford, is a top adviser on my staff. Her group is also tired of seeing blighted communities full of people living paycheck to paycheck and never getting ahead. Instead of just complaining about the way things are, they offered ideas to change them. When their ideas weren't seriously considered by some of our elected leaders, they took action themselves. The abandoned building behind me that is about to be transformed will be the third project of Professional Women of Power. The King's Kingdom Plaza in Silverville was the first. It brought two hundred new jobs to local residents there, and it is going strong. Try to find a parking space there on the weekends. The place is a booming source of pride for Silverville. The second project was the repopulation of the old Greendale Industrial Park. There is a local soft drink bottling company, there is a candle factory, there is a furniture maker, and there is a cosmetics maker. Where there were once four vacant buildings, there is now an industrial park that found new life. Three more companies plan to build and operate out of the Greendale Industrial Park in the next year. There will be well over a thousand full-time jobs with health benefits for local people to find their livelihoods and vocations. All these projects were possible because of people with a vision. Talks are already underway for a fourth project in the town of Carter. Nancy Bradford and Everett Avery of my staff are discussing ideas for the long-abandoned iron-and-aluminum factory with Carter mayor Orlando French and his staff.

"There are places like this all across our state. There are people with ideas and vision all across our state. As governor, I will put the two together and rebuild local economies. In the past, when local economies were strong, people did well. I'm not promising to bring back the past, but I want to bring new life to communities so they can do well again. Progress isn't going to happen overnight, especially after forty years of celebrating victories that have long since passed. Progress will only happen with the support of the people. Communities must learn to support their communities. People must learn to shop local, get involved, and share ideas and vision. When communities came together in the past, new schools, hospitals, and community centers were built. We can't build a better future if we stop building. As governor, I want to be the leader that helps launch hundreds of these projects across our state. People are tired of waiting for trickle-down economics to work. Foundations aren't built at the top. Anybody with common sense knows a foundation goes on the bottom and supports the growth that springs from it. Elect me governor, and let's build a foundation that will support prosperity for our future and prosperity that will continue for future generations."

Theodore pauses for a long and loud applause.

The girl in the front row that lifted her top has recruited four other friends to flash their breasts at Theodore. Theodore winks and gives them a thumbs-up and waits until the crowd quiets.

"I'm sure the press is eager to get to questions about my platform, my speech, my staff, and my candidacy. Let's get you, media folks, some answers."

"Aren't these projects just pet projects of Professional Women of Power that you are shamelessly promoting in your platform?" a reporter asks.

"If ideas like this came from other organizations, I would be promoting them as well. I'm not ashamed of progress. I don't think we should be. Just because the Professional Women of Power came up with these ideas and moved these projects forward doesn't mean other organizations can't apply the same ideas to their communities. They are just the first group to try something new and different. I've seen what they've done, and I like it. I admire the hard work that went into making them happen. Nancy Bradford is on my staff for her ideas. She encourages copycats of her group's successful programs. She is willing to share her ideas. She has ideas that will help our state government make projects like this happen on a larger scale from border to border. Pick her brain. She will be speaking to communities and town councils over the next few weeks and showing them how to get started."

"Won't tax breaks for programs like this hurt tax coffers of local communities?"

"What's hurting tax coffers in our communities now is the tax break we give to box stores and restaurants that get tax exemptions but don't invest in the local communities. Look at the Walmart up the road. They came to Cannonsburg eight years ago and offered to build a store to boost the local economy and bring people into the area. They would only do it if they got a ten-year tax exemption and if Cannonsburg paid the costs of updating the roads and infrastructure to accommodate their highway access needs. Walmart came in with their own contractors, with their own materials, and with their own people. When they opened, they hired over two hundred local employees, and now they reduced that number a little under a hundred. The ten-year tax exemption is up in less than two years, and now Walmart is negotiating a ten-year tax exemption with Merkley Township two miles down the road. If Merkley agrees, they will get a new Walmart and the one in Cannonsburg will close and become a vacant blight. The tax breaks that hurt communities are the ones where the community gets nothing in return."

"Are you against the fair capitalist market?"

"How fair is it that small businesses that invest in the community can't get a break but box stores that don't give back to the community don't have to pay taxes?"

"Are you saying Walmart doesn't give back to the community?"

"Walmart considers giving Girl Scouts permission to sell cookies in their parking as giving back to the community, and they get a tax break for it."

"Walmart brings people into Cannonsburg. They are holding up their end of the bargain, aren't they?"

"Walmart is bringing people to Walmart. They are going nowhere else in Cannonsburg because small business can't compete with them. The building behind me slowly became vacant and blighted when Walmart came to town. Is that a fair capitalist market? Are the cheap, foreign-made goods they sell employing members of the community?"

"How can you guarantee programs like this will work in the long run?"

"I can't guarantee it. What I can guarantee is these programs are trying something different to benefit communities. There is action being taken. Change doesn't happen when we just stand still and complain about what's happening. Action is needed."

"How do you plan on changing the shopping habits of people and getting them to come to these local businesses?"

"Change is never easy or comfortable at the start. I hope that community leaders and area chambers of commerce would promote local business. Local businesses have to do their part and promote themselves. People will change their habits if they are shown better alternatives. It's going to take time. I'm not promising instant gratification."

"You are running for governor. How would you help these programs at the state government level?"

"At the state level, I can push for our legislature to find ways to cut the red tape for these projects, make resources available, offer grants, offer tax break incentives for local investment, stop the tax breaks for the businesses that don't invest in our state, and welcome business that wants to grow with a community and not just in it."

"How is your economic plan different from Gene Douglas's plan?"

"What you would have to do is go to our website and look at our economic plan and go to the Gene Douglas website and look at his economic plan. I'm familiar with my economic plan. I'm confident in it, and I would like the opportunity to move it forward for the people of this state. I'm not familiar with his because I am busy with mine. It's up to the voters to make the comparison and decide what is best for them."

"You worked for Gene Douglas, you have to be somewhat familiar with his platform. Aren't you using that insider information to your advantage?"

"I don't have any inside information. I knew what I knew when I was his campaign manager. I don't have any access or insight beyond what he says to the public or posts on his website. I'm not trying to outdo him. I am putting my ideas out there. If the people like mine, they will vote for me. If they like his better, they will vote for him."

"Gene Douglas got rid of the Whitneys because of their corruption and fraudulent practices. Wouldn't it be likely that he would associate with those type of campaign investors again in order to push his campaign to victory in exchange for favors from our government?"

"I know you are trying to get me to sling mud. I'm not going to do that. I believe that Gene learned a hard lesson by associating with the Whitneys, and I believe he is smart enough to not let it happen again. If he does, I expect the press to find out about it and keep him honest."

"You talked about economics today, but what are some of the other issues you will be addressing?"

"My next stop today is in Smithborough, where I will be meeting with the Homes for the Brave organization. They have some ideas how to refurbish old hotels and condominium complexes into homes, support centers, and social organizations for veterans. Tomorrow, I will be in Capital City talking to the State Public Library Association. They have some ideas to bring together public schools, adult education, and manufacturing companies to train a workforce for the jobs that will be available in our communities. My press caravan is full, but I encourage other members of the press to follow us to these places and listen to these ideas with me.

"Unfortunately, that is all the time I have for questions from the press. I want to come out and meet some of the people that came out today, and then we have to move on to our next stop. Thank you all for coming out today."

Theodore makes his way into the crowd. He shakes hands and makes small talk with some of the people. He does a brief stand-in interview with Grace Downwood and returns to the crowd. The girls who showed their breasts approach Theodore and talk to him. They ask him to sign their breasts, and he graciously does. He then waves to the crowd and walks back to the van with Delores and Sweet Barn.

"Nancy will be with us in a few minutes. She is talking to some of the reporters about some of her community-rejuvenation projects," Delores says.

"That's good. People are interested in what we are saying. I think this went really well," Theodore says.

"It went well, but I think you are going to be the only governor that has girls that show you their boobies," Sweet Barn says and giggles.

"That's one of the perks of running for public office. I'm not complaining."

"Me either. I like seeing boobies."

"I know both of you are thinking with the tiny brains in your penis and those girls voluntarily showed you their breasts, but did you have to wink at them and give them the thumbs-up? And why did you sign their cleavage? There was a news camera filming you autographing their breasts. You know that will make the evening news. What did you write on them, anyway?"

"I wrote, 'Your breasts are nice, but your brains will get you further,' and signed my name."

"At least it's a positive message. We might not win this election, but the Tits for Teddy foundation will be increasing their membership," Delores jokes.

"If you want to join, you can. All you got to do is dump your junk. I will gladly sign your breasts."

"I can't believe people might actually vote for you to be their governor."

"I am the breast man for the job," Theodore says, and Sweet Barn laughs.

"Very clever, Theodore," Delores says.

CHAPTER 33

The Theodore Graham for Governor campaign staff sits at the meeting room table, reviewing the progress of the campaign. They are looking at headlines, public commentary, and polling data. Theodore walks into the meeting.

"Good Monday morning, my minions. How are we doing?"

"You're nearly an hour late," Delores says.

"I have two jobs. We have a staff meeting every Monday at the *Weekly Beat*, and I was helping some of my young writers. It's my job. It's the job I will be returning to when I lose this election."

"I think you should take this campaign a little more seriously."

"I'm guaranteed to lose. I believe I am giving it more seriousness than it deserves."

"You have to at least hit Gene Douglas on his platform this week."

"I didn't want to make this a nasty campaign from the beginning. I'm not going to start now. The voters will decide which platform they like better and vote accordingly."

"You give the voters too much credit. Contrary to what your fifth-grade teacher told you when you ran for student council, politics is a popularity contest. Tim, how are we trending?"

"Surprisingly, there wasn't a lot of fluctuation over the weekend. The Gatesville festival was good for politics but really didn't do anything for either campaign. If anything, it prevented you from improving our numbers. Here's what some of the public comment from the web are," Tim Collins says and puts a page on the big screen at the front of the room.

It was refreshing to see politicians and their staff interacting in a friendly manner. The Gatesville festival put the nastiness aside and raised money for worthy charities.

Teddy Graham is one heck of a guitarist, but he's not the right choice to be governor.

The friendliness at the Gatesville festival between the two candidates is just a big act. This is just another clever rouse from the two-party system to sell the people a load of shit.

I don't think it's appropriate that a man seeking the governorship of our state should sign the cleavage of young girls with loose morals.

Gene Douglas has the personality of a roof shingle. Teddy Graham has a fun personality, and I think people will be more inclined to work with him.

The Teddy Graham campaign is bush league. A few shitty stores opening in a shitty strip mall isn't going to fix the economy of our state, but I guess he has to appeal to the do-gooder vagina vote.

Gene Douglas has the connections and the business savvy to bring big industry back to our state. The pizza shops and tree-hugger essential oils and all natural honey stores that Teddy Graham is promoting may be nice, but they will make no difference in the grand scheme of things.

Gene Douglas has proven to associate with scam artists. So that makes Teddy Graham a scam artist and Gene Douglas a foolish man. I'll probably whack off to department store bra ads on Election Day instead of voting.

Teddy Graham has a way with the ladies. He has beautiful women on his staff, and girls show him their breasts at his events. I would rather be hitting all that instead of wasting my time with government stuff.

Theodore Graham is the first candidate in a long time that is actually talking about doing something different to get this state moving again. He got my vote. Embrace the change, folks.

Sherman Jones is a better candidate than both of these losers, and he's dead.

It's sad that the Democrats can't find a decent Democrat to run. They chose a circus act candidate that will probably win. If the people vote Teddy Graham, it makes him their clown.

The choice is going to be a tough one. Gene Douglas and Theodore Graham both put their friendship above their political beliefs. They are both good men. It's going to come down to their positions on the issues.

Finally, there is a candidate listening to the ideas of the people and promoting those ideas to get this state going again.

I wouldn't kick Teddy Graham out of my bed for eating crackers because I slept with a lot of crumbs. Meoooooow!

"So that's what people are saying on the web. It's a pretty even mix, and it shows that Teddy can get laid just about anywhere in the state."

"Nice. We should start a Fuck the Vote campaign."

"It's Monday, Teddy. Time to use your head brain and give your penis brain a break until next weekend," Delores says.

"You said you wanted me to take this more seriously. I floated the idea of fucking my way to the governor's mansion, and you shut it down."

"Moving on. Pam, what's the press putting out there?"

Pam puts a list of the headlines on the big screen. "It is a pretty even mix, just like the public opinion. We have some positive and negative headlines. Take a look for yourself."

NEW IDEAS, TOO LITTLE, TOO LATE FOR DEMOCRATS, the *Morning Sun Gazette*

GRAHAM LISTENING TO IDEAS, DOUGLAS DOING THE USUAL, the *Gatesville Courier*

GRAHAM COMES OUT WITH PRICEY LIBERAL AGENDA, the *Capital Register*

GRAHAM PROMOTES SUCCESSFUL PROGRAMS IN PLATFORM, the *Harmon Herald*

THE GATESVILLE FESTIVAL AND FRIENDLY OPPONENTS, the *Weekly Beat*

WOMEN, MINORITIES, AND MR. GRAHAM: SOCIALIST HEAVEN, the *Capital Beat*

SNORE! WHERE'S THE MUDSLINGING THAT PEOPLE WANT? the *Hatsboro Republican*

"Those are the highlight headlines from our official announcement Wednesday up until the Sunday morning news cycle. Most of this morning's headlines are about how great it is that both candidates and their staff spent time together at the Gatesville festival. You should have just played with Ernie Douglas's band on Friday night, taken advantage of the photo ops, and gotten back out on trail Saturday and Sunday. This was basically a wasted weekend."

"I hung out with my friends and played music. I don't consider that a waste."

"Gene Douglas went to campaign events on Sunday while you decided to play guitar hero for an extra day. You could have made some appearances at some of the events you sent your staff to. You ended up looking like an uninterested candidate."

"I am the uninterested candidate. You had the chance to run Nathan. He was at least interested in the job," Theodore says.

"I'm going to run in four years. I wouldn't have the numbers you have this year. On brighter note, though, fund-raising has been going well. There have been a lot of contributions coming in through the website and in the mail. There are a bunch from community revitalization groups that believe in your economic platform. Nancy Bradford, she's going to be on the road all week talking to community leaders about starting their own projects. Your platform seems to resonate with voters, and it's bringing in contributions," Nathan Winters says.

"See, Delores and Pam, I'm doing well."

"Not well enough. We need to do better," Delores says.

"This week, we will be campaigning with most of our Senate and House of Representative candidates in their areas. We are going to incorporate my economic platform with the communities they serve. It's going to be a strong week for us," Theodore says.

"It's not going to be strong if you don't appear strong. You have to at least start hitting the Gene Douglas platform. He hit yours yesterday."

"I didn't see it. What did he say?"

"Of course you didn't see it. You were busy entertaining at his charity event and making him look good. He was smart enough to get back to work and get ahead while you were having a good time."

"I'm sure the people see I was committed to raising money for worthy charities by sticking around at the festival."

"The drunk stoners that hung out for the day might appreciate you hanging out, but the media was bored out of their mind with the friendly opponent's story. It was a stale story by Saturday night. Russ Dewitt saw that and got Gene some Sunday coverage. He has the news cycle until at least lunchtime today," Pam says.

"What did Gene say that's going to hurt us?"

"Tim, get Gene's speech from last night on the screen."

Tim clicks a few keys on his computer and gets Gene's speech and press conference on the big screen. The staff focuses their attention on the video clip.

"See for yourself," Pam says.

"Good evening, everybody. It's my great honor to announce that the Gatesville festival this weekend raised over half a million dollars that will go to veterans hospitals, emergency responders, police officers, and

the picturesque Gatesville Fairgrounds. I want to thank everybody that came out for such great causes. I believe my opponent is still there sitting in with some of the bands, playing today. I thank him too. He really is a gifted guitarist."

The crowd applauds. Gene waits for the crowd to quiet itself.

"I'm here to talk to you about my economic plan. My economic plan doesn't have all the bells and whistles that my opponent's does. Mine doesn't depend on unlikely factors that probably won't happen. His plan is like traveling from Florida to Texas by going through Maine. There's a lot of unnecessary steps. My plan follows what historically worked for economic recovery. I'm going to go with a plan that has been proven to work."

Gene waits for the applause to wind down.

"Taxes in this state are too high. Governor Harmon spent the last eight years in office letting taxes go up, letting jobs go out of state or overseas, and battling an assembly that wanted nothing more than to compromise so we could get the state economy going strong. The Democrats wasted their time. They wasted our time."

Gene waits again for the applause to quiet.

"My plan is simple. Lower the taxes and give business incentives to come to our state. There is plenty of room for growth. My plan will bring manufacturing jobs back. Once I am in office, I will make sure there are shovel-ready sites for companies to build lasting employment opportunities for our citizens. When the taxes are low and the red tape is eliminated, companies will come and good-paying jobs will be available. I've run businesses over the years. I've run my own profitable businesses. I sat on boards of successful corporations. I've advised CEOs on opportunities that would benefit them. I've chaired multimillion-dollar business projects that produced billions in profit. I know a thing or two about fiscal responsibility, and I will bring that experience with me to the governor's mansion. I'm sorry I didn't talk about a complicated economic plan that might work in thirty or forty years. I've always found better success by keeping it simple."

"That wasn't a bad speech. He outlined his plan and played the crowd," Theodore says.

"Don't praise him. He just tore your economic platform to shreds and made us look like a bunch of fools," Delores says.

"How did he hold up with questions from the press?"

"He didn't take questions. He let Channel 3 News and Barry Barnhardt cover the event. They broadcast his speech, showed clips of him talking with people and shaking hands. He didn't let the press question him. Now the press will start questioning our plan instead of his."

"Crap! That's a pretty good tactic."

"Yeah, no shit. I know you don't want to make this election personal, but you have to attack his platform, or our guys won't win their assembly races. This was the original plan. You are getting them elected. Remember? This was the agreement. Do your job!" Delores says.

"That's why I wanted you to be my campaign manager. You're not afraid to tell it like it is. Give me a little bit of time. I will think of something. If you'll excuse me, I'm going to work on some of my speeches for this week. I will meet you at the caravan for this evening's events," Theodore says and leaves the meeting room.

"Wow, Delores, how did you do that?" Tim Collins asks.

"Do what?" Delores says.

"Put Teddy Graham in his place and let him leave the room knowing he was wrong."

"I'm not sure. This is the first time I have been successful doing so. Now that you pointed it out, I'm kind of scared to see what comes next."

CHAPTER 34

Theodore is sitting on a sofa and going over some notes. He busies himself while waiting to make a speech for his campaign event. Delores is answering e-mails and working on the schedule for the next week's events. They sit in silence as they work. A stagehand knocks on the door and enters the room.

"You'll be going on in about twenty minutes, Mr. Graham. I will send somebody in to get you five minutes before you go on."

"Thanks for the heads-up. I'll be ready."

"Are you going to hit Gene's economic plan in this speech?" Delores asks.

"Not yet. He's going to get hit soon enough."

"You told me you are going hit him on his platform when you left yesterday's meeting. You didn't do it in any of your speeches last night, and now you're telling me you aren't going to do it? When are you going to do it? We got to get enthusiasm to the base."

"I'm going to make a better presentation for our platform than he will for his. I will beat him there. I'm not going to have to go on the attack."

"Our ground team is out there getting pounced on by the press with questions on our platform. Their hands are tied because you won't attack. They need you to attack so they can move our narrative forward."

"It's all going to work out. You've got to trust me."

"I don't trust you, and I think you are wasting a big opportunity if you don't attack his platform tonight. The Seniors for Society organization is made up of elderly people that you can depend on to get to the polls. You want to get some of them to vote for you so we can get our guys in the assembly."

"The Seniors for Society typically vote Republican. You can almost count on them to go into a voting booth and voting straight party. I picked this event to talk about welfare reform. Welfare reform is an issue that resonates with this group. I will win some of their votes with the contents of my speech. These people are so loyal to the Republican Party that they would vote for a Republican monkey that throws poop before they would vote for Jesus if he was a Democrat."

"This is the perfect place to hit the Douglas platform. Hit him in front of his own people. You are wasting an opportunity. Why won't you listen to me?"

"I did listen to you. I did something about it as I promised."

"You wanted me to manage your campaign. I had strong doubts, but I thought, if we were working toward the same goal for once, we could be successful. Attaching my name to yours was a big mistake. Managing a loser that is afraid to attack his friend isn't going to look good on my résumé."

"That's what you think of me? You think I'm a loser?"

A stagehand enters the room. "You're going on in five minutes, Mr. Graham."

"Okay, thanks," Theodore says. "Come on, Ms. Daniels. You have to come out with me and at least look like you support your loser."

"Teddy, I didn't mean it like that."

"I have a speech to do. We can talk about our future moving forward when I am done."

The host of the event announces Theodore, and he makes his way onstage. Delores claps for him as he makes his way, but she is visibly upset about their conversation. The crowd gathered in the ballroom gives tepid but respectful applause.

"I know the majority of you are Republicans and I don't have a lot of supporters in this room, but I thank you all for being gracious enough to accept my offer to speak to your group. Many members of my staff urged me not to speak here. I was told that most of you loyally vote Republican so I would be wasting my time talking to people that most likely won't change their minds. Obviously, I disagreed. Here I am. I disagreed because Seniors for Society is the most active group of voters in our state. Talking to voters is never a waste of time and only talking to voters who support me doesn't make much sense. I want to be the governor for all the people in our state, not just the ones who like me. Since you are the most active voters, I believe you are the most informed voters at the polls each Election Day. When you accepted my offer to speak at your annual banquet, I told my staff, Seniors for Society members actually listen to the candidates so they can go into the voting booth with knowledge guiding their votes. I can't thank you enough for giving me this opportunity and taking the time to listen to what I have to say."

The crowd applauds his introduction.

"I picked this event to launch the next part of my platform. I read the Seniors for Society website and newsletters. I read the editorials your members send into the local newspapers. I've listened to the radio talk shows your members call into to voice their opinions. One of the most frequent issues this group talks about is welfare reform or entitlement reform, for as much as it is talked about, nothing ever gets done about it. Why isn't anybody listening to what you have to say? Why is the problem getting worse and not better?"

Theodore pauses for slightly more enthusiastic applause.

"I have a plan for welfare reform. I'm sure most of you are like me and are tired of seeing people being handed money for nothing. You all worked hard to earn what you have, and when you see people getting handouts for doing nothing, it makes you ask, What's the point of working hard if you can get money for nothing? The welfare system as it is now only makes each generation lazier and lazier. There is no excuse for it. America was built with hard work. Hardworking Americans worked too hard making it the great nation it is. I don't want it to be destroyed by people constantly looking for a handout."

Theodore pauses for more applause.

"Welfare is money for nothing, and the taxpayers are handing it out. This has got to stop. Welfare works if it gives a hand up to people that truly need one, but it fails when we give it as a handout to people who make welfare their lifestyle. Look around your communities. Look at your civic organizations. Look at your parks. Look at your town halls. Look at your community centers. There is lots of work to be done at all these places. Our justice system sentences people to do community service to pay their debt to society when they are found guilty of a crime. Why can't we have welfare recipients doing some of this community service to repay their debt to the taxpayers of this state?"

Theodore waits for applause to quiet itself.

"The welfare system has been in dire need of reform for years. Politicians promised to fix the system but never did. There hasn't been a welfare reform bill introduced in our state legislature for over thirty years. How can that be? All these promises without action. I call those politicians bullshit artists, and it's time to put an end to this bullshit."

There is louder and longer reaction from the group.

"I actually have a welfare reform plan. I'm introducing it to Seniors for Society first because I want to let you know that I have been reading and listening to what your organization has been saying for years and I agree with you. My plan isn't going to fix it overnight, and I am not a snake-oil salesman that will offer an empty promise just to get your vote. Welfare reform is going to take some work. We're going to have to talk to community and county leaders and see what community service can be done. We are going to have to get the state legislature to pass bills that will administer and oversee the system. We are going to have to reform food stamps so working people that are clipping coupons to try to make ends meet aren't in the checkout line behind freeloaders that are buying surf and turf with money they didn't earn."

Theodore waits for a long round of applause to calm.

"My plan will be posted on my website later this evening, and I will be taking questions about it at a press conference tomorrow. I urge you to take a look at my website. Watch my press conference. Call my campaign headquarters with questions and follow my campaign. My platform was created by the concerns of the people, not by my quest for power. I'm not a candidate that's going to hide from your scrutiny. My goal isn't to win an election and become governor, my goal is to win the election so as governor, I can work hard to solve problems that face our state. If I am elected governor and am working hard to make this state better, I'll be damned if I will let freeloaders let my hard work be in vain."

The crowd rises to their feet to applaud.

"Thank you for having me here tonight. I'm going to come out and hopefully meet a few of you before I have to go. Seniors for Society, you are great people, and it was a pleasure being here. Thanks for listening, and never stop letting your voices be heard," Theodore says and exits the stage.

Delores is at the side of the stage, clapping, as Theodore makes his way to the wing. "That was a great speech. I didn't expect this event to go this well."

"Not bad for a loser. I'm going to go meet some people from the crowd, and I will meet you in the van in fifteen minutes. We can continue our conversation from earlier then."

Theodore makes his way to the front of the stage and talks to some of the crowd during the intermission. He shakes hands and gets some pats on the back from people who enjoyed his speech. After his brief meet-and-greet session, he leaves the venue to where Sweet Barn and Delores are waiting for him in the campaign's conversion van.

"Teddy, about earlier—" Delores starts, but Theodore interrupts.

"It's my fault. I failed to take into consideration that you attached your professional name to me when you signed on. It was ignorant of me to assume that after the election, you will go back to your superintendent job and live happily ever after. I never considered that you might have other career aspirations and life goals. If being my campaign manager may hurt your future, I won't hold you back. You can resign if you want."

"I just want you to hit Gene's platform like he's hitting ours. I see what you're doing with the transparency angle, but we can't take all the media scrutiny when he isn't getting any. You have to call him out on his plans so the people can see there is no depth to them and he is all just well-crafted lip service."

"You told me I was wasting too much time at the Gatesville festival. You told me to do campaign appearances on Sunday, but

I didn't listen. I stayed at the festival and played guitar and raised money for Gene's charities. Russ Dewitt was smart to make Gene do a campaign event on Sunday. He was even smarter by not allowing questions from the press about his platform but raising questions and suspicion about ours in the speech. He played us. He played me. What bothered me the most is that he made your team look foolish because I didn't listen to you. Delores, I wanted you on my campaign because of your brilliance and focus. I lost sight of that, and I let us all down, especially you. I owe you an apology. I'm sorry. If you choose to stay on, I promise I will listen to you."

"I'm not resigning. It would make things worse. Sunday was a setback, but I'm sure if we put our heads together, we can overcome it. Your speech tonight is certainly going to help. There was TV coverage of the event, and you got a standing ovation from a typically Republican crowd."

"I said yesterday that I would think of something to hit back at Gene's tactic. Remember that reporter that was leaving my office the day you came by to get me to run for governor?"

"The one that was dressed like a nightclub slut? The one with a pole dancer's name?"

"Yes, Sasha."

"I knew it was some harlot name."

"Well, I gave her the chance to write a feature editorial on the Douglas campaign event on Sunday night. It's in today's *Weekly Beat*. Maybe her editorial will help us hit Gene's campaign like you asked."

"I don't know how an editorial from a slutty reporter that offered herself to you in order to advance her career will help, but I will take a look. You didn't sleep with her, did you? The last thing we need is a sexual harassment claim hanging over our campaign."

"I didn't sleep with her, but the temptation was there. I gave her a chance to use her writing talent to get ahead instead of her sexual prowess. Read her article and tell me if I would have been better off sleeping with her."

Delores pulls out her iPad and finds the *Weekly Beat* online edition and scrolls to the editorial page and finds the article.

My Chance to Shine Stolen by Gene Douglas
by Sasha Monet

All my life, I dreamed of being a journalist. I wanted to report the world to the people. From middle school and all through high school, I was actively involved with the school newspaper. A few summers, I attended a young journalist camp. In college, I studied hard and worked my way up to being a feature writer for the daily collegiate newspaper. Upon graduation, I was ready to take on the world and be the best journalist this world did see. I was ready to report the world to the people.

To my ignorance, journalism, in reality, wasn't what I thought it was. All through middle school, high school, college, and my times at journalism camp, I was handed assignments and told where to go and what to write about. I assumed that was the way it was. My writing résumé landed me an entry-level reporting job at the Weekly Beat. *Landing the job was easy. Keeping it was where I struggled. I was never taught how to find stories. I expected my boss to tell me what to write and I would write it well. Things don't work that way at the* Weekly Beat. *My boss is Theodore Graham.*

Theodore Graham is a feature writer, an editorial writer, and the managing editor of the paper. He also has taken charge of the young writing staff. He encourages all the young writers to go out in the world, ask questions that will uncover stories, and follow those stories to their conclusion. I didn't possess that skill. I struggled because of it. A normal boss would have just fired me, but Theodore Graham, as most people know, isn't normal. He's noted for doing things differently. Instead of ridding himself of my lack of skill, he took time away from his work and went out in the field with me. It took some time, but I started finding stories. I even landed a few articles in the paper because of his help. I was no longer regretting my choice to be a journalist. I was becoming confident in my choice. I felt Theodore Graham, my boss, was finally getting confident in me, because he lent me the press credentials to cover the Gene Douglas for Governor event Sunday evening.

I wanted to do well with this story. I wanted to write a great article about our gubernatorial election. I wanted to ask pointed and tough questions so I could deliver the facts to the people who are trying hard to be informed voters. When I arrived at the event, I was told by Gene Douglas's campaign manager, Russ Dewitt, that the press was allowed to listen to the candidate's speech but would not be allowed to ask follow-up questions. I was heartbroken. This was my time to shine, and that opportunity was taken away by a campaign that has chosen to shirk transparency. The press release only highlighted the positives of Gene Douglas's speech and allowed no flexibility for follow-up. I left the event with unanswered questions swirling in my mind. Freedom of the press was foiled by closed-agenda politics. I hope other journalists feel as cheated as I do. I had a job to do. I had questions. But I was forced to leave without answers.

In Gene Douglas's speech, he mentioned bells and whistles of his opponent's economic plan that won't work. I wanted him to explain to me what those bells and whistles were and why they wouldn't work. He said his plan follows what historically works for economic recovery. I wanted to know what history he could cite that supports and offers evidence of his statement. He said his plan is simple, lower taxes and give businesses incentive to come to our state. What incentives is he giving? How much will his incentives cost taxpayers? Isn't his plan trickle-down economics that hasn't worked for thirty years? He said his plan will bring manufacturing jobs back to the state. What companies did he talk to about his plan? What do companies want to make here? How many jobs will his plan create? He talked about eliminating red tape in our bureaucracy so business wouldn't be deterred by burdensome regulations. What red tape? Is he going to cut redundancy? Is he going to gut safety regulations? Is he going to cut environmental protections and natural resource restrictions?

At the end of his speech, Gene Douglas touted his business record and résumé. He says he has run successful businesses over the years. Which ones? Is the publishing company that filed for bankruptcy four years ago considered successful? He said he advised CEOs about opportunities. What CEOs did he advise? What advice did he give? Did they follow that advice, and was it successful? All these questions went unanswered because he refused to take questions from the press.

A lot of controversy surrounded the Douglas campaign in its early stages, his involvement with Mort Whitney, his campaign manager Dick Ratzinger paying an arsonist to burn down a newspaper, and the head of his super PAC breaking campaign finance laws. I thought a campaign with that kind of controversy in its past would be up front and transparent for the media and the voters. I guess I was wrong. I guess I shouldn't sweat it. More experienced journalists aren't calling out the Gene Douglas campaign for its lack of transparency. They aren't questioning his lack of details. They didn't even question why they aren't permitted to ask ques-

tions. I just learned to ask questions and wanted to show my boss what I've learned. But I didn't get the chance to shine. All I wanted to do was find out if Gene Douglas's platform is a real deal for voters or if it's a paper-thin platform just for show.

Delores puts her iPad down on the table. "Why didn't you tell me about this article?"

"You were busy being mad and calling me a loser."

"That slutty reporter of yours lit a media wildfire for Gene's campaign. He's going to be bombarded tomorrow. She used your trick of calling out other journalists for their poor journalism too. Did you write this article for her?"

"No, I didn't write it for her. I just told her to write about what she learned from the event. She's a quick learner and not a bad writer either."

"Score one for the pole dancer. Russ Dewitt is going to snap when the press attacks the campaign for his press-avoidance strategy. You fixed your mistake. Teddy, I'm sorry I doubted you."

"I forgive you. Please don't resign. Can I get a hug?"

"I'm not resigning, but we're not hugging. I don't want you to think that I am starting to like you."

"I guess a blow job is out of the question?"

"Most certainly is."

CHAPTER 35

Theodore walks through the security gate and up the driveway of the Douglas mansion. He makes his way to the front door and repeatedly rings the doorbell until Issac opens the front door.

"Good Sunday morning to you, Issac."

"Theodore 'Furshizzle' Graham, the man that is both praised and cursed in this house. Why, I myself was just cursing you."

"Aw, man. Why were you cursing me?"

"I'm not deaf, and I don't have Alzheimer's. You only have to ring the doorbell once."

"I'm sorry. I have Parkinson's in my one finger, and that was the one I chose to ring the doorbell with," Theodore says and holds up his index finger and shakes it.

"I'm sorry to learn of your terrible self-invented affliction, Mr. Graham. I don't know how you cope."

"It's not easy, but the ladies seem to enjoy it."

"I imagine you are quite the finger-banger, sir. You've managed to take the lemons the lord handed you and make lemonade with them. Props to you. I kindly ask that on your next visit, you choose a nonshaky finger to summon me with the doorbell."

"I'm sorry, Issac. I'll try to remember on my next visit. I have a few gifts for you to make up for my poor doorbell-ringing finger choice," Theodore says and places three joints in Issac's shirt pocket.

"I thank you, Mr. Graham. It is Sunday. I am done early today. Perhaps the wife and I can enjoy one of these treats and watch *America's Funniest Videos*. Piñata stick accidents and groin shots are so much more entertaining while enjoying the intoxication of your fine herb."

"*AFV* is a lot funnier on weed. I should come over and watch it with you and the wife."

"I don't want your Parkinson's finger in the same room as my wife."

"Probably a wise choice. Is the man of the house around?"

"Yes, the man of the house is on the patio with the lady of the house. They are waiting for your arrival. I must warn you, the lady of the house is on her fourth mimosa."

"Good to know. I will try not to cause one of Sandy's famous drunken meltdowns."

"You can try, but history shows that you usually fail. Need I escort you to the patio and announce you, or can you manage on your own?"

"I can find my way. Thank you, my friend."

"You are most welcome, Mr. Graham. I do always enjoy our verbal exchanges."

Theodore strolls through the long hallway to the rear of the house. Gene is busy reading newspapers in the patio lounge. Sandy is stretched out on a deck chair, getting some sun. She is on her stomach, with her face resting on a towel, her eyes closed. The string on her bikini top is untied and dangling over the sides of the chair. Theodore closes the patio door gently and sneaks along the pool and dips his hand in. He drips the cold water on Sandy's back, and she jumps up, topless.

"Teddy, you son of a bitch!"

"It's only slightly past ten in the morning, and I already saw your breasts. Today is going to be a good day."

"Don't you see enough breasts at your campaign events?" Gene asks.

"I do all right at my events, but not all of them are as nice as your wife's. I spoke at a senior citizens' center the other night. A few ladies showed me their breasts. I just wanted to iron them."

"Some guys have all the luck. I don't get breasts shown to me at my events."

"That's because your events are usually one big sausage party. You got to get some more women involved in your campaign."

"Sure, I can pander to the women and minority vote like you do."

"That's not all what it's cracked up to be. One of those senior citizens that showed me her breasts at my event the other night was a black lady. Since I saw her breasts, the California Raisins singing 'I Heard It through the Grapevine' is stuck in my head."

Gene walks over to Theodore and shakes his hand and gives him a hug. "It's good to see you, my friend."

"I'm glad to be here. I can't believe we are going to watch people talk about us on television together. Do you think we should be high for this?"

Sandy ties her bikini top and walks over to Teddy. She gives him a hug and a peck on the cheek. "We definitely should be high for this. Maybe a little drunk too."

"Didn't you have four mimosas already this morning? I don't think you need to be high as well."

"I didn't ask what you thought, dear. Let's get baked."

Theodore removes a joint from his pocket and hands it to Sandy with a lighter. "Knock yourself out, young lady. It's Sunday fun day."

"Thank you, sweetie," Sandy says, lights the joint, and takes a drag. She passes it back to Theodore.

Theodore takes a drag off the joint. "Here you go, buddy, join the party."

"I can't be doing that shit. I have a campaign event to go to later."

"So do I, but I'm going high."

"You're good at being high. Me, I can never figure out if I said the things I was supposed to say or if I said the things I was actually thinking. I'm gonna play it safe."

"Suit yourself. The show's just about to come on. Would it be possible to enjoy a beer with the show?"

"You know where they are, help yourself. You and my wife, I don't know how you two do it, fucked up before noon on a regular basis."

"That's what makes us fun and interesting people. You got to loosen up, honey."

"She's right, Gene, we are fun and interesting. Sandy is interesting because she prowls on the edge of drunken sluttiness."

"You've seen them once today. You better start throwing money if you want to see them again," Gene says.

"If you throw enough money, I will give you a private dance," Sandy says.

"Annnnnnnnd the four mimosas found their voice. Here we go," Gene says.

"Let's negotiate that lap dance later. Our people are going to be on television, talking about us. Let's watch the show."

The three of them make their way to the television in the patio lounge. Gene sits down, and Sandy sits next to him. Theodore reaches around Gene to pass Sandy the joint. Sandy takes the joint from Theodore and reaches around Gene to pass it back.

"Just switch seats if you two are going to pass that back and forth the whole time."

"Somebody fell out of the grumpy tree this morning," Theodore says as Sandy switches seats and sits next to him. Gene turns on the television, and the three of them turn their focus to the screen.

"Good Sunday morning to you and welcome to a special edition of State of the State This Week. I'm your host, Walter Carl, and this is the 'Candidate's People' edition of our show. Every four years, we do this special edition of our show. Staff members and associates of each of the gubernatorial candidates make up our panel and we discuss the candidates and the issues. Joining me today are the campaign managers for both candidates, Delores Daniels of the Theodore Graham campaign and Russ Dewitt of the Gene Douglas Campaign. Also joining us are Orlando French, the mayor of Carter; Marty Price, policy strategist for Gene Douglas; Pamela Eynon, Democratic Party trustee and adviser for the Graham campaign; and Jim Peterson, trustee and board chairman of the Douglas Youth Honors College. We should have lots to talk about. Stay tuned.

"Welcome guests. I guess I should start with Pamela Eynon. You serve as a trustee for the Democratic Party of our state, and now you are an adviser for the Graham campaign. Doesn't it bother you that the Democratic candidate isn't even a Democrat?"

"Of course it bothers me, but I can hope that Theodore has a change of heart when he is in the governor's mansion."

"How can your party feel confident with an independent that may not always reflect the values of the party?"

"Theodore Graham has vision and wants to get the state moving in a forward direction again, just like the Democrats do. A lot of his values reflect our party's values. He listens to people with ideas and figures out how to apply ideas to find solutions to the problems facing our state."

"Russ Dewitt, you are Gene Douglas's campaign manager. What do you think of Theodore Graham's candidacy and the platform he is pushing forward?"

"Mr. Graham isn't a native of our state. He has only limited knowledge of our issues, and he has no previous political experience to help him navigate the legislative process. I think Mr. Graham means well, but he's not a good fit for our people and his policies will be costly and ineffective for the taxpayers."

"Delores Daniels, you are Mr. Graham's campaign manager, how do you respond to Russ?"

"Mr. Graham has been a resident of this state for nearly five years. He's worked here. He's paid taxes here. He's voted here. He's taken the time to get to know the people here. People seem to like him. Mr. Graham's platform was created by the concerns of the people, and he is proposing to actually take action to fix the problems facing the working class. People have heard the 'lower taxes will attract businesses that create jobs' campaigns for decades. The taxes have never been lowered, unemployment rates continue to rise, and businesses are leaving the state. Theodore Graham is doing something different. Doing things differently is kind of like the definition of change."

"Orlando French, you are the mayor of Carter and you have lent your support and gave your endorsement to Theodore Graham. Why?"

"I support Mr. Graham because he has supported me and the people of Carter. Our town has been struggling economically for years. We have housing issues. We have jobs issues. We have blight. Our police and emergency services budgets are stretched thin. Before the governor's campaign even started, Mr. Graham came into our town, got to know our people, helped our city council navigate some of the legal challenges of our dwin-

dling budget resources, and he did it all because he cares and wants to see people do well. If he is our governor, I see my town starting to move forward. I believe in my heart that he is legitimate and sincere."

"At the beginning of the campaign, you were a supporter of Gene Douglas. Now you support Mr. Graham. What changed that loyalty?" Russ Dewitt asks.

"I was supporting the Gene Douglas campaign when Theodore Graham had your job and was your boss. Two campaign managers later and the switch to a trickle-down economics platform that hasn't helped my town, that's what changed my mind."

"Delores Daniels, you are the superintendent at the Douglas Youth College, an employee of Gene Douglas, and Theodore Graham's former boss. How did you end up being the campaign manager for your former subordinate and the opponent of your current boss?" Walter Carl asks.

"To be clear, personally, I'm not a fan of Mr. Graham. Professionally, Mr. Graham is one of the most brilliant minds that I've had the privilege of working with. When people want to change the way things are, he listens. When people have ideas to make change happen, he finds ways to apply those ideas. His economic platform isn't his own creation. He saw organizations like Professional Women of Power who were committed to restoring prosperity to neighborhoods and incorporated them into his platform. He's not in this race to take credit for the work of others. He's in it to see progress. I am his campaign manager because I believe in him. I don't have to like him to believe in him, do I?"

"I guess liking him isn't a requirement, but do you think you will ever like him?"

"He makes it difficult to not like him. The more we campaign and the more we are out talking to people, the more I'm surprised by the people that come forward and thank him for helping them. From his young reporters at the Weekly Beat to the people of Carter to the young lawyer he helped get into a major law firm, there are always nice things he does. I almost started liking him when he made Sophia White, the mother of his security team, our official campaign mother. That was touching, and I saw how sweet Theodore Graham could be. I was just about to start liking him, and then he told me not to. I was asked to do this job *because I don't like him. He said he needs my dislike for him to keep him grounded."*

"Gene Douglas was working with Professional Women of Power at the beginning of the campaign. Aren't you just trying to steal our ideas to get votes for your candidate?" Russ Dewitt asks.

"Gene Douglas was working with Professional Women of Power when Theodore Graham was his campaign manager. When Mort Whitney and Dick Ratzinger, the campaign manager before you, got involved, Professional Women of Power didn't hear from the Douglas campaign. When you became the third campaign manager, how come you didn't reach out to the organization to learn more about their prosperity projects for communities?"

"Jim Peterson, you've been a longtime friend of Gene Douglas. Your children all attended the Douglas Youth Honors College. Your wife is an educator there and has published a few economics textbooks through the Douglas publishing house. What do you have to say about this campaign?" Walter Carl asks.

"My ex-wife, Claire, is an educator and publisher through the Douglas business ventures."

"I didn't realize you were divorced, I'm sorry."

"It's okay, Walter. It was a mutually-agreed-on divorce. I fully support Gene Douglas. He will do great things for this state. He will bring jobs. He will lower taxes. He will restore the infrastructure of our communities. Theodore Graham is just a loser with no respect for authority. The only reason he is running for office is that he has the chance to get back at Gene Douglas for firing him. Theodore Graham will destroy this state with his crazy plans."

"I take it you've had some experience with Mr. Graham when you sat on the board at the Douglas school?"

"The Douglas Youth Honors College got lucky when Theodore Graham left. He was destroying the academic curriculum. He was a bad influence on the students at our school. I spent many hours on the phone talking with parents who were unhappy with Mr. Graham's loose morals and questionable teaching methods. Delores, I don't know how you can sit here on this show and praise a psychopath that nearly destroyed your career as an educator."

"You think Mr. Graham is a loser. Did you decide that before he took the Douglas debate team to the semifinals in his first two years at the school, or did you decide that when he took the team to the national debate finals and won? Your son was a secondary alternate on that team, wasn't he? Did you think he was a bad influence on the students when the GPA of the student body increased every year he was a working there? I am having a hard time figuring out why you are calling Theodore Graham a loser."

"I don't like him for the same reason that you don't like him, Delores. I question your loyalty to Gene Douglas, the guy who gave you a break and made you the superintendent of a nationally recognized school."

"I am thankful that Gene Douglas hired me, but I believe he hired me based on my résumé. I do my job at the school and do it well. You know that, and there is no need for you to question my loyalty. I don't think we dislike Theodore Graham for the same reasons. I don't like him because he challenges the system, succeeds, and points out how ridiculous the system is. You dislike him because he had an affair with your ex-wife. Maybe we are both jealous of him, but for different reasons."

"That's not appropriate, Ms. Daniels. My personal life has nothing to do with this gubernatorial campaign."

"It sounds like it has everything to do with your dislike for Theodore Graham," Pam Eynon chimes in.

"I don't like him because of what he did to the Douglas Youth Honors College."

"I never worked with you or Delores at the honors college, but the way I understand it, Theodore Graham was hired by Gene Douglas as an educator and debate coach. As an educator, he improved the school's GPA. As a debate coach, he took the team to the finals and won. Enrollment at the school is at capacity for the coming school year, and there is massive construction project underway to accommodate more students in the years to come. What did he do that was harmful to the school? Did he not respect your figurehead position of authority on the board?"

"I just don't like the guy, and he will be a disaster for our state. I don't understand how he brainwashes you women."

"How he brainwashes us women? I think your jealousy of Mr. Graham is eating away at your better senses. Your ex-wife, Claire, is one of the most brilliant women I know. She didn't have an affair because she was brainwashed. She had an affair with Teddy Graham because he respects her brilliance, her work, and listens to her ideas. It's not brainwashing that Mr. Graham does. It's consideration for other people he offers to people he respects. It doesn't hurt that he is handsome either, but maybe if you showed Claire even a smidgen of consideration for her work, you might still be happily married and not be bitter toward a guy you envy," Delores says.

"Things are getting a little heated on our show today, but I do want to move on to one of our other guests. Marty Price, what are your thoughts on this whole gubernatorial race?" Walter Carl asks.

"I worked for the Douglas campaign when Theodore Graham was running it, and I am still working for it with Russ Dewitt in charge. I believe Gene Douglas is the best guy for the job, and I think he will make a great governor. I'm voting for Gene. I do have to say that I have never admired the friendship between two people more than I admire Gene and Theodore's. If politics don't destroy this friendship, nothing will."

"What do you think, Russ, would Theodore Graham be the right guy for Gene Douglas's lieutenant governor or vice versa?

"Their friendship is admirable, but I don't know if it would be wise to release that dynamic on the people of our state," Russ jokes.

"How about you, Delores? Would you be in favor of having them on the same ticket?"

"I'm going to have to agree with Russ on this. Pick one or the other. Who knows what would result if they ran together."

"Well, that's all the time we have for today. I like to thank my guests for talking to us and giving our viewers a little insight to the candidates. I'm your host, Walter Carl, and I thank you for tuning in to this special edition of State of the State This Week. Join us next week as we discuss the issues that face our state."

"I never thought of us running on the same ticket," Gene says to Theodore.

"I never thought of that either, but what surprised me the most was, Delores Daniels, she thinks I'm handsome."

"You are handsome, Teddy. That's why that slut bag Claire Peterson fucked you," Sandy says.

"Mimosa number six chimes in!" Gene says.

"I'm not voting for you, Gene. You can't even count. This is mimosa number seven."

"At what number mimosa do your breasts come out?"

Sandy lifts her bikini top and shows her breasts to Theodore. "Usually they come out after ten, but for you, Teddy, it only took seven."

"Sandy, must you?"

"It's okay, Gene, I don't mind."

"Of course you don't mind, but I paid for them and I mind."

Sandy puts her breasts away. "Don't be upset. You guys are such good friends. There's one for each of you."

"I can't believe Delores mentioned the whole Claire affair, though."

"I can't believe she got that upset when Jim Peterson called me a loser. Delores doesn't usually stick up for me."

"Teddy and Delores sitting in a tree, K, I, S, S, I, N, G. First comes love, then comes marriage, then comes a little Furshizzle in a baby carriage."

"Don't get too carried away, Sandy."

"I think I'm going to have to get going. I have a feeling I am going to have to think about doing some damage control after this show."

"Yes, I have a feeling I will be getting a call for an emergency staff meeting."

"I have a feeling I will be getting a call from Claire."

"Just show her your penis. That shut her up before," Sandy says.

Theodore hugs Sandy, and she gives him a peck on the cheek. "Thanks for having me over. How about you cut back on the mimosas and have some more of these?" He takes two joints out of his pocket and hands them to her.

Gene shakes Theodore's hand. "I guess we got to get back to fighting each other on the campaign trail, but I enjoyed your visit."

"Soon we will be doing this in the governor's mansion," Theodore says and leaves the patio and disappears into the house.

CHAPTER 36

The Theodore Graham for Governor campaign staffers are busy sorting through newspapers, cataloging news videos, analyzing Gene Douglas's campaign ads, and jotting down notes. The staff looks tired. They are irritable and worried about the coming days of the campaign. Theodore enters the room smiling and cheerful before the morning meeting.

"Good morning. Why does everybody look so glum? It's Friday! Embrace the Friday feeling."

"It's kind of hard to be happy when we've been being shelled with negative ads and defending ourselves in the press for the past week," Pam Eynon says.

"Don't worry, be happy. Isn't that what Bobby Mcferrin advised?"

"How can you be this nonchalant? This is your character that's under fire, and your unwillingness to care or defend yourself is only letting the press continue to write negative things."

"I said from the beginning that I'm not going to be part of a negative campaign."

"You're buddy Gene Douglas said he wasn't going to run a negative campaign either, but ever since our shit show on *State of the State This Week*, the Douglas campaign has been hitting us with negative ads from their super PAC and leaking incriminating pictures and stories about you. You don't even seem to care," Ed Reese says.

"I've been going to our events. I have been talking about and explaining our platform. We've been lining up community leaders and organizations that are interested in bringing about change. I've been talking to the press honestly."

"When the press asks you about the character attacks and accusations, you dismiss them or ignore them and go on to reporters with questions about our platform."

"That's what we're supposed to be doing, talking about the issues and our plan. Right?"

"That's what candidates are supposed to say, but fighting back is what they are supposed to do. You have to fight back."

"At the next event, I'll announce that I won't pick Gene Douglas as my lieutenant governor if he doesn't stop being a big meany. You think that will work?"

"You're joking about that, but there are a few newspapers—one of them the *Weekly Beat*—waxing hypothetical about you two ending up on the same ticket," Pam says.

"Wouldn't it be nice if friends could put aside their differences and work together for a good cause?" Theodore says and starts singing. "We are the world. We are the children. We are the ones who make a brighter day, so let's start giving."

"This isn't the eighties, and we aren't trying to guilt people into feeding foreign brown children. We have to do something about this. Can't you at least call your friend and ask him why he's not sticking to his word about not going negative? At least find out why he's doing this."

"Gene hasn't been returning my calls since the last time I saw him."

"When was the last time you saw him?" Pam asks.

"We got together for brunch and drinks to watch *State of the State This Week* last Sunday. I left his place for an emergency campaign meeting here. We decided to let what's done be done and keep plugging our platform as the right way to go. That's exactly what I've been doing since. The Douglas campaign went a different route. I don't control their campaign."

"Our strategy isn't working. Your strategy isn't working. The negativity is hurting us, and the final polling data before the election will be coming out in a few weeks. We aren't going to accomplish what we set out to do," Ed Reese says.

"We set out to get Democrats to win their assembly races. My candidacy was based on this. It's all senior staff in here. We all know what the deal was from the beginning. Nobody in here can say they expect me to win this election. How badly is the negativity hurting the state House and Senate races? Tim, you're the pollster and stats guy. What are you learning?"

"Well, like Ed said, the official polling won't be coming out for a few weeks, but the day-to-day polls that follow the press cycle aren't helping us any. None of the numbers I have are gospel, but the projections that I've made with these numbers show Gene Douglas extending his lead."

"By how much?"

"Like I said, these numbers aren't law. They're only projections based on day-to-day polling of small sample groups. The projections have you at 38 percent, Gene at 59 percent, and there is a 3 percent margin of error. That means if you cover the entire margin of error, you will lose 59 to 41."

"So I lose by a bigger margin. What's the problem there?"

"The problem is, if the race isn't tighter, our people will believe that voting won't make a difference and won't bother going out to the polls on Election Day. The Democrats will lose the state races we need to win the majority in."

"Can we make up this ground and tighten the race before the final polling cycle?"

"We can do it, but we have to change our course and we have to do it quickly. Time is something we can't afford to waste."

"What are our options? Does anybody in here have any suggestions?"

"We've got to fight fire with fire. You got to hit Gene with negatives. You will have to hit him personally. I know you know how to hit him. You've made something of an art form of taking out people who come at you," Ed Reese says.

"I don't like where this is going. I gave up six years as the coordinator for the Young Republicans because of the flip-flopping and corruption of the Douglas campaign. He went back on his word about getting the young people more involved in the process, and he got in bed with the Whitneys, who were trying to purchase him and the state government. I left the Republicans because I no longer recognized the party values as my own. I will leave this campaign if it's going to be the same way," Kevin Baker says.

"Kevin, we're not going to change our values. There is nobody better with the ground operations and motivating our volunteers in the field than you. We will figure something out. Don't leave yet. I need everybody in this room to help turn this around," Theodore says.

"Maybe we can put some negative ads in the media until the official polling comes out. Then we come out strong on the issues until Election Day," Nancy Bradford says.

"What's our budget look like? Can we afford to do something like that?" Ed Reese asks.

"Nathan, that's your wheelhouse. Do we have the funding?" Theodore asks.

"The ads we did promoting our platform cost us a bunch. We are pretty limited as to what we can do. We have enough to make a few new ads, but not enough to flood the market. Whatever we put out there, we have to make it count. Your super PAC isn't really a super PAC. It's got about two million dollars behind it. Gene Douglas's has over thirty million at his disposal."

"I didn't even know I had a super PAC, but what they do with that funding is up to the super PAC. I'm not risking the violation of campaign finance laws. How about these state races? Are the guys that are attaching themselves to my coattails putting up anything for our fight?"

"We got a few contributions from some of them."

"Some of them? How much are they putting up?"

"Rick Kashire put up five hundred dollars for our campaign. His was the biggest contribution. Most of them are one-hundred, fifty-, or seventy-five-dollar donations."

"You've got to be shitting me. This party gets me to run for governor with the purpose of not winning but to help state representatives and state senators win seats in the assembly. They better start getting behind our campaign. We are the hands that feed them. You're awfully quiet, Delores. What are your thoughts?"

"I was kind of hoping we would put our heads together at this meeting and come up with an approach. I'm not sure which way to go. We have to get the candidates we are helping to help us. I agree. Anna Martinez and Fred Miles, how about the three of us schedule a meeting with these assembly candidates so we can get everybody on the same page?" Delores says.

"I'll start making some calls after the meeting," Fred Miles says.

"I'll help Fred with that, but I did get a call last night from Jason Munch's campaign. They said if we don't do something about the negative attacks, he is going to start distancing himself from us and our policies," Anna Martinez says.

"How much did Jason Munch help us with our campaign?"

"He didn't donate any money to our campaign. I'm not sure if he even publicly endorsed you," Nathan says.

"Fuck him! Get me his phone number. I will call him after this meeting and tell him that if he doesn't get on board, I will pull support away from him. Actually, pull some support from him right now because he isn't shit without our help. Kevin, pull our ground operations out of his district until he gets on board. Pam, pull our press agents off of him and have them ignore his calls until we tell them differently. He's not getting shit from us."

"Put the warning out to all of them. We will pull our resources away from their campaigns if they aren't supporting us. Their races are theirs to lose if they don't do better to help us," Delores says.

"All well and good, but what are we going to do about our campaign? What are we going to do about our numbers? Tim said that time isn't something we have the luxury of wasting," Ed Reese says.

"We have to figure out how to take the sting out of the attacks on us and attack Gene Douglas without making it appear we are being negative," Delores says.

"No shit, Delores. That's why we're here. We wouldn't be having this meeting if you and Pam had not let yourselves be baited into arguments with Russ Dewitt and Jim Peterson on television. Why in the hell did you mention Teddy's sex scandal?"

"I don't . . . I can't . . . I didn't mean . . . I only wanted to. I can't do this now," Delores says and grabs her briefcase and quickly leaves the conference room.

"Delores, wait! Don't leave! This isn't your fault!" Theodore yells and moves toward the door.

"Let her cool off. She's had a rough week. I'll go to your events with you this afternoon. Give her time to think," Pam says.

"Ed, that was totally uncalled for. We're on the same team. I need everybody in this room on the same page and working together. The blame game is only going to make the situation worse. If anybody isn't willing to put the past behind us and figure out how to move forward, leave right now. We can't afford to implode!" Theodore says.

"Teddy, I'm sorry."

"I understand the frustration. My past dealings and actions are the problem. If you are going to blame anybody, blame me. I should have been more forthcoming with the shit that could be used against me. I wasn't. I fucked up. Be frustrated with me. Ed, please apologize to Delores."

"I will. I'm sorry. I was speaking while hotheaded."

"Let's just put that in the past and get rolling. What am I being hit with? I see you all compiling media clippings and videos. Tell me the list and give me what you have, and I will see what I can come up with."

"You're getting hit for not sticking with your career in law. They are hitting you with your womanizing, alluding that you are sexist. You are getting faulted for pandering to minorities. There are pictures of you smoking marijuana. Your political experience and knowledge of politics in the state are being questioned because you are not native. Gene's super PAC put out an ad that you are antigun and will regulate people out of their Second Amendment rights. The newest attack, they are questioning your commitment to being the governor if you are elected," Pam says.

"Okay, that's quite a list. I'm pretty much an asshole. The Democrats should have done their homework before getting on board with me," Theodore says.

"We did our homework, and you are the best we could come up with. That's the problem."

"That's kind of sad, but we have to work with what we have. We have me. Pam, you will be with me this afternoon. Anna, do you think you can join us? You're the one that's most knowledgeable on our day care and health platform for children. I need your expertise."

"Definitely. I will be where you need me."

"Thank you. Kevin, hook me up with some appearances with our ground operations in other areas of the state this weekend. I only need events where I am showing my face and support for good causes. I want events where I'm not speaking and doing press conferences. Make sure they are events where my presence doesn't distract from their purpose."

"You got it. I will e-mail you a list of the events. Pick the ones you think are the best, and I will set everything up."

"Perfect. I will contact staff members and put them where I need them to be. Don't turn your cell phones off. We will meet here again on Sunday night at seven, and we will discuss how we will own the news cycle by lunchtime on Monday."

"How are we going to turn this around?" Nancy Bradford asks.

"That's why I need until Sunday night. Everybody is welcome to bring their suggestions to the meeting. If I can get in touch with Gene Douglas over the weekend, I will try to find out why he went negative. I have a feeling that Russ Dewitt is telling him to cut ties with me until after the polling data comes in."

"You have my number, and I am where you need me to be," Nancy says.

"That goes for all of us," Ed says.

"This kind of talk sounds like teamwork. That's what we need. That's how we're going to come out on top," Theodore says. He packs up his briefcase and leaves the room.

CHAPTER 37

Theodore walks from Harmon to Douglas Hills. He walks past all the classroom buildings of the youth honors college, through the block of administration and business offices, to the row of Cape Cod homes that serve as faculty housing. In the middle of the row, there is one Cape Cod home that is surrounded by well-maintained flower gardens with meticulously-cared-for roses and hanging plants. Theodore knocks on the door of that home.

Delores Daniels opens the door. "Not now, Teddy. I can't deal with the circus that surrounds you right now."

"You didn't answer your phone. You didn't respond to my texts. You didn't check your e-mail. I tried a few birdcalls. You didn't answer them, but I believe I may have agreed to pull a jewelry heist with a sinister crow."

"Please go away. I will talk to you at the staff meeting on Sunday."

"I walked all the way over here from Harmon. I brought you a bottle of wine and a six-pack of beer. I'm embarrassed to say that I have no idea what you like to drink."

"You walked the two miles from Harmon carrying a six-pack of beer and a bottle of wine? Are you insane? You are running for governor, you can't be alone in the open like that!"

"No paparazzi followed me. One guy yelled, 'Suck my farts, Teddy!' when I walked by, but I didn't take him up on his offer," he says. "I want to talk to you about this morning's meeting."

"I really don't want to talk about any of this mess. I appreciate you getting people to cover for me while I sort things out, but you're the last person I want to see right now."

"Well, you could have answered your phone and told me that. You could have sent me a text or answered my e-mail. You could have unfriended me on Facebook, and maybe I would have understood, but your radio silence made me put on my walking shoes. Please talk to me for a few minutes," Theodore says and puts the bottle of wine on the porch table and takes the beer out of the paper bag.

"There are only five beers."

"It's a two-mile walk over here. I got thirsty."

"That's all you need, a reporter or even just a passerby to send a picture of you walking the streets, drinking a beer. You are a candidate for governor, and you are breaking open-container laws in two towns. You have an open alcohol container in a school zone."

"I have a couple of joints in my shirt pocket too. I'm in a 'drug-free school zone.' I could get in a shitload of trouble. Personally, I would prefer a 'school-free drug zone,' but that's just me."

"Say what you got to say, Teddy."

"I was hoping for a conversation just like you were hoping for a conversation when you came to my apartment to talk about me running for governor. I regret not talking with you that night. I was needlessly dismissive of you. I don't want you to regret not talking to me tonight."

"All right, come on in."

Theodore picks up the bottle of wine and follows Delores inside. "Who does your landscaping and garden work? You have the nicest yard on the block."

"Gardening is how I relax. I like taking care of flowers and growing things. I have an herb-and-vegetable garden out back."

"Do you know anything about growing weed? You could probably save me a ton of money if you do."

"Have a seat," Delores says as they make their way into the parlor.

"You don't have a television. How do you know which way to point your furniture?"

"The television in my office is plenty. I don't like the nonsense television spews."

"Yes, television is pretty mindless. I like *Jeopardy* and *Mr. Ed* reruns. What's with all the boxes?"

"I was packing up some of the knickknacks, clutter, and things I don't use often."

"Are you planning on going somewhere?" Theodore asks.

"I don't know. Maybe. I might have to. I'm not sure anymore."

"Why would you have to move? You're on paid sabbatical. You'll be going back to work after the election in November."

"It's this whole mess. After the election, I don't know if I will be able to go back. There's always going to be mistrust between me and the school administration. My credibility on the board will always be in question. I'm starting to regret my choice."

"This is because of me. You don't have to tiptoe around my feelings. I can take it. I did put you in a bad position."

"I made the choice. I could have said no and been done with you."

"I'm glad you didn't. This campaign wouldn't be half as successful as it is without you. You run a tight ship, and the staff works like clockwork. From the volunteers to the fund-raising, to the event schedule, to the campaign logo and merchandise and all the speaking engagements, it's a smooth operation. I don't have to worry about the little details with you in charge. I picked the best campaign manager. I don't regret that decision."

"Our campaign is losing ground because of me. The Douglas campaign is attacking us hard because of me. I will probably lose my job at this school because of the election. If they don't find a way to fire me, they will make it so uncomfortable to be there that I will have to quit."

"Don't let what Ed Reese said at the meeting this morning bother you. He said it out of frustration."

"He called me to apologize for blaming me. I know he said it out of frustration, but he was right."

"No, he wasn't right. That's why he apologized. Russ Dewitt has hated me since the first day he met me. I was his boss, and when I was let go from campaign, he didn't move up. He only got to where he is because of Gene Douglas's missteps. He's the third-choice campaign manager, and Russ knows he wouldn't have that job if some-body better than him was willing to step in amid the turmoil. Russ couldn't wait for Gene to give him the green light to go negative against me. Jim Peterson is just an insecure man of no substance. He inherited his wealth. His Ivy League degree was purchased and not earned. The board of the Douglas school is his only real position of power. I undermined him any chance I got. Jim Peterson is just a vengeful, bitter man. Don't blame the negativity hitting the cam-paign on yourself."

"I mentioned your affair with his wife on a television show. I lowered myself to his level and opened the gate for the attacks on our campaign. It was very unprofessional. Now we probably won't achieve our goal of taking back the state assembly."

"The campaign isn't over yet. Don't give up."

"Closing that gap in the polling numbers is going to be close to impossible."

"I'm not done trying, and I need you more than ever."

"I think I would do more harm than good. I lost my cool on that show and let them get the best of me. I don't seem to be able to get it together since."

"I should have come here to talk to you right after the show, but you won the argument and made Russ and Jim look stupid. I was proud of you."

Delores reaches in the six-pack holder and takes a beer out. "I'm having one of these beers. My nerves are shot."

"Go ahead. You deserve one. Maybe one of the joints in my pocket will help with your nerves."

"I'm not going to start smoking pot."

"It helps me. I thought it might help you too," Theodore says and takes a beer out of the six-pack holder. "We didn't get to have a drink over a conversation when you came to my apartment. I'm not missing the chance this time around."

"I was so mad at you that night. I probably shouldn't have come unannounced, though. The committee put a lot in your head. I knew how you overthink things, and when I saw the floor of your apart-ment covered with information, I knew you were stressing over the decision. For some reason, I thought I could talk to you as a person and help you think things through. I'm not sure that you would be running for governor if we did talk. I kind of guilt-tripped you into running."

"Things happened the way they did. We can't change the past. I made the right decision. I picked the right campaign manager, and I picked a great staff. Together we put together a beautiful political platform for the people."

"Do you think you made the right decision? You could have been doing other things with your time. You could have been pissing people off with your newspaper, playing guitar, and getting high."

"I'm still doing all that and running for governor. I'm not a half-bad multitasker. You must have taught me a thing or two over the years."

"Yeah, you really didn't change at all."

"I like me. Not many serious people do. I'm more of a novelty. I do what I do to make me happy. If I didn't, the echoes of the judgmental people who don't like me would eat at my mind and I would live a miserable existence plagued by constant doubt."

"That's a good way to be, I guess."

"There's one thing I have wanted to ask you since your appearance on *State of the State This Week*."

"I'm afraid to ask but curious. Go ahead, ask me what's on your mind."

"How come you attacked Russ and Jim like you did? You are one of the people that don't like me, but when they attacked me, you and Pam pounced on them. Pam defended me, but you went in for the kill. I couldn't figure out why. Why did you defend me so hard and with such devotion?"

"I don't know why I did it. I don't like you. I guess I'm just sick of those rich, pretentious jerks attacking you. If Gene didn't hire you, the school would be filing for bankruptcy and closing. The school is hurting without you now. His publishing house would have closed if you didn't publish there. You made his campaign great, and even after he fired you, you used your newspaper to expose the trouble that surrounded him. You truly are a good friend. Most people wish they had a friend like you."

"Good friends are important to me. I don't have many. The close ones, I want to keep. But what made you go after Jim Peterson so hard? Why did you bring up Claire? My whole Claire affair made your job harder than it had to be."

"I wanted to hurt him like he was trying to hurt you. I knew your affair with Claire cut him deeply. Jim Peterson thought that because he was a man, he had the right to rule over and control her. I don't agree with how your affair took place, but I was happy it freed her so she could let her brilliance pave her way. She's leaving the school at the end of this school year to work on the president's economic advisory team."

"Yeah, she told me. She can do anything and will be ten times as wealthy as Jim in no time."

"How come you and Claire didn't stick together? You would have made a great power couple."

"We weren't a long-term type of couple. I think my purpose was just to free her so she could succeed on her merits."

"You may be freeing me. It might be time to move on after this campaign."

"Does that mean we have to have sex?"

"No! But working with you made me want to look at other opportunities. I was content working at the school until I retired, but maybe you are showing me better options."

"Maybe it is. You saved that school and ran it well, but you can do so much more and so much better somewhere else. You are a lot like Claire, but instead of having a controlling husband holding you back, you have a career that's holding you back. You're not going to make the school any better or take it any further than you have. You should go after what makes you happy. There's no law against setting new goals," Theodore says.

"Is that what you do?"

"I grew up poor. I lost my mother when I was young, and my father lived a miserable life. He worked himself into an early grave so I could be one of the rich people that bossed him around. My parents never took the time to be happy. They sacrificed everything because they wanted me to be happy. When I realized happiness was a choice, I chose to be happy and fulfilled my parents' wishes."

"Is happiness really a choice?"

"For me it is, and I am happy I made it. I do what makes me happy."

"With all the mess surrounding your campaign? Balancing your job as a journalist and a politician makes you happy?"

"The chaos is fun, and the good people around me make me happy. I'm not really concerned with the outcome. It will work out how it works out."

"I am jealous of you. That's probably why I hate you so much."

"On *State of the State This Week*, you said I was handsome. I was flattered by the compliment. Do you really think I'm handsome?"

"I might not like you, but you're pretty easy on the eyes."

"Why, Delores Daniels, I would have never—"

Delores leans over to him and kisses him on the lips. Theodore goes numb with surprise.

"I'm sorry, I don't know what came over me. It must be the beer. I'm not much of a drinker."

"Have another one if it will help you do it again."

Delores takes the beer out of Theodore's hand, puts it on the coffee table, moves closer to him, puts her arms around him, and kisses him again.

"Do you still hate me?"

"I have a feeling I may end up hating myself for this. Shut up and keep kissing me."

CHAPTER 38

Theodore enters the meeting room of the campaign headquarters on Sunday evening. Staff members are seated and ready to get to work.

"I hope everybody made the best of what little free time they had this weekend. Thanks for the extra efforts. Last week was a tough one, but I am hoping, after this evening's meeting, we can turn it around."

"We've been bouncing ideas back and forth before you came in. We made some notes," Ed Reese says.

"Awesome, let's hear what you came up with."

"We will talk about them item by item and craft our statements from there. Tim Collins, you want to start with Teddy's law career."

"Okay, I'll start. They are claiming you left a multimillion-dollar career in law because you couldn't handle the pressure. We can say you kept your credentials as an attorney. You can still practice law but you just don't choose to do so."

"That's true. It's pretty much what I did. If we go that route, we will have to sharpen the language so it resonates."

"Let's move on to the attacks about Teddy's womanizing. Nancy, do you want to handle that?"

"Sure. This is an easy one. You are an adult that has consensual relationships with other adults. You are single and aren't cheating on a spouse or being disloyal to a committed relationship."

"That's probably the right way to go, but since I brought up Claire Peterson on television, they may paint Teddy as a home-wrecker," Delores says.

"I'm pretty sure they are itching to hit me with that. It's going to be tough to get around, and we will bring unwanted attention to Claire."

"Let's table that for now. We can't get her embroiled in our battle," Delores says.

"What about the gun rights attack?" Ed Reese asks.

"I don't even know where that attack came from or what it's based on. We have nothing about guns in our platform, nothing in our literature, nothing on our website, and have never discussed it in a speech. I think they are just saying it to get the gun lobby endorsement and gun owners against us," Everett Avery says.

"I think that was something Gene's super PAC put out."

"It doesn't matter where it came from. It's all over social media. The gun-rights people are merciless when they feel threatened."

"Yeah, I know. I can't believe I have to defend myself over this shit! Goddammit!"

"Calm down. I know you're frustrated. We'll figure this out," Delores says.

"I'm sorry. I'm very frustrated. I want to sell our platform and not downplay my life choices and missteps to please a bunch of fickle mush-heads that are too fucking stupid to think about the issues."

"Let's move on. They shared some pictures of you smoking marijuana. What are we going to say about that?" Ed Reese asks.

"We can say you were experimenting with marijuana and it was only a phase," Nathan Winters says.

"Experimenting? I just got done with an experiment three hours ago. I started my scientific study with marijuana when I was in college, and I am still working on my study. It's a decades-long phase. I like to be thorough. Once my study is complete, I will decide if marijuana should be legalized or not."

"We can say the pipes and paraphernalia pictures are tobacco pipes and you were indulging in some social and legal tobacco use."

"I don't think anybody will buy that, plus there are other people in those pictures that can come forward and say we were smoking marijuana. We don't want to be caught in a lie. I don't want to lie about that either."

"Is there any dirt on Gene you can throw back at him?" Ed asks.

"Of course there is. I went to college with him. But I don't want to go negative and stoop to their level."

"You're going to have to do something. We have to improve our numbers. Where's the Theodore Graham the Democrats wanted on their team? Welcome to politics, Teddy. It's an ugly game, and it's played dirty. You have to start playing the game how it's played."

"Hate the player, not the game. Is that how it is? Gene is playing the game and getting voters to hate me, the player?"

"He is now, but we're here to help you turn it around," Delores says.

"I'm going into my office for a bit. I'm not accustomed to feeling this much anger. I don't want to vent it toward the staff that's trying to help me. Please excuse me."

"He can't just walk out like that. He called this meeting. We're here for him," Ed says.

"Leave him go for a bit. He'll be back. He just needs to clear his head," Delores says.

"There are a lot of things I would rather be doing on a Sunday night than waiting for Teddy to grow a set of balls."

"Do you want me to go talk to him?" Nancy asks.

"No. I'm the campaign manager. I will get him back in here."

Delores walks down the hallway to Theodore's office and knocks on the door. "Teddy, it's Delores. Can I come in?"

"I wanted a couple of minutes to decompress. Can't I even get that?"

"I thought if I gave you a hand job, that might help."

Theodore opens the door in one quick motion. "Come on in."

"I knew that would get me in here, but I am teaching you a lesson in politics. I made a promise that I'm not delivering on."

"I had a feeling it was too good to be true, but you made out with me on Friday night. It seemed like the next logical step."

"Friday night is behind us. Now we have work to do."

"I thought you were going to say Friday night was a mistake."

"I'm not sure what it was—I haven't decided yet—and I don't have time to analyze it. I have a campaign to run."

"If I drop out of the race, could we kiss some more?"

"I'm not making out with a quitter."

"I'm not quitting. I'm just not sure what to do. I hate that I have to go on the attack. We put an awesome platform together. All of us did. This whole staff worked so hard. I believe in it. I want the voters to see how good it is. I'll lose either way. If I go negative, I let myself down. If I don't hit back, I let my team down. My anger comes from being stuck in the middle of the two."

"You're not supposed to win the election. Don't overthink it. Let's just figure out how to do enough to fill the assembly seats we need to."

Theodore opens a desk drawer and pulls out a large manila envelope. "In this envelope is exactly what we need. It's the counterpunch that will get us out from under the thumb of Gene's negative attacks. It would probably be a knockout punch. Having this has been torturing me, and I don't know if using it is the right thing to do."

"What's in it?"

"If I tell you, this has to be our secret and has to remain a secret until I decide what to do with it."

"You can trust me. It will stay between us. What's in the envelope?"

"Last week, amid all the negative attacks on us, a young friend of mine, Wayne Arnold, came to me with this envelope. Wayne was a student of mine at the community college. He is my local weed guy. We get together to play guitar. He's hung out and played guitar with me and Ernie Douglas. He sat in with bands and played with Ernie in recent weeks. He also has some entrepreneurial aspirations and is looking to leap into the adult entertainment world."

"What's in the envelope?"

Theodore opens the envelope and removes some pictures and hands them to Delores. "There are some pictures of Ernie Douglas smoking marijuana. There are some pictures of him doing lines of cocaine. There are some photos of Sandy Douglas nude and some pictures of her in sexually explicit poses in different stages of undress."

"These pictures will destroy the Douglas campaign."

"Yes, but that's not all. Remember those *Girls Gone Wild* videos from the nineties?"

"Yeah, I remember them. They were those drunk, slutty college-girl videos they advertised late at night. They appealed to the little young perverts that were entering puberty and the dirty old men who weren't getting any attention from their wives."

"Yes, they're the ones. Anyway, Sandy Douglas appeared in one of those videos when Gene, Sandy, a few of our other college friends, and I went on spring break one year. Wayne found a copy of it. It's in the envelope."

"That video could hurt the Gene Douglas campaign deeply."

"It could, but I also mentioned that Wayne Arnold was trying to get into the adult entertainment industry. There is a new video of Sandy Douglas. Wayne is trying to round up some women from the *Girls Gone Wild* videos to make *Girls Gone Wild: The MILF Years*."

"What's a *MILF*?"

"It's an acronym for 'mother I'd like to fuck.'"

"Well, that's clever."

"I'm not sure how clever it is, but Sandy Douglas is in raw video footage of one of those videos performing oral sex on somebody that isn't Gene. There is also a release form signed by Sandy Douglas allowing her video to be released in exchange for a percentage of sales and distribution."

"Oh my god, she is such a whore! This will destroy the Douglas campaign. This will destroy her beauty pageant organization."

"It will also probably destroy the Douglas Youth Honors College. All this information, if it's made public, will destroy the Douglas family. I can hit back with this stuff and put myself out front. It might even win me the election. It would hurt the school and education there for future generations. It will hurt Sandy. It will hurt Ernie and his future. It will hurt my friends. I don't know if I could play this dirty. I don't think I could live with myself if I played dirty with this information."

"I can't, in good conscience, ask you to use this. What are you going to do?"

"I don't know. Maybe . . . I'm not sure. Ummm. I'm not going to use it. We still have to figure out what we are going to do. I thought an idea would come to me over the weekend, but it didn't. Is that hand job totally out of the question? It might knock something loose and get my mind going. It may help me think of something."

"The hand job is not an option, I'm sorry."

Delores goes around his desk and kisses Teddy on the lips.

"I got it!"

"Got what?"

"I know what we're going to do to. Let's go back to the conference room."

"I just gave you a kiss. Where did this come from?"

"You're one heck of a kisser. Let's go."

Theodore charges into the conference room. "I know how we're going to fight back and get us moving in a positive direction again."

"What do you have?" Ed Reese asks.

"We're going to own the criticism, embrace it, and turn it back on the Douglas campaign. Delores, Nancy, and Ed, I need you to stick around. The rest of you can go home and be with your families. Our press conference is tomorrow at ten. Be back here at nine."

"Delores, what did you say to him?" Nancy asks.

"I'm not sure if it was something I said or something I did, but I hope I don't regret it."

CHAPTER 39

Delores is quizzing Theodore on points of his speech and asking him questions the press may ask. Other members of the campaign staff are mingling with the crowd and talking to some supporters and volunteers.

"You seem to have the talking points down, and you handle the press questions well. I think you're ready. Do you feel ready?"

"I feel ready. I can't thank you enough for staying late last night and getting me ready. You, Nancy, and Ed really brought this all together. I have a feeling this is going to work. We will turn this around and do what we set out to do."

"I can't believe you were able to talk Claire Peterson into participating in this."

"She will probably be glad to clear her name in the press. I know they have been hounding her for a comment. We were fortunate that Gene had the good sense to protect the school from the media. It indirectly sheltered her because she lives and works there."

"I still feel horrible about bringing her up on that show."

"I imagine she isn't really happy with you for doing so, but what's done is done."

"When she is here today, I don't know if I am going to be able to look her in the eye."

"Now is your chance to find out. Here she comes."

"Good morning, Teddy. Ms. Daniels," Claire says.

"Thank you for doing this," Theodore says.

"I have to clear my name and get the press out of my business."

"Claire, I can't tell you how sorry I am for bringing you into this and mentioning you on that show."

"Well, Ms. Daniels, you did bring me into this. The last thing I wanted was to be mentioned on the news for an extramarital affair. I still can't understand. You, of all people, you reduced yourself to gossip. This was way out of character for you. Since I've known you, you always conducted yourself professionally and above the fray of petty chatter. What happened? I'm going to be working for the president of the United States as an adviser on his economic panel. I didn't need this. This made me look like a slut and casts shade on all that I've worked for."

"Claire, I am truly sorry. I don't know how I can make it up to you, but if there is a way, please let me know," Delores says.

"Maybe a little bit of casual lesbo heavy petting would help," Theodore says.

"Shut up, Teddy," Delores and Claire say simultaneously.

"I'm just trying to help. I hate to see you guys mad at each other. I just thought some lesbo action would help reduce the tension. It seems to help in some of the porn videos I've seen."

"You're not helping."

"I did enjoy seeing you put my ex-husband in his place and calling him for the stupidity that spews from his mouth. I could have done without the attention, but it is what it is, I guess. I will consider this a favor for Teddy. He rescued me from my shitty marriage. If it weren't for him, I would still be married and miserable."

"I am sorry, Claire."

"I will make a good statement for your campaign, Delores."

"Thank you, Claire. You will be great," Theodore says.

"It's ten minutes before we go on. I'm going to round up the staff and get them in their places. Claire, do you want to follow me? You will be sitting next to Rose Fayweather," Delores says.

"Rose is here? She's not here to clear her name of a sex scandal, is she?"

"No, she plays hard to get, but if she gave me the green light, I'd hit that."

"Gross, she's seventy-eight!"

"Age doesn't matter. She still knows how to work it. Plus, she's worth like a gazillion dollars."

"I never pegged you for a gold digger, Teddy, buy it's nice that you are pushing her pet project."

"Claire, I ain't saying I'm a gold digger, but Rose Fayweather ain't dealing with no broke African American."

"I'm not sure if I like the politically correct Teddy Graham," Claire says.

"We have to get going. Teddy, I will introduce you, and you can do your thing. Did you figure out what you are going to do with the contents in that envelope?"

"I'm going to send Gene a text right now. The rest is up to him."

Claire and Delores make their way to the stage and gather the rest of the staff. Theodore takes his cell phone out of his pocket and sets it to vibrate so it doesn't ring during his speech. He composes a text message to Gene.

> *I know you aren't returning calls or texts. I imagine that is on the advice of your staff. I am about to address some of the negative attacks your campaign launched against me. While preparing for this speech, I received some information to hit you with. As your friend, I couldn't, in good conscience, use it, but I think you should know about it and have it in your possession. I would like to meet you alone, without our staff, and without Sandy. I will give you what I have. Please respond and let's set up a meeting.*
>
> *Love,*
> *Teddy.*

Theodore shoves his phone back in his pocket. Delores is now at the podium. She looks to Theodore on the wing of the stage to see if he is ready. He gives her the thumbs-up.

"Good morning, friends, supporters, citizens, and members of the press. This morning, candidate Graham is going to begin by answering some of the press inquiries we have received in the last few weeks. Copies of the press release can be obtained through Pam Eynon, and there will be a transcript of the speech posted on our website later today. After Mr. Graham addresses these press inquiries, he will introduce another part of his platform. There won't be a press Q-and-A session with the candidate here because we have another campaign event to get to. There will be opportunity for the press to ask questions at our headquarters at two this afternoon. Thank you. And now, it is my great pleasure to introduce you to the next governor of our great state, Mr. Theodore Graham."

Theodore walks onto the stage, past the podium, and over to his staff seated there. They all stand to shake his hand, pat him on the back, and encourage him. He leans down to Sophia White, his official campaign mother, and gives her a hug. She gives him a peck on the cheek and points to the podium. Theodore steps to the podium and waits for the applause to quiet.

"Good morning, folks. When I decided to run for governor, I didn't want it to be politics as usual. I didn't want to run a mudslinging campaign full of personal attacks on my opponent. I wanted to put together a platform that would start addressing the issues that politicians have promised to address for decades but never have. I wanted to be a campaign of substance. This is a campaign of substance, and it is because of the people seated here on this stage. These are the people that have been here from the beginning. I'm still on my first campaign manager, while my opponent is on his third. My staff worked hard to put our platform together. We've had our disagreements and some heated arguments, but we had them with the same goal in mind. From our conflicts, we find solutions. Our goal is to serve our citizens. We work as a team to figure out the best way to do so. I'm proud of our platform. It's what I have been touting and talking to the people about from the start. Sadly, some negative attacks have been launched against me. I didn't want to have to stop talking about my platform to defend myself, but I understand that the press has a job to do. These negative attacks have raised some questions. It is the job of the press to ask them and report the answers to the public. I want to be open, honest, and transparent with the people who I am counting on to vote for me. I will give the press and the people the answers they want."

Theodore waits for the applause to calm.

"One of the questions raised by my opponent is about my career in law. They accuse me of leaving a multimillion-dollar career at one of the top national law firms in the nation because I was incompetent and couldn't handle the pressure. I left Zimmer, Gregor, and Holtby because I didn't like writing legislation for lobbyist firms. These firms represented corporations and special interests that wanted legislation written in their favor so they could close the doors of opportunity for their competition and start-up companies. It was the same thing Morton Whitney was trying to do with my opponent's campaign. That's not how a fair-market capitalist system is supposed to work. Capitalism only works if there is a level playing field for all. I didn't like what I was doing, and guilt over what I was doing wouldn't let me sleep at night. I could have kept that job and made millions of dollars for destroying the capitalist system, but I chose to walk away. As for leaving because I was incompetent or couldn't take the pressure, well, you can judge for yourself. In my press release, and later on our website, I have included letters from all the recruiting firms, law firms, and lobbyist groups that have offered me jobs in the last few months. I will also post my law license. It's still active. I keep up my credentials. I can work as a lawyer if I choose, but that's not what I am choosing to do now. You can decide for yourself if you think I am incompetent or not."

Theodore waits for a longer applause to quiet.

"My opponent's campaign also accused me of being a womanizing sexist. I don't believe I am. I am a bachelor. I have never been married, and therefore, I have never been divorced. I've enjoyed a pretty active dating life over the years, but I'm not actively searching for a wife. I'm not saving myself for marriage, and I am certainly not going to feel ashamed for enjoying myself with the company I keep. My relationships are consensual. My sex life isn't a conquest, and I've always felt that I have been respectful of women. Sadly, in politics, innocent bystanders get pulled into the mud. One of these innocent bystanders is here with me today because her name has been mentioned in the press. I want her to have the opportunity to clear her name and avoid future media speculation. I'm going to invite her up to the podium to tell her side of the story. Claire Peterson, would you come up here?"

Claire comes to the podium to applause, and Theodore steps aside.

"Thank you, Teddy, for this opportunity. I didn't care one bit to have my name mentioned during this campaign. Unfortunately, it was, and it was mentioned negatively. I did have an extramarital relationship with Teddy Graham. I do not regret it, however, not even a little. Everything happens for a reason. The reason, I believe, is my indiscretion was needed so I could be rescued. The love had gone out of my marriage many years before I even knew Teddy. I have PhD in education and one in economics. I have a master's degree in American history and an MBA in business. Knowledge was something I treasured, and I continued to obtain as much as I could. As a teacher at the youth college, I met my now-ex-husband, Jim, a very wealthy man. I was young and thought getting married was what I was supposed to do. Once I was married, my now-ex-husband expected me to stay as a teacher at the school where he was a trustee until I retired and we could live happily ever after. I had other aspirations, and I wanted to apply my knowledge in other areas and try my hand in other careers. My ex-husband would have none of it and belittled the education and degrees I earned. Along came Teddy Graham. Here was a man who talked to me and not down to me. He asked me questions and listened to my answers. He valued my opinions and readily took my suggestions. He respected me for what I worked for. I was attracted to him because he made me feel good about myself. It doesn't hurt that he is a handsome man, but he made me feel happy to be in my own skin. I gave into temptation and broke my marriage vows. Again, I don't regret it. The attacks launched against him for being a sexist womanizer are false. The attacks stem from jealousy. Women want to be with Teddy. Guys want to be Teddy. After this coming school year, I will be leaving the Douglas Youth College and going to Washington to work on the national economic platform. I wouldn't have been able go after this opportunity if it weren't for Teddy Graham, who rescued me from an unhappy life. Once I explore my career and finish sucking the marrow out of life, if some woman doesn't snare Teddy Graham, I will take another run at him. Thank you, Teddy. Thank you for letting me speak on your behalf today. I'm repaying the wonderful favor you have done for me."

The crowd applauds. Claire gives Theodore a hug and returns to her seat.

"That is one brilliant woman. I believe she will turn Washington on its head and do some of her most brilliant work yet. If you want to know some more brilliant women, look at my staff, Delores Daniels, Nancy Bradford, Pam Eynon, Anna Martinez, and Sophia White. I have the deepest respect for each and every one of them," Theodore says to loud applause.

"Another attack made against me was from my opponent's super PAC. They are claiming I am antigun and, if I'm elected, I will legislate the people's Second Amendment rights away. I don't know where that came from. Guns aren't mentioned anywhere in my platform. In response to this attack, I will be posting pictures of some of my hunting trips over the years. One of my favorite pictures is Gene Douglas and me posing with the deer I shot on one of our hunting trips to Montana. That deer held the state record until only a year ago. I own guns. I'm responsible with them. They have gunlocks and are stored in a safe. My hope is that other good gun owners will come forward and show future generations how to be good gun owners too. That's my stance on guns."

Theodore pauses for more applause.

"One of the other attacks, and one that I've heard from the beginning, is that I will pander to women and minorities. I have women on my staff. I have black people on my staff. I have a Hispanic woman on my staff. You can check their credentials and résumés. You will find they are all intelligent and respected people. I trust them to help me form relationships with the people of this state. I want to do well by all our voters and not just the ones that look like me. This is my choice. If you have a problem with diversity and learning diverse points of view, then you obviously have a problem keeping an open mind."

The crowd comes to its feet and applauds and cheers.

"Thank you. Thank you," Teddy says and waits for another calm in the crowd.

"My favorite attack is the leaked pictures of me with marijuana and marijuana smoking paraphernalia. I am not denying using marijuana. I'm not about to lie and say that I didn't inhale. I'm not going to tell you that I tried it and I didn't like it, because that would be a lie. I think recreational marijuana use should be legal. Look at the extensive research done on marijuana, and you will see that it is safer than alcohol, tobacco, many prescription medications, and other illegal drugs. That's my view on it. There will be some details about it on my website so you can read for yourself. One of the pictures leaked by my opponent is of me with a bong. If you look in the bottom left corner of the picture, there is a hand in the frame. On that hand is a Harvard class ring with a fraternity symbol. The only person I could think of with a ring like that is Eugene Douglas. It's not up to me to say if he was there or not. It's not up to me to say if he smoked some marijuana that day or not. The members of the press can do their job and ask those questions of my opponent."

Theodore again gives the audience a chance to react.

"The last point I will address is my commitment to the job of governor when I win this election. It was said that I would get bored, frustrated, or too pressured by the job. My opponent's campaign says that I would resign and turn my back on the citizens of this state. I came to this state because my opponent asked me to work at his school. My record in that job speaks for itself, but feel free to check on it. My opponent hired me as his campaign manager and fired me from that job. I didn't quit. I was hired by the *Weekly Beat* and signed a two-year contract with the paper. I still have that job, and you can read my articles in that publication on a regular basis. The biggest reason I will commit myself to the job as governor is the people up here onstage with me. It would be a sin if their hard work was a waste of their brilliance and time. They didn't let me down. I'm not about to let them down. I'm not about to let the voters who support me down."

Theodore waits for more applause to subside.

"I believe I answered the attacks honestly. My website is open to the public. Do yourself a favor. Go there and make an informed decision about me. The press, I hope, will quote me fairly and accurately. Now I want to talk about another aspect of my platform. I chose to do my speech in front of the Fayweather Building here in Harmon for a reason. This building has been here a long time, and it has always been in the Fayweather family. Originally, it was the office building for a whale-oil fuel company. After the whale oil industry disappeared, it was the office building for the timber and paper industry. It then became the business offices of the local textile industry, and from there it became the executive offices of a retail brokerage. Last year, the brokerage closed, and it currently sits empty. In June of next year, this building will house the Fayweather Public Library and Education Center. It will have all the educational, research, and leisure reading resources of a modern library, and it will offer affordable credited college courses, career training, technical training, and lifestyle improvement instruction for the people of Harmon and its surrounding communities. The teachers of these classes will be qualified and certified instructors volunteering their time to help better the people of our communities. There are vacant office buildings in communities all across our state that can be repurposed for the same communal and educational opportunities. As governor, I want to push for more of these projects and give our citizens opportunities to better themselves. This idea was presented to me by one of the most dedicated, lifelong educators that I ever had privilege of working with, Mrs. Rose Fayweather."

Rose Fayweather makes her way to the podium as the crowd cheers. She hugs Theodore and positions herself behind the podium.

"Thank you, Mr. Graham. I've always believed that it takes a village to raise a child. Thus, the village should have all the resources it can to teach and prepare each of God's children for the world. Rather than let this building lie vacant or be sold to a private interest, I want it to be my legacy as an educator for future generations.

It will be a building full of knowledge and opportunity. It can help the people who are struggling financially get an education and open the doors for their betterment. It will help those who lost factory and manufacturing jobs learn skills and trades. It will be a place where those seeking to better themselves can go. This will be a house of opportunity for the people of Harmon. Ignorance is no excuse when the chance to educate yourself is within your grasp. Thank you, Mr. Graham, for helping move this project forward. We need you as our governor so you can bring opportunity to all the people of our state. Knowledge is power, and knowledge is my gift to this great town."

Rose Fayweather gets loud, enthusiastic applause. She hugs Theodore and returns to her seat.

"Thank you all so much for coming out today. I hope I answered the questions that were on the minds of the people and press. Please check out the campaign's website and feel free to talk to my staff. Check out the Fayweather Educational Project online and see how wonderful this opportunity is. If you like what you see, please vote for me. Thank you."

Theodore exits the stage to loud applause and cheers. He reaches into his pocket and pulls out his cell phone. He has felt it vibrate while he has been speaking. There is a text message from Gene.

Meet me at my office on campus at nine
tonight. We can talk then. Gene.

Chapter 40

Theodore walks across the youth honors college campus to the administration building. He is wearing a baseball cap, sandals, cargo shorts, and a Rolling Stones *Steel Wheels* concert tour shirt. There is a beer bottle sticking out of one of the pockets of his shorts and a manila envelope sticking out of another. He scans his faculty identification in the scanner at the main door of the admin building and heads inside. He walks down the hallway to the back of the building and sees Gene sitting in his office at his desk, reading a newspaper.

"Whazzzup, nigga!" Theodore says.

Gene is startled and jumps out of his seat. "Goddammit, Teddy! Why do you do that?"

"Well, if I give you a heart attack, there's a good chance I will win this election."

"Look at the polling numbers. I will beat you, dead, disabled, or alive."

"My speech today and my press conference this afternoon should help improve my numbers."

"Yeah, you might get a percentage or two, but did you have to point out my class ring in that picture? My press office is getting calls and asking if that is my hand in that picture of you with the bong. They are asking if I smoked marijuana."

"I covered for you. I didn't tell them you did. I know how baked you were that day, but I wasn't ratting you out."

"Thank God for small favors. But since you pointed the ring out, the press is asking the questions."

"It's their job to ask questions. What did you tell them? Did you lie?"

"I didn't answer yet. We have an early-morning meeting so we can figure it out. Your little stunt made quite a mess for my campaign."

"You're the one who went negative. We agreed privately we wouldn't go negative, and we said publicly we wouldn't go negative. You went back on your word. I had to hit back."

"We had to go negative after Delores mentioned the Claire Peterson affair."

"You didn't have to. You did because Russ Dewitt got put in his place by women from my campaign. They called him out on his false narrative."

"Why are you fighting me so hard? You aren't going to win this election. Why couldn't you just let it go?"

"I can't make it look like I rolled over and died on the Democrats. They put their hope and money behind me. I have to at least look like I give a shit."

"You could talk about your platform instead of attacking me."

"That's what we agreed to do, but you broke that agreement, remember?"

"I'm just listening to the advice of my staff."

"Did your staff tell you to ignore your friend? You wouldn't take my calls. You wouldn't answer my texts. I knocked on your door, and Issac turned me away when I knew damn well you were home. You didn't answer e-mail, and you wouldn't even *like* my Facebook statuses with cute kitten pictures."

"Russ thinks it would be best if we didn't talk to each other until after the election."

"I think Russ is afraid if you talk to me, I will undermine his authority. Why do you listen to him? I thought our friendship was stronger than this."

"Hey, how did you get in the building, anyway? It's after five. All the buildings are locked."

"Way to change the subject. I used my faculty ID."

"You don't work here anymore. You didn't turn your ID in?"

"Nobody asked me to."

"That means you still have full access to campus. You still have access to my campaign headquarters."

"Yeah, I guess I do. I don't go in there, though. That place always smells like mothballs and dog farts. For that, I blame Russ Dewitt mostly."

"Give me that ID right now."

Theodore reaches in his pocket, pulls out the ID card, and tosses it on Gene's desk. "There you go, buddy."

"I don't have all night, and I have a lot of work to do tomorrow because of your little speech this morning. Why are you here? What do you have that I should see?"

"I don't want to hold you up, so I will get right to it. When you were hitting my campaign with your negative attacks, my staff and my supporters wanted to hit you back. One of my supporters gave me this envelope. It contains things I could have leaked to the press and blended into my campaign rhetoric about you. The material is personal and would cut you deeply. I couldn't use it against you. Our friendship means more to me than the election."

"Well, aren't you the martyr?"

"Before your sarcasm and condescension changes my mind, have a look for yourself," Theodore says. He removes the manila envelope and throws it on the desk.

Gene grabs the envelope and begins to open it. "I can't wait to see what this is." He pulls out the pictures and looks them over. "Where did you get these?"

"I'm not telling you that, but I am giving them to you. As far as I know, they are the only copies."

"I hope to Christ they are. There are pictures of my son doing drugs. I'm not surprised he smokes marijuana, but cocaine? Did you know about this?"

"I had no idea until I saw these pictures."

"These nude pictures of Sandy are new. Who took them?"

"I don't know who the photographer is, but they are Sandy's current set of tits. I've seen them, I like them, and I remember what they look like during my special alone time."

"Teddy, this isn't funny. What's going on? Why are you doing this to me?"

"I'm not doing this. I was given this by a supporter to use against your campaign after you hit me so hard. I could have probably sunk your campaign with this. I could have sunk everything with this."

"Yeah. This would ruin me. It would ruin my son's future. It would ruin Sandy, and it would ruin all that I have. Why would you do this?"

"Again, I didn't do this. I'm not using it against you. I love you too much to hit you with this."

"What's this release form with Sandy's signature? It has a current date. How come the name of the people entering this contract with her are blacked out? She did the *Girls Gone Wild* years ago."

"Apparently, there is a director looking to make a sequel."

"What do you mean?"

"There's some video on that unmarked disc you should see. Do you have a DVD player in here?"

Gene picks up a remote and turns on the television. He grabs another remote and aims it at the DVD player and opens the disc carriage. He gets up and places the disc in the machine and returns to his desk. "Why isn't it playing?"

"I don't know. Do you have it on the right input setting?"

"Maybe I have to have it on channel 3."

"It's still not playing."

"Maybe it has to be on channel 4."

"It's a DVD player, not a VCR. Try pushing the Video Input button."

"Where's that button?"

Theodore stands up and looks over Gene's shoulder to see the remote. "Third row of buttons down from the top far left button. The one that says VIDEO."

Gene pushes the Video button, and the screen switches to Sandy on her knees in lingerie and performing oral sex on a man whose face can't be seen. "What the hell is this? That's my wife. What's she doing? That's not me."

"No shit. It's definitely not you. I saw you in the shower at the gym."

"This is no joke, Teddy. Is it you?"

"No! It's not me. I wish I were hung like that. I would never do that to you. The release form is her agreeing to do *Girls Gone Wild: The MILF Years*. I guess she wanted to try acting again."

"Is this real? Did somebody doctor a video and put my wife in it?"

"It's real. Look at it. You know what your wife looks like. It's her."

"I can't believe this. I can't believe you showed me this."

"It's better that I showed you personally rather than have you see it on the news."

Gene slumps his head onto his hands. "My son's a junkie. My wife's a whore. What am I going to do? What should I do?"

"It's not my place to tell you what to do. It's your family. You got to deal with it. I would rather you deal with it as a family without media scrutiny."

"Are there any more copies of this floating around out there?"

"As far as I know, no. There are definitely some of the original *Girls Gone Wild* videos out there, but it's hard to recognize Sandy in it. With all the plastic surgery, it's easy to deny it's her."

"Do I have to brief my staff on this in case somebody else puts it out there?"

"Don't embarrass yourself and lose the respect of your staff. I doubt this will surface."

"Does anybody on your staff know about this?"

"Delores knows about it, but she's the only one."

"Great. She'll get mad at Russ Dewitt again and leak it on television like she did with the whole Claire Peterson thing."

"She won't do that. She regrets mentioning the whole Claire affair. It hurt our campaign."

"What should I do, Teddy?" Gene pleads. "You have to help me."

"You got to figure this out yourself. Talk to your wife. Talk to your son. Don't do anything irrational. Maybe have Sandy demonstrate the oral skills she was applying in that video on you. It looks pretty intense."

"This isn't funny. This is my life, and it's crumbling around me."

"No, it's not funny. I'm sorry. I'm going to get going. You have a lot to think about, and you don't need me here," Theodore says. He pulls the beer bottle out of the pocket of his shorts. "You don't have another one of these I can grab for my walk back to Harmon?"

"You walked here?"

"I like to walk, and I hate my new car. Your last campaign manager paid the arsonist that torched my car. Since I lost my old Buick, I don't enjoy being a motorist."

"You walked over here with an open bottle of beer and the envelope containing the information that could destroy me in your pocket? Somebody could have mugged you and leaked this information to the press."

"Good thing I didn't get mugged. Do you have a beer I can take for the walk back? I would like a 'road soda' to keep my whistle wet."

"This is a school, not a bar."

"I just thought you might have a couple bottles of suds tucked away somewhere."

"There's a couple in the minifridge by the bookcase."

Theodore makes his way to the minifridge and opens the door and grabs a bottle of beer. "Do you mind if I take two? It's a two-mile walk. A beer per mile would be great."

"Yeah, take what you want."

Theodore takes a whole six-pack out of the minifridge. "I'm going to play some guitar tonight, and I'm almost out of beer at my apartment. Thanks, buddy."

"Did you just take all my beer?"

"Yes. You told me to take what I want."

"You come to my office, destroy my life with an envelope full of bad news, and you take all my beer."

"You want one? I'll give you one out of my six-pack."

"Just go, Teddy."

"I'm going now, but if you need to talk, you know my number. I know your campaign staff told you not to talk to me, but you have a lot on your plate. If you need a friend to talk to, call me."

"I'm sorry I ignored you."

"That's politics," Theodore says. "I'll see you on the campaign trail, old friend."

Theodore leaves the office with a five-pack of beer. Gene opens the beer that Theodore left behind for him and takes a sip. He looks at the pictures on his desk and throws the television remote at the wall.

CHAPTER 41

Theodore Graham Headquarters

Senior staff is assembled around the large conference table. They check e-mails and the social media while they wait for the meeting to begin. Theodore enters the conference room with boxes of doughnuts under his arm.

"Good morning, staff. I smell freshly brewed coffee. I brought a shitload of doughnuts for us to enjoy. The doughnuts are a small way of saying thank you to all of you. No matter what the polling numbers say, you all deserve thanks for your hard work. Everybody has worked hard, and I can't say thank you enough. Hopefully, these doughnuts convey a bit of my gratitude."

"Sophia White stopped by earlier and dropped off a couple plates of homemade chocolate chip cookies and brownies for this morning's meeting," Delores says.

"Fuck these doughnuts," Theodore says and tosses them on a table at the side of the room.

"Tim Collins is still getting the polling data. He's running late. He will be here in a little while."

Theodore takes his seat. "The waiting is the hardest part. I long for the days when candidates just ran for office on their beliefs, plans, and values and hoped for the best. The polling data wasn't as important. We wait for the quarterly polling because it's 'official,' but in the electronic age, there is monthly polling, weekly polling, daily polling, and hourly polling. Why? Do we need to check in that often to see how we're doing? Maybe we do. I see how often people check in on

Facebook to see if their friends 'like' and 'share' what they post. We're like insecure dogs constantly seeking approval and pats on the head."

"I don't know why there's so much polling, but we can see what voters are saying while we wait for Tim to get here with the official numbers," Pam Eynon says.

"Public opinion, the sometimes-unpleasant side effect of freedom of speech. Let's see what the people are saying."

"I looked at some of the public comments since you addressed the negative attacks. I was surprised to see how well you did. Embracing the attacks worked. I had my doubts, but you proved me wrong," Ed Reese says.

"I had my doubts too. So what's the public saying?"

Delores connects her laptop to a projector and turns it on. A public comments section from a political social media site appears on the big screen at the front of the room. "See for yourself. We're not doing too bad with the public."

Theodore and the other staff turn their attention to the screen.

> *I think Teddy Graham is crazy for turning his back on the millions he could have been making as a lobbyist lawyer. Because he did, I believe he is a man that practices what he preaches.*
>
> *Claire Peterson is a fool for putting her career ahead of starting a relationship with Teddy Graham. He's handsome, is smart, and has a good heart. Most women would kill to get a man that has a third of the qualities Teddy has.*
>
> *Theodore Graham is the man. Girls show their tits at his events. I used to have to go to NASCAR events to see that many breasts. Now I just have to follow local politics.*
>
> *I do not support Theodore Graham's nonchalant attitude toward marijuana use, but he's honest about it. Most candidates hide from who they really are. Mr. Graham embraces it. It's refreshing to see.*

I applaud Claire Peterson for getting out of her loveless marriage, where she wasn't respected. I need to do the same. Teddy Graham, please fuck me out of my misery.

I don't care what the media or the candidate himself says. Theodore Graham panders to women and minorities. I look at his campaign staff and can't tell if it's the line at the welfare office or It's a Small World in Disney World.

Why the hell would you leave a multimillion-dollar career in law because of your conscience? For that much money, he could afford to pay people to get offended for him.

Usually, candidates try to hide, deny, or spin the negative attacks levied on them. Theodore Graham addressed them and spoke honestly about them. He must have been high. I like his honesty.

Teddy got my vote. The guy is honest about himself, and the people around him say good things without being forced.

Sandy Douglas is hot, but Theodore Graham surrounds himself with hot women. His penis should write a book.

Theodore Graham is offering change. Fuck him! It's just more liberal policy that won't work and will cost the taxpayers a fortune. We're sick of paying for failed fairy tales.

People want things to change and things to get better. Theodore Graham is the guy who is offering a plan and not just promises. Put your money where your whiny mouths are, people. Vote for the change you want, or shut your mouth while the world around you gets shittier.

I wish I were as good with the ladies as Teddy Graham, but I have a feeling his governorship will look like a The Benny Hill Show *chase seen. How can he govern with all those good-looking women around him?*

Theodore Graham came clean and was honest about himself. Gene Douglas spent the last few months covering up the crooked path his campaign was following. The better choice should be obvious.

An honest politician? No fucking way! Mr. Graham, drop out of the race now before the ugly game of politics ruins you. The cesspool of corruption destroys good people. I don't want to see Mr. Graham become a victim.

Finally, a pot-smoking politician that is honest about smoking pot. Sadly, all the religious and Nancy Reagan, 'Just Say No' voters will keep him out of office. Just legalize it already.

Theodore Graham smokes pot now, but if we elect him governor, he will be shooting cocaine, snorting heroin, and smoking acid.

Please go back to teaching, Mr. Graham. Our youth need to learn from your mind now so they can build a better future tomorrow. With you as governor, they're only going to watch you turn into a greedy crook.

Delores turns off the projector. "That's some of the public commentary. Most of the feedback is positive. I'm sure our polling numbers improved."

"I'm glad other people see that I surrounded myself with hot women. That was my goal from the start. I didn't want a staff full of uggos."

"All this time, I thought the goal was to put a good platform together to serve the people. I didn't know you were building a harem. I don't know if I should be honored or offended," Nancy Bradford jokes.

"You should be honored. Did you notice that the men on my staff are pretty homely? That's intentional. They make me look better."

"I'm just as good-looking as you," Kevin Baker says.

"True, but you're good with the young voters. You help us recruit the young hotties."

"Claire Peterson came out and spoke on your behalf to prove you weren't a womanizing sexist. I think she would regret doing that if she heard this conversation," Pam says.

"I hope everybody knows I'm kidding. You should all know me by now, especially after all the great work we did together and the amazing campaign we put out."

"Haha, you said 'put out,'" Delores jokes.

"Delores, you made a sex joke. You are human."

"I can't believe I said that out loud. I've officially known Teddy Graham too long."

The conference room door opens, and Tim Collins walks in. "I'm sorry I'm later than I said I would be. Traffic in this town is terrible, but we now have the official polling numbers."

"How did we do?" Pam asks. "We just looked at some of the public commentary, and it was pretty good."

"The polling numbers seem to line up with what the public is saying. I think most of us will be pleased," Tim Collins says.

Tim hooks his laptop to the projector and presses a few buttons. A polling spreadsheet can be seen on the screen. "These numbers are a lot better than we expected."

"Are these numbers accurate?" Delores asks.

"They are the official election polling numbers. I hope they're accurate. We improved across all the demographics—up with seniors, up with the working class, up with minorities, up with young voters, and way up with women voters. Claire Peterson speaking on our behalf resonated. The biggest surprise was the gains with senior citizens. The welfare reform plan is the biggest reason, according to the surveys."

"Are we going to do what we set out to do?"

"I had to look at the numbers twice and then a third time. I didn't believe what I was reading. All the state assembly races we want to win, the numbers show those candidates winning. Some of them will win by double-digit percentages. There are also five seats we didn't expect to win that are now competitive. We have a chance at picking up those seats. Some of those candidates are up by a percentage point or two, and some are within the margin of error."

"This is great news. These numbers are awesome! What about the overall for the governor's race?" Delores asks.

Tim switches the page on the big screen. "Here's the overall. Gene Douglas leads us 50 percent to 48 percent. There is a 2 percent margin of error. Teddy, you are technically able to win this thing."

"Shit!"

"You would have to cover the entire margin of error to reach the 50 percent mark. It would then become the difference of a few thousand or few hundred votes."

"What's the plan from here?"

"We tout our platform at our events. We highlight the parts of our platform that appeal to the crowds we are speaking to, and we take it to Gene Douglas in the debate," Delores says.

"We didn't even discuss a lieutenant governor to run on the ticket with us. We have to officially announce at the debate so their name can go on the ballot," Ed Reese says.

"We're not supposed to win, so I don't want to raise hopes, but I think Nancy Bradford is the one we should name. Her work with community leaders and professional organizations to get towns to rebuild their local economies is the centerpiece of our platform. I would be willing to put anybody from this staff on the ticket with me, but I think Nancy is the best fit for what we want to accomplish."

"I was going to suggest Nathan Winters, because if Teddy weren't running for us, Nathan would be. I do agree with Teddy, though. Nancy's plans, her connections to business leaders, and her leadership ability are the best fit," Pam says.

"It's not about taking turns. It's about doing what's right for the state. I don't mind being passed over for Nancy," Nathan says.

"You're not being passed over, Nathan. If, for some fucked-up reason, I end up winning this shit show, I would want you leading the budget office. You're pretty handy with the numbers."

"I would gladly accept that position."

"We didn't even ask Nancy if she would be interested," Delores says.

"I'm not sure what to say. We never expected to win this thing. Now there's a chance. Can I have some time to put some serious thought into this?"

"Take all the time you need, but hurry the fuck up. We only have until debate night."

"We have a lot to think about, but we also have a lot of work to do. We have events to attend, speeches to write, and a platform to present. It only gets worse next week. We will be here for some late nights doing debate prep. Put your lives on hold for a bit. Teddy, I need to go over the schedule with you. Everybody, great job on the polling numbers and keep doing the good work you're doing. I will text all of you with the information for our next meeting," Delores says, concluding the meeting.

Gene Douglas Headquarters

The Gene Douglas campaign staff sits in their meeting room. They sit silently, stunned as they examine the latest polling numbers. Staffers are jotting notes, thinking of strategies, and starting to feel a little panic.

"Are these the real polling numbers? How can this be? Teddy Graham can actually win this race," Gene says.

"Unfortunately, they are," Marty Price says.

"Mother fuck! How did this race get this close?"

"Teddy's counter punches to the negative attacks landed, and they hurt. I wanted to hit him with some negatives again, but you wouldn't let me," Russ says.

"We're not going negative again."

"We put some major distance between you and Teddy when we attacked him. If we hit him again and make it stick, he's not going to have time to hit us back," Russ says.

"We're not going negative again!"

"Why the hell not? You see the numbers. We have to do something."

"Teddy could have punched back a lot harder than he did, but he didn't. He could have raised the whole Dick Ratzinger thing and played up the victim role of the arson attempt. He could have thrown Mort Whitney in our faces. We are still funding our campaign and super PAC with Whitney money. Mort is facing jail time for corruption and fraud charges."

"That's the beauty of it. Teddy agreed to be the good guy and publicly said he would not go negative. If he goes negative when we punch him again, we can call him out on his hypocrisy."

"We're not going negative! Think of something else."

"I don't get you, Gene. Do you want to win or not?"

"I want to win, but not like that. If Teddy hits me with what he can hit me with, I stand to lose a lot more than an election. He can damage my family and good family name if he wants to."

"Speaking of your family, where's Ernie?

"He went up to Mirror Lake on a retreat. He will be up there for a while."

"My sister-in-law went to Mirror Lake for drug rehab a few years ago. She's doing pretty well now. What kind of retreat is Ernie up there . . . oh, I get you. Never mind," Marty says.

"What do you mean? That's great news. Ernie is in drug rehab. We can say he is there because he hung around Teddy too much," Russ says.

"Russ, you have thirty seconds to apologize for that statement, or I'm firing you. I don't give a shit if I have to find a fourth campaign manager."

"I'm sorry, Gene, but we can use that to our advantage."

"I wasn't kidding about firing you. Try that apology again."

"I'm sorry, Gene. We won't use Ernie's rehab."

"That's better. Ernie's whereabouts don't leave this room. Is that clear to everybody?" Gene asks and looks around the room and sees his staff in agreement.

"We'll think of something, Gene. We will keep hitting him on the taxes, minorities, and his lack of family values. We can showcase you and Sandy for your family values stance."

"We're going to have to limit my wife's appearances. She doesn't want to be in the spotlight."

"Are you kidding me? Sandy had all that plastic surgery because she loves the attention and spotlight. Is she in rehab too?"

"No, she's not in rehab. I just want to limit her exposure and only have her make the photo op appearances we need to."

"What's going on, Gene? Is there problems at home? Is there something we should know about?"

"What you don't know could fill a fucking book!" Gene says and gets up to leave the room. "I'll be in my office a while. I don't want to be disturbed. I'll be ready for the speech at the VFW later."

"What got into him? He's miserable," Russ says to the remaining staff in the room.

"I don't know, Russ, but if I were you, I would stop pressing his buttons. Something is obviously going on at home. You best let that alone and start getting this campaign ready for the debate," Marty says.

"He better cheer the hell up. Nobody is going to elect a grouch to be their governor."

"Maybe we can try that, Russ. We can liken him to Oscar the Grouch. Oscar the Grouch looks like a nugget of weed. People like weed," Marty jokes.

CHAPTER 42

Theodore and Delores are in one of the green rooms at Channel 6 studios. Delores is quizzing Theodore on platform details as Theodore paces around the room. He is getting the answers right but appears nervous.

"Teddy, you got this. You know the answers. You know the platform. You speak well. Don't be nervous. You are ready."

"I just don't want to fuck up."

"Being a fuck-up is your thing. Own it. You are the guy who fucked his way up to being a gubernatorial campaign."

"Is that a compliment?"

"You're the most brilliant fuck-up I know."

"You saying the f-word is unsettling."

"I've gotten pretty good at cursing since I started working with you."

"I would think working with the teenagers at the youth college would have made you a seasoned swearer, but it took me to get you cursing."

"The students have an excuse for their behavior. They're teenagers. You're a grown man."

"Wouldn't it be neat if I were retarded and won this election and then, in my acceptance speech, I let the people know they elected a retard?"

"I hate that word, but it will be a story come true if you win this thing."

"Are you one of those women that hate the word *moist*?"

"I never had a problem with *moist*."

"It's a recent trend I just learned of. *Moist* makes some people, mostly women, wince. I never had a problem with it until I learned it bothered some people. When I heard the word *moist* in the past, I thought of cake. Now when I hear it, I think of vaginas."

"I might have just started to have a problem with the word *moist.*"

"Haha, I got you to think about vaginas."

"You may have ruined cake for me too."

There is a knock on the green room door. A cheerful young man enters the room. "Hello, I'm Stanley, one of the debate coordinators. You will be going on in a few minutes. I'm here to give you the rundown of how the debate is going to go and answer any last-minute questions that you may have."

"Sounds good. Lay it on us. Give us the plan, Stan."

"You will be waiting on the left wing of the stage. Mr. Douglas will be doing the same on the right. There is a monitor there where you can watch what's going on until you get introduced. A stagehand will let you know when you are introduced and when to go on stage to take your place behind your podium. You will meet Mr. Douglas in the middle to shake hands. You with me so far?"

"So far, so good."

"Great. When the ON-AIR light comes on, you will see the camera shots panning over the studio audience. After that, Walter Carl will introduce the other moderators, Grace Downwood and Brad Utes. He will then introduce Mr. Douglas, and he will go to his podium. He will do the same for you. Walter will explain the debate rules, and the debate will begin. At the end of the debate, Walter will wrap it up and thank everybody. A stagehand will send your family out onstage to be with you for the last two minutes of the broadcast. All of you can shake hands and make small talk as the credits roll. Your microphones will be shut off at the end of the debate, and the applauding audience will be the only thing heard on the air. That's about it. Do you have any questions?"

"What do you think about the word *moist*?"

"It makes me think about chocolate cake."

"I used to be the same way, but now it makes me think about vaginas."

"All right. Somebody will be in to take you to the stage wing in a few minutes," Stanley says and leaves the room.

Delores stands in front of Theodore and looks him over. She straightens his collar and his tie and pulls his suit jacket down to make it firm.

"You are ready, Teddy. You are going to be great."

"I'll do what I can."

"What's wrong?"

"It's how this thing ends. The debate will be over, and Sandy and Ernie Douglas will make their way out onstage to stand with Gene. I have nobody coming out to stand with me. It just kind of hit me. I have nobody to stand with me. I'm a loner."

"Sandy Douglas is a cheating, phony slut. Ernie is a spoiled, rich-kid cocaine addict. They are phony, hollow people."

"Phony or not, at least it looks like he has people that stand by him. He has the optics."

"Don't get hung up on unimportant details now. I have all the faith in the world in you." Delores pulls Theodore close to her. She kisses him on the lips.

"I hate pretending to hate you."

"Don't fall apart on me now, Delores. You have to hate me. I will, however, take another one of your hateful kisses. They are pretty sweet."

"I hate that I enjoy kissing you, Theodore Graham."

"I like that I enjoy kissing you. Too bad I have to go onstage soon. We don't have enough time for hot, naked action."

"Thank God for small favors."

There is a knock on the door. "We need you on the stage wing, Mr. Graham."

"Make our team proud," Delores says and gives Theodore a peck on the cheek. Theodore leaves the room and follows a stagehand to the wing of the stage and waits for the debate to begin.

The camera pans through the studio audience as the broadcast begins. It moves through the crowd to the stage, where the debate moderators are seated. The focus is on the three of them and then on the debate moderator and host, Walter Carl.

"Good evening and welcome to our gubernatorial debate. I'm Walter Carl, host and moderator of this evening's discourse between our great state's candidates. Tonight, we will hear from our state's Republican and Democratic candidates seeking the office of governor. We will have the opportunity to get to know the candidates a little bit better. We will learn of their strategies to move our state forward. We will also learn the candidate's choices for lieutenant governor. We will hear from those running mate choices a week from tonight in the lieutenant governors' debate. Joining me as moderators for tonight's debate are Grace Downwood of Channel 6 News and local political analyst Brad Utes. Let me now introduce you to our gubernatorial candidates."

Walter Carl pauses while the studio audience applauds.

"For the Republicans, we have a member of the founding family and controller of the nationally acclaimed Douglas Youth Honors College, the owner of the Douglas Community College, the operator of the Douglas publishing company, and former town council president of Douglas Hills. Please welcome Mr. Eugene Douglas."

Gene comes onto the stage from the wing. He smiles and waves to the applauding crowd. He takes his mark at the center of the stage.

"For the Democrats, we have a lawyer, an educator, and the debate coach that took the Douglas Youth Honors College debate team to win the national debate championship. He now serves as managing editor, feature writer, and an editorial columnist for the newly revamped, *Weekly Beat*. Please welcome Mr. Theodore Graham."

Theodore enters the stage area and waves to the studio audience as he makes his way to center stage. The crowd applauds. Theodore and Gene shake hands and take their places behind their podiums.

"Welcome, gentlemen. I just want to go over some of the rules for tonight's event. We will start off, and each of you will get a chance to tell the people why you want to run for governor. After your introductory statement, you will be asked questions by our moderators. Each of you will have the chance to offer a brief rebuttal. We ask the candidates to do their best not to talk over the moderators or each other, and we ask our studio audience to keep their reactions brief so we can keep this debate moving along. Mr. Douglas, we will start with you. Why do you want to be governor of our great state?"

"I'm a native of this state. I was born and raised here. My family planted roots and committed themselves to giving to the community around them. My family built an educational foundation to provide future generations with a quality education. I've been successful as an educator, an entrepreneur, and a leader. I want to be governor so I can share my skills and bring success to the people of our great state. As governor, I want to help the people achieve the luxury of limitless prosperity."

"Thank you, Mr. Douglas. Mr. Graham, same question. Why do you want to be governor of our great state?"

"Originally, it was to pick up women, but if you look at my staff, I did all right. I'm not native to this state, and I don't come from an area where every building around me has the same last name as I do. I came to this state to be an educator. I got to know the small towns, countryside, and cities. I took some time to enjoy all this state had to offer and take in the beauty within it. Most importantly, I got to know the people here. The people here helped me call this great state home. There are brilliant minds, hard workers, folks with kind hearts, and people who always work to make tomorrow a better day. I listened to the people. I heard their concerns. I listened to their dreams. I share their hopes. This great state is full of wonderful and amazing people. I want to be governor so I can serve the people I had the privilege of getting to know. I want to see the friends I made during this campaign live successful lives. I want to see the people around me have opportunities. I want those people to have hope for the future. I want to work alongside those hard workers and carve out a better tomorrow. I want to lay a foundation so future generations can continue to build better futures for their future generations."

Walter Carl waits for the applause to calm. "Now, let's turn it over to some questions from our moderators."

"Mr. Douglas, your fiscal and economic platform and your opponent's are very different. Can you tell us why yours is better for our state?" Grace Downwood asks.

"My opponent has a very ambitious economic platform. It's very complex, and it depends too much on things that are unlikely to work. My economic platform follows one of my core beliefs, keeping it simple. My plan calls for managing the state budget, eliminating waste, cutting red tape, reducing the size and reach of government. A better-managed budget will keep taxes low. Low taxes will attract business and industry to our state. More business and industry will bring more jobs. More jobs bring down unemployment, and lower unemployment makes the people of our state prosperous."

"Mr. Graham, do you have a rebuttal? Would you like to talk about your economic plan?"

"My opponent's plan may be simple, but it's not a new plan. It's a plan that's been in place for nearly forty years. It's been offered by many politicians before, and it hasn't been successful. The red tape is still there. The waste keeps piling up. The size and reach of government hasn't changed—it's grown, in fact. Industry hasn't come. Taxes continue to go up, and our state is operating on a deficit budget. It's a simple plan that simply hasn't worked. My opponent is proposing a plan that citizens are tired of waiting for. My campaign staff looked at our communities. We looked into programs that are improving communities. We looked at business organizations and listened to business leaders that are community-minded. We listened to what the people need, and we came up with a plan that is different. Our state was better off when we had strong local economies supported by strong local business and industries staffed by local people. Tax incentives for national corporations that don't invest in our communities end up costing our communities. Incentives for communities bring communities together to find success. My opponent says my plan is complex and depends on too many things that won't work. Well, history is on my side. When there were strong local economies, people did better. History, in recent decades, has shown that trickle-down economic plans haven't worked. It's up to the people, though. Do they want to keep doing something that fails, or do they want to try a different approach and embrace change for the better? It's the voters' choice."

"Mr. Graham, you have been an employee of your opponent. You were a teacher and a debate coach at his school. You were his former campaign manager. How can the voters believe your candidacy is legitimate and not just a way of getting back at your former boss?" Brad Utes asks.

"I have been friends with Gene Douglas since freshman orientation at college. Our friendship, I wouldn't trade for the world. Gene Douglas is one of the great people of our state. I liked working for him. I liked teaching. I liked coaching. I liked publishing through his publishing house. I liked running his campaign. It was obvious that our politics differed when I was running his campaign. He chose to let me go. I was happy to make a clean break and move on. Sherman Jones passed away, and there was an open spot in this gubernatorial race. People in the Democratic Party with similar political beliefs followed my career. They asked me to fill this open spot. I didn't want to run against my friend, but I wanted to see the people around me succeed and have better opportunities. This was my chance to bring different ideas to life. I feared, if I didn't run, I would live to regret not trying. My campaign isn't about revenge. My campaign is about change. I'm offering a new plan to the voters. If they like it and want to get on board, I ask them to vote for me."

"Mr. Douglas, any rebuttal?"

"My friendship with Mr. Graham, I wouldn't change for the world. I never expected him to run for governor against me, but having him as my opponent has made me a better candidate. I had to let him go from my campaign because of our political differences. His plans for my campaign would have been disastrous for the people of our state. I want to win with a good plan and not lose with a bad one."

"Mr. Douglas, at the start of your campaign, Tim Collins was on your staff. Kevin Baker was in charge of the Young Republicans. Professional Women of Power was backing your campaign. All three of them are now backing the Theodore Graham campaign. According to recent polling, you lost a lot of support that traditionally voted Republican. How can you explain this shift?" Grace Downwood asks.

"There was some controversy that surrounded my campaign because of some of my financial backers. I lost some support because I made some bad decisions. Do I regret some of the losses? Yes, of course I do. Would I like to have their support back and have them working with me? Definitely. My door is open to all voters of this state. I hold no hard feelings. When I win this election, I hope I will be able to work with all these people and organizations and hear their ideas and concerns."

"Mr. Graham, any rebuttal?"

"The controversy surrounding my opponent's campaign was unfortunate. I hated seeing my friend being so controlled by corrupt actors and hurting his credibility by associating with them. As for the support he lost and I gained, I like to think it is because people believe I will listen to their voices and hear their ideas. Those voices and ideas were what my campaign staff used to develop our platform. I have their support because they can hear their words in my proposals, see their dreams being built into my plans of action, and believe I will do what's best for our home state."

"Mr. Graham, you've been photographed using marijuana on different occasions. You've voiced your opinion for the legalization of recreational marijuana use. What message does that send to people fighting the heroin epidemic in our state? What does that say to our emergency responders who are battling increasing instances of meth-amphetamine labs and street drug manufacturing?" Brad Utes asks.

"First, I would start by comparing apples to apples. Marijuana is not meth or heroin. The science for all three is out there. Meth destroys a body. Heroin destroys lives and families. Marijuana has been scientifically proven to be safer than legal alcohol and tobacco. I'm not advocating for mandatory marijuana use—I'll let the people make their own choices—but I want them to be informed when they do so. The heroin epidemic and methamphetamine problems are directly related to economics. I believe the problems increase as trickle-down economics continues to fail."

"Mr. Douglas, any rebuttal?"

"Drugs are a problem that are tearing our communities apart. I don't understand my opponent's nonchalant attitude toward drug use. When I'm elected, I will make sure that law enforcement, emergency responders, and medical professionals have all the resources they need to fight our drug crisis."

"How are you going to fund those resources with a trickle-down economics plan? You said you wanted to reduce government spending and red tape. How are you going to lower taxes and increase funding and resources to fight a failing war on drugs? Are you going to overcrowd our prisons at the taxpayers' expense? How much is your drug plan going to cost taxpayers? How much success will it have?" Theodore asks.

"The safety of the citizens of this state is my number one priority."

"That's my number one priority too. If marijuana is scientifically proven to be safer than alcohol and tobacco, why not legalize it, tax it, and use proceeds from legal marijuana to intelligently battle the problem of harmful drugs? You have to find ways to pay for your plans. My platform has done that by proposing legal marijuana use. Proceeds from marijuana can fight the battle with harmful drugs, be invested in education, be invested in communities, be invested in infrastructure, and to properly fund law enforcement and emergency responders that are tasked with the safety of our citizens. That's what you said your number one priority is. Do you fund your number one priority with your plan?"

"Mr. Douglas, your platform talks about tax incentives for business and industry. What incentives are you offering? What businesses are interested in operating in our state if there is enough tax incentive to do so? Would you require those industries to headquarter in our state?" Grace Downwood asks.

"My first priority is jobs for the people. These tax incentives bring industries that bring jobs. There have been a couple of mining and timber industries that have expressed an interest in operating in our state. There are some natural gas pockets the fracking industry is interested in. There is a company proposing to reopen some of the old oil fields and use modern technologies to clean unusable oil and make it usable. There are some major retailers interested in building warehouses in our state. I'm happy to give incentives and tax exemptions for job creators in our state. I think those industries would give up on doing business here and go elsewhere if we are going to dictate where their corporate headquarters have to be."

"Mr. Graham, your rebuttal?"

"I'm just wondering if there is a difference between your number one priority and you first priority. Anyway, mining, timber, refurbished oil—these are all dying industries. Modern technology has diminished the need for these industries. Solar, wind, hydroelectricity, and geothermal limited the need for fossil fuel and unrenewable resources. New technologies for the same purpose are cheaper, are cleaner, are more efficient, and hurt less of our natural resources. Fracking doesn't have solid science behind it that says gas extraction can be done safely without polluting groundwater. Why give tax incentive to dying industries that pollute? Retailers build warehouses to reduce their transportation costs. Why give tax incentives and make taxpayers pay for infrastructure improvements so out-of-state corporations can save money? I want to save our own in-state corporations money. If these companies don't want to fully commit to our state, our state shouldn't commit to giving them tax breaks. Our state budget is operating in a deficit because of this type of economics. Companies got tax incentives, and the state got nothing in return. The taxpayers now have to pay for this budget gap. When the state gives a tax incentive, it's making an investment. A smartly run business looks for a good return on investment. Gene, you invested in me with your schools, I gave you a great return on your investment. Look how your business improved when I came on board. The state should operate the same way. I'm not opposed to tax exemptions and incentives, but there has to be a return on those investments. We can't simply give money away to our corporate buddies at the taxpayers' expense."

"We're running out of time for this evening's debate. We've heard some highlights of both campaign platforms and had the candidates elaborate on their positions. It's now time for the candidates to announce their running mates who will serve as their lieutenant governors. We will have the chance to get to know these people in the media in the coming days, and we will hear them debate right here next week. Let's start with Gene Douglas. Whom have you chosen as your running mate?" Walter Carl asks.

"There were a lot of qualified running mates, but I had to choose the one who best suited my platform and shared my values. I chose a person with experience and a proven track record. My running mate has served six terms in the state House of Representatives. He chaired the budget committee during his last term and submitted three balanced budgets. My running mate is Representative Albert Wood," Gene says to applause.

"Mr. Graham, whom have you chosen as your running mate?" Walter Carl asks.

"I would be willing to have any member of my staff as a running mate, but I chose the one whose work has become the centerpiece of my economic platform. This woman has proven that community revitalization can be achieved and prosperity can be brought back to struggling towns. It was her belief in improving local economies that inspired her to form Professional Women of Power. Her organization merges communities with businesses to create opportunities. Her track record of success is proven, and having her as my running mate will bring that success on a statewide level. My running mate is Nancy Bradford!" Theodore says to applause.

"Thank you, candidates. With the time we have remaining, we will give both candidates the opportunity to make closing statements. Since we let Mr. Douglas make his introduction first, we will let Mr. Graham go first with his closing statements. Mr. Graham?"

"My campaign doesn't stem from my personal aspirations to be governor. It stems from listening to the people around me. My plans are made with the wants of the people in mind. I've incorporated new ideas and new approaches because doing the same thing over and over isn't working. To make things better, change is required. I want to do differently to make tomorrow a better chapter in the history of this state. It's going to take work. It's going to require coming together as people and as a proud state. I am going to do the work to bring us together so we can all have the opportunity to prosper. If you believe that we can make the future better, please vote for me on Election Day. Thank you!"

"Mr. Douglas, your closing statement."

"I've run successful schools and a successful publishing house. I served on a town council that has always turned in a balanced surplus budget. I have proven myself to be a fiscally responsible conservative. I believe lower taxes and less government will bring our state prosperity. That prosperity will be shared by the great people of our great state. Vote for me on Election Day so I can use my proven ability to serve the interests of the people. Thank you.

"That's all the time we have. On Sunday, there is a special edition of *State of the State This Week* with both candidates and their running mates. It is your chance to learn more about the people in our gubernatorial race. Before we go, I want to say thank you. Thank you, candidates. Thank you, fellow moderators. Thank you, studio audience, and thank you, viewers at home, for tuning in. Goodnight and pleasant tomorrow!" Walter Carl concludes the program.

Gene and Theodore shake hands. Sandy and Ernie Douglas come onstage, greet Theodore, and stand with Gene to pose for the photo opportunities. Delores Daniels, Sophia White, and the Douglas Youth Honor's College debate team greet Theodore onstage. Theodore hugs Sophia and high-fives and hugs members of the debate team he took to the national championship. Ernie Douglas crosses the stage to be with his former debate teammates.

Delores hugs Theodore and whispers in his ear, "I know these aren't blood relatives, but this is as close to family as I could get on such short notice. You're loved by all these people."

Delores gives Theodore a peck on the cheek. His eyes glaze over as he holds back happy tears. He is deeply touched by the love he feels from those surrounding him.

CHAPTER 43

Theodore and Nancy Bradford wait to do their appearance on *State of the State This Week* in one of the green rooms of the Channel 6 studios. Nancy paces around the room as Theodore reads the Sunday paper.

"Nancy, you have to relax. You will be fine, and you will do a good show. You are well-spoken. Don't worry about Albert Wood."

"I'm only a little worried about Albert Wood. Last time our campaign was on this show, one of your sexploits was mentioned and we got shelled with negative press. I just don't want that to happen again."

"I'm not planning on mentioning one of my sexual adventures. Are you?"

"I'm not planning on mentioning one either, but Gene knows about our little stint in the hospitality suite when he spoke to Professional Women of Power."

"He won't bring it up. Gene's not like that, and he knows I can hit him with some unsavory things. Just focus on our platform and talk about the successes of your group."

"You don't have a low opinion of me because of my behavior that night, do you?"

"Seriously? I chose you to be my lieutenant governor if I win this thing. That night, there was a connection and a physical attraction between us. We acted on it. It was great. Your work is what earned my respect and admiration."

"I didn't know what came over me that night until I heard Claire Peterson talk about your affair with her. You made me feel appreciated for my work, for my mind, for my personality, and for my body. I was intentionally a bitch to you, yet you broke through my defense mechanism."

"That's what it's all about for me, bitches and hoes."

"I guess I am both. I was a bitch, and I threw myself at you like a whore."

"You were more like a slut. Whores charge money. You did it for free."

"You're welcome. I think."

"If you were a lawyer, you could consider it 'pro boner' work."

"I still don't understand how you might become governor of our state."

"I don't get it either. I'm still waiting to wake up and realize all this is a dream."

"How come you never settled down?"

"A therapist would say my commitment issue is because I saw how much pain my mother's unexpected death caused my father and I didn't want to live with the same pain. I believe it's because I just haven't found the right one."

"Is there a right one for you?"

"So far, I haven't found one, but I am still conducting tryouts. Are you interested in a follow-up interview?"

"I'm not going to say no, but the work we are doing means more to me than another roll in the hay with you."

"We are doing great work. I'm proud to have you on my team. How come you haven't settled down?"

"I'm childless and divorced twice. Being an independent, smart, and powerful woman intimidated both of my husbands. Those tough-guy biker types I was attracted to turned out to be a bunch of pussies. Now, I'm reaching the bitter phase of my life."

"I wish I had some relationship advice to give, but look at my behavior and track record. It's not my wheelhouse."

There's a knock on the green room door. "Mr. Graham, Mrs. Bradford, we're going to need you to take your positions on set now."

"Let's do this. Just stick to the platform and talk up your work," Theodore says as they leave the green room.

"What are you going to talk about?"

"Sports bras. I'm not sure if I like them or not. I've been both turned on and turned off by them. I think that will be a useful discussion."

"That is an issue on the minds of many voters. I'm almost sure of it," Nancy says as they get on set.

Theodore and Nancy greet Gene and Albert onstage. The host, Walter Carl, and journalist Joan Mowrey come on set and greet the guests. Stagehands get everyone's microphones in place and do a sound check. The set director gives the signal for "one minute to air."

"Good Sunday morning to you and welcome to *State of the State This Week*. I'm your host, Walter Carl. Joining me today are gubernatorial candidates Eugene Douglas and Theodore Graham. With them are their running mates, Nancy Bradford of the Theodore Graham campaign and Representative Albert Wood of the Douglas campaign. Our journalist on the panel today is Joan Mowrey of the *Harmon Herald* and *Morning Sun Gazette*. Welcome to the show. We have a lot to talk about today," Walter Carl says and leads into the opening music of the show.

The theme music ends, and Walter Carl begins the show.

"Gene Douglas, you are leading in polls by a small percentage, how do you think your numbers did after the debate?"

"It was a good debate. The voters had the chance to see the difference in the platforms, and they can see clearly how costly my opponent's plans would be for the state."

"Mr. Graham, what did you think of the debate?"

"I had a lot fun at the debate. You, Brad, and Grace did a great job. Gene and I didn't kill each other. I'm not sure how the polling numbers changed. I hope I made some gains. One of things I noticed after the debate was the increased activity on our website and people calling our headquarters with questions about how to get involved in some of our initiatives. It's great to see the voters educating themselves on the issues and getting active. My plans are new to the voters, so they are getting informed. Most of them already know how trickle-down platforms have failed the state for the last few decades."

"Before we talk to your running mates, tell us why you chose the people you did. Gene, why did you choose Albert?"

"Albert's record speaks for itself. He's an experienced legislator and knows how our state assembly functions. He chaired the budget committee and passed balanced budgets. His experience is going to be a great asset. I chose Albert because he works hard for the people and knows how to get things done."

"Mr. Graham, how come you picked Nancy?"

"When I moved to this state, the newspapers were full of articles about lost jobs, vacant storefronts, empty strip malls, abandoned industrial sites, bankrupt towns, and blighted communities. No matter how much worse those problems became, government wasn't addressing the issues. I read an article about this Professional Women of Power organization trying to revitalize communities. The article captured my interest, and I wanted to know more. I went to their website. The new ideas for improvement made a lot of sense. I remember thinking how much more successful Professional Women of Power could be if they had the backing of our state government. When I found myself running for governor, picking Nancy Bradford to help me move this state forward was an obvious choice. She knows how to rebuild communities and get things done. She's a doer."

"Now, let's meet these lieutenant governor candidates. Albert Woods, what do you bring to the Douglas campaign?"

"I bring experience. I know how our state works. I know how to get a bipartisan budget passed. When Gene asked me to be his running mate, I was honored. Gene shares the same conservative values I do. We both want to reduce taxes, reduce wasted money, reduce the size of government, and bring back prosperity to our state."

"Nancy Bradford, what do you bring to the Graham campaign?"

"It's not what I bring to the campaign, it's what I want to bring to the state. People are tired of watching their communities die. People are tired of waiting for politicians to deliver on their promises of prosperity. I got tired of going to elected leaders with ideas only to be talked down to, dismissed, or ignored. The politicians that didn't do anything about the problems facing their communities are the reason I formed Professional Women of Power. We took action where politicians have failed. When we win this election, we can apply better resources to rejuvenate communities, develop small businesses, create jobs, and build strong local economies. Strong economies diminish poverty and some of the side effects that go with it."

"Isn't your organization, Professional Women of Power, only made up of women who feel they aren't getting the recognition they want in the real workforce?" Joan Mowrey asks.

"I hear that criticism about our organization from people who are ignorant of it. I'm not sure what you mean by 'the real workforce.' If you look at the members of our group, you will see it is made of successful entrepreneurs, CEOs, millionaires, developers, inventors, lawyers, accountants, and doctors. All these are respected professions in the 'real workforce.' Our members are recognized in their professions. Many have won awards and high honors in their fields. I don't know how it is where you work, Joan, but I know you have won awards and recognition for your writing. How come you haven't been promoted to a managing editor? You worked for the *New York Times*. How come your experience doesn't get the recognition it deserves? You write for three newspapers. With your background, you should be running them. Who's holding you back? Is it men in power who talk down to you and dismiss your ideas?"

"This isn't about me. This is about your organization. Isn't it a private women's club that wants a pat on the back?"

"Professional Women of Power became a women's group because when I was looking to form a community-revitalization group, the only ones that showed up for the meetings were women. They were women who wanted to make better towns to do business in, better towns for their children, and towns with more opportunities for its residents. Joan, if you want to know more about my organization, join me this week. The organization is a well-managed machine. We have a management structure. We have an infrastructure. We have a research and development branch. We have a media relations, advertising, and promotions department. We have a community education and outreach staff. Come out with me this week. I will be visiting some of our successful projects. I will be checking up on the progress of projects already underway. I am meeting with community leaders that like what we did and want to know if we can bring the same success to their communities. I will also be touring some vacant industrial properties and brainstorming with some business leaders to bring life and jobs back to those facilities. If you want to know more about my organization, come out with me and get informed about us instead of speculating and assuming. We can use your talents and insights, Joan. You're a brilliant woman. I would love for you to see what we do and have you join us."

"I didn't realize I was so highly respected by you. I may just set that up."

"Please do, Joan. We need smart women like you. We may even pick your brain," Nancy says.

"I've served six terms in the House. I've seen hundreds of organizations like Professional Women of Power come and go. They come with grand ideas and they go because they fail, but before they fail, they cost the taxpayers a ton of money," Albert Wood says.

"Name one," Theodore says.

"I can't name one off the top of my head," Albert says.

"You said you've seen hundreds. I just thought you would be able to remember at least one."

"Well, Mr. Graham, I don't remember their names, but I have worked on the budgets and I saw all the waste those programs have caused."

"You served in the House for six terms. In your sixth term, you chaired the budget committee. Didn't you lose your last election because your budget cut four billion from education and two billion from Emergency Responder Services programs?" Theodore asks.

"The budget committee had to make tough choices. Unfortunately, some cuts had to be made."

"I guess you were in a tough spot. I remember Joan's article about the cuts in the budget from education and emergency services. The cuts coincidentally totaled the same amount as the subsidies given to out-of-state companies as incentive to develop and create jobs here. That was a very good article, Joan."

"Thank you, Mr. Graham. I remember writing that one very well."

"You should republish it for your paper's website. It might give the voters some more information to be better informed when they go to the polls."

"Mr. Graham mentioned education. Public education is underfunded in many districts across our state. Gene, you're an educator and the owner and operator of a nationally renowned youth honors college. What will you bring to the state with your experience? How does your platform address education's financial struggles in our state?" Walter Carl asks.

"It's all budget management. Once we eliminate some of the redundancy, waste, and poorly spent money, we can invest in education."

"You've mentioned cutting some of the redundancy and waste in your platform, but you haven't been specific. Can you tell us some of the things you would cut?" Joan Mowery asks.

"We got to cut costly programs that hurt the state. The platform of my opponent, Mr. Graham, is entirely made up of programs that will cost the taxpayers a fortune."

"Gene, you accuse our campaign of promoting costly programs, but if you go to our website, you can see how the cost of our programs are covered. I went to your website, and I can't find specifics. Are you going to cut subsidies to companies like Morton Whitney's who try to purchase government? Are you going to cut tax incentives to out-of-state companies? I look at your plan and wonder, How long will it take you to fix the budget so companies can come here and create jobs? How long will it take you to eliminate redundancy? How long will the people have to wait for your platform to be successful? How long will it be until people see results?" Nancy Bradford asks.

"I had great results with my schools and publishing house. I had good results with Douglas Hills when I sat on the town council. We passed surplus budgets."

"Douglas Hills always passes surplus budgets. The majority of Douglas Hills is your for-profit private school that has nonprofit status and doesn't pay taxes. Douglas Hills was partially annexed by Harmon, so Harmon does trash pickup, road maintenance, snow-plowing and takes care of the parks in Douglas Hills. How come taxes collected in Douglas Hills don't go to Harmon but taxes collected in Harmon go to Douglas Hills? No wonder it's a surplus budget. The results with your schools weren't really that great until you hired people like Delores Daniels and Theodore Graham. Your publishing house was in bankruptcy protection until Mr. Graham and Claire Peterson started publishing there."

"I made the decisions to hire the right people. Delores Daniels and Mr. Graham did great work. They were definitely assets."

"I appreciate you saying so. I enjoyed working for you. I enjoyed teaching. I enjoyed the students. I enjoyed most of the faculty. Jim Peterson was pretty much a douche, but he's a nobody, really. When I win this election, I will consult with you on some of my educational programs," Theodore says.

"You're not going to win this election," Gene says.

"Yes, I am."

"No, you're not."

"Yes, I am. My platform is better than yours."

"No, you're not. My platform will work."

"Now you're being childish, Gene."

"No, you're being childish."

"Walter, I don't want to have this childish argument with Gene. Please ask us another question," Theodore says.

Gene turns red with frustration for being baited by Theodore's childish discourse.

"Okay, let's move on. Albert, you haven't been in elected office for seven years. Do you think you can work with the state assembly in the state that it is in now?"

"Our assembly seems dysfunctional because Matt Harmon, our current governor, a Democrat, won't work with the assembly to pass commonsense legislation. Once Gene is in office, the state can actually pass much-needed reform."

"So what you're saying is that your party is only bipartisan when you have the majority and can pass budgets and legislation that suit the will of the party. I guess that's why the assembly is being obstructionist with Governor Harmon. Putting party over state, that doesn't seem very bipartisan," Nancy says.

"The Democrats do the same thing."

"Albert, you make childish arguments just like Gene," Theodore says.

"No, I don't."

"Walter or Joan, can one of you help us move along?"

"Speaking of bipartisanship, if you are elected, Mr. Graham, and the assembly has a Republican majority, will you be willing to work with them?" Joan asks.

"Of course. I put the good of the state over the will of the party. If you remember, I am an independent running on the Democratic ticket. If you look at the history of this country, there were instances where conservative solutions were the best way to go. There were also instances where a liberal solution was a better fit. I don't want to waste time lumping and labeling points of view. I want to find solutions. To find solutions, you have to listen to both sides. That's why I will not become a Democrat or a Republican. Sometimes the two-party system becomes an obstacle."

"How about you, Gene? Could you work in a bipartisan manner?"

"Certainly. I look at how well my opponent and I worked together over the years. We have come from different upbringings. We have different political views. We disagree on many issues. Somehow we managed to work together and found great successes and lasting friendship."

"We did a lot of good together, my friend."

"We are getting close to the end of our show, but there is one question I want to pose to our unique set of candidates. Has this campaign taken a toll on your friendship? And how do you see your friendship moving forward after the election? Theodore, let's start with you," Walter Carl says.

"This election definitely tested our friendship. There were some trying events. But somehow, we worked through it. No matter how this election goes, Gene will always be my friend. He is a good man whom I trust, and I will always seek his council in his areas of expertise. I love the guy."

"Gene, same question."

"I love Teddy. He's always been a good friend. Even when we were at odds in this election, he put our friendship in front of the politics. When I'm governor, I would be silly if I didn't seek the advice of his brilliant mind."

"A strong friendship, very good. That's all the time we have for today. I would like to thank our guests, Gene Douglas and Theodore Graham. You can see the lieutenant governor candidates meet again at their debate on Wednesday night. Nancy Bradford and Albert Wood, we look forward to seeing you debate. Thank you, Joan Mowrey, for asking some tough questions today. Thanks for watching *State of the State This Week*. Join us next Sunday morning. Have a great Sunday and a great week ahead!" Walter Carl says, and the end credits roll.

The host and guests make small talk and shake hands after the show. Theodore and Nancy return to the green room to gather their belongings.

"You did great, Nancy. You are going to eat Albert Wood alive at the debate."

"I hope I can."

"We cleared the schedule on Wednesday. We have the day to do your debate prep. You will be more than ready. You really called Joan Mowery out on her bullshit."

"Somebody has to. I hope she takes me up on the challenge to follow me this week."

"I think maybe a writer from the *Weekly Beat* will shame her into joining you by writing about it."

"You really know how to use the press to your advantage, don't you?"

"Public shame is a heck of a motivator."

"Indeed," Nancy says.

CHAPTER 44

Election Day, 1:30 a.m.

"Who let the dogs out? Woof! Woof! Who let the dogs out?" Theodore's ringtone wakes him.

"Arrrghhh waaarg. Hello?" Theodore says. "You got to be kidding me! I'll be right there. Don't let anybody leave."

Theodore jumps out of bed and quickly dresses. He picks up his cell phone and makes a call.

"Sweet Barn, I'm sorry to bother you in the middle of the night. I need your help. I need you to meet me at the Bumpin' Club as soon as you can. Grab your brothers, Lizard Eddie and Funky Brian, if you can. I'm sorry, buddy, I hate to bother you with this. Thank you, Barn."

Theodore leaves his apartment and makes his way to the Bumpin' Club. Sweet Barn and Lizard Eddie are waiting outside when he gets there.

"Funky Brian can't be out late at night because of his probation. He says he can't be prowlin' at night. Mama said no," Sweet Barn says.

"I wouldn't disobey Mama Sophia either. The three of us can handle this," Theodore says and knocks on the door of the club.

"She's a drunken mess. I didn't want to call the cops. She was grinding on guys on the dance floor. She was buying everybody shots. She was showing her tits and starting to strip. She was challenging some of the girls to fights. She was passed out for a bit, but she's starting to stir. I have her back in a corner booth, but the spectacle of her draws a crowd," Wayne Arnold says when he opens the door.

470

"Fucking great! Take me to her."

Theodore follows Wayne to a corner booth. There's a small circle of people snapping "selfies" and taking pictures with their phones.

"Teddy-Fucking-Furrrrrrfuckingshizzzle-Graham, today's the big day, honey. You're going to lose, but that's okay, because it will all work out for us," a drunk Sandy Douglas slurs from the booth. Her dress is crooked and half-off.

"What are you doing, Sandy?"

"I came out to celebrate a little bit. After all this governor shit is out of the way, I am leaving that dial tone of a husband of mine. Gene, Eugene. Euuuuuuuuuugene—that's a funny word. I'm divorcing that miserable fuck. Come on, Teddy, light a joint and let's celebrate."

"What are we celebrating?"

"That I'm done with Gene. After the governor shit is over, I'm filing for divorce. Then we can finally be together. We should have been together from the start," Sandy slurs.

"Dude! That's the other governor guy. He's fucking the other governor guy's wife. No shit! I love politics. I got to get a picture of this," a college-age kid with his hat on backward says and holds up a cell phone.

"Get that phone out of my face before you lose it," Theodore says.

"No way, dude. Once I get outside, I'm going to post this. This shit is going viral."

Lizard Eddie grabs the kid's wrist and takes the phone out of his hand. He snaps the phone in half, drops it on the floor, and stomps on it. "You dropped you phone, sir."

"Dude, not cool."

"You're lucky I broke your phone and not your neck."

"Sweet Barn, line everybody up. Wayne, get her keys and park her car out front next to our van. You, backward-hat douchebag, get me a pen and paper," Theodore says.

"Teddy, what are you doing? It's the night before Election Day. Take me back to your place, and I will make it Erection Day for you. I'll fuck you better than Claire Peterson."

"You're making a fool of yourself, Sandy."

"I'm gonna make you so happy, Teddy. It should have been us all along. I'm going to be such a slut in bed for you once I leave my loser husband!" Sandy shouts, tries to stand up, and passes out.

"Everybody line up! I'm checking IDs, writing your names down, checking your cell phone pictures and videos, and deleting anything that involves this incident. If you don't cooperate, my associates, Sweet Barn and Lizard Eddie, will deal with you. You don't want that. We just saw Eddie snap a cell phone in half. Choose wisely. As far as any of you are concerned, this incident never happened," Theodore explains to the small crowd of people. "If any of this ends up on TV or in the press, everybody on the list will be getting arrested for the ecstasy and other drugs they have on them. I will spend the rest of my life making all your lives a living hell. Don't think for one second that I can't."

"You're not touching my cell phone. I don't care who you are," a college-age kid says.

"Eddie, you want to handle this."

Eddie picks the kid up with one hand and throws him over his shoulder. He slams him down on the bench of the booth. "Give me that cell phone before I have to hurt you!" Eddie says. The kid appears scared and dumbstruck. He hands his phone to Eddie, and he hands it to Theodore.

Theodore looks at his cell phone and scrolls through the pictures and videos. "You tea-bagged her when she was passed out? Really? No wonder you've never seen a for-real vagina."

Theodore deletes the photos and videos. "Eddie, show these folks what you will do to their phones if they don't cooperate."

Eddie takes the phone out of Theodore's hand and holds it up so everyone can see it. He snaps it in half. "Is that what you wanted, Teddy?"

"Good job, Eddie. Anybody else want to be difficult?"

Sweet Barn and Theodore write names down and check phones. They delete any incriminating photos and videos.

"Eddie, carry her out to the van and lay her down. Wayne, you ride in the van with Eddie and keep her under control in case she wakes up. Sweet Barn, you drive her car and follow us to the Douglas mansion."

Eddie throws Sandy over his shoulder, and the five of them make their way outside to the front of the club. Eddie rests Sandy on one of the bench seats, and Wayne sits by the door. Sweet Barn gets in Sandy's little red convertible.

"Sweet Barn, you got to switch jobs with Wayne," Theodore says.

"I can drive her car home, Teddy. It's no problem."

"You're a black man that is over seven feet tall and 350 pounds. Your head sits two feet above the windshield of this tiny red convertible. You might draw the attention of any law enforcement we may encounter."

"I didn't think of that, Teddy. You're going to be a great governor."

The convoy of vehicles, the conversion van, the little red convertible, and Theodore's new Buick Lacrosse, leaves the club. They drive through Douglas Hills and make their way up the driveway of the Douglas mansion. Gene is waiting outside in his bathrobe.

"Did you have to have a convoy of vehicles come up my driveway in the middle of the night? What if somebody saw this? What if the press saw this? This would look bad for the election."

"Why is your drunk, slutty wife my fucking problem?"

"I don't know what to do about her. I can't control her. She's a mess."

"Again, how does your mess become my mess? Grow a set and take control, Gene. You're worried about the convoy of vehicles coming up your driveway. If you had seen some of the pictures I had to delete off cell phones, you would have bigger worries. If any of them make it on the six o'clock news this morning, Election Day will be very, very painful for you."

"Where do you want me to put Debauchery Barbie?" Lizard Eddie asks.

"Take her in the house and put her on the sofa in the front room," Gene says. "This is the last thing I needed. I have a busy day ahead of me."

"You have a busy day. Have you forgotten I'm your opponent? I have a pretty full day ahead of me too. She isn't my wife. You better figure out how to get her under control, or you will have a very short and embarrassing political career ahead of you."

"I'm sorry, Teddy. I just don't know what to do."

"You better figure it out. This is the last one of Sandy's drunken meltdowns I'm going to deal with. If I were just an opponent and not a friend, I could have just sat back and watched the morning news destroy you," Theodore says. "Are we ready to go, fellows?"

"She's still passed out. I took her shoes off and put her on the couch. I tossed a blanket over her," Lizard Eddie says.

"Let's go. Do you guys mind dropping Wayne off at the Bumpin' Club? I got to try to get some sleep for the big day tomorrow," Theodore says.

"We'll drop him off. You need your beauty rest, Teddy," Sweet Barn says.

"I'm sorry, Teddy. Thanks for getting her home. Good luck in the election tomorrow."

"Fuck you, Gene."

The conversion van and Theodore's Buick Lacrosse leave the Douglas mansion. Theodore drives back to the *Weekly Beat* building and goes into his apartment. He looks at the clock. It's 4:20 a.m.

"It's four twenty! I might as well celebrate with a joint," Theodore says to himself and pulls a joint out of his nightstand.

Election Day, 5:30 a.m.

"Who let the dogs out? Woof! Woof! Who let the dogs out?" Theodore's ringtone wakes him.

"Arrgggh. Hello? Good morning, Delores. I know I sound like shit. I had a rough night. I'll explain later. I will be there as soon as I can."

Theodore gets out of bed and grabs a pair of cargo shorts from the floor and a Van Halen concert T-shirt and gets dressed. He takes the garment bag with a freshly dry-cleaned suit and gym bag as he leaves his apartment. He gets in his car and drives to the campaign headquarters.

"Morning, folks."

"Teddy, you look like shit. Why are you dressed like that? It's Election Day. Did you lose your mind?" Pam Eynon asks.

"I had a rough night."

"You left here at nine last night and said you were going to get a good night's sleep. What happened?" Delores asks.

"A friend's wife had a drunken meltdown. I had to help him out and get her home safely."

"You weren't with Sandy Douglas, were you?"

"Not by choice. It was a rescue mission."

"Your eyes are red and shiny. Are you high?"

"Yes. I might be a little high. The clock said four twenty when I got home. I had no choice but to celebrate."

"Today is not the day to be yourself, Teddy. What the hell are you thinking?" Pam asks.

"The rough night wasn't part of my plan. I have a freshly dry-cleaned suit in my car. I'm going to shower here, and I will be ready to roll. Let's get to the business at hand. Please get off my back."

"Okay, let's just get started. Kevin has our volunteers at just about all the polling places across the state. They will be handing out pins and pamphlets. Nancy Bradford has an interview with Barry Barnhardt that will be on at eleven thirty before the lunchtime news. She will be talking about building local economies, promoting small businesses, and shopping local. Everett Avery and Fred Miles will be speaking at a couple of polling places and doing some interviews. Anna Martinez will be speaking at the voters' lunch this afternoon, and she will be doing the same at the voters' dinner in Hurleysville. There will be a team of senior staff making some stops at some of the polling places to talk to some of the voters. Teddy, the polls open at eight. You will do a brief speech at Harmon City Hall, and you will then walk across the street and vote. Please vote for yourself. After you vote, you will be doing a stand-in interview with Grace Downwood. I suggest you get some Visine so you don't look high," Delores says.

"I will be ready for all this, don't worry."

"I sure as hell hope so. Looking at you now doesn't instill confidence in me. From Harmon, we will get in the van and be making stops at five polling places. This afternoon, we will be back here, looking at the exit polls and seeing how the day unfolds. We will determine if we have to take any actions when we see how things are going."

"How do the daily polls look, Tim?" Ed Reese asks.

"They are too close to call. Gene leads us in some areas of the state. Teddy leads him in others. Some are mathematical ties. I can't even begin a guess on this. Public commentary doesn't give us any insight either. It's an even match."

"Let's look at some of the public comments," Theodore says.

Tim taps a couple of keys on his computer. A comments page from a political social media page appears on the screen. "Here you go, Teddy, check it out."

Not much of a choice in this election. One guy will fuck you over. The other guy will fuck your wife. Either way, we're fucked.

Teddy Graham has new ideas. This is what we have been whining about for decades. Make the right choice, folks.

I hope Teddy Graham wins. He's dreamy. If he wins, I will be able to say that I pleasured myself while fantasizing about the governor.

Teddy Graham is a liberal pussy with ideas that will kill our state. Vote for lower taxes and commonsense approaches. Vote for Gene Douglas.

Gene Douglas got my vote. I'm not voting for a stoner pervert.

Nancy Bradford is a bitch, but she's a smart bitch. Go, Graham!

A trickle-down plan hasn't worked yet. I'm tired of waiting. I'm trying something new. Teddy, you got my vote.

I'm voting for Gene Douglas, not because he is going to do a good job, but because his wife is a drunk whore who can't keep her clothes on. The sex scandal and the new nude photos that will get leaked are going to fill my spank bank with hours of pleasure.

Good luck, Teddy! You will be good for our state. I hope the people are smart enough to see this. I'm tired of all the politics."

Then why are you on a political page? Retard!

"That's the public commentary. The last two people commenting continue arguing and calling each other names for the next two pages. Do you want to see more?" Tim asks.

"No, that's plenty. Thank you," Theodore says.

"Teddy, you better go get showered and cleaned up so we're on time," Delores says.

Theodore stands up and looks around the conference room. "Before I clean myself up, I want to say a few words. Not all the senior staff is here, but please pass my sentiments along to all of them. I never dreamed of being the governor. Even after I became a candidate, I never even thought for a minute about being in the governor's mansion. This morning, I look at all of you. I think about the hard work we did. I honestly believe in the platform we put together. No matter what happens, I am proud of this team and grateful for having all of you on my side. Tonight, at the election night party in the Gatesville Hotel Ballroom, we can celebrate an amazing campaign, win or lose. Drinks are on the Democratic Party. We can win this thing. It's totally possible. If all of you are still going to be on my team if we win, then let's get out there and make sure we win. Thank you. I love all of you."

"We love you, Teddy. Now go get cleaned up," Pam says.

"I'm going. I'm going," Theodore says.

Election Day, 7:55 a.m.

Theodore and Delores are standing on the side of the Harmon City Hall, waiting until it's time for Theodore to do his Election Day speech. Theodore is cleaned up and looking sharp in a fresh suit.

"You cleaned up nicely. I was a little worried when you came into the conference room this morning. You looked like hell. What the hell went on last night?"

"Sandy Douglas went out on a bender. I guess Gene is ignoring her since he found out about her posing for nude pictures and *Girls Gone Wild: The MILF Years* appearances."

"Can you blame him?"

"No, not at all. I wouldn't want to be in his shoes."

"He should just cut her loose."

"Gene would love to have that option. Unfortunately, he's trapped. He needs her for public appearances. She is eye candy, and when she, Gene, and Ernie are together in front of the press, they look like the perfect, happy family. The general public wants that happiness. They don't know it's only an illusion. If he wants a second term as governor, he has to keep her around. He's basically stuck with her for eight years."

"I guess a bitter divorce battle would overshadow his legacy."

"Oh, would it ever! And it would be bitter. Gene is trapped by his family legacy, and Sandy has him trapped financially."

"Didn't he get a prenup?"

"There's a prenup, all right, but it wasn't from Gene. Sandy's mom, Bambi Wilson, was a noted stripper in Kentucky. She was also a noted gold digger and inherited the fortunes of many lonely widowers. She was also a crazy, dominant beauty pageant mom that would take Sandy around the country to compete in pageants. Gene's parents' sponsored one of those beauty pageants. Gene went crazy over Sandy. Bambi Wilson saw this and knew the wealth of the Douglas family. She talked Sandy into marrying Gene so she would be set for life. The marriage came with a tight, well-crafted prenup from Bambi's shyster Southern lawyer. If Gene divorces her, she gets nearly two-thirds of the Douglas estate, the schools, the mansion, and a ton of money. Gene had me examine this prenup a bunch of times to look for loopholes. I couldn't find one. He would be better off if she dies."

"What if she divorces him?"

"She never will. She threatens to leave him for me all the time, but she knows how much she will lose. After I showed Gene how stupid he was for signing Sandy's prenup, he had me put one together for him. She signed it on the morning of their wedding. If she files for divorce, she gets two million dollars and their beach house in Delaware. I told Gene to bail on the morning of their wedding and her prenup would never be relevant. He didn't listen."

"Don't you think she would take the money and run?"

"Sandy Douglas can't live on two million dollars. She would burn through that in a year or less."

"So how did last night involve you?"

"I got a call from a friend of mine that knew who she was. He called me because he knew that I knew Gene. I could have just called Gene and told him to go get his wife, but he wouldn't be smart enough to cover the trail of damage she did."

"How much damage did she do?"

"I spent the better part of the early morning hours deleting pictures and videos from the cell phones of drunk and drugged millennials. If those had hit the news, today would be a very different day for us."

"Your commitment to your friendship is admirable, but why won't you ever take advantage of the things that can give you an advantage?"

"I'm very afraid of karma. My conscious and idle thoughts would torture me. I would always feel guilty if I exploited somebody's pain for my own personal gain. I don't want to be old and senile with that kind of guilt swirling in my head."

"You're a very complex man."

A sound technician walks over to Theodore and Delores. "Looks like we got the sound system all figured out and operational. You can do your thing whenever you're ready."

"Thank you. Are you voting for Theodore Graham today?" Theodore asks.

"Who?"

"I guess he's not a big politics guy."

"It appears that way. Do you want me do introduce you?"

"No. I'll just go on and make my speech. Just signal the press that I am going on."

"You look good, Teddy. Do a good job up there. I want you to win."

"You do?"

"I hate that you're making me say this. Teddy, you are a good man. I enjoyed being your campaign manager. You worked hard and deserve to win."

"You're supposed to hate me. That's your job. Do it."

"After today, my work here is done. You can fire me now if you want. I can get a jump on my freedom from you."

"You're not getting off that easily."

Delores gives Theodore a peck on the cheek. "Go do a good speech."

Theodore walks up to the podium and waves to the small crowd gathered in front of the stage. A few girls up front flash their breasts at him before he begins. He winks at them and gives them a thumbs-up.

"Good morning and happy Election Day. The right to vote is the cornerstone of our democracy. Your vote is your voice. Your vote is your choice. I'm here this morning asking for your vote. I want to hear your voices in my corner. I want to be your choice. I've listened to the people. They told me they want jobs. They told me they want stronger communities. They told me they want strong local economies. They told me they want quality education for their children. They told me they want welfare reform. I heard what the people were saying, and with the help of a dedicated and knowledgeable team, I crafted a platform based on what the voices of the people told me. Today is the day to use your voice. Today is the day to make your choice. I believe in the people. I believe in my plan to serve the people. I believe in me. It would be my honor to have your vote. Now, if you will excuse me, I am going to exercise my right to vote. I am using my voice and making my choice for what I believe is the right path moving forward. Thank you. I hope you will all give me the opportunity to work for you."

"That was a short speech," Delores says when Theodore goes back over to her.

"Short but full of sound bites for a full day of local media coverage."

"You know how to play the press. Now, let's go across the street and cast your vote."

Delores and Theodore cross the street and make their way to the Harmon Volunteer Fire Company, Theodore's polling place.

The media, with their cameras, follow behind to capture the images and spectacle of the process. Theodore cheerfully greets the people in line at the polls. He shakes hands, makes small talk, and jokes around with some of the voters. He thanks the staff working the polls as he waits for an open booth to cast his vote. When a booth opens, Theodore enters and pulls the curtain closed behind him. The media cameras continue to film him.

"No whammies, no whammies, come on, big bucks!" can be heard from Theodore as he is in the voting booth.

When he is done voting, Theodore whips the curtain of his booth open and shouts, "Tahdah!"

One of the volunteers at the polls places the I VOTED sticker on Theodore's lapel and poses for the photo op. Theodore walks back over to Delores, who is waiting for him.

"Did you vote for yourself?"

"Sure did. I want to win."

"It's a far cry from where we started, isn't it?"

"Maybe it's where we need to be."

"Let's get your interview over with so we can get on the road and visit some other polling places."

Grace Downwood comes over to Delores and Theodore. "We are set up on the side of the firehouse. I figured we can do your interview with one of the fire trucks as the background."

"Perfect, let's do it."

Theodore follows Grace to where she wants him to stand. She gets him positioned and positions herself in front of the camera. She gives her cameraman the signal to begin rolling.

"Good morning, I'm Grace Downwood of Channel 6 News, reporting from Harmon on this gubernatorial Election Day. Standing with me is the Democratic candidate Theodore Graham. Mr. Graham, how do you view your chances at winning the election today?"

"This is going to be a close race. I believe my chances are good. I listened to the people. I was surrounded with an amazing staff and built a platform around what the people were telling us. At the end of the day, I'm hoping to be called Governor-Elect Graham. Today is the voters' day, though. This is the people's democracy, and it's their voice that will shape its future."

"Do you think your platform resonates with the people?"

"It was crafted by what the people told us they wanted. I hope so. I'm running to serve the people, not to serve myself."

"This was a unique election. You and your opponent are long-time friends. One of you will win today. Do you think that will put a strain on your friendship?"

"We've been friends a long time. It's a strong friendship that I wouldn't trade for the world. Our friendship had its ups and downs over the years. We celebrated a lot of good times. We've leaned on each other in rough times. I like to believe this election won't change our friendship. We both wish each other success."

"You were a long-shot candidate. You're not a traditional politician. Do you see yourself making a career in politics? Would you seek a second term for governor if you win?"

"I would have to win a first term before I start thinking about a second. If I do a good job for the people and they want me to keep doing a good job for them, I would run again. I'd serve at the pleasure of the voters."

"How would you incorporate Gene Douglas's supporters into your platform if you win today?"

"I'm seeking an office that serves all the people of the state, not just my supporters. I have an obligation to hear their voices and work for them."

"Do you think you can work in a bipartisan manner?"

"Certainly. I will the take the same oath to serve the people that all politicians take. That is my contract with the people. If I don't honor that contract, the people will have me removed. One advantage I have, I'm an independent."

"The Democrats put you on their ticket. Will you become a Democrat when you are in office?"

"No. I never want to put party loyalty in front of the good of the people. The two-party system has limited progress in many cases because each side wants to win. It's not the parties that should be winning. It's the parties that should be working together to make sure the people win."

"It's Election Day, and this interview is going to be on television. This is one more chance to appeal to the voters. What do you say to the voters that are heading to the polls?"

"I say thank you. I would like people to vote for me, but it's their choice. They will pick the candidate that best matches their values. I say thank you because I am grateful for the voters that participate in our democratic process. A government of the people won't work if the people aren't involved."

"Well, Mr. Graham, thank you for talking with me today. Good luck in today's election."

"Thank you, Grace, for taking the time to talk to me."

"I'm Grace Downwood, Channel 6 News, reporting on this gubernatorial race from downtown Harmon," the reporter says and signals her cameraman to quit rolling.

"Do you think you're going to win, Teddy?" Grace asks off camera.

"I have no idea. It's too close to call. If I do, are you interested in being my press secretary?"

"Win the election first, then we can negotiate. Good luck. You got my vote."

"If I win by one vote, I will know it was yours. Have good day covering this shit show."

"It's going to be a long day."

"It's not even nine o'clock, and my day has already been too long," Theodore says.

"When this is all over, let's go on a vacation where we can live in our bathing suits and consume unlimited drinks with umbrellas and lots of rum in them."

"That's sounds like a fine plan, Ms. Downwood. We'll talk," Theodore says and goes back over to Delores.

"Now you're going to run away with a TV reporter," Delores says.

"Jealous much, Delores?"

"I'm not jealous."

"I'm all in favor of running away on vacation with you. Are you into rum?"

"With you, I would need something stronger."

"There will be weed too."

Election Day, 12:30 p.m.

Sweet Barn sits behind the wheel of the campaign's conversion van. His brother Lizard Eddie rides shotgun in the captain's chair next to him. Delores and Theodore are seated at the table in the back, going over some notes and speech points.

"Earlsburg is the last polling place we have to visit, then we can go back to headquarters for the rest of the afternoon and keep an eye on the election results, exit polls, and see if there is anything we have to go back out in the field to address. You're starting to look tired. Maybe we can let you get a nap in before we go to our election night party."

"I'll be fine. Sweet Barn and Lizard Eddie helped me out at the Bumpin' Club last night. If they aren't tired, I'm not tired," Theodore says.

"I'm tired as shit, Teddy. I need some coffee or Vivarin. Do they still make that stuff? I remember the commercial, 'Revive with Vivarin.' Remember that, Teddy? Maybe you need some of that," Sweet Barn says.

"You two helped Teddy out last night?"

"Yes, that Sandy Douglas is one nutty lady," Sweet Barn says.

"Yeah, Teddy, you better watch out. She's crazy. She said she was going to get a divorce so you two could be together. I would consider that a threat," Lizard Eddie says.

"Yeah, you're better off playing with yourself, Teddy. She ain't worth the headache," Sweet Barn says.

"Thanks for the advice, big guy."

Delores's cell phone rings. "Hello, Kevin, what's up? You've got to be kidding me! How many are there? Okay, let me talk to Teddy and get back to you."

"That doesn't sound good. What's going on?"

"Apparently, there's a group of about fifteen or so protesters that found out we are coming to Earlsburg. Americans for the American Way of Life is the name of their group. They are carrying flags and signs, and they are planning to give you a hard time when you get there. Should we cancel the Earlsburg stop and find another one?"

"Is there any media going to be there?"

"Our press caravan is there. They were going to capture some of the photo ops and get some sound bites if they could."

"No. If they have media of their own, it will look like we chickened out because of them. I will speak directly to their group. Let's see what we can find out about their organization. Maybe they have a website or something on the internet."

"Are you sure about this? Kevin said they looked like a pretty unruly bunch."

"Look at the size of the men in the front of this van. I don't think I have too much to worry about when these two guys have my back."

"Damn straight, Ms. Delores. You have no worries. Teddy, you're like our brother. We got your back," Lizard Eddie says.

"Where's your brother Brian?"

"Teddy told him to eat an all-egg breakfast and sent him on special assignment at the Douglas Hills Country Club," Sweet Barn answers.

"What special assignment at Douglas Hills? That's Gene's Election Day center."

"It's just a little something I did for my own amusement. I hope it bears fruit," Theodore says.

"I'm sure something's gonna happen. He ate eighteen dollars' worth of eggs at breakfast this morning. I'm glad he's not with us," Sweet Barn says and laughs.

"What am I missing here?"

"It's fart stuff. Don't worry about it. Let's just worry about our next stop."

"I don't want to know about fart stuff. You guys act like a bunch of sixth graders when it comes to flatulence. I will send Kevin a text and let him know we will be there."

Delores sends a text to Kevin Baker. Theodore and Delores search the web for information about Americans for the American Way of Life. They both jot some notes down and pass them back and forth. Sweet Barn pulls into the parking lot of the Earlsburg community center. A group of protesters gathers outside the van. A few uniformed police officers direct the crowd to step back from the van. Sweet Barn parks the van, and the protesters begin to chant.

"Stop the liberal agenda! Graham will get slammed! Vote no on tax-and-spend!" the protesters chant.

"You want to get out now?" Lizard Eddie asks.

"Give it a minute or two. Let the media cameras get set up and let them chant a little more," Theodore says.

"Stop the liberal agenda! Graham will get slammed! Vote no on tax-and-spend!" the protesters continue to chant.

"Okay, it looks like the media is rolling. Sweet Barn, you walk around the van and meet Eddie on this side then let me and Delores out."

Sweet Barn and Lizard Eddie are on the passenger side of the van. Lizard Eddie slides the side door open. Theodore steps out and takes Delores's hand as she steps out of the van. The protesters continue to chant. Theodore turns and faces the crowd.

"Good afternoon, Earlsburg. It's great to be here with you all on Election Day," Theodore says but is barely audible over the chanting.

"Stop the liberal agenda! Graham will get slammed! Vote no on tax-and-spend!"

"I see some of you are in disagreement with my candidacy. Let's talk about it."

The crowd chants louder.

"We can't have a discussion if you are chanting. If you want to talk, let's do it. If you want to chant and talk over me, I can go talk to my supporters and ignore you. That will be a lot easier for me, and your concerns will go unheard," Theodore says and begins to walk toward the community center.

"Your liberal policies are killing the taxpayers of this state. Your policies are un-American, and we won't stand for it!" a man from the crowd shouts.

"What's your name, sir? Are you the spokesman for this group? What is the name of your group?" Theodore asks.

"My name is Red Hurley, and I am the president of this chapter of Americans for the American Way of Life."

"Red, it's good to meet you. I've heard of your group. I just read an article on your website. Voters for Gene Douglas, the super PAC of the Gene Douglas Campaign donated thirty-five thousand dollars to the local chapter of the Americans for the American Way of Life so you could remodel your lodge right here in Earlsburg. Does that donation have anything to do with why you are protesting my stop in your great town?"

"Mr. Douglas supports our group because he believes in the American way of life. Not like you and your socialist-communist agenda."

"Socialism and communism are two very different forms of governance. I can't be both. What makes you think I am socialist?"

"Your policies are killing our state. Because of you, our taxes are too high. Your liberal agenda is stealing our freedoms."

"My policies aren't doing anything at the moment. I haven't been governor yet. You can go right into that community center right over there and vote against me. If enough of you vote against me, you won't have to worry about my policies. I'm not sure where you got your information, but my policies, I made very clear that they were made based on what I heard from the people out on the campaign trail. Those people told me they were tired of their communities falling apart. They told me they were tired of people on welfare getting everything for nothing while hardworking people pay for it. They told me they want jobs. They told me they want better education for their children. You can go over there to one of my campaign volunteers, and they will gladly give all of you a pamphlet that outlines what I want to do for the state."

"You're going to take our rights away. You're going to take our freedom of speech from us. You are going to stop good gun owners from owning guns. You can't be trusted."

"I don't know where you get your information. I have no plans on taking any rights away. I want you to have freedom of speech because this is a government of the people, by the people, and for the people. How can I listen to the people if I take your freedom of speech away?"

"But what about our gun rights? You will make laws in this state that violate our Second Amendment rights from the Constitution."

"Red, you are dead wrong. If I do anything to violate your Second Amendment rights, I am also hurting my Second Amendment rights. This is why I will not mess with your right to bear arms."

Theodore bends down and pulls up his pant leg. There is a pistol in a holster strapped to his ankle. "The right to bear arms shall not be infringed!"

Members of the group applaud Theodore for having a gun.

"What do you want to see next? My lifetime NRA membership? My concealed weapon permit? How about you take your group to the Douglas campaign and ask him to show you his weapon. I guarantee he will take your gun rights away before I would even consider it." Theodore pauses and waits for a response from the group. The crowd goes quiet.

"I like your group, Americans for the American Way of Life. I'm proud to be an American, and I am proud to know there is a group like yours that has the guts to come out and stand up for what you believe in. Now, what do you think is better in the long run for Earlsburg, a thirty-five-thousand-dollar check from a politician's super PAC or a fellow gun owner that will bring jobs to Earlsburg and a quality education to your children? You tell me. Americans for the American Way of Life, you have your right to vote. Today is the day to use that right to stand up for what you believe in. Go vote!"

"If I already voted for Gene Douglas but changed my mind, can I vote again?" a man from the group asks.

"Sorry, sir. You were supposed to go in as an informed voter. Let regret be your lesson," Delores says.

Theodore shakes hands with some of the people in the crowd. He motions to Lizard Eddie to open the van door. Theodore waves to the crowd as he makes his way back to the van. Delores follows him. They enter the van, and Eddie closes the door behind them. Sweet Barn drives the van out of the community center parking lot.

"You really turned that crowd around. I don't know how you do it," Delores says.

"The spokesman for their group was wearing bib overalls without a shirt underneath. It's Earlsburg, where the long buses are full of what the short buses used to be. His mind wasn't hard to change. If showing him my gun didn't work, I would have had some of my supporters show him their breasts. Boobies have a lot of persuasive power, you know."

"I know you were a hunter and owned guns, but I didn't realize you carried one on your ankle."

"Oh, this?" Theodore says and lifts his pant leg and removes the gun. "This isn't a real gun. It's a squirt gun full of vodka that looks real." He pulls the trigger of the gun and shoots a blast of vodka in his mouth.

"Why would you need a squirt gun full of vodka?"

"In case I need a drink."

"Why can't you get a flask like a normal person?"

"I'm campaigning to be governor. People shake hands with me and hug me all day. I can't have them feel a flask in my jacket pocket. They'll think I'm an alcoholic."

"They already know you're a stoner sex hound. What's one more vice?"

"I know, right? People are too uptight these days."

"Sometimes my sarcasm doesn't translate well," Delores says.

Election Day, 2:20 p.m.

Theodore and Delores return to headquarters to monitor election results. Tim Collins is sitting at the conference room table, looking at exit poll charts and up-to-the-minute election results. Ed Reese and Pam Eynon are cataloging media reports.

"We're back. Did you miss us?" Theodore says.

"I missed Delores a little bit. You, not so much," Pam jokes.

"How are we doing? Do we have to go back out again?"

"Let me put it up on the big screen, and I can show you what we got so far," Tim Collins says and clicks a few keys on his computer. A series of charts appears on the screen.

"That looks like a Boston bus route map, not election numbers. I hope you can translate all these hieroglyphics for me."

"That's why you hired me, Teddy," Tim says. "Right now, Gene is leading you by half a point with seventy percent of counties reporting their midday count."

"So I am losing?"

"Not by much, and surprisingly. If we look at the exit poll charts from eight this morning until ten, you did way better than expected. The majority of early voters are senior citizens, so you broke even with Gene in that demographic. I call that a victory. Those voters normally vote Republican, and you got half of them. Russ Dewitt probably saw those numbers and sent those protestors and their press people to Earlsburg to interfere with your campaign stop."

"The way you handled that, Teddy, was a thing of beauty. The media captured the whole interaction between you and Americans for the American Way of Life. It's all over the news, and they are really chatting up the donation that the Douglas super PAC made to their organization. You made that protest backfire on the Douglas campaign," Ed Reese says.

"It's great that it's all over the news. You will probably steal a good chunk of gun voters from Gene. Channel 6 News did some research and found out Gene Douglas hasn't renewed his concealed weapon permit in over twenty years. Your sweetheart, Grace Downwood, is talking it up during every update she gives. If Gene straps on a gun to impress the gun voters and to show he's like you, he's breaking state law and could be arrested. Teddy, I honestly can't tell if you are a genius or a moron. The lines are blurred."

"I like to think that I am a highly functional moron."

"I had no idea you had a weapon strapped to your ankle. With your smart mouth, I can understand why you do."

"It's a squirt gun full of vodka. Teddy isn't Rambo," Delores says.

"Seriously?"

Theodore pulls the vodka gun out of its ankle holster and shoots a stream of vodka into his mouth. "Yep, I'm armed with a vodka gun. It takes a good guy with a vodka gun to stop a bad guy with a vodka gun."

"You're unbelievable! You fooled protestors with a vodka gun. Aren't you worried about talking to the public with booze on your breath?"

"When I take a squirt of vodka, I pop an Altoid in my mouth. It smells like I just used mouthwash."

"I never met a more functional alcoholic or addict in my life," Ed Reese says.

"Quick, put on the news. They're evacuating the Douglas Hills Country Club," Pam says.

Delores turns on the television.

"I'm Derrick Snyder, reporting live from the Douglas Hills Country Club that has just been evacuated because of a possible gas leak. The Gene Douglas for Governor campaign rented the country club for its Election Day events. During a supporters' luncheon in the main dining room,

491

a foul odor, possibly gas or propane, blanketed the room. Dining room staff quickly called emergency responders and moved all the attendants of the luncheon outside and safely away from the building. Firefighters are inside, monitoring the air and checking the kitchen and heating system for gas leaks. We have no further information on the leak at this time. The activities for the Douglas campaign, the remainder of the luncheon, the Gene Douglas staff dinner, and the election night ball are uncertain at this time. We will update our viewers with any further information as it comes in. I'm Derrick Snyder, Channel 4 News, reporting live from Douglas Hills," the reporter says as a large black man walks behind him smiling and giving a thumbs-up.

"Isn't that black guy walking behind Derrick Snyder one of your security team?" Tim Collins asks.

Theodore starts laughing hysterically. "Yeah, that's Funky Brian." Theodore continues to laugh and giggle. "He did a way better job than I expected. I owe him one."

"You sent him to the country club to cause a gas leak? Are you a fucking psychopath?" Ed asks.

Delores starts to laugh. "Oh, now I get it. The fart thing you were talking about in the van."

"What am I missing? If there's an explosion, people could get hurt or killed."

"Calm down, Ed. I bought Funky Brian a big breakfast this morning and sent him over to the Douglas Hills luncheon this afternoon. Eggs don't agree with his belly, and they make him very gassy."

"You mean the evacuation over there is because of egg farts?"

"Yep. It went better than I ever imagined it could have. I just wanted him to crop-dust the people attending the luncheon so they all had foul faces when news cameras panned the room."

Theodore snickers, giggles, and begins to laugh uncontrollably.

"I'm always wishing you would just grow up already, but this immature prank may be one of the best ever," Pam says and begins to laugh.

"Hold on, Russ Dewitt is going to be interviewed," Delores says.

"I'm Derrick Snyder, Channel 4 News, with an update on the gas leak at Douglas Hills. I'm here with Russ Dewitt, the campaign manager of the Douglas campaign. Mr. Dewitt, how does the gas leak affect your campaign's Election Day events?"

"The campaign staff and country club staff are discussing alternative options in case we can't use the country club. We hope we don't have to relocate. We are just grateful for the quick thinking of the country club staff in getting everyone safely out of the building. We are especially grateful for the emergency responders who quickly responded and who are currently investigating the leak. They are brave men and women, and we can't thank them enough for what they do."

"Thank you, Mr. Dewitt. Standing with me now is Harmon Fire Chief Patrick McHenry. He's here to give us an update on the gas leak situation. Chief McHenry, what can you tell us?"

"My firefighters arrived on scene. There was a strong odor thought to be gas in the main dining room. We had crews checking all gas lines, fittings, and heating units for possible gas leaks. Our gas-monitoring devices didn't detect any raised levels of propane or natural gas in any areas. There were some elevated, but not dangerous levels of methane in a few areas throughout the main dining room, but those levels have dissipated to zero. My crews are just double-checking everything, and the day's activities at the country club will be able to resume shortly."

"What would cause a raised level of methane gas in a building like this?"

"We couldn't pinpoint a source for methane. Methane gas can be found in decomposing organic materials, pockets of methane in the soil, and human and animal flatulence."

"Do you think the influx of methane gas inside was a pocket of methane coming up from underground?"

"I highly doubt it. The methane levels weren't high enough for an underground gas event. My guess would be it was from a human in the dining room or it was wafting in from one of the restrooms at the facility," Fire Chief McHenry says and begins to laugh a little.

"Good news for the Douglas campaign. The gas leak may have only been a gas leak from a supporter. Gene Douglas's Election Day activi-

ties will continue momentarily. I'm Derrick Snyder, reporting live from Douglas Hills Country Club."

Theodore and his staff are all laughing at the news report. "Farts are funny. I don't care who you are," Theodore says and continues to giggle.

Delores shuts off the television. "That's enough fart humor for today. We have some work to do. Teddy, let's go over your speeches for tonight's events. You have a speech to do when you arrive at the Gatesville ballroom. We will put together a victory speech and a concession speech so we are ready for anything. Let's put our heads together and come up with a list of the people we have to thank, the people we have to acknowledge, and the points we want to drive home."

"I wish there were more fart stories to watch. That was fun. Funky Brian is the best. But I guess we best get to work."

"Tonight, when you get to the Gatesville Hotel, you will be doing a speech. The people you will be talking to are your senior staff, field volunteers, some donors, and a few business leaders. You will do your speech sometime after eight. You may want to keep that speech on the lighter side. They are your supporters, and they will have just had dinner and will be starting to feel the early effects of a few cocktails. Thank-you sentiments and praise. Teddy, are you with me?

"Uh um hah, huh? Yeah, I'm with you. I was just resting my eyes."

"You looked like you were asleep."

"I'm," Theodore begins to say and yawns. "Oh, I'm sorry. I'm fine. Let's continue."

"There will be a couple of presentations we will be making to some staff members for their exceptional work. We have some plaques and gifts to hand out. Nancy Bradford will make a brief speech after you and announce the people getting those awards. You can hand the awards to the recipients and shake their hands. Rose Fayweather's birthday is today. We want to acknowledge her day and her contributions to our election and platform. Teddy, are you paying attention?"

"Huh? Yeah, Rose Fayweather likes birthday cake. Gotcha. I do too."

"Teddy, you're falling asleep. Your Sandy Douglas escapade is catching up with you."

"I'm fine. Go ahead. I'm ready."

"Now, the senior staff talked about it. We have to mention or honor Sherman Jones in either a concession speech or victory speech. If it weren't for his passing, you wouldn't be here. Teddy. Teddy!"

"He's out cold. He's sound asleep," Pam says.

"His late-night adventure getting Sandy Douglas out of trouble is catching up to him."

"The shots of vodka from his squirt gun aren't helping him stay awake either," Ed Reese says.

"He's got to get a nap, or our night is going to be ugly."

"There's not much going on this afternoon. The two o'clock polling numbers are in. Teddy made up that half a point at 85 percent of counties reporting. It's a dead heat. If you want to send him home to get a little rest, I think it will be okay. If we need him, we can call him," Tim Collins says.

"Do you want me to call Sweet Barn and have him take him to his apartment?" Pam asks.

"I have to swing by my place and pick up my outfit for tonight. I can drop him off on my way. Teddy sent Sweet Barn and Lizard Eddie home to get some rest so they are fresh for tonight," Delores says.

"Okay, we will call you if we need you."

"Teddy. Teddy. Teddy!"

Theodore opens his eyes wide and appears confused. "What's going on? What's the problem here? Let's get these speeches done."

"Teddy, you were sound asleep. I'm taking you back to your apartment so you can take a nap."

"I'm fine. I just dozed off."

"You're not fine. You're going to take a nap. Don't fight me on this. Don't make me pull rank. We can't have you being a slurring mess tonight."

"Okay, okay, I'm not really that tired, though."

"Let's go. You can rest for an hour or two, shower, put on a change of clothes, and get ready for your party tonight. You and Gene are now at 50 percent apiece. Tonight might be a victory party."

"After my nap, I'm going to have to refill my vodka gun if we're going to win."

"You have a good chance, big guy. After two o'clock, the younger voters go to the polls, the workers vote on their way home from work, and the people that forgot to vote get to the polls. You're strong in all those demographics, especially with the stoners that may forget to vote," Tim Collins says.

"We can only hope my stoner buddies come through for us."

"Let's hope they aren't too paranoid to go outside. Now, go home and get a nap."

"Yeah, come on, Teddy. Let's get you home," Delores says. Theodore gets up from his seat and follows her.

Election Day, 3:50 p.m.

Delores pulls her Prius in front of the *Weekly Beat* building. She turns off her car and shakes Theodore's shoulder to wake him. "Teddy, wake up. We're here."

"Um, grrrr wah. Okay, I'm up. I'm ready for this speech."

"We're at your building. You can go get a nap now."

"You wake me up to tell me to go to sleep?" Theodore says. "Thanks for dropping me off. You can send Sweet Barn to pick me up later."

"I'm not just dropping you off. I'm going in with you and making sure you lie down for a little while. If I don't make you take a nap, you'll go in there, smoke one of your joints, play some guitar, or work on one of your writing projects."

"Are you going to lie down with me? We can have a little fun first."

"No, don't get cute. I will be back to pick you up later. Give me your cell phone. I'm not letting that disturb your nap."

Theodore hands her his cell phone. "Here you go, but what if I have to poop? I won't be able to take care of my farm in Farmville or play Angry Birds."

"Read a magazine while you go, just like the cavemen did."

Theodore and Delores get out of the car and make their way inside the building. They take the elevator up to the top floor to Theodore's apartment and go inside.

"Do you have a fresh suit for tonight?"

"Yes, ma'am. There is one hanging in a garment bag on the back of the bedroom door," Theodore says.

"Good. Get out of that suit and get into that bed."

"You like to get right to it, Delores, but I like to be romanced. I'm not slutty and easy. A little foreplay wouldn't kill you."

"You're sexual résumé begs to differ. Now get into bed, relax, and go to sleep so I can get going."

"You're not going to join me? You won't help me update my sexual résumé?" Theodore gets into bed shirtless and in his boxer shorts. "Can you at least tuck me in and give me a kiss before I go night-night?"

Delores leans down and gives Theodore a kiss on the lips. "I hate myself for enjoying your kisses and getting tangled in your web of nonsense."

"It's not that bad, is it?"

Delores's cell phone beeps. She takes it out of her purse and checks it. "That was a text from Tim Collins. The latest polls have you up by a full point."

"Seriously?"

"That's what he says," Delores says and holds up her cell phone to show Theodore the text. "We might actually win this thing."

"I'm scared for the citizens of our state."

"After your fart-prank, gas-leak thing, I'm scared too."

"Can I ask you a serious question?"

"I know you are planning to go back to your job at the Douglas school when this is all over, but I was wondering if you would consider being my chief of staff."

"Win first then ask me again later."

"I think you would be perfect for the job. I've never seen a person that can coordinate and manage complex projects and staff like you do. I wouldn't be up by a point if it weren't for you. You run a well-oiled machine. You did it at the school, and you did it for my campaign. This campaign wouldn't have had half the success it had without the skills and brains you brought to the table. If I win this thing, I need somebody with your skills to manage the staff, keep me briefed on what I need to know, and keep me grounded when I start to take things too far. You kept me grounded and focused. As you know, there aren't very many people that can do that. I would be a successful governor if you would be my chief of staff."

"Oh, yes, not many people can keep you at bay. You've given me something to think about. Let's see where we are at the end of the day. If you win, we can talk about it then."

"Fair enough. If I lose this election, I also have a favor to ask you."

"I'm sure I can talk the board into letting you coach the debate team. Professor Dannonberry is the temporary coach until they can find a replacement, but they are doing a horrible job looking for one. The team won't even make it to the playoffs this year. Some of the kids quit the team already."

"That wasn't what I was going to ask, but if I lose this thing, I will consider it and talk to Gene about it. Jim Peterson would hate it if I came back."

"He sure would. The board is actually looking into replacing him this spring. They want to run another trustee against him for his spot."

"That would be the best thing for that school. Jim Peterson is just a grouchy old man with outdated and out-of-touch views of the world."

"So what is the favor you wanted to ask me to do if you lose this election?"

"I would like you to go out to a nice dinner with me. Preferably in a restaurant without a drive-through or plastic trays to bus when we are finished eating. I want to have a dinner with you so we can talk to each other and not about the school, not about the campaign, not about speeches, and not about press conferences. I want to have a dinner where I can get to know you."

"Are you asking me out on a date?"

"Yes, I guess I am."

"But only if you lose?"

"I would love to have a nice dinner with you either way, but I want you to have dinner with me because you want to and not because we are working together and you have to."

"What brought this on?"

"When I was at your house and you kissed me for the first time, I felt cared about. It felt like it was more than just a kiss brought on by physical attraction."

"You're so tired you're delirious. How about you close your eyes and take that nap? I'll stick around until you fall asleep."

"You didn't answer that question either. The way you dodge questions, you should be the one running for office."

"You put a lot to think about in my head. Let's get through the rest of this Election Day. Okay?"

"Fair enough. Can I at least get a kiss before I nap?"

Delores leans down and gives Theodore a long kiss on the lips. "Is that good enough for now?"

Theodore looks dumbstruck and fumbles with his words. "That was . . . it was . . . I never. That was . . . perfect."

Delores leans down and kisses him the same way. "Now get some rest so you are ready for tonight."

"If you keep kissing me like that, you are going to have to get naked and crawl into bed with me."

"Go to sleep, Teddy."

Theodore quickly falls asleep, and she gives him a peck on the cheek before she leaves.

Election Day, 7:50 p.m.

Delores drives her Prius behind the Gatesville Hotel and parks in the rear employee lot. Theodore, in the passenger seat, looks around the small poorly lit parking lot.

"Did you park back here so we could have a quickie in before we go to the party?"

"Really? Is there nothing else on your mind besides sex?"

"I'm thinking about getting high too. Do you want to get high and have a quickie?"

"I set myself up for that," Delores says and shakes her head. "I parked back here so we can go in the back door and go right into the staff room. Everybody is waiting for us, and you are going to have to make a speech very shortly."

"I am ready to do the speech. Don't worry. This is the big night, let's enjoy it."

"I'm still the campaign manager. I'm managing you. Now, let's get inside and get up to speed."

Theodore and Delores get out of the car and make their way through a private door to the building. Inside, the campaign staff is sitting in a lounge, reading exit poll statements and going over the schedule of events for the night.

"It's about time you guys got here. We were starting to get a little worried. How was your nap?" Ed Reese asks.

"It was productive. I feel like ten bucks."

"You look a lot better than you did this morning and this afternoon," Tim says.

"What's going on here? Any new polling numbers? Anything we need to know?"

"That's why we love you, Delores. You're no-nonsense and get right down to business. Come on in. Sit down. Have a drink or three. Have some hors d'oeuvres and relax. It's going to be a long night," Ed Reese says.

"Looks like you've had a few cocktails already, Ed. An alcoholic beverage sounds nice. I can use a nice, strong vodka martini," Theodore says.

"Jerry, get Mr. Graham a vodka martini," Ed Reese says. "That's Jerry. He is our personal waiter for this evening. Delores, what are you drinking?"

"A white wine would be great."

"So, Tim, what are we looking like with the vote count?"

"The last update I have is after the six o'clock count. There were 85 percent of counties reporting, and you are still up by a point. The polls will be closing in about four minutes, and I should be getting another count update before eight thirty. Since the governor's race is so close, I don't expect to get the final count until after eleven o'clock tonight. Ed Reese will be good and drunk by then."

"It looks like he's on course to be good and drunk by eight thirty. By eleven, he's going to be shit-faced plastered."

"Hey! I resemble that remark," Ed says.

"No worries, buddy. Let's have a good time tonight. What are the exit polls saying? What's going on out there now?"

"Gene Douglas went out and did some appearances and press interviews. He's been down a point since two o'clock this afternoon. I imagine he is concerned and making some last-ditch efforts to get the last of the voters."

"What's he saying?"

"The usual. He's calling you another tax-and-spend Democrat that will bankrupt the state and cost the people jobs."

"A classic from the Republicans' greatest hits album," Theodore says. "How are we doing in the assembly races?"

"If nothing else, we will have accomplished our goal of taking the majority back in both the Senate and the House. Some of our candidates are going to win by landslides. Some have healthy leads. There are two or three races that are too close to call now, but Democrats will have the majority. If you win this thing, you will have a majority state Congress to work with."

"That will be great, as long as they aren't going to pass a bunch of whiny, costly liberal policies. I will have veto power, and I am an independent. If we win, we work for everybody."

"I'm just hoping they all put their money where their rhetoric is. We need progress, not bullshit."

"You know what? Fuck it. We can worry about that later. Let's enjoy this night," Theodore says as he takes his vodka martini from Jerry, the waiter. "I hope you didn't pull a Cosby and roofie my drink, Jerry. You're not a closet Gene Douglas supporter, are you?"

"No, sir, I voted for you. I'm just here to earn a little extra weed money."

"Attaboy. See, Tim, that's what America is all about, people working hard for the things they want out of life. It doesn't get simpler than that."

Delores moves to the front of the room. "May I have everyone's attention, please?" she says. "We aren't done yet, people, let's not celebrate too hard. I want to go over tonight's itinerary."

"Come on, Delores, relax a little," Ed Reese says.

"Pace yourself, Ed. You're not that good at drinking."

"Boooooo," Ed slurs.

"Okay. I just got word that the polls have closed across the state. We won't hear anything more about the results until we get the final results, probably sometime after eleven. In a few minutes, Teddy, you are going to make your welcome speech and introduce Nancy. Nancy, you will make a brief statement and recognize some of our outstanding volunteers with appreciation plaques and gift bags. Teddy, you will stand next to her and hand the plaques and gift bags to the recipients. Thank them, shake their hands, and pat them on the back. After the presentations, the DJ will play music and we can mingle and talk to our supporters. Please keep the conversations light and polite. At eleven, we will all assemble back here and wait for the polling results. Does anybody have any questions?"

"I don't have a question, just a statement. I just got a text. As of eight o'clock, we are still leading Gene Douglas by at least three-quarters of a point with 87 percent of counties reporting," Tim says.

"That's great news," Delores says. "Teddy, are you ready?"

"I'm ready. Let's get this party started. Do you want to introduce me?"

"Yes, I will introduce you," Delores says. "Everybody, if you want to make your way to the senior staff table in the ballroom."

"Ladies and gentlemen, welcome to the Gatesville Hotel ballroom. The polls have just closed. All the work in the field is done. Now all we can do is wait to see what the majority of voters said. I hope you all had a chance to take a nap today. It's going to be a long night. We don't expect to get the final results until after eleven o'clock. The waiting is the worst part. While we wait, the man we are all here to support would like to say a few words to all of you who are here in support of him tonight. Please welcome to the stage the next governor of our great state, Mr. Theodore Graham!"

The ballroom erupts with applause as Theodore makes his way onstage. He hugs Delores and thanks her before he takes his place behind the podium.

"Thank you, Ms. Daniels. Thank you all. It's hard to believe that at the beginning of this campaign, I was my opponent's campaign manager. As we moved forward in the primary, it became clear that we had differences in opinion as to which direction his campaign should go. It was obvious that he wanted to go the traditional route by promising low taxes for wealthy businesses so they would create jobs and rescue our working class. That's been tried for decades and failed over and over. If we had agreed on that strategy, I would be over at the Douglas Hills Country Club, waiting for the election results with my longtime friend. As his manager, I wanted to make him a candidate that makes things happen instead of just letting him be one that only makes empty promises. I was let go from that campaign. My ideas didn't align with his. I thought I was done with politics, and I was grateful to be out," Theodore says and pauses.

"A longtime public servant, the man who is supposed to be standing up here speaking to all of you tonight, suddenly passed away. The Democrats lost a great man and a great civil servant when Sherman Jones was taken from us. His passing left it seem as if a campaign of empty promises would emerge victorious and another gubernatorial term absent of progress would hurt the citizens of our state." Theodore makes a dramatic pause and looks around the room.

"It's been said before, 'Desperate times call for desperate measures.' Well, here I am, an independent, running on the Democratic ticket. It doesn't get much more desperate than that," Theodore says, and the crowd laughs.

"When the state's Democratic Committee came to me and asked me to run for their party, I thought they were high. Then I remembered that I was the one who enjoyed marijuana, so I had to double-check and make sure I wasn't high. I wasn't high at that moment. They really wanted me to run for governor on their ticket. I really didn't want the job. I would rather get high. I didn't feel that it was I who could make a difference. In fact, I knew it wasn't me," Theodore says and pauses.

"Then I sat down with some of these people. I listened to their ideas. They listened to mine. We started brainstorming. We set some common goals. With those goals in mind, we came up with a plan to achieve them. Once we had a plan, we put a team together that could make those plans come together. When I saw how well the team worked together, I changed my mind. I wanted the job. I wanted to help make a difference. I wanted to be among the brilliant minds that want to build a better tomorrow for our state and for our people. Well, here we are. Tonight, we wait and see if the people of our state believe in our plan and our message. I believe in it because I believe in the hard work of the people surrounding me. It is them that I thank for giving me this amazing opportunity," Theodore says and pauses for applause.

"There are many people I owe my deepest thanks. First of all, to the Democratic Party, for trusting me with this opportunity. Next, it's to my amazing staff. Ed Reese, Pam Eynon, Tim Collins, Kevin Baker, Nathan Winters, Anna Martinez, Everett Avery, and Fred Miles. I have to thank my security staff. They were always where I needed them to be when I needed them to be there, and they had my back the whole time. Sweet Barn, Lizard Eddie, and Funky Brian, thank you. I love you guys, you are like my brothers. With three brothers like I have on my security team, I definitely need somebody to keep me in line and morally guide me. Sophia White, I made her my campaign mother. Without her guidance and tough love, I wouldn't have made it this far. Thank you for adopting me and welcoming me as family at your table. You made me feel at home in your home. I felt like family. Family is so important to have. Sophia, your heart is the heart of this campaign, the heart of our family. I love you." Theodore pauses for applause.

"The volunteers can't go unrecognized. They are the ones out there knocking on doors, talking to people, and coming out for what they believe in. They volunteer because they believe that tomorrow can be better if we work together. They do it for free, and their work is what makes a campaign successful. Volunteers, give yourself a round of applause. Your work made a difference, and I am forever grateful for your time and support." Theodore pauses again.

"Coordination is the key to any successful organization. I picked the best campaign manager in the world. Without her, this campaign would resemble a monkey humping a football. This woman is amazing. She did a job that few could do in the short time we had, and she made it look easy. She kept all arms of this campaign working together and running smoothly. Delores Daniels, thank you for your brilliance and hard work. You were the oil of our political engine. No member of our staff can deny you were the one who kept us running. Ms. Daniels, from the bottom of my heart, well done and thank you, thank you, thank you, and thank you again to infinity." Theodore pauses.

"The next person I want to thank is the creator of the centerpiece of our campaign. She got tired of waiting for politicians to deliver on their promises of jobs and better communities. She went out and found others like her that were sick of waiting too. She formed Professional Women of Power and started doing, with her community-minded group, what she and our citizens were tired of waiting for. She is a woman of action. I think, after this campaign, she's going to want to change the name of her organization. When men in the community started seeing successes, they wanted in too. Jobs are being created. Blight is being refurbished and renewed. Infrastructure is getting the attention it needs. Industries are being built. Communities are getting local-minded businesses. People are shopping local. All this is because of this woman who was tired of waiting and decided to act. Nancy Bradford, the candidate I want as my lieutenant governor, showed me how you can roll up your sleeves and bring prosperity back to once-prosperous areas. Nancy, thank you for making me believe once again that progress is within our reach." Theodore waits for the crowd to calm.

"Nancy would like to come out here and say a few words and recognize some of the efforts of the great people that went above and beyond to deliver for the people. I'm getting tired of talking, and I'm sure you're getting tired of listening to me. Plus, there's and open bar and I am getting thirsty. So let me turn it over to the better half of our gubernatorial ticket. Please welcome Nancy Bradford!" Theodore says to loud applause. Nancy hugs Theodore and takes the podium.

Nancy makes her speech and gets a great reception from the crowd. Theodore and the staff socialize and make small talk with their guests and supporters. The ballroom is lively and fun. The atmosphere is relaxed and celebratory. The staff and attendants take advantage of the open bar at the expense of the Democratic Party. Ed Reese takes a little more advantage of the open bar than he probably should be. They dance to the music the DJ is playing. They busy themselves while they wait for the results of the election to be final.

Election Day, 11:00 p.m.

Delores makes her way through the ballroom and gathers staff members. She gets Pam Eynon, Anna Martinez, and Nancy Bradford off the dance floor and sends them to the private staff room. She sends Ed Reese and the other staff socializing around the bar to the lounge. She sees Theodore telling stories and joking with a group of giggling young volunteers and walks over to them.

"Excuse me, ladies. I must take our candidate away from you for a bit. We will be getting the final election results soon."

"Hey, Delores," Theodore says. "This, ladies, is the model of professionalism you should strive for. You should start a mentor program, Delores. You could shape and influence young minds like this group of young women here."

"Thank you, Theodore. Girls, the first lesson I would teach you is to stay away from men like this. Please excuse us," Delores says.

"You were quite a hit with those young ladies. They were hanging on your every word and giggling at everything you said. What were you telling them?"

"At first, I was talking about the campaign and our platform, but when I realized they were starstruck, I knew it didn't matter what I said. I was just talking about Woody Woodpecker cartoon plotlines."

"Are you going to take one of them home and show them your Woody Woodpecker?"

"Only one?" Theodore jokes. "Actually, when I leave here tonight, I'm going to sleep for a week. You're welcome to join me. My cuddling skills are noteworthy."

"Tempting offer, but I think I may have to pass on it," Delores says as she and Theodore enter the staff lounge.

"Here's our candidate. Jeremy, get our boy Teddy another vodka maternerini," Ed Reese says.

"Ed, our waiter is Jerry, and it is a vodka martini, not what you said. Looks like the booze was treating you well tonight."

"Yeah, buddy! Best day ever! We're gonna win. Gene Douglas can suck it."

Delores goes to the center of the room. "Listen up, folks. We will stay in here until we get the election results. Make yourselves comfortable. It may be a while. Tim, do we have any idea when they will be calling?"

"I just talked to the election officials. They are double-checking the numbers and making sure all counties are reported."

Ed Reese staggers to the center of the room. "I just want to say a few words and brief statements and a few words. Everybody, everyone, all of everyone did fanterrific job with this champagne. I never wanted the opportunity to work with such great people, but I was amazing. No matter what happens or whoever this turns out, I just want everyone to know I love like they are family, like they are brothers and sisters and shit. We did a good job and should be proud of yourselves. When we go back out in that barroom, I have a feeling that Teddy will be the next president of our great straight."

"Thank you for that alcohol-induced gibberish, Ed. The bartenders took good care of you," Theodore says. "I hope I can be the next president of this state."

"You are running for the gubernatoriumal race," Ed slurs.

"Right you are, buddy. What is the news saying about the race?"

"The TV is just a bunch of noise about nothing. These reporters are reporting about news that hasn't happened. Channel 6 has you the projected winner. Channel 4 has Gene the projected winner. Channel 5 has a squirrel on that para-sails. Fox News says Obama is responsible for every broken shoelace in the history of man, and Channel 9 has reruns of the *Dukes of Hazard*," Fred Miles says.

"Ooh, put on *Dukes of Hazard*. Let's see what scheme Boss Hogg is up to and how old Bo and Luke are going to have to save the day," Theodore says.

"Let's turn off the television. It's not going to tell us anything official," Delores says.

"Aw, come on, Delores. Cooter is in this episode. How did he get the name Cooter? I've heard some women refer to their lady part as a cooters."

"It just dawned on me that in a few minutes, you might be the next governor. A chill of doom came over me just now," Delores says. "Please turn off that television."

Tim Collins's cell phone rings. "It's the election bureau. This is what we are waiting for." Tim puts the phone up to his ear. "Hello. Okay, I will gather them and call you back. Okay. Thank you."

"What's the story, Tim?"

"They want me, you, Nancy, and Teddy on the official call. We can do it on speakerphone," Tim says.

Tim puts his cell phone in the middle of the coffee table. The four of them congregate around the phone while the rest of the staff mills around behind them. Tim dials the election bureau and places the call.

"Hello, Tim, this is Sheldon. Do you have your people gathered?"

"Yes, everyone is here," Tim says.

"Mr. Graham, do you want me to tell you the results first and have me repeat them for your staff? I have to ask, because your campaign is your namesake."

"No, you can tell me in front of everybody. This was a team effort."

"Okay. With 100 percent of polls and counties reporting, the Gene Douglas campaign won the election by 8,343 votes. Do you need me to repeat that?"

"You're kidding me! We were up by a point since two o'clock this afternoon," Nancy says.

"I'm sorry, ma'am. Those are the final results. Since it is less than a ten-thousand vote difference, the election rules put a mandatory recount in effect, but with the electronic voting machines, that number is unlikely to change. I'm sorry. Your campaign put up one hell of a race. You can all be proud of that."

"Thank you, Sheldon," Tim says and hangs up his phone.

"Well, that's that. Eugene Douglas is the governor-elect," Theodore says.

Ed Reese runs across the room and grabs a wastebasket. "Wrettcchhh argggaahhhh" can be heard through the room.

"We can all hold our heads high, except Ed, of course, because he is drunk, vomiting in the waste can. We put one hell of a team together. We put a solid platform together. My purpose for running was to get the majority back in the state assembly. We did what we set out to do. Mission accomplished. Great job, everybody!" Theodore says.

"Teddy, I'm sorry," Delores says.

"Don't be sorry. We achieved our initial goal. Anything more than that would have just been extra gravy."

"But you wanted to win."

"Yeah, wish in one hand and shit in the other. That's what they say. Right?"

"So what's next?" Nancy Bradford asks.

"I call Gene and congratulate him. Then we go out into the ballroom and I make my concession speech. After that, we pick up the pieces and move on. I don't have to be governor for us to continue our work of helping communities and people."

"I'm sorry, Teddy. I really thought we were going to win this thing," Nancy says and hugs Theodore tightly.

"Wreeeetccccchh argggggg yaaak" is heard from Ed Reese, who is still vomiting in the wastebasket.

"You okay over there, Ed?"

"I'll be fine. It must have been something I ate."

"Thirty whiskey sours isn't considered food."

"But they had cherries in them."

"Oh, yeah. Sorry, my bad. I got to go call Gene now," Theodore says.

"Tell him I said to fuck off."

"I will pass along your salutations, Ed," Theodore says and exits the building to make his call. The staff is teary-eyed as they watch him go outside.

"Hello, Teddy, how are you?" Gene says as a lot of commotion can be heard in the background.

"You know how I am. I just called to congratulate you. You have fulfilled your legacy. I'm happy for you, my friend!"

"Forgive me, Teddy, for being overjoyed. I waited a long time for this. You put up a heck of a fight!"

"This is your moment. Enjoy it. I kind of feel bad for you, though."

"Why would you feel bad for me?"

"Because you actually have to be the governor and do the work of the governor."

"Yeah, that kind of sucks. Plus, I have to move to the capital, and the governor's mansion is smaller than my family mansion."

"Sounds like one-percenter problems to me. I wouldn't wish your problems to a monkey on a rock."

"Teddy, thank you. Running against you made me a better candidate, and you always remained a true friend. You could have sunk me with my involvement with the Whitneys and the misadventures of my whore-bag wife, but you didn't. I would like to think I would have done the same, but greed has made me do some shitty things to good people."

"Hey, since I won't be doing any governor shit, I only have my day job at the paper now. I have some free time. I heard rumors there's a debate coach job open up at the school. I wouldn't mind trying to win nationals again. I miss working with those young minds."

"The job is yours. I think Jim Peterson's asshole will fall out when I tell him the news. Do you want me to videotape it for you?"

"Please do. I love tormenting that guy. Well, hey, I imagine you got a pretty big party going on over there, so I will let you go. I just wanted to say congratulations and well done."

"Thank you, Teddy. You ran one heck of a campaign. Hey, come on over for dinner tomorrow night. We can get high and let Sandy get passed out drunk and draw penises on her face."

"It's a date. I will see you then, my friend," Theodore says and hangs up the phone. He goes back into the building to the staff room.

"Are you all right?" Delores asks.

"Yes, I was offered a job as a debate coach. I took it."

"The kids will be so happy. You love that job. You will be happy."

"I do love that job, plus I would have a really sexy boss. Sometimes she's a bitch, but she's sexier when she is."

"You insult me and compliment me in the same sentence. I don't even know how to react."

"Doesn't matter. You're going to turn me on no matter what."

"Let's go get your concession speech out of the way," Delores says. "Are you sure you're all right?"

"Yeah, I'm going to be fine."

Theodore goes on the ballroom stage and whispers to the DJ. The DJ stops the music. The room goes silent. All eyes in the room are on Theodore. The media cameras stand by and ready themselves to begin filming.

"Hello, everybody. I have the news that everybody is waiting to hear. The Eugene Douglas for Governor campaign has beaten the Theodore Graham for Governor campaign by 8,343 votes. Gene Douglas is going to be the next governor. It's official. I concede the election to Eugene Douglas," Theodore says and pauses. The audience boos loudly.

"I know this isn't the news that any of you want to hear. We all wished for a different outcome. I myself wished for a better outcome. This is how democracy works. The people cast their votes for the candidate who they believe will best serve them. The people have spoken, and they have chosen Gene Douglas.

"From the boos, I can tell you are disappointed, but you shouldn't be. The beauty of this campaign was its working platform. I surrounded myself with people who are doers in their communities. My staff was made up of people who are actively addressing the wishes of the people and the needs of their cities and towns. There are no reasons to quit on those efforts. We can't give up. Those efforts are noble, and there have been differences made in people's lives. We haven't lost our will to do well, and most importantly, we still have our voices. We must continue to make our voices heard."

Theodore pauses for tepid applause.

"I'm not going to stop using my voice. I work for the *Weekly Beat*. I can still share my voice with the people. I'm going to use my voice to ask Gene Douglas where those low taxes are. I'm going to ask Gene Douglas where the jobs he promised are. I'm going to ask him when he is going to rebuild our communities. I'm going to ask him where the funding for education is. I'm going to ask him when his welfare reform plan will take effect. I'm going to ask him if he will work with newly elected congressmen that want to see our platform of progress move forward. I am going to use my voice, and all of you should use your voices. He made promises to the people. It is up to us, the people, to hold him to the promises he made. If he isn't delivering on the promises he made and our state is still facing the issues we are facing now, you can damn well bet, in four years, I will reassemble this team, this group, and these volunteers, and together, we will call Gene Douglas out on his bullshit platform and make him a one-term governor. Gene Douglas, you are warned. Deliver on your word, or face us again."

The crowd erupts into loud applause.

"With that being said, the Democratic Party is still paying for an open bar. Let's hit it hard! We have cause to celebrate. We came together for a good cause. We did amazing work in a short period. The Democrats took the majority in both the Senate and the House. Lord willing, we have a shitload of tomorrows to work hard to make better. Thank you for standing by me and getting behind me. I couldn't have asked for better people. Now, let's not lick our wounds—let's celebrate our good work!"

Theodore exits the stage. He is approached by Grace Downwood.

"Teddy, do you think I could get an interview?"

"Sure. Why the fuck not?"

"Let me get my cameraman in place, and we can do it right here in front of your banner."

"No problem," Theodore says as the reporter positions the shot.

"I'm Grace Downwood, Channel 6 News, reporting from the Gatesville Hotel ballroom. Standing with me is Theodore Graham, who lost this year's gubernatorial election by a narrow margin. Mr. Graham, what do you have to say about today's election?"

"The people of our democracy have spoken, and they chose Gene Douglas. I want to say congratulations to my friend Gene for a well-fought campaign and wish him good luck in the governor's office. I also want to thank the people that worked so hard for my campaign. It was a gallant effort, but we fell a little short."

"What's next for Theodore Graham?"

"In the immediate future, a hangover. I'm getting drunk tonight."

"What comes after that?"

"I still have my job at the *Weekly Beat*. I plan to be a journalist, and I plan on being the journalist that will hold Gene Douglas accountable for his promises. The people voted for him because they believe his plan. The people are expecting lower taxes, more jobs, better education, balanced budgets, and safe, prosperous communities. I want to make sure he delivers for the people and not for special interests. If he lets the people down, he will face me once again. The people won't be fooled twice."

"Do you think the Douglas plan will fail?"

"Similar trickle-down platforms have tried and failed in the past, but Gene has the opportunity to make a difference. He can work with his Congress. He can listen to community leaders. He can listen to people with ideas. He has the power to succeed. It doesn't matter what I think. The choice is his."

"Can we expect to see you again in four years?"

"If Gene Douglas isn't delivering for the people, there's a good chance."

"You are close friends with Gene. Does this hurt your friendship in any way?"

"No, not at all. We are having dinner together tomorrow night, and when I called to congratulate him, we decided that I should come back to the Douglas Youth Honors College and coach the debate team. I want to bring another national championship back to our state."

"That's good news for the school and the state. Thank you for taking the time to talk to me tonight."

"Thank you, Grace."

"There you have it from the Theodore Graham campaign. Look out, Gene Douglas, you better stick to your promises. I'm Grace Downwood, Channel 6 News, reporting," the reporter says, ending the interview.

"I'm sorry you lost, Teddy. You would have been a better governor."

"It is what it is. Thank you," Theodore says and walks away.

The Morning After, 2:20 a.m.

Theodore is sitting on the stoop in back of the Gatesville Hotel, smoking a joint and drinking a bottle of beer. The majority of the staff and guests have left for the night. Delores is inside, saying goodnight to the few remaining guests. Jerry, the waiter, comes out the back door of the building carrying a bag of garbage. He takes a whiff of the air around Theodore.

"Something smells really good out here."

"Sit down and enjoy some of this joint with me."

"Let me get rid of this trash, and I will be happy to smoke with you," Jerry says and throws the bag in the dumpster. He sits next to Theodore.

Theodore passes him the joint. "I'm sure you can use some of this after dealing with these drunk folks all night."

Jerry takes the joint and takes a long hit off it. "I don't mind the drunk people, I'm used to it. I'm just pretty bummed you lost the election. I was really hoping for change."

"I was kind of looking forward to trying to make it happen."

"I've been voting for fourteen years, and nothing has changed. The issues are the same. Does it ever change? Will it ever change?"

"Humans don't change. Change is the boogeyman that hides in our closets or under our beds. Change is doubt that lives in our minds. Change won't come until people have faith in their ability to make change and face the boogeyman. I lost because I am that boogeyman. I offered something different," Theodore says and takes a puff off the joint.

"I believed in you, if that's any consolation."

"Having you smoke this doobie with me after the day I had is all the consolation I need."

"Do you think Gene Douglas will do a good job?"

"Gene Douglas won't do better or worse than any other governor. He is money, and money follows money. The ones that have it figure out how to get more of it out of the ones who have less of it. That's the way politics works. Always has. Always will. It's all bullshit, and it's bad for you."

"How can you go back to working for Gene Douglas as a debate coach at his pretentious honors school after all this?

Theodore takes a hit off the joint. "It's all personal leverage. I'm going to be highly critical of him in the *Weekly Beat*. He can't really make a counterattack on me if I am a winning debate coach that is making his school money and bringing him notoriety. He's stuck in the middle, so he has no choice but to do the right thing. Sometimes you get the most bang for your buck if you play the hero, victim, and villain, but it can be a lonely life."

"You are a calculated man, Mr. Graham."

Delores comes out of the back door. "I smell that you guys are still celebrating."

"Jerry and I are just talking about politics. Did everybody leave?"

"Yeah, just about. Last call is over. There are few people finishing their drinks."

Jerry stands up. "I should get going and help get everything cleaned up. Thanks for the buzz."

"It was my pleasure, Jerry. Stay away from politics," Theodore says as Jerry disappears into the building. "Have a seat, Delores."

Delores sits next to Theodore on the stoop. "Are you soon ready to get going?"

"You're my ride, unless you're calling me a cab."

"You're a cab."

"Why, Ms. Daniels, you made a simpleton's joke. I'm rubbing off on you."

"I will take you home. I do believe I owe you an answer."

"I did lose the election. You're right, you do owe me an answer. Have you decided?"

"Yes, and yes, I will have dinner with you. I want to have dinner with you."

"That's great news. Do you think—" Theodore says and is interrupted when she gives him a long kiss on the lips.

"I didn't want you to ruin the moment with your words."

"Good call. I have a tendency to yammer when I should shut up."

"Yesterday, you asked me if I would take a nap with you. I didn't, but I was wondering if the offer is still on the table for when I take you home tonight."

"Of course the offer is still there. I really need to hold someone I care about close to me."

"I need the same thing. I need to be held. This has been one tough day."

"Remember when I was in your office being reprimanded for playing that song on the debate team bus?"

"Yes, you almost lost your job over it."

"What song was I playing?"

"It was 'Pop the Pussy' by 2 Live Crew."

"That's right."

"Why are you asking me that now?"

"Because when we get back to my apartment, I want to pop, pop, pop, that pussy."

"Let's start with a nap first and see if we want to get Naughty by Nature and Down with 'OPP' after our dinner," Delores says and gives Theodore another long kiss on the lips.

THE END

About the Author

Daniel Urban grew up in Coaldale, Pennsylvania, a small working-class town in the Anthracite Coal Region. He attended Penn State University, where he earned his bachelor's degree in communications. After college, he returned to the area of his roots with the hopes of putting his degree to work for him. He worked a multitude of jobs, as a grocery clerk, as an exterminator, as a marketing consultant, and as a lab technician at a magnesium powder manufacturer. As a strong believer in the value of community, he spent time volunteering as a firefighter, a scout leader, a labor union leader and participated in various community improvement and beautification projects. Though the future he envisioned when he returned home from college wasn't what he had hoped, it was the triumphs, tragedies, struggles, resilience, and humor of the people he had the privilege of getting to know that inspired his imagination and love for stories. Becoming a writer became his dream. In 2015, his then-fiancée and now wife, Tracy, was offered a career opportunity in the New England states. He left the life he knew and headed north with the love of his life and settled in the Quiet Corner of Connecticut and calls the welcoming town of Willimantic his new home. Daniel is now working hard on making his writing dreams come true.

CPSIA information can be obtained
at www.ICGtesting.com
Printed in the USA
FFHW021103091118
49312211-53567FF